# THE PAIN OF COMPASSION

Thanks
MIKKO !

Enjoy !

# Eyes of the Deluti

## Book 1

# THE PAIN OF COMPASSION

## by Roland Boykin

Cover design by Benita Prins.

# ẟEDICATION

This book is dedicated to my friends and family who have stuck by me through this whole process. I would especially like to thank the folks at the Kitsap Writers Group, and my writing partners:

Michelle Van Berkom

Carrie Lawrence

Meghan Skye

# TABLE OF CONTENTS

# PROLOGUE

# END OF AN AGE

Now was the time to finish this. Only Demitrios, the last surviving Deluti High Lord, had the power to locate and if possible, destroy the Dark Lord. He rode at the forefront of the Army of the North, an alliance he had forged between Northern Ogre, Mountain Wolves, the light-shifters of the Elintria and Humans. That alliance proved to be the turning point in a war that had lasted for decades. The Dark Lord of the South refused to acknowledge the intelligence and fighting abilities of the Elder Races. For that reason, his army was comprised entirely of humans and their sorcerers, whom he treated little better than slaves.

The Army of the North advanced steadily across the Plain of Sarglon and approached the Stagwood Forest. Ahead of them stretched an ancient, densely packed wood. The Dark Lord had established his final defensive line there to protect his fortress at Bryhom. At the High Lord's signal, the army positioned itself for attack with archers and sorcerers to the front, followed by ogres, wolves and human swordsmen. The horsemen were positioned as rear guard due to their disadvantage in the thick forest.

As the first volley of arrows darkened the sky, and fireballs sped towards the forest, lightning strikes sent by the Dark Lord's sorcerers began falling among the archers. Holding position, the sorcerers and archers continued to provide covering fire until the wolves, ogres, and Elintria assassins reached the edge of the forest. The swordsmen then followed to sweep through in their wake. Riding among them, Demitrios provided as much protection as he dared, but every death added to the burden of sorrow weighing on his heart.

His personal shield protected him from attack but did not block out the pungent odor of ozone and the sickly sweet stench of burning flesh. They had left behind a plain littered with the bodies of human and animal, but in the forest, Demitrios knew they would have the advantage. The wolves and ogre were formidable predators and the Elintria would quickly eliminate anyone firing from the trees.

A sudden immense gathering of power alerted the High Lord to the presence of his enemy and the shocked realization of the terrible mistake he had made. The forest was a trap. With the last of his energy he sent out a powerful mental command to the entire army to abandon the forest immediately. Face buried in the mane of his horse to keep from being swept off, they careened through the forest with the roar of an inferno pursuing them. Tendrils of smoke trailed from the burnt ends of the horse's tail as they escaped through the western edge of the forest and ascended to a rock strewn meadow. The horse, lathered and trembling, stopped a few paces away from the body of a man slumped against the side of a large boulder. Demitrios fell from his saddle and stumbled over to his brother. The face of his twin was beyond recognition.

Compassion overwhelmed all other emotions as he

gazed at the burnt and blackened body before him.

"Why have you done this to us Scorpios?" he cried. "Your lust for power has destroyed the last members of our race. The Council of Five have given up their lives and forged their spirits into the five Amulets of Focus. Those amulets are now hidden from you throughout both kingdoms. The Deluti are no more. You have placed the future of this world in the hands of the humans."

The body of his brother convulsed, one eye cracked open, and a hiss escaped through burnt and blistered lips.

"Kill me."

"I can not. Regardless of what you have become, you are still my brother."

Anger invoked by the senseless destruction and death his brother was responsible for, rekindled the power of a Deluti High Lord in him. He rose to his feet and stood straight and tall. "You will live, but your wounds will never heal. Suffer with your injuries and the knowledge of what you have done to our people."

Demitrios walked over to stand next to his horse and stared at the smoking ruin that had once been the Stagwood Forest. With a faraway look in his eyes, he continued.

"Many generations from now, the blood of the Deluti will return through the line of humans even stronger than before and our time on this world will come to an end. I have foreseen it."

Back in the saddle, he turned away from the broken body on the ground and whispered, "Goodbye, brother."

He never looked back.

# Chapter One

# A Whisper from the Past

Flickering torch light cast shifting shadows across the courtyard as two figures faced each other in the center of a practice circle. It would be several hours before the sun cleared the eastern wall of the Keep and its glow would chase away those shadows. Pre-dawn dew glistened from every surface and added to the chill of a late spring morning. It failed to match the frost that surrounded the Baron's two youngest sons.

The sound of wooden practice swords connecting in a

series of thrusts and parries filled the air, then quieted as the combatants circled each other looking for an opening. Formed from the same mold as his father and brothers, Micah easily outweighed his younger brother by fifty pounds of muscle that filled out his chest and arms. This provided him no advantage over Navon, who had developed a skill and speed unmatched by anyone in the Keep.

Once again they came together amid a flurry of swinging swords, neither giving ground to the other until the younger brother landed a solid hit to an upper arm.

"You will pay for that, Navon."

"Perhaps, but I will never again allow you to abuse me, Micah. Not only am I a better swordsman, after my naming ceremony tonight we will be equals in this family."

With a growl, Micah rushed him only to have Navon nimbly sidestep and smack him across the shoulders as he charged past. "I've heard a rumor that Father plans to put you in charge of the latrines after your naming."

"At least Father chose wisely when he put you in charge of the pig farms. They match your personality perfectly," Navon retorted.

No longer interested in sparring, Micah cast aside his wooden sword and attacked his brother open handed. Navon dropped his practice blade and calmly stood his ground in the face of his brother's rage. At the last moment he grabbed one of Micah's arms and using his momentum, spun the older boy to the ground.

Spitting dirt, Micah slowly rose to his feet, eyes narrowed to slits. Drawing his knife, he hissed, "With that hair and pretty face of yours, you'll fit right in with the women's bower once I'm done with you, little brother."

The arms-master, who had been watching from the shadows, strode to the middle of the circle and focused his fierce continence on Micah. "In all the years I have served the Baron, never has a member of this family pulled steel against another. You are a disgrace to the name of Roddell. Your father will determine what becomes of you, but for now, remove yourself from my sight."

He turned his back on Micah and studied Navon who now stood with downcast eyes. After enough time had passed to force the young man to look up, Master Drummel spoke. "That's better. From this day forward, never cast down your eyes before any man. Now, since I distinctly forbade sparring without supervision, I expect to see you in the armory right after you break your fast. Maybe a day spent repairing armor will help you remember when I give an order."

Navon nodded and turned away, the arms-master's words barely registering. Foremost in his mind was the hate he saw in his brother's eyes before leaving the practice yard. That look disturbed Navon more than he cared to admit.

*       *       *

Every other lamp was lit in an attempt to keep the shadows at bay in a Keep designed for defense that lacked windows on the ground floor. Winter carpets still covered the floors as the stone had yet to catch up with the warmth of the coming summer. His mother's touch was evident in the placement of spring flowers under several oil lamps. Their fragrance helped to remove the musty odor of the winter damp.

Navon made his way down the stairs and into the passageway leading to the dining hall with a lighter step than usual, that morning's confrontation a distant memory. He had looked forward to this day for many years and took extra care in his appearance. Everyone's eyes would be upon him as the Baron announced his son's coming of age and assigned him his first official duties as a member of the ruling family.

After a nod and a smile from his oldest brother, Altair, and a respectful bow towards the Baron and his Lady Mother, Navon solemnly took his seat at the lower table amid the excited whispers of his siblings. Micah was nowhere to be seen.

The Baron stood holding a goblet in one hand and turned to Navon with an unreadable expression before he muttered a curse that only his wife could hear, "Damn the Deluti! This is not right." He flung the goblet to the floor and stormed out of the room.

In the ensuing silence, Navon slowly slid back his chair, got up and carefully placed it under the table, then retraced his steps toward the lower entrance to the dining hall. Safely alone out in the corridor, he began to run, taking the stairs two at a time. Hot tears of shame and rejection burned his cheeks as he tried to distance himself from the looks of sympathy on the faces of everyone in the Great Hall. Why? Why had his father done that to him? Was he really such a disappointment?

The sound of heavy footsteps on the stairs alerted him to the eminent arrival of his brother, Altair. He ran into his room and wiped the tears from his face. No one was going to stop him now that he had made his decision to leave.

His brother walked in and stood for a moment watching him pack before he spoke. "Are you sure you want to do this, Navon?"

"No, but what choice do I have Altair? Father made his feelings perfectly clear and you could see from the look on everyone's face that they also understood what was happening. I am outcast and no longer have any hope for a future as part of this family."

The youngest of the Baron's children, Navon had been given a small room on the upper floor of the Keep. A giant oak rooted in the center of his room would have been as nothing compared to the presence of his brother. He wished Altair would just leave him alone with his misery but his brother's concern also gave him comfort. Altair had always been there when Navon needed a shoulder to cry on and never laughed at his fears of being different.

Navon stood in front of his small wardrobe, his light blond hair falling forward to conceal the tears that threatened to flow again. Altair approached him from behind and placed a comforting hand on his shoulder.

"Do you know how eagles learn to fly, little brother?"

Unable to speak, Navon shook his head.

"The chicks spend weeks standing on the edge of their nest just flapping their wings. It builds up their muscles. Then one day, the parents will push a fledgling out of the nest. He will either learn to fly or fall to the ground where he will die. I think Father just gave you that push."

When he didn't respond, Altair turned his brother around and with a finger under Navon's chin, raised his head, wanting, needing to look him in the eyes. "You have no idea how much I envy you, little brother. The rest of us will always be chained to this Keep or at least to our little corner of the country. Do you remember all those fantastic tales of the world that traveling bard regaled us with at last summer's festival? You are free to travel and experience those faraway places for yourself, while we are prisoners here to our duties and responsibilities. From the day you were born, we have all felt that you were someone special and that someday you would have to leave us."

Altair reluctantly released his little brother and quickly moved towards the door. Once there, he turned back with as fierce a look as Navon had ever seen on his brother's face. "Learn to fly, Navon. Never forget that you are a Roddell. If you are ever in need, send word to me and I will come regardless of what Father says."

Micah disappeared around the corner as Altair closed the door to Navon's room. Chuckling at his little brother's misfortune, he rushed up the stairs to the rooftop and the dovecote there. Quickly penning a short note, he attached it to the leg of a very special pigeon. As the bird faded from sight, he smiled in satisfaction. *Some fledglings are pushed out of the nest, hit the ground, and die.*

Unable to concentrate on his packing after Altair left, Navon sat on the edge of his bed trying to make sense out of what his brother had said. A knock at his door jarred him out of his thoughts. Wondering who it might be, he heard a soft voice outside calling.

"Navon. May I come in?"

By the Eyes! It was his mother, the last person he expected. She had never come up to his room before, so why now? He swung open the door and answered with a bow. "Of course you may come in, Lady Mother."

All the excuses for why he was packing melted away as he watched his mother calmly survey the room while holding a plain wooden box in her hand. The box was like nothing he had ever seen before. The edges had darkened with time and the simple design spoke of an age long past.

"Long ago it was foretold that when evil once again made its presence felt in the world, the Eyes of the Deluti would return to combat that evil. That day has come and is why I am here. I have something that has been in my family for many generations. I became the bearer of this box on the day my mother passed from this world. Inside is the amulet of a Deluti." She opened the box and removed a triangular amulet that contained three luminescent eyes and was attached to a small gold chain. "Once you put this around your neck, the amulet will disappear and only you have the ability to remove it."

"Why are you giving this to me?" he asked, unable to keep the hurt and frustration from his voice. "You have many sons and daughters who are more deserving of this than I."

"Navon, no one in living memory has worn this. Tradition says that the bearer of the box will know who is to wear the amulet or who to pass the box on to for the next generation. The moment you were born, I knew you were the one to wear it but that I was not to give it to you until you were ready to leave. There is a power in you,

Navon, and the amulet will help you focus that power. Please put it on, my son. It is yours."

With trembling fingers he reached for the amulet. The loop in the chain appeared to be too small to slip over his head. The chain began to glow and Navon felt a tingling travel up his arms and into his chest. The glow quickly faded and the chain separated, revealing a tiny clasp.

At a gasp from his mother, he raised his eyes and stared in awe as the box disappeared in a flash of light. He reached behind his neck with the ends of the chain where they snapped together to become a solid loop once again. From the look of wonder in his mother's eyes, he knew the amulet was no longer visible. Unnerved by the touch of the chain, he froze as a voice in his head whispered, *"Go north."*

\*　　\*　　\*

Far to the north, in a castle hidden deep within the Mountains of Mists, the Ancient One raised his head and smiled. Far to the southwest, across the Straits of Durmont, the Stagwood Marshe trembled as Scorpios clenched his scarred fists in a fit of rage. The slave who had been serving him burst into flames, reduced to a small dusting of ash on the floor.

\*       \*       \*

In the morning, wearing comfortable leather pants and vest over a light green shirt with a touch of lace at the cuffs and neck, Navon gathered his things and went down to the kitchen. It was early enough that he should be able to avoid everyone in the family. Now that he had made his decision, he was eager to be on his way.

He asked the cook to wrap up some sausages in bread that he could eat while he traveled, then noticed the furtive looks of the kitchen staff. As Navon had feared, this is how the people in the keep would treat him if he remained, and reinforced his decision to leave. The cook's words as he handed him the sausage rolls were unexpected, "May the Eyes of the Deluti watch over you wherever you go, m'Lord."

The guard at the outer gate barely acknowledged him as he trudged through, un-strung bow in his hand. Sword and knife were hung from his belt, a quiver of arrows over one shoulder and his pack and bedroll tied to his back. The pack was only large enough to hold a few of his prized possessions, some clothes and his herb pouch. The old healer at the Keep had taught Navon everything he knew about healing lore, so the pouch should come in handy.

Defending himself wouldn't be a problem even though he would never achieve the brute strength of his brothers. The Keep's arms-master judged that Navon had the quickest hands of any swordsman he'd ever taught and his skill with a bow was un-matched by anyone in the Keep.

He might only be sixteen summers, but felt he had taken his first step to becoming a man. Raising his face to the warmth of the morning sun, he strode away from the Keep with a spring in his step. *You were right, big brother. It is time for me to fly.*

*     *     *

A solitary figure stood on the ramparts of the Keep long after Navon had faded from view. *Forgive me, my son, for what I had to do. Your path in this life was set the day you were born and I fervently hope I was able to prepare you for it. You will always be my special son.* Turning away, Baron Rodgier d'Roddell disappeared into the Keep, his beard glistening with tears that no one would see.

# CHAPTER TWO

# ODD MEETINGS

Constructed with blocks of white granite quarried from the nearby mountains, the Keep pushed the limits of wealth that a minor Baron could display. The d'Roddell family home stood centered in a large valley and was the oldest structure in the south-eastern region of Marlinor. Rumors hinted that the Keep had originally belonged to a powerful Deluti lord. Alternating fields of winter wheat and spring corn filled the valley in a patchwork pattern of green and gold. In the foothills of the mountains to the south were pastures for sheep and a few cattle. Far to the east were the pig farms where the prevailing breezes prevented the distinctive aroma from enveloping the Keep. Workers dotted the fields to either side of the road, tending to the young crops.

Several farmers, leading small horse carts, passed Navon on their way to the Keep. Some were on their way to deliver their required tithe to the Baron and some to sell their goods at the local market. All gave him a friendly greeting and never mentioned how odd it was to see him walking with a pack over his shoulder. He had decided not to take a horse from his father's stable, the extra responsibility more than he felt he could handle. Navon also hoped that a man walking would present a less tempting target than someone on a fine horse.

Several hours of walking brought him to the edge of the fields and into the forest. The gnarled limbs of ancient elm and oak had grown together forming a canopy over the road. With it being well into spring, walking down the cart path was like traveling through a long green tunnel. Small rays of sunshine penetrated the tree tops, dancing across the path in front of him. He heard the faint rustling of small animals going about their lives in the underbrush, and laughed at the antics of tiny finches trying to snap up as many gnats as they could in the flickering beams of light.

Memories of his brother's visit and the strange encounter with his mother kept floating to the surface of his mind no matter how hard he tried to bury them. He just wasn't ready to deal with the implications right now. Lost in thought, he took several steps before the deathly quiet of the forest announced that he was no longer alone.

Two very large wolves sat in the middle of the path with their eyes fixed on Navon. He felt the hairs on the back of his neck stand up, and as a single drop of sweat ran from his temple, he slowly reached for his sword. None of the training he had received prepared him for this. When they made no threatening moves, his fear subsided, but he remained alert. These were no ordinary wolves. The older and larger of the two sat with his head at a height equal to Navon's chest. Both bore distinctive light grey patches on their dark fur, perfect coloring for blending in among the rocks and patches of snow high in the mountains. What in the Name of the Eyes were northern mountain wolves doing this far south?

Navon relaxed and took his hand away from his sword. If the stories were true, he wouldn't stand a chance against one mountain wolf, much less two. He was completely at their mercy and they both knew it. As if his relaxing had been a signal, the older wolf stood up, gave a short bark and headed off of the path into the forest. The younger one rose to follow, but stopped at the edge of the path to look back. He directed another short bark at Navon, and then melted into the brush. The meaning was clear. They wanted him to follow.

After traveling a short distance into the forest, they came to a small clearing where three more adults and three pups, the size of normal wolves, waited. Unsure why the wolves had led him here, he hesitated. At the edge of the clearing, Navon spotted one of the wolves lying on her side with a crossbow bolt embedded in her thigh. Ignoring the soft warning growls from the other wolves, he rushed forward until he was confronted by the three young but very protective pups. He slowly set his pack and bow on the ground, knelt down to unpack his herb pouch, and talked to the pups as soothingly as he knew how.

A sharp bark from the elder male caused the three to move aside, but they kept their eyes fixed on Navon while still emitting soft growls. Inspecting the wound, he saw the head of the bolt had not passed all the way through. He would have to try and bring it back out the same way it had gone in. Fortunately, the bladed head had gone in parallel to the muscle tissue causing little damage. Unfortunately, the barbs on the head were designed to cause maximum harm when pulled back out.

The wolves and the forest around him faded from his awareness as he poured all his concentration into pulling each strand of muscle tissue away from the barbs as he slowly backed the bolt out. The she-wolf seemed to understand the need to lie perfectly still until he was done. Navon used a tincture of yellowleaf and queensfoot to mask her pain and stem the flow of blood, but occasionally he would hear a quiet whimper. At those times he became aware of her pain as if it was his own.

When the last stitch had been tied off, he sat back on his heels, surprised at how drained he felt, and the orange glow of the sun indicated how late it had become. A growling stomach reminded him that he had planned on reaching the town of Twin Oaks tonight and hadn't packed any extra food. As he wondered what to do, one of the wolves returned to the clearing with a rabbit and laid it next to him. The she-wolf stood up, slightly favoring her hind leg, and gently touched her nose to his. That was disconcerting to say the least, since she actually had to lower her head to his. The pups had fallen asleep, but jumped up at the sound of a soft bark from the elder. Seeing their mother standing on all four legs, they padded over with tails wagging and rolled over on their backs in front of Navon. Another bark brought them to their feet as the rest of the wolves stood up to leave. Each one nodded to him as they filed past until all had slipped silently into the forest.

On the edge of his endurance, he managed to start a small fire, then skin and roast the small rabbit. After eating half, he barely remembered to wrap the rest of it in the cloth left from his breakfast roll-ups before passing out.

*     *     *

Navon woke from a night of eerie but non-threatening dreams to find the sun already well above the horizon. He sat up and looked around, dismayed by the sorry state of his camp and himself. Herbs and bloody cloths were still scattered on the ground where the she wolf had lain. Stiff joints made him groan as he stood slowly and watched dirt and leaves fall from his clothes. By the time he finished eating the last of the rabbit and cleaned up the mess, the stiffness had subsided to a tolerable level. Satisfied, he strapped on his weapons, threw the bedroll over his shoulder, and found his way back to the cart path.

All that morning, Navon walked along the path completely unaware of the forest and the sights and sounds that he had enjoyed the day before. He could not understand the meaning of his encounter with the wolves. Their intelligence was un-mistakable, yet they had treated him with a certain amount of respect. Why would they treat him that way? How had the she-wolf been able to lie perfectly still as he removed that bolt? Any other animal would have had to be restrained to keep them still. And why had time seemed to stand still while removing the bolt, when it had actually taken many hours?

Unable to fathom any answers, Navon tried to turn his thoughts to the road ahead but once again they were interrupted. This time he heard loud voices on the path up ahead, just around the corner. Not wanting to stumble into anything, he slipped into the forest and crept up to where he could see what was happening. Three large men surrounded an older boy and were apparently taunting him. One man had a crossbow slung over his shoulder and all three had a sword at their side. The boy held them off by brandishing a knife in each hand, but Navon was afraid that the men would quickly grow tired of their game. If one of them drew a sword, it would be over for the boy.

He strung his bow, nocked an arrow, then jumped up on the fallen tree he had been hiding behind and shouted.

"Let the lad go and be on your way!"

The reaction he got was not what he had expected. As the man with his back to him spun around, the boy jumped forward and thrust both knives into the small of the man's back, dropping him instantly. At the same time, one of the other men yelled.

"It's him! Don't let him get away!"

As the man with the crossbow inserted a bolt and raised the weapon to his shoulder, Navon reacted without thought and put an arrow in the man's throat. The last one drew his sword and rushed forward, but before Navon could decide whether to nock another arrow or draw his own sword, the man pitched forward, the hilt of a knife protruding from his back.

As the impact of what he had just done sank in, Navon found himself on his hands and knees with his meager breakfast in a puddle on the ground. His stomach continued to heave even after nothing was left.

"Next time it won't affect you as hard," the boy commented knowingly, then added. "You can thank me at any time."

Navon stood up on trembling legs and watched as the boy pulled his knife from the back of the last man, wiped the blade clean, and then meticulously sorted through the pouches of the three men. This was not a boy as Navon had originally thought, but a wiry young man. Certainly the calm and quiet manner in which the young man spoke indicated a maturity beyond his apparent years.

"What do you mean?" Navon asked, still confused. "Why would I want to thank you, and what won't affect me next time?"

"I didn't say it wouldn't affect you the next time you have to kill someone, just not as strongly," the young man replied calmly, handing Navon back his arrow. "It wouldn't be wise to leave this in a man's throat since most people around here will recognize the fletching pattern of your house." Looking him in the eye, the young man continued. "You can thank me for saving your life, Navon d'Roddell."

"What are you talking about?" Navon demanded. "I

distinctly remember finding you surrounded by three very large men with swords, and when I confronted them it gave you a chance to escape. In another moment they would have tired of their game, and you would have died. I believe it is you who should be thanking me."

Crystal blue eyes met steel grey, locked and held. Navon had to look away first, suddenly unsure of himself. Something in those eyes pulled at his soul like nothing he had ever felt before.

Eyes still fixed on Navon, the young man explained. "Yesterday, I overheard those three muscle heads bragging about what they were going to do with all the gold they would soon have. When they left the village this morning, I followed until they reached this bend in the cart path. Realizing they planned to ambush someone rounding the curve, I skirted ahead intending to turn back whoever was approaching. You were already too close, so I confronted those fools instead, hoping to make enough noise to warn you away. I should have known your honor would never allow you to run."

"When I saw you surrounded and threatened by those men, the thought of running away never entered my mind."

"Never lose your faith and your sense of honor as they will serve you in the days to come. You have a powerful enemy, Navon. Each one of those men had five gold crowns in his pouch. Standard practice is to pay half at the start of a job, and the other half when the job is finished. That much gold could only mean the Royal family or possibly one of the Dukes."

"This doesn't make any sense," Navon complained. "I'm only a younger son of a minor Baron. Why would I have any enemies? I'm sure the Royal family doesn't even know I exist. Besides, I only just decided to leave the Keep night before last."

"I don't know, Navon, but I must leave you now," the young man apologized. "Remember, you are in grave danger wherever you go. The future is uncertain, but I hope we will meet again. May the Eyes watch over and protect you."

"Wait! I don't even know your name!"

"Emma, but all my friends call me Em," she replied, heading down the path toward town.

"But..." he stammered. "That's a girl's name!"

"And just what did you think I was, Navon?" she called back over her shoulder with a mischievous laugh.

Navon shook his head and walked back to retrieve his pack from behind the fallen tree. *What is wrong with me? How could I have missed the fact that she is a girl? And how did she know my name?* Well, it was simple once he thought about it. Everyone in the surrounding area probably knew the names and descriptions of the Baron's entire family. How far would he have to travel before people no longer recognized him?

As he skirted around the dead men, his attention was drawn to the distinctive design of the crossbow bolt lying next to the man he had shot. Navon nodded his head in satisfaction and turned back to the path thinking, '*That one will never shoot at wolves again.*'

He broke into a run, intending to catch up with Emma and apologize. She was nowhere to be seen. He resumed a more leisurely pace and thought about the things she had said. By the time he reached the eastern gate of Twin Oaks he had convinced himself that she had it all wrong. Those men must have mistaken him for someone else. How could anyone have possibly known that he would be on the path today? Besides, everyone knew that girls were too emotional and were always over-reacting. Yes, that must be it. He felt much better about the situation as he stopped at the gate for directions to the nearest inn.

Navon looked around with interest as he followed the Guard's directions. Twin Oaks was the largest town in the eastern reaches of Marlinor. It was surrounded by a defensive wall of upright logs with three gates; one to the north and one each in the east and west walls. A small detachment of the Crown Guard was garrisoned at the western edge of town to provide peace-keeping and to man the gates.

He approached what appeared to be the correct inn as indicated by the sign out front and saw that despite being very old, it was in good repair. The second story overhung the front wall forming a covered porch area for patrons to use during the hot summer months. Tired and emotionally drained after the events of the past several days, he looked forward to a nice hot meal and a soft bed.

At the door to the inn, Navon could see the inside through the large windows in the front wall. A long counter lined the right side of the inn, and to the left was the common room with a large fireplace built from the local river rock. In the center of the common room were two long tables with benches and a scattering of small tables along the walls. Everything looked old and well used but clean.

When he entered the inn, the few patrons in the common room turned in surprise and regarded him with curiosity. The innkeeper quickly hid his surprise as he set down the mug he had been polishing and bowed to Navon with knuckles to his forehead.

"Welcome to the Dancing Badger, m'lord. How may I serve you?"

"A hot meal and a room for the night will serve me admirably," Navon replied.

"I think you will find the first room to your right suitable. Would m'lord prefer to eat in his room?" asked the innkeeper.

"The common room will do fine. I would also like to ask you a few questions after my meal, if that would be agreeable."

"Of course m'lord," the innkeeper answered, eyes narrowing in suspicion. "I would be honored to answer any questions you may have."

Located at the back of the inn, just past the end of the counter and next to the swinging door to the kitchen were the stairs to the second floor. Once inside the room, Navon tossed his pack and bedroll on the bed, which looked surprisingly clean and comfortable. He moved to the washstand and stared into the mirror. The reason for the curious stares when he first entered the inn became clear. His hair was in total disarray, and his clothes were still dirty and wrinkled from sleeping on the forest floor. The blood stains on his shirt from the wolf and the rabbit made him look away with a shiver.

A quick wash, a change of clothes and after running a comb through his hair, Navon felt he was now presentable. As the aroma of roast venison filled the air, he hurried downstairs just as the innkeeper emerged from the kitchen with a steaming platter in one hand and a mug of ale in the other. Following him to a corner table, Navon barely acknowledged the innkeeper's bow before digging into his meal. He'd always preferred the basic, hearty fare of the common folk over some of the elaborate meals the cook at the Keep prepared.

All too soon he pushed away an empty platter and raised his mug, signaling he would like a refill. As the innkeeper approached, Navon gestured to the chair opposite him at the table, his prepared speech ready.

"Please be at ease and join me for a moment. I am on a quest for the Keep's healer to find a special herb he says can only be found in the far north and I would prefer not to travel alone. Do you know of any group or trader who will be traveling in that direction?"

"I haven't heard of anyone m'lord, but I know someone who I can ask." The innkeeper's attitude changed to one of concern as he leaned forward. "Certainly m'lord wouldn't need protection on the road, or have you heard of some danger recently?"

"No, nothing like that," Navon denied. "It's just that it can get lonely on the road, and having someone to converse with makes the trip shorter."

"As you say m'lord. As you say. Please excuse me as I must get back to my other patrons. If I hear of anything, I will inform you straight away," he promised.

Navon wondered at the innkeeper's nervousness. Maybe he was just uncomfortable talking to someone of a higher station. Thoughts of the innkeeper soon gave way to an image of that comfortable looking bed upstairs. With a full meal and two mugs of stout ale making his eyelids droop, he headed up to his room with no other purpose other than to get a full nights' rest.

After a night filled with dreams of snow covered mountains, strange beings, and a sense of impending danger, Navon broke his fast in a somber mood. Even the impish smile from the innkeepers' daughter as she brought him his breakfast, failed to lift his spirits. Coming through the door from the kitchen, the innkeeper spotted Navon and rushed over.

"Good news m'lord," he beamed. "I just received word that a group of men, who arrived last night from the Capitol, are leaving this morning for Brighton Ferry. I'm sure they would be honored to have the Baron's son accompany them."

Navon listened closely as the innkeeper gave him directions to a stable near the north gate. After settling his account, he hustled upstairs with a renewed sense of purpose. Weapons strapped on and with pack in hand, he hurried along the dirt street as fast as was seemly for a Baron's son. His upbringing would allow nothing less. The village was larger than he had imagined, and the shops that lined the street made him wish he could take the time to stop. The innkeeper had warned him however, the men planned an early start, and he would have to hurry to catch them before they left.

Anxious, Navon rounded the last corner and was relieved by what he saw. A small coach, with two canvas covered wagons lined up behind it, stood ready to depart. Thank the Eyes, he'd made it in time. As he approached the open stable door, rehearsing how he would introduce himself, an odd thought crossed his mind. Shouldn't there be someone outside tending the horses? It was his last conscious thought before darkness overtook him.

# Chapter Three

# A Betrothal

Sofia woke with a start. A ray of sunshine had discovered a gap in the thick blue drapes covering her bedroom window, and playfully danced over her eyelids. Cursing, she escaped from the tangle of blankets on her small four poster bed, and pulled her long blond hair out of her face. She padded over to the window on bare feet and jerked open the drapes. Sunlight flooded her room from a traitorous sun already well above the horizon. Normally, the warmth of an early morning sun on a crisp spring day would fill her with joy and comfort.

Unfortunately today was not a normal day.

A quick check of the sitting room revealed that no one had disturbed her rooms since last night. By the Eyes, someone was going to pay for this oversight. After a couple of irritated jerks on the servant's bell rope, she stalked over to her wardrobe, and with a grimace, pulled out the gown made especially for this occasion. She would much rather be riding or sparring with the old arms-master, but the Queen required her daughters to appear at court only four days out of the year, and today was one of those days.

The Princess returned to the sitting room just as Floanne, her maidservant, slipped through the door, and quickly closed it behind her after a fearful glance up and down the hall.

"Your Highness," she exclaimed. "Are you still in pain? How may I help you?"

"What are you talking about? Where are the rest of my servants, and why do you look like the Eye of Death is lurking out in the hall?"

"Princess Darnelle commanded all the servants not to disturb you this morning on fear of dismissal. She told us you were suffering from a terrible head pain and needed to sleep. But when you rang the bell so urgently, I was afraid for you and came as swiftly as I could. I was alone in the servant's hall when you called so no one knows I am here. Please m'lady, don't tell Princess Darnelle I disobeyed her."

"I will deal with my sister later. Right now I need you to help me prepare for this morning's audience with the Queen."

Sofia gently brushed a tear from the cheek of her maid, then continued, "Fear not Floanne. Your loyalty to me is appreciated and will be rewarded. Now, let us remind the Court just who and what I am."

*     *     *

In the northern reaches of Dahlian, at a point where the River Susala and the Red River converged, sat Mount Barltok. On a promontory that pointed west toward lush farmland, stood a tower of rock that had split away from the mountain like a crystal shard. On the pinnacle of that shard perched an ancient castle named the Rose Palace. Built in an earlier age, when the Deluti ruled the land, it was so named not only by the pink granite used in its construction, but also because it was patterned after the blossom of a wild rose. A large, domed, reception hall dominated the center with two story wings in the shape of petals arranged in a circle around it.

With an eye for defense as well as beauty, the Palace was connected to the mountain by a single bridge that appeared to be an extension of the very stone itself. Storerooms and a large cistern had been carved out of the rock below to supply the Palace in the event of a siege. The road from the bridge traveled down the gentle slope of the mountain to the capitol city of Kiplar spread out below.

Her Majesty, Queen Oliva Salidoris, sat on display in her Crystal Throne at the northern end of the Great Hall. Today was the first day of summer and one of only four days she required her three daughters, the four Governors, and the local nobility to attend her. Dark and curly shoulder length hair, adorned with golden threads containing delicate pink blossoms and tiny green leaves, framed the face of a mature yet strikingly beautiful woman. The intricate Crown of Dahlian, nestled atop the curls, appeared to anchor the golden threads in place. A sleeveless, floor length gown, was the color of spring wheat in celebration of the new season. The gown was trimmed with the same profusion of leaves and blossoms at the hem and waist, with the neckline cut just low enough to hint at the femininity hidden within.

Intense hazel eyes, partially hidden behind lowered dark lashes, scanned the courtyard as she greeted her guests with a nod and a distracted, but benevolent smile. The fingers of her right hand continued to tap out a rhythm on the arm of the throne despite her best efforts to still them. Today's major announcement involved an agreement that had been reached concerning Princess Sofia. An agreement that her daughter was completely unaware of, and the Queen was concerned what her hot tempered daughter's reaction would be. At a discreet signal from the Queen, the Seneschal lowered his head to hers.

"Any word as to the whereabouts of Princess Sofia?" she whispered.

"No, Your Majesty. The servants are being uncommonly tight lipped. No one has seen the Princess since late last night."

Just then a movement at the southern entrance to the chamber caught the Queen's eye like a breath of air rustling the leaves of a single tree branch. A young woman, dressed in a blindingly white gown with folds of sheer lace down the sleeves and around the neck, strode down the aisle. Back straight, every muscle loose and in perfect balance, her eyes never seemed to move, yet saw everything. The lethal grace of her movements was a testament to the years of clandestine lessons she had received from the Palace Guard's retired arms-master.

A wave of silence spread out from the Princess as the sea of courtiers parted before her on the way to the Throne. Even from far away the Queen could see the anger smoldering in the eyes of her youngest daughter. Knowing Sofia wouldn't have created a dramatic entrance on purpose, something or someone must have delayed her. The Queen's suspicions were confirmed as she caught the barely suppressed smirk and look of disdain on the face of her middle daughter, Princess Darnelle.

The Queen stood to address the court, purposely ignoring Sofia's attempt at an apology. She fervently hoped her daughter would contain her infamous temper this day.

"People of Dahlian. May the blessings of the Eyes continue to look down upon our land. The Governors inform me that the crops are healthy, our herds of cattle and sheep are thriving, and the mines continue to produce precious gems and gold. Our Master of War reports that the Army and the Navy are strong and prepared. However, I have no intention of testing those claims by initiating another war with Marlinor as I relish the security of peace. To this end, Princess Francine has been negotiating tirelessly with the King of Marlinor. Today we joyously announce the betrothal of Princess Sofia to Prince Mathias, the youngest son of King Charles."

She waited for the cheers and applause to die down before continuing. "To honor this announcement, I call for a day long celebration throughout the land. Let the Proclamation be sent forth!"

As the clamor reached a new height, the Queen turned to her daughter with a raised hand to forestall the objections she knew were coming. It wasn't needed. Sofia stood motionless, the color of her face reflecting that of her gown. Eyes like blue topaz regarded the Queen, then looked away as she descended the steps of the dais and slowly walked away. Her steps were no longer graceful as she ignored the well wishers and exited the chamber. Unable to bear the sight, the Queen turned away as she fought to dismiss the memory of the emptiness in her daughter's eyes.

Sofia managed to make her way back to her rooms through a fog of despair and disbelief. Of all the things she had envisioned for her life, being married, especially to a Malinorian, had never been one of them. Deep inside of her, where the cauldron of anger normally simmered, sat a cold emptiness. Floanne, sensitive to the mood of her mistress, moved quietly about the rooms, laid out a change of clothes, and poured the Princess a cup of chilled wine. At a knock on the sitting room door, Floanne quickly hid in the bedroom.

Queen Oliva entered and stopped just inside, then quietly closed the door behind her. The Princess stood motionless, staring out of her window.

"You will leave in the morning with an escort of ten men commanded by Lt. Marton. You may take along one maid. The men will escort you to Seaside where a ship will be waiting to take you and the escort across the Straits of Durmont to the capitol city of New Bratan. There you will be met by King Charles and Prince Mathias."

Gliding to a side table, the Queen carefully set down a small bejeweled chest.

"Inside of this chest is an ancient wooden box, the contents of which are unknown. No one has been able to open it for many generations. The box has been part of the Royal Treasury since the time of the first Queens of Dahlian and is believed to contain an item of great power. King Charles's only requirement for the betrothal was the gift of this box, so you will present it to him immediately upon meeting. How he even knew of its existence is a mystery."

Unused to being ignored, the queen ordered, "Face me while I am speaking."

She involuntarily took a step back as Sofia turned to face her. Out of lifeless eyes spun a darkness that threatened to draw the color out of everything in the room. Determined to finish what she had started, the Queen continued.

"My daughter, your sacrifice will benefit our country immeasurably. As your Queen, I demand it of you. As your mother, I ask it of you."

Receiving no response, the Queen turned and made her way back to the door and risked one final look at her daughter on the way out. As the door clicked shut, a breath of sound escaped Sofia's lips, "I have no mother."

Unable to think, Sofia continued to stand long after the Queen was gone. A movement drew her attention to the bedroom door where Floanne stood transfixed. With faltering steps, her maid walked across the room as if being pulled by a rope straight to the jewel covered chest.

Once there, Floanne's hands slowly grasped the lid and raised it. Eyes bright with wonder, she trembled slightly as she reached inside and lifted out a wooden box darkened with age. A smile danced at the corners of her mouth as the box appeared to open on its own accord, and she was bathed in a golden light. Closing her eyes with a sigh, the lid of the box closed, and she returned it to the chest.

As the glow around her maid diminished, the Princess heard a voice, as if someone was speaking to her from the bottom of a well.

*'The bearer of the box is found. Guard her life with your own.'*

Sofia shivered and pulled back from the abyss where her shock and despair had led her. The sharp edge of her reasoning flared to life and cut through the events of the morning. She was being manipulated for someone else's gain, but would have to deal with it later. Right now she needed to make plans and prepare for her departure in the morning.

"Floanne! What are you doing over there?"

"Your Highness? I... it is such a lovely chest!"

Tearing her eyes away, Floanne bounced across the room, hands clasped together.

"This is so exciting! Are you really going to Marlinor? And to be escorted by Lieutenant Marton. He is so handsome! I have always dreamed of sailing on a ship. You have to beware of pirates though, or so I've heard. And the King! They say he is so strong and handsome that women fall down at his feet!"

Laughing at her maid's excited ramblings helped to lighten Sofia's mood, and put her in the right frame of mind for what she had to do.

"It will take more than a pretty face to make me fall down at the feet of any man," she snorted. "And don't you worry about pirates. Our ships are a match for anything those thieves will have." Turning toward the bedroom, she continued. "Now, I need to get out of this gown and leave to make certain arrangements. While I'm gone, I want you to pack only the two large travel chests. When I return I'll have one of the Guard escort you to your quarters so you can pack without being disturbed. I want us both ready to leave first thing in the morning." Not receiving a response,

Sofia turned back to find her maid frozen like a deer caught in the gaze of a hungry wolf.

"Floanne? What is wrong? You heard the Queen. She said I was allowed one maid and you are the only one I would trust to travel with me."

Fear filled eyes regarded the Princess as Floanne trembled, "No one in my family has ever left the Rose Palace, Your Highness. We have always served the Queens of Dahlian. My grandmother told me that a curse had been placed on our family, and anyone who tried to leave the Palace would die before reaching the end of the bridge."

Putting an arm around the shoulders of her maid, Sofia steered her towards the bedroom. "I imagine your grandmother told you that just to scare you into not leaving the Palace and getting into trouble. Don't you worry, Floanne. I will protect you with my life." With a sense of unease, she wondered, *why would I say such a thing?*

\*      \*      \*

Sofia awoke early the next morning, refreshed and with a renewed sense of purpose. After a peek into the sitting room, to check if Floanne was still asleep in the trundle bed brought up for her last night, Sofia hurriedly dressed herself. What she would be wearing today under her gown would be frowned upon by nearly everyone, but she was taking no chances. The gown she had chosen was the color of freshly tilled earth with long sleeves and loose fitting enough to hide what was underneath. The mornings were still cool which gave her the excuse of wearing a light cloak for added concealment.

She left her bedroom for the last time and almost ran into her maid who was coming to wake her. Floanne immediately dropped into a curtsy. "Please forgive me, Your Highness! I didn't mean to sleep so late."

"You are forgiven. I sometimes enjoy dressing myself in the morning, and it is not as late as you think. Now go and ring for our breakfast. I want to check the travel chests one more time before I send them down to be loaded."

Servants arrived with breakfast along with two guardsmen who would carry the chests down to the courtyard where the escort was assembling. As she ate, Sofia went over in her mind the precautions she had taken, and the preparations she had made last night. She had also decided last night to conceal her anger and act like a dutiful daughter when the Queen came to send them off. Sofia had no intention of giving anyone the satisfaction of seeing how upset she really was. The sadness she felt at the thought of leaving surprised her. The Palace was the only home she had ever known, but she had never felt comfortable in the role of a Princess. Whatever the future may hold, Sofia doubted she would ever return to the Rose Palace.

A knock at the door heralded the arrival of Lieutenant Marton to escort her down to the courtyard and the coach waiting there. Calf high boots so black they looked wet, every button and buckle of his uniform gleamed. With the twin golden braids of his rank proudly displayed on each shoulder, he was the epitome of an officer in the Queen's Guard. Short blond hair, a neatly trimmed mustache, and square face with a strong chin, were typical of most men from Dahlian. Standing just over six feet made him taller than average.

Plumed helmet under one arm and his hand on the hilt of his sword, he executed a perfect bow to the Princess, and then gave a slight nod to Floanne. Sofia hid a smile as she watched her maid attempt to brush her skirts with one hand, pat at her hair with the other, while preventing the two travel bags from slipping off of her shoulders.

Unable to pass up the opportunity, the Princess

commented, "Since my maid has apparently lost the use of her tongue, Lieutenant, please come in and be welcome."

Floanne jerked her head around to glance at her mistress, the look of admiration quickly changing to one of chagrin as Sofia's smile caused her to blush even brighter.

"Lieutenant Ronald Marton at your command, your Highness," he began. "It is with the greatest pleasure…"

"Save your speech for one of my sisters, Lieutenant. I'm sure it is a good one, but I want to get this over with."

Wisely keeping whatever else he had planned to say to himself, Ronald held out his left forearm. Once the Princess laid her hand on it, he escorted her down to the courtyard. The ten man escort stood next to their horses ready to mount at a signal from their Lieutenant. The Queen arrived with her Seneschal and the four Governors, then gave a short speech praising her daughter's courage and the sacrifice she was making for her country.

As the people cheered, the Queen came over to stand in front of her daughter. Searching Sofia's face for any sign of emotion, the Queen sighed, "May the Blessing of the Eyes comfort and protect you."

"Thank you, my Queen."

After bowing to the Queen, the Princess spun on her heel and climbed into the coach before the Lieutenant had a chance to assist her. Bowing to his Queen, he proceeded to his horse and the entire escort mounted as one. Riding to the head of the column, he raised his arm and motioned the escort forward. The sound of trumpets mixed with the cheers of the people as the Princess and her escort slowly disappeared through the palace gates and onto the bridge.

*     *     *

High atop the Palace, a young woman watched the proceedings below.

"Is everything in place?"

"Yes, Your Highness. Half of the men will be waiting at the planned location. The rest of us will follow at a discrete distance. It should be easy."

"Do not fail me Erik. Every one of them must die. The only thing I require is that you bring me the chest." Watching the coach enter the gate, she continued. "Mark my words. I *will* be Queen. Those who have served me well will be rewarded." She turned to the swarthy faced man with a look that made him shiver. "Those who fail me will never know the end of their suffering."

*   *   *

The blood drained from Floanne's face as the coach passed through the gates of the Palace, and began to travel across the bridge to the mountain. Sofia gently took hold of her maid's trembling hands and gave them a reassuring squeeze. Tear filled eyes turned to regard her mistress.

"I am so afraid, Your Highness," she whispered.

"I will let nothing harm you, Floanne. In just a few moments we will be across the bridge and free. If something does try to prevent you from leaving, I will deal with it."

At the end of the bridge, the coach shuddered to a halt, the horses frozen in their harnesses. The air inside of the coach rippled as a shimmering mist formed the outline of a man's face and a disembodied voice declared.

"This one is not allowed to leave the Palace. Return or she will die."

The Princess stood up and planted herself directly in front of the terrified Floanne.

"I have sworn to protect this woman with my life. If you attempt to take her, you will have to take me first. As a Princess of this realm, I command you to let her go."

An ancient power buried deep inside of Sofia's soul

began to stir. The spirit hesitated, recognizing that power, and then relented.

*"So be it. The responsibility for the safety of this woman and the item she carries falls on you. You are now marked as* Guardian.*"*

A searing pain above her right breast knocked Sofia back onto the seat just as the coach lurched forward and crossed the end of the bridge to the mountain path.

"Oh look, Your Highness," Floane exclaimed. "We are across the bridge, and I am still alive. You were right. It was just a silly story my grandmother made up to scare us."

"I told you that no harm would befall you as long as we are together," Sofia said as the pain in her chest swiftly faded from memory. "Now let us enjoy the ride through Kiplar as we still have a long journey ahead."

# CHAPTER FOUR

## TOGETHER AGAIN

Emma watched from the shadows across the street as Navon disappeared inside the stable. *'Was I ever that young and foolish?'* she wondered. Maybe he wasn't foolish, just innocent of the ways of the world. It was such an obvious trap, she had been sure Navon would realize what was happening and leave Twin Oaks as fast as his feet could carry him. Unfortunately, the setup worked perfectly, and he was now in the hands of his enemies.

What to do? Her orders were clear; observe from the shadows and only interfere if his life was in danger. Her instincts told her these men had no intention of killing Navon, and would keep him alive at all costs. But she would do everything in her power to prevent them from delivering the boy to the Dark Lord.

Four heavily armed men exited the stable and took up positions around the wagons. A small man, with a hood up to conceal his face, was followed by two more men dragging the unconscious boy between them. The leader and one of the men entered the coach. After helping them lift Navon inside, the other man climbed to the driver's seat and grabbed the reins, ready to leave. Emma could do nothing here in the village, especially against six armed guards. She would just have to follow until an opportunity presented itself.

The kidnappers pushed their horses hard all day, with only a short rest in the early afternoon. As long as they stayed on the main road through the old forest, Emma would be able to keep up. Descended from the Elintria, an ancient race of tree dwellers, she could travel through the trees just as fast as the men on the road as it meandered back and forth through the forest. She would have to attempt a rescue tonight before the road entered the river plains sometime tomorrow.

As night began to fall, the kidnappers stopped in a clearing alongside the road. There they set up three small tents for the guards and one large tent for the leader and Navon. Apparently, the guards were trained as two man teams, which meant that they were professional soldiers in someone's employ. That would make a rescue even more difficult.

While Emma stood hidden behind some brush and watched the men as they set up camp, a wickedly curved blade appeared in front of her face, and a large hairy hand covered her mouth. Just as silently the hand and knife disappeared. She wasn't afraid, she was seriously irritated. Sebastian was the only person she knew who could see her when she didn't want to be seen, and could sneak up on her so easily. He was an ogre she had hoped never to see again. By the time they reached his small camp, she had resigned herself to the fact they would have to work together again.

"So little one," he growled. "I be thinking it not so smart you to be rescuing the boy alone, yes."

"Sebastian, you big hairy oaf. What are you doing here? And don't call me '*little one*'."

"I just camping here be," he smiled. "South I going,

you be finding. Lucky, you be finding me."

"Don't tell me you were sent to watch over the boy also?"

"No," he chuckled. "I be sent over you to be watching, Em. Sometimes knife in your head bigger be than knife in your hand, yes."

"Wipe that dumb smile off of your face, Sebastian," she said glaring. "It's still only the two of us against six professional soldiers, and I have a bad feeling the leader is more than he appears."

"No little one. Many, not two," Sebastian nodded as a number of large grey shapes slipped into the clearing. The largest stopped in front of Emma and sat back on his haunches.

"Silverstar," she whispered, wrapping her arms around his neck and burying her face in his fur. "My heart sings at the sight of you. It has been so long, I thought I would never see you again."

"Later reunion time be," Sebastian rumbled. "Now boy be rescuing, yes."

"You are right, but first I must eat," she said pulling away from the elder wolf. "I hope you have some extra food. I've been running through the trees all day to keep up with the horses."

"Surprised I be, you not be stealing acorns from squirrels, or snatching insects while be running through trees. Only bread and cheese I be having."

"Very funny. *'Oh great hairy one'*. I see you haven't improved your speech in the last year either, have you?"

"I can speak properly when I want to Em. Right now, wanting to I not be."

Emma snorted at the smug look on Sebastian's face. Inwardly she was impressed since most of the ogre never bothered to learn more than a few words. He must have been practicing very hard since she last saw him.

She glanced first at Sebastian and then to the wolves while licking the crumbs from her fingers. "A simple plan is best, I think. The guards work in pairs, so when one pair comes to relieve the other, we will have four together in one spot. The wolves should be able to eliminate them quickly. At the same time, Sebastian, I want you to slip inside the tent of the last pair and put them to sleep permanently. Hopefully, the sorcerer will come out of his tent when he hears the commotion. When he does, I'll enter the tent, free Navon, and make our escape."

At midnight, everyone was in place. As with any plan,

it was good until the first blow was struck. Four grey phantoms shot out of the night from different directions, the men on watch and their relief were dead before they hit the ground. Sebastian slipped inside the sleeping men's tent and emerged a few seconds later, blood dripping from the tip of his blade. Unfortunately, not a sound was heard coming from the leader's tent.

Afraid of what she might find, Emma rushed through the tent opening, and was confronted by a grey haired, wiry old man wearing a bright red robe. He stood against the back wall of the tent, holding Navon in front of him like a shield, with a knife pressed to the boy's throat. A dark red stone sitting on a small table flared to life, bathing the inside of the tent in a ruddy glow.

"So, Light-Shifter, it is you. My Master was wise to give me a mage stone with the power to un-mask you. Now leave and don't trouble me again, or the boy dies."

"You and I both know your Master would be very displeased if the boy was to die, Sorcerer," Emma sneered. "If you somehow managed to escape me, then surely your Master will succeed where I have failed."

"It appears we are at an impasse. I…"

Whatever the sorcerer had been about to say came out

in a gurgle of blood as the point of a sword appeared just below his chin. The knife at Navon's throat dropped from lifeless fingers as the mage stone winked out.

"Impasse over be," growled a voice outside of the tent. A moment later, Sebastian entered through the flaps. "Happier the boy be, I am thinking, if light be for seeing," he observed.

She and Sebastian had developed their night vision to the point that they were comfortable in the dark. The boy however, was completely blind and probably very frightened. Lighting a candle with the tip of her finger, she turned to find Navon huddled in the corner with the fallen knife clutched in his bound hands.

"Emma," he stammered. "Is that really you? Everything was quiet while Master Geron read at the table. Then there was a noise outside, he jumps up, pulls me to my feet with a knife at my throat, and tells me if I make a sound he will kill me. The candle goes out, then this red light appears, and there you are standing in the middle of the tent. Then I feel Master Geron fall and then ..." Navon snapped his mouth shut to stem the flow of fear driven words. He shifted his focus to Sebastian instead and whispered, "Who *is* that, Emma?"

"I told you before, Navon, my friends call me Em and that big, hairy oaf is Sebastian. You are among friends now and safe for the moment."

Navon stood and massaged his wrists after Emma cut him free, then heaved a great sigh of relief. "I sure am glad that's over!"

"No young one," Sebastian rumbled. "For you just beginning it be."

\*     \*     \*

Listening to Floanne's excited commentary on the sights and sounds of the procession through Kiplar was just as entertaining as the actual event. Her maidservant's wide-eyed, childlike innocence was enough to dampen the growing apprehension Sofia felt about what might befall them on the road to Seaside. The Queen had declared a day of celebration, so the Princess decided she might as well enjoy it while it lasted.

When they reached the outskirts of Kiplar, the drummers, trumpeters and the extra escort saluted the Princess, and then started their return to the Palace. Lieutenant Marton positioned five men to ride ahead of the coach while the other five rode rear guard as he rode alongside. He leaned forward in his saddle to speak to the

Princess.

"We will stop tonight at the Vinebridge Inn, Your Highness. With an early start in the morning we should reach Whitecliff by tomorrow night, and then arrive in Seaside by the next afternoon."

"Thank you for that information, Lieutenant. I'm sure I would have figured that out myself eventually. What I want to know is whether you and the escort will be joining us on the ship to Marlinor."

Keeping his expression perfectly neutral, Marton answered. "The captain of the Silverfin has been ordered to take whatever steps are necessary to guarantee your safe arrival in New Bratan. The Queen charged me personally with your safety until the time you are presented to the King. The escort will board the ship to provide extra protection in case of a pirate attack."

With a glance at Floanne, who was gazing out of the other side of the carriage, Sofia turned back and locked eyes with the Lieutenant. In a lowered voice she hoped her maidservant wouldn't hear, "Never drop your guard, Ronald, even after we reach Marlinor. Things are not as they seem."

That night at the inn, the peace and quiet did nothing

to diminish the foreboding Sofia felt. Early the next morning as they crossed the bridge the inn was named after, even Floanne's delight at seeing an artifact left over from the age of the Deluti had no effect on Sofia's mood.

Around noon, Lieutenant Marton called a halt for lunch in a clearing alongside the road. He kept half of the escort in the saddle and positioned to watch both directions of the road. The sun was directly overhead in a cloudless blue sky with the temperature still rising. The tender shoots of the surrounding trees and bushes heralded the arrival of summer, and the color of the grass in the clearing was a shade of green that would only last for a short time. Fortunately, the road was still damp enough from the winter; dust was not the problem it would become in the following months.

The Lieutenant dismounted to assist the Princess and her maidservant from the coach. After he received a nod from Sofia and a blushing smile from Floanne, Ronald turned to re-mount his horse just as a bolt from a crossbow thudded into the side of the coach next to him. A moment later the driver of the coach fell from his seat with a bolt in his back. Riders, with weapons drawn, could be seen approaching from both directions.

"Lieutenant, you and the others ride out and engage those horsemen before they have a chance to use their horse-bows," the Princess ordered. "I will stay here and take care of the men with crossbows."

Ronald had heard the rumors about the Princess, and took a chance she knew what she was doing. Having made his decision, he jumped back onto his horse and drew his sword. "Sergeant, take two men and join the others to the west. The rest of you follow me."

Before they could move, two more bolts whistled out of the forest on either side of the road. One of the men crashed to the ground, hit in the chest, while the other bolt glanced off of the sergeant's helmet.

Sofia ordered Floanne to lie flat on the floor of the coach. She reached under the seat and pulled out a sack containing a small crossbow, and a bundle of bolts she had hidden there the night before leaving the Palace. The Princess ducked under the coach and spotted the archer hiding in the trees as a ray of sunshine reflected off of his helmet. A single shot in the throat dropped him. The other archer was smarter and farther away across the road. Only when she saw another bolt flash out from behind some brush did she fire, reload and fire again.

The young guardsman, who had been knocked out of his saddle, still lived and tried to crawl towards the coach. Sofia hoped she had eliminated the threat from across the road. She sprinted over with crossbow at the ready to help the young man to his feet, and turned back toward the coach. Before they could return, a rider appeared out of the woods, jumped up to the driver's seat of the coach, snapped the reins and sped off down the road towards Whitecliff, with Floanne trapped inside.

As the team of horses galloped past Lieutenant Marton, the last two attackers broke off and followed the coach. Ronald appeared to be the last one alive from the escort except for the young man still being held up by the Princess. To the west all was quiet except for the thrashing of a wounded horse. Several others were standing where their reins had been dropped, the area littered with the bodies of dead men and animals.

The Lieutenant galloped back to the Princess and stumbled after climbing out of his saddle, blood running down his leg from a deep gash in his thigh.

"Your Highness. Are you injured?"

"I am unhurt, Lieutenant," she answered as she helped the young guardsman to the ground. "Which is more than

I can say for you. Quickly now, before you fall down, undo the buttons on the back of my gown so I am free to move."

Ronald stared at the buttons for a moment before he reluctantly pulled off his gauntlets and began the task of un-doing them. He fumbled at first, trying to keep his eyes averted, uncomfortable, until he saw what was hidden underneath. Sofia shrugged her shoulders and let the gown slide down her body into a crumpled pile at her feet, revealing a full set of hardened leather armor.

"Now, Lieutenant, lie down right here so I can stop your bleeding," she ordered, and began to rip strips of cloth from the gown. She hurried over to the guardsman's horse and grabbed the med kit and the bladder of water that every man was required to carry.

Pulling a small knife from the sheath at her waist, the Princess proceeded to cut away the material around the wound in the Lieutenant's leg. He did his best not to flinch as she cleaned it, but his occasional sharp intake of breath made it clear she needed to quickly sprinkle crushed Twinkleberry powder in the wound to lessen the pain. With needle and thread she deftly sewed the flesh together. Funny, she couldn't sew a stitch into cloth, but somehow this was different.

Sofia looked up from inspecting her work and found the Lieutenant gazing at her with a wondrous look on his face.

"Princess, where did you learn how to do that?" he asked, the admiration clear in his voice. "I felt nothing."

"You would be surprised at the things I have learned," she retorted. "Now, lay still and rest while I do what I can for our young guardsman."

Sofia stood up to stretch and heard a sound behind her just as Ronald hissed a warning. She spun around and came face to face with the archer from across the road. The shaft of a crossbow bolt protruded from the right side of his chest, his arm hanging useless. Held steady in his left hand was a loaded crossbow aimed directly at her.

The burning ember of her anger had been smoldering deep inside ever since that day at the Queen's Court, and became an inferno that threatened to burn away all reason. How dare these men threaten her life, kill her escort and kidnap her maidservant? Along with the rush of desire to kill the man, came the realization that deep within lay the power to see it done with just a thought. Before she could act on that revelation, the attacker began to waiver, the crossbow clattering harmlessly to the ground as he slowly collapsed and died from loss of blood.

The Princess turned away and knelt beside the injured guardsman. She felt an overwhelming need to bury her desire to kill under a desire to heal. Forcing the anger back down, she was able to feel compassion for the young man as she saw the pain in his eyes.

"What is your name?"

"Gilfor, Your Highness," he answered through clenched teeth.

"Be brave, Gilfor. I need you to live. Now, lay perfectly still so I can get this breastplate off of you and remove that bolt."

The breastplate had absorbed most of the force from the shaft of the crossbow, but it had still penetrated his chest. After the breastplate was removed, Sofia was still unable to see the head of the bolt. It appeared to have gone in between two ribs and possibly punctured a lung. She would have to work quickly.

Again using her small knife, she cut away the leather and cloth surrounding the wound, at last exposing the bolt head. After cleaning the area as best she could using a little water and a strip from her gown, she sprinkled more crushed Twinkleberry leaf onto the wound to slow the bleeding and to deaden the pain.

The world around her slowly faded away as Sofia focused all of her attention on the tedious work of slowly removing the barbed head from the young man's chest. Awareness returned as she tied off the last stitch and attempted to straighten up.

The muscles in her back and neck protested at the movement being forced upon them, which caused Sofia to groan out loud. Slowly turning her head, it became obvious that the Lieutenant had disobeyed her and was not resting where she had left him. She spotted him leaning over a fire stirring something in a pot. Horses were picketed in a line just off the road with saddles and packs stacked neatly to one side.

"Lieutenant Marton. Why aren't you resting as I ordered, and how have you managed to accomplish so much in such a short length of time? I won't have you tearing that wound open and bleeding to death."

At the sound of her voice, Ronald quickly ladled some stew into a bowl and brought it and a water bladder over to her.

"Here, drink some water and eat before you attempt to

stand," he instructed.

About to give him an earful for taking that tone with her, and tell him she wasn't hungry or thirsty, the world began to spin and her traitorous stomach growled loudly. Without a word, the Princess gratefully accepted the water and drank half before she could stop herself. Handing her the bowl, Ronald took the water, gently raised Gilfor's head, and managed to get him to drink while Sofia continued to kneel next to them, soon staring into an empty bowl.

"Here, let me get you another. To answer your question, Princess, I have been able to accomplish a few things because you have been working on the boy for over an hour."

Muttering to herself, Sofia attempted to stand but her legs felt like stumps and wouldn't move. "Help me up, Ronald. I must get the blood in my legs moving again."

Rather than merely giving her a hand, he bent over, grabbed her by the arms and lifted her up. She gasped as the blood rushed into her legs like a river of molten fire. Leaning against Ronald until her legs would support her, Sofia noticed that he had taken the time to change clothes. She glanced at his thigh, then looked him in the eyes.

"Your leg?"

"Apparently it wasn't as serious as we first thought. It feels fine now." With a significant look he continued, "There is barely a scar."

He led her over to the fire and re-filled her bowl. As she stood there, eating more slowly this time, she spotted the two groups of bodies the Lieutenant had lined up at the edge of the clearing.

"Did you recognize any of the men who attacked us?"

"No, Princess. Nor could I find anything that would tie them to a particular country or province." Searching her face, he accused, "You knew this was coming."

"I suspected it, but I wasn't sure whether they were after me or the item I carried in the coach." She turned and stared off to the east as she felt a faint pull on her heart. "Either way, Ronald, as of this day, Princess Sofia Salidoris of Dahlian no longer exists. If you wish to join me, your life will be forever changed also. Nothing is more important now than following that coach and rescuing Floanne."

# CHAPTER FIVE

## TIME TO BELIEVE

Navon glanced down at the dead sorcerer, and then back to the ogre. He had heard tales of ogres who spoke, but you had to listen closely to what they said. What Sebastian just said made no sense. "I don't understand. What is just beginning for me?"

"It's alright, Navon. Ogres are hard to understand sometimes, especially Sebastian." Emma gave the ogre a warning glance, and then continued, "Sometimes he says things he shouldn't."

She did not know what the Ancient One had told

Sebastian about Navon, but her orders were clear. Shadow and protect Navon if needed. Say or do nothing that might influence him as to where he was going and when. It was up to the amulet to guide him now.

"You two have seven bodies to bury while I look over things here in the tent. The sooner that is done, the sooner we can get some sleep. I, for one, have had a very tiring day."

Navon nodded in agreement and turned back to the body of the sorcerer.

"No, young one," Sebastian cautioned, touching his shoulder. "His body, many spells be. Ogre I be, and magic no touch ogre."

Navon stepped back for a moment and studied the ogre. Sebastian was at least several hand-spans taller than even his brother Altair. Leather pants, vest and boots, were the only clothing covering the ogre's hairy body. A large, two-handed sword was strapped to his back with several short swords and knives attached to the wide belt around his waist. Navon shivered at the thought of coming face to face with Sebastian in a fight.

He suddenly felt drained, and slowly made his way over to the table to sit down, the events of the last few days weighing heavily on his mind. As he sat there and stared at the candle on the table, the memory of Emma lighting it with a touch of her finger flashed before his eyes. Raising his head he saw the look of sympathy on her face and blurted out, "You're not human either!"

"No, Navon, I am not. My people come from a race of tree dwellers. I have a small amount of power that enables me to shift the light so I become invisible to anyone who looks in my direction. I am the largest of my clan and was chosen and trained by the Ancient One for other duties."

"The ugliest Em also be," Sebastian chuckled.

"Sebastian!" Navon cried out as he surged to his feet. "That was very un-kind and totally un-true. I think Emma is very pretty and you owe her an apology."

"It's alright, Navon," Emma said, blushing, and then glared at Sebastian. "He is just jealous. Sebastian is so ugly, whenever he goes home they hide all the little ones so he won't scare them to death."

With a huge smile that showed off his fangs, Sebastian headed for the opening of the tent. "Come, young one, work we have. Answers later be."

As Navon and Sebastian began the arduous task of digging seven graves for the dead men, Emma carefully moved about the tent and inspected what she found, but touched nothing. She did not have a natural defense against magic like Sebastian. The sorcerer appeared to have been reading a history of the nation of Marlinor. It lay opened to a page depicting a map of the region with several of the Keeps circled in red. What that meant, she had no way of knowing, but noted the names of the ones circled. It might prove important later.

The tent was neatly divided between the sorcerer's area and the small corner allotted to Navon. All of his weapons were carefully stacked behind the sorcerer's cot. Even though the old man had the boy under some sort of spell, he obviously hadn't trusted Navon with possession of his weapons. Once Sebastian cleared out everything that might be spelled, there should be enough room for the three of them to spend the night in the tent. Emma hoped that Navon would be too exhausted to ask any more questions tonight. She had no idea how to answer them. Tomorrow would not be a good day.

In the morning, Navon rolled over in his cot and came face to face with three hairy muzzles with fangs and yellow eyes that danced with excitement. The pups started nipping playfully at his blankets and the cot, threatening to tip it over.

"Alright, alright!" Navon laughed as he swung his legs out. "I'm getting up, but what are you three doing here?"

The young wolves turned and trotted toward the entrance of the tent, their job done. Just before passing through the flaps, the female turned, showed him what could only be described as a wolf smile, and continued with her tail flagged out playfully behind her. Shaking his head, Navon pulled on his boots, and then reached over for his sword, belting it on. He finally accepted the fact that Emma must be right, his life was in danger. He swore he would never be caught defenseless again.

The bright morning sun pushed away the darkness that had been shrouding Navon's thoughts. Sebastian sat next to a fire with a steaming kettle hung over it, stirring something that smelled surprisingly good. As soon as the ogre spotted Navon, he ladled some of the stew into a bowl and motioned the boy over. Emma and the wolves were lying together at the edge of the clearing. She leaned against the shoulder of the elder male, running her fingers through his fur. The pups sat around a stump by the fire, apparently waiting for Navon to join them.

"Sit down and eat, young one," Sebastian suggested, handing him the bowl. "Em and I talking be," he started-- then stopped, growling. He took a deep breath before continuing. "Em is right, I must practice my speech. Navon, we know you have many questions, but most things you will have to discover the answers to on your own. I will tell you what I think is safe to be telling you."

Sebastian stared into the fire for a moment, collecting his thoughts before he addressed the boy again. "Young one, the Elder Races have been waiting a long time for someone like you to be chosen. We live longer, and have longer memories than humans. What for you has become a distant legend is still very real for us. The number of Elder lives lost to the hatred of the Dark Lord will never be forgotten. He still lives, Navon, and his power is growing. You and others like you will be needed to prevent him from searching out and destroying all non-human life on this world."

Navon sat motionless, spoon frozen halfway to his mouth as he tried to focus on the ogre. '*Why me?*' was his first thought, then '*Why not me?*' What had been the point of becoming the best swordsman and archer he could be, plus studying the herb lore with the old healer, if it wasn't for the purpose of protecting and caring for others? The impact of what Sebastian told him slowly began to sink in. It took a moment before he could speak.

"But I thought the Dark Lord was defeated at the end of the Deluti War."

Emma, feeling sorry for the ogre as he struggled with his speech, answered from her place among the wolves. "He was defeated, Navon, but the High Lord was unable to take the life of his own brother. Instead he cursed him to live with the pain of his injuries and the memory of how his lust for power brought about the total destruction of the Deluti. I believe the Spirit of the Deluti cursed the Ancient One to live with the shame of *his* failure to rid this world of a terrible evil."

Something in what Sebastian had said ate away at one of Navon's assumptions until he finally asked, "Emma, how old *are* you?"

Sebastian let out a hoot of laughter as Emma stood up and glared at him. "Laugh it up fur face. One of these mornings you will wake up with little pink ribbons in that beard of yours."

She ignored the ogre's continued laughter and turned back to Navon, whose face was red with embarrassment.

"My age is not important and none of your concern. What is important is that we get you safely to the Ancient One before others are sent out to capture you. He will be able to explain all of this better than we, and help you learn about your power."

Navon sat there with his head hung down and berated himself for such uncouth behavior, when Emma's last word brought his head up with a jerk. "Power? What do you mean?" Unbidden, the image of the she-wolf's thigh sprang up before his mind's eye. It was completely healed without even a scar. He forced the image back down, not wanting to deal with it.

"Navon, anyone with even the slightest bit of ability, will sense the aura of power surrounding you. I happen to know that the power now comes from the amulet you wear, only because the Ancient One told me it had chosen you. Others will not know, and will try to use your power for their own gain."

Absently stroking the fur of the wolf pup sitting beside him, Navon felt he needed to change the subject fast before he became overwhelmed and made a worse fool of himself.

"What of the wolves? Do they have special abilities

also?"

"Because of their size, the wolves are just as intelligent as any human, and smarter than some I know," she answered while looking at Sebastian, who only grinned. "What makes them special is their ability to communicate mind to mind. They don't have speech like you and I, but through images and emotions they get their point across. Silverstar believes that eventually you will be able to sense their thoughts."

"Silverstar?"

"My oldest and dearest friend," Emma replied lovingly, her arm around the elder wolf. "He leads this small pack along with Drifting Snow, the one you healed. These three youngsters are theirs. Thunder Dancer, Shadow, and Moonlight, who appears to have taken a liking to you."

As their names were called, each pup cocked their head in his direction, except for Moonlight, who laid her muzzle on Navon's leg and gazed up at his face. Other than his brother Altair, he had stayed away from close relationships with anyone in the Keep. He believed they would not want to be his friend because of his differences. The young wolf's eyes drew him in and enveloped Navon in a warm golden glow that shone with more than acceptance and understanding; acceptance of who he was and understanding of what he might become. The wonder of having a true friend began to erode the walls he had raised to guard his heart.

Unable to sit any longer, Navon stood up and stared into the forest without seeing. *'Walk,'* whispered a voice from deep inside of him. "Please excuse me. I must walk," he announced to no one in particular. Bending over to pick up his bow and quiver of arrows, he turned toward a small path leading into the forest. "Maybe I will get lucky and bring back some fresh meat."

Emma and Sebastian could only watch in stunned silence as he left the clearing with Moonlight at his side, the other two pups close behind. They had not meant to drive him away.

Navon walked the path that appeared before him as it meandered through the trees. This forest was much older than the one surrounding his home as the trees were larger and farther apart. Their dense canopy of leaves blocked out most of the sunlight, which kept the forest floor open except for the occasional plant able to survive the gloom.

Moonlight's presence beside him provided a much

needed anchor for his soul. His hand on her shoulder was a link to the real world while his mind tried to grapple with fantasies suddenly come to life. The Deluti were legendary beings from the far distant past who had disappeared from the world, yet supposedly one of their Amulets of Focus had chosen him. For what? What did that mean?

Bright sunlight, blinding after the dim light of the forest, forced Navon to stop and shade his eyes. He stood entranced by the vision spread out before him. A large, white stone structure with a delicate spire in each corner, dominated a circular clearing. It was both the most beautiful thing he had ever seen, and the most frightening. Nowhere was there any sign of life, not even a single blade of grass marred the white perfection of the clearing. The dirt path he had been on ended a few feet in front of him where it became a road paved with perfectly fitted stones. He glanced to either side and saw that even the branches of the forest giants dared not pass the boundary of white.

The pups stood rooted in place as they looked to Navon for reassurance. Was it safe for them to continue or should they turn back?

Seemingly stronger and closer, the voice in his head spoke again, *"You must choose. If you return you will never be more than you are now and the Amulet will go to another. The path before you will hold many rewards, but is filled with danger. Once you start on that path, you can never turn back"*. As Navon sought the eyes of the young wolf pressed up against him, the voice continued. *"The she-wolf is the only one who may accompany you. She is bonded to you now and forever. Her life is in your hands."*

Moonlight gazed up into his eyes with such intensity that, for the first time, he felt a presence in his mind not his own. Compassion and encouragement slowly filled an empty space inside of him he never knew existed. Navon returned her look, hoping she could feel the gratitude and affection he felt for her.

"Altair believed in me, my mother believed in me, and now you," he said aloud and turned back to the clearing. "Maybe it is time to start believing in myself."

That said, he pulled out his sword and resolutely stepped forward onto the paved road, Moonlight close by his side. When the last hair on her tail passed the line of the boundary there was an intense flash of light, and the entire clearing, including the young man and the wolf, was gone. The forest re-appeared as if nothing else had ever been there.

Thunder Dancer and Shadow huddled together in terror until their eyes adjusted to the darkness of the forest. As soon as they were able, they raced back down the path, howling in misery, convinced their sister was lost forever.

*     *     *

Far to the west, on the coast of Marlinor, sat the bustling city of New Bratan. The Capitol enclosed the mouth of the White Feather River where it ended its long journey from the farthest reaches of the interior. Not only did the city enjoy the advantage of a thriving river trade, it also oversaw the largest natural harbor on the west coast. The Bay of Salia provided shelter from the fierce storms that blew out of the north, and being the homeport of the King's Navy, it was a safe haven from pirates.

The King's Palace overlooked the entire bay, and for several miles in all directions from a position atop a point of land at the north end of the bay. Designed by men and built by ogres, it was sometimes referred to as the Iron Fortress and had never been conquered by any enemy.

In a small chamber, adjacent to the Royal Audience

Chamber, King Charles d'Rodare met with his Council of Dukes.

"Today, my friends, marks a turning point in the history of our country. Duke d'Lorange has worked tirelessly on my behalf these last several weeks negotiating with the Queen of Dahlian to secure a lasting peace between our two nations."

The King then passed the golden Cup of Truth to his closest friend and advisor seated to his right at the round council table. Tradition held that in council, only the person holding the Cup was allowed to speak, and they must speak the truth.

"Marcus, if you will."

"Thank you, Majesty. As you all know, we have been at war with the nation of Dahlian for as long as anyone can remember." He paused for a moment to make sure he had the attention of the other Dukes, and then continued. "What has it gained any of us? We have all lost family members to a useless war that has proved nothing. We finally have the opportunity to end this conflict now and forever. The Queen of Dahlian has agreed to the betrothal of her youngest daughter, Princess Sofia, to King Charles' son, Prince Mathias."

Duke Anthony Strumant pushed back his chair, almost knocking it over, and stood to his full height. With a face that appeared carved in stone, he stared at the King, and then leaned forward with his knuckles on the table.

"Majesty, this is preposterous. There can never be peace with those witches." He continued through clenched teeth, "Why wasn't I consulted on these negotiations?"

The King, equal in stature to the Duke, was not intimidated and calmly answered as Marcus returned the Cup. "Sit down, Anthony. You have made your views perfectly clear in the past, and even though we all held similar views, it is time for change. I believe you will also find that this treaty will open up a whole new market of eligible young men for those daughters of yours."

With a harrumph, the Duke re-seated himself at the table, ignoring the smiles of the others. "Very well. But would someone please enlighten me as to the additional benefits of such a union."

Benjamin al'Fortuna, the Eastern Duke, signaled for the Cup. He had been quiet up to this point, but began to tick off points on his fingers.

"One. Our trade, especially through your port here in New Bratan, will certainly double or more. Two. While we have been fighting each other for control of the Straits of Durmont, Rogosh the Pirate has been stealing us blind. Our combined Navies should be able to send him packing back to his island and keep him there. And finally, though I have been unable to substantiate this, rumors from the east say the Elders are upset about something and coming out of their seclusion in the mountains."

Duke Strumant, still ignoring the Cup, glared at everyone seated there. "I will agree that your first two points would be a great benefit to our country if we can trust the Dahlians that far. What I do not understand, Benjamin, is why we should be concerned by rumors of the non-humans?"

"Anthony, my old friend, it is not the Elders we should be concerned about. It is what they are telling the people. They say the Ancient One has warned them the Scarred Mage has become more powerful than he was before, and is once again threatening our lands. My friends, we all remember the tales of the massive destruction and loss of life caused by the Dark Lord. There are no more Deluti left in this world to protect us if he is truly still alive. The combined armies of our two countries may not be enough to save us."

A dark, foreboding silence fell among those at the table as childhood memories played out in their minds. Memories of great-grandparents who struggled to convey the horrors passed on from their ancestors who survived the Deluti War. One by one, each man raised his head to face his King.

The Cup of Truth already before him, King Charles took a moment to collect his thoughts before he answered the questioning looks of his Dukes. "My friends, this is dire news indeed, if true. However, before we become overly concerned, I feel we should take the time to ascertain the validity of these rumors. Benjamin, I must ask that you return to the east and personally visit your Barons to gather whatever information you can. It would be preferable if you could speak directly with one of the Elders. In the meantime, Marcus, if you would be so kind, I want the proclamation sent out to announce the upcoming betrothal, and individual invitations sent to all the Barons requesting they attend the formal banquet."

The King stood up from the table with the Cup held before him and continued with a smile. "It will take an ogre appearing at court to personally convey the truth before I will believe that the Ancient One or his brother is still alive after all these years."

As the others rose from their seats, he bid them a good day. "May the Eyes watch over us, my friends."

*     *     *

In a secret room, deep within the Duke's mansion, there hung a special mirror. This mirror, however, did not reflect a person's image. A single large feline eye, the vertical pupil surrounded by a dark red iris, filled the mirror. No matter where the Duke stood in the room, the eye always appeared to be staring right at him, even though he had never seen it move.

The eye in the mirror was not the reason for his unease. The image that would replace the eye, when he uttered the words of calling, still turned the blood in his veins to ice. The memory of that first contact, over a year ago, remained branded in his mind with fire and pain.

*A voice in his head woke him from a deep sleep. It commanded he arise and follow its direction. When he tried to ignore it, pain such as he had never felt before forced him to obey. The voice then directed the Duke to a door hidden behind a tapestry inside his office. It guided him through a series of secret locks that opened the door to the mirror room.*

*The moment he opened the door and spoke the words forced out of his mouth, a hideous, scarred face replaced the eye, and took him, mind, body and soul. All of his memories, emotions and plans paraded past the edge of his awareness as the Dark Lord sifted through them. After an eternity, the image in the mirror released him and spoke for the first time.*

"I am Scorpios, your new lord and master. You may continue your plans to usurp the Crown, I care not, but you will do and say what I tell you or the pain you experienced earlier will become a fond memory."

The Duke took pride in his ability to not show fear, but was unable to prevent the beads of sweat that formed on his brow in anticipation of this meeting. He had learned long ago not to lower his eyes in the presence of his master, so he kept his eyes fixed on the mirror as he spoke the words of calling.

The scarred face of his master appeared to be distracted before those hate filled eyes locked onto his. "Ah, my little Duke, the would-be King, what have you to report?"

"The terms of the betrothal were agreed upon by both rulers, and Princess Sofia will leave the Rose Palace in the morning along with the chest you required. They should arrive here in the Capitol within the week depending on the weather in the Straits. Also, just as you foresaw, the boy was driven from his home by his father, but the men I hired to capture him have not reported back. I must believe they have failed."

On anyone else, the smile that appeared on the face in the mirror would have given the Duke some hope. The cruelty of that smile convinced him that the Dark Lord was aware of his heightened fear, imagining the punishment he would receive for his failure. The smile widened, confirming his fear.

"Fear not, my little would-be King. Your men were never more than a diversion to set up the boy for the real abduction. I have a team planted in the village that will accomplish the task. I expect to hear of their success very soon. However, I suggest that in the future, you hire men with more intelligence to accomplish any task that I have set before you."

The Duke knew this to be more than a suggestion, and could only nod. "Yes, my Lord."

"Now, no one there will be able to open the jeweled chest that the Princess is delivering, so I will send someone to you who will open it and remove the item inside. He will replace it with something dear to the King. My man will remove the hidden locks so the King will be able to open it himself at a ceremony you will arrange."

Once again, that smile twisted the face in the mirror. "What the King discovers inside the box will guarantee your needed diversion as he initiates another war with Dahlian. Plan wisely, my little Duke. I am sure my brother is aware of your ambition and is watching."

# CHAPTER SIX

# DEATH OF A PRINCESS

"Ronald, whoever planned this ambush must have given orders to leave none alive. I know my sister Darnelle is ambitious, but this seems above what even she is capable of. It appears I have even more reason to leave the country now. The men who escaped will report that the Princess and the Lieutenant survived, therefore we must effectively disappear."

"And how do you plan to accomplish that, Princess?" he asked around a mouthful of stew.

Sofia chose to ignore the sarcasm in the lieutenant's

voice as she continued. "You and I will become successful caravan guards, mercenaries if you will. I'm sorry, Ronald, but everything that has a Palace mark on it will have to be left behind. Choose the best armor and weapons from amongst the attackers to replace your own. I have already made certain that the weapons I carry bear no markings, and in this outfit I look nothing like a princess."

After a quick glance up at the Princess, he shook his head. "Your hair."

"What?"

"Princess, you could be dressed in sackcloth, but with your face and that hair, someone will recognize you. We can't do anything about your face, but something will have to be done about your hair."

Mind racing, the Princess scanned the clearing for something, anything she could use. With a slight smile, she began to braid her hair and loop it around her head. She picked up Gilfor's discarded helm and set it on her head, covering her hair.

Ronald nodded in approval, and then scooped up some ashes from the fire. Dipping a fingertip in the ashes, he gently smeared a small amount onto her eyebrows, then stood back and smiled.

Sofia regarded the lieutenant with suspicion. "Now what?"

"Well, every good merc has a nick-name. I think yours should be Surly Sofia."

"Ha ha, very funny. Now get busy, Ronald the Wretched, we're wasting time."

With a chuckle, he began unbuckling his armor and headed for the line of corpses. Looking down at the bodies of his men, he felt a surge of sorrow, regret, and anger. This was supposed to have been a mission of honor, not a rendezvous with death. He was proud of them, especially since there were twice as many dead attackers. His men had acquitted themselves well.

Sofia scooped up the last of the stew into a bowl and brought it over to the young guardsman. "Here, eat this and then rest. I need you strong enough to ride. Your mission is just as important as ours. The Queen's life may be at stake."

Gilfor's voice already sounded stronger. "Just tell me what to do, Your Highness. I won't fail you."

"Will anyone in Kiplar recognize you if you go there?" Gilfor shook his head no and continued to eat.

"Good, this is what you will do."

*　　*　　*

The sounds of the galloping horses and the spinning coach wheels were like thunder in Floanne's ears. From the moment the coach lurched forward and slammed her against the leg of the rear bench, she had held on to that leg with all of her strength, unable to let go. Eyes squeezed tightly shut, tears formed a puddle under her face.

Before she left the Palace with the Princess, she had never moved any faster than her feet could take her. Riding in the coach had been so exciting, and the speed at which they traveled took her breath away. Now, the one glimpse Floanne had dared through the wildly swinging coach door made her squeeze her eyes even tighter.

She repeated the words of her mistress over and over in her mind. *"I will let nothing harm you, Floanne."* The Princess must still be alive. Somehow, Floanne understood their lives were now tied together, and could sense her mistress. But would the Princess be able to catch up in time to protect her from these terrible men? What did they want?

After what felt like hours, she heard one of the riders

outside yell. "Slow down! There is a farmhouse ahead where we can hide the coach."

The thunder diminished to a low rumble as the coach slowed, then swerved off of the main road. They came to a stop as she heard the creaking of rusted hinges, then moved again into darkness. The coach leaned to one side as the driver climbed down.

"You two find a lantern and give us some light. Take two of the horses from the coach and hitch them up to the wagon that should be here. The sooner we find that jeweled chest, get it loaded in the wagon and leave, the happier I will be."

"Eric, what about the Princess' jewels?"

"You fool. What would you do with them? Who do you know with enough gold to buy them who wouldn't hesitate to kill you to get his gold back? Just leave them. They are not for the likes of you or me."

Having completed the task of hitching up the wagon, one of the attackers went to look inside the coach while Eric searched the large travel chests strapped to the top. The first thing he saw upon opening the door was a pair of bare white legs.

"Well, well, well.... Eric, looks like I found

something better than jewels. The only thing I like better than a good fight, is an unwilling wench."

Eric, jeweled chest under one arm, climbed down and glanced inside the coach. "Keep your britches tied up, Bron. I want to be gone from this place now. She's just the Princess's hand maiden and worth nothing. Kill her."

"Eric wait," the youngest of the three spoke up. "I enjoy killing someone who has raised his sword against me, but I don't like to kill for no reason. Besides, she is worth considerably more than you think. I know a man in Whitecliff who will pay a lot for a virgin."

The silence stretched as Floanne's fate hung in the balance. Eric quickly took the measure of the defiant young man, and decided that now was not the time to test him.

"Since you are new to the group, Harlo, I'll let that slide for now. However, the next time I tell you to kill someone, I will expect immediate obedience. Do you understand me?"

The young man's eyes never left the face of his leader as he nodded once. Harlo had his own plans, and they did not include the other two men. He ignored the look of undisguised lust on Bron's face as he brushed by and gently pried the young woman's fingers from the bench leg. He carried the maid, unresisting, over to the wagon and laid her inside. His Master had foreseen Princess Darnelle would try to double-cross him and keep the chest for herself. It did not concern him whether the Princess received the jeweled chest now. The item they all wanted was no longer inside. Somehow, Princess Sofia and her hand maiden had removed the item from the chest and hid it in the skirts of this young woman. He could sense the power within the item, but his Master had warned of the consequences were he to touch it.

Floanne made no effort to struggle, or make any sound. From the moment she heard Eric say *"Kill her"*, her consciousness fled to a far corner of her mind where it huddled and wept, repeating over and over, *"Princess, help me."*

*     *     *

Gilfor left on his way back to Kiplar with instructions to contact the old arms-master, Master Horshall, and tell him everything. Dressed in the Lieutenant's armor, he would not stop until just outside of the Royal City. There he would discard the armor and royal trappings. The uniform should prevent anyone from impeding his progress, and spread rumors of a Lieutenant of the Palace guard racing back to the Palace alone.

Sofia and Ronald left the clearing soon after, dressed as merchant guards with serviceable, but unmarked armor and weapons. The only exception being Ronald's sword. They would claim it was a gift from a wealthy merchant. In fact, that wasn't far from the truth since it had been a gift from his father.

They had been on the road for over an hour, alternating the gait of the horses so as not to harm them. Another hour and they would switch to the backup horses. The slow, steady pace chaffed at Sofia like an ill fitted breastplate, but she knew better than to abuse the horses. Her anger continued to burn its way to the surface and push for more speed. Added to that, the overwhelming compulsion to find Floanne, both confused and frightened her with its intensity.

Sofia was just about to call for another burst of speed when Ronald pulled up, his horse struggling to keep its balance as he pulled the animal around and headed back the way they had just come. Her anger erupted and took control. His horse reared up on its' hind legs and screamed as they both tumbled to the ground.

Unable to move, she watched the terrible scene unfold before her. *What did I just do?* The outward flare of her anger vanished as if smothered by a bucket of water, and then re-kindled inward. *What is wrong with me?*

The horse scrambled to its' feet, apparently not seriously injured. A groan from the man on the ground forced Sofia to move. Afraid of what she might do to her own horse, she jumped off and ran over to where Ronald lay in a crumpled heap. She knelt down beside him and searched for any injuries.

"What happened?" he gasped.

"Your horse reared and you fell off," she replied, unable to face the pain and uncertainty in his eyes. "Are you hurt?"

"It will be uncomfortable sitting a saddle for awhile, but nothing appears broken," he winced as he sat up. Ronald grabbed the arm she put around him to help and tried to catch her eye. "What really happened, Princess?"

"That's not important right now. What I want to know is why you stopped and turned around."

He decided to let it go for now, but promised himself he would push her for answers later. "I am not much of a tracker, but anyone could have followed the tracks of that coach, and those tracks turned off of the road at this point. It only makes sense they would have someplace to hide the coach before they rode on into Whitecliff. I think we should find the coach, not only for any clues they might have left behind, but also the possibility of some shelter from the coming storm. Besides, it will be dark soon, and I don't relish the thought of sleeping under a tree."

After Sofia helped him to his feet, she finally took the time to survey their surroundings. The sun was visible just above the horizon to the west, and dark clouds approached from the north. The area around them offered only open fields with an occasional stand of trees. Not a pleasant spot to be caught in a downpour.

"Forgive me, Ronald. It appears that I have been spending too much time reacting, and not enough time thinking. You are absolutely correct. We must find shelter for the night, and whatever clues the attackers may have left behind. They might give us a better idea of what to expect tomorrow."

They traveled a short distance from the road, and came upon a small farm house and barn on the other side of a rise in the lane. Apart from a few chickens in the yard, nothing else could be seen or heard. Swords drawn,

Ronald approached the house while Sofia headed for the barn.

He soon emerged from the house, slammed his sword back into its scabbard and approached the barn, his jaws clenched. Sofia appeared at the side door of the barn and motioned him inside.

One look at his face and she rejected the question she had been about to ask. "You were right. We would not have been able to catch them tonight. They took two of the horses from the coach and hitched them up to a wagon of some sort. This happened some time ago as the horses they left behind are completely cooled down."

Her observations confirmed what he had suspected after seeing the wagon tracks heading into and out of the barn's main doors. "At least they will be traveling much slower now, and will have to stop for the night. We still have a chance to catch them before they reach Whitecliff."

Sofia stood with her eyes closed, arms folded across her chest as if in a hug. A barely perceptible change in her expression caused her face to look softer and slightly wilted. Opening her eyes, and in a voice minus the usual arrogance, she admitted. "This is very difficult for me, Ronald. For the first time in my life, I am unsure of myself."

"We have both been thrust into a situation neither of us has had to face before, Princess. Why don't we take care of the horses, see what there is in the coach we can make use of, and then eat. Afterwards we will talk."

The Princess was uncommonly quiet as they went about their individual tasks. No caustic remarks resulted when he took charge and gave orders to her just as he would to any of his men. Ronald became seriously concerned, not only for her, but for himself as well.

They settled down on a couple of overturned buckets in a corner of the barn. A small brazier provided some light and comforting warmth as the rain on the roof could be heard over the moaning of the wind. Ronald glanced over at the Princess, and knew he would have to initiate the conversation.

"I think the first thing we need to talk about is your new found power."

"Power? I have no idea what you are talking about."

Her eyes never left the glowing coals, but Ronald recognized the signs of fear on her face. He had seen it enough times on the faces of the young guardsmen he commanded.

"What are you afraid of, Princess?"

"I am afraid of nothing, Ronald. Even if there was something to be afraid of, I won't let it deter me."

"Princess, the absence of fear is death. When we feel fear, it reminds us that we are still alive, and gives us the strength to stay that way. You cannot deny the fact you healed Gilfor and me with something more than herbs and stitches. And what about this afternoon? It was you who stopped my horse dead in its tracks and nearly killed us both, wasn't it?"

For a moment, Ronald felt his own fear as her eyes locked onto his, surprised he couldn't feel the heat from the fire burning within them. The flames flickered and died to be replaced by shame.

"By the Eyes, Ronald!" she cried. "I didn't want to hurt you. I was angry, and just wanted you to stop. A power rose up inside me, and I acted without thinking. I am so sorry."

"Apology accepted. At least you have finally admitted to yourself there is a power in you. It is enough for now. What I would like to know is what is so significant about your handmaiden? I agree with you that those men probably had orders to kill everyone, yet she still lives.

You have given up your crown to rescue her. Why?"

Sofia leaned forward to add more coal to the brazier, her eyes once again focused on the glowing embers before she answered. "I don't fully understand it myself, Ronald. She carries an item of great power. I cannot describe it since I have never seen it, but I have felt its power. Somehow, it made me swear to guard her life with my own. I must find her."

Ronald jumped up and started to pace back and forth, mumbling to himself. "By the Eyes, it must be one of the lost Deluti Amulets of Focus. That means the Princess ... I never dreamed ..." At which point he stopped to stare with apprehension at the Princess.

"Ronald, what are you babbling about? Sit down and talk to me."

He slowly returned to his bucket, eyes still locked on Sofia, trying to gather his thoughts. How could he convince her that what he suspected was true?

"Princess, I may be a simple soldier, but I love to study history, especially the history of the Deluti wars. As you may remember, the High Lord Demitrios ruled the world through the Council of Five. Each of the councilors wore an amulet that helped to focus their power, as a symbol of their position. Toward the end of the war, the councilors gave up their lives by forging their spirits into each one of the amulets."

Sofia was never interested in history, but when Ronald began to speak of the Deluti, the hairs on the back of her neck stood up, and she felt something stir deep inside of her. "Why would they do such a horrible thing?"

"None of the Five were as powerful as the Dark Lord, even with their amulets. If he had defeated any one of them and gained the power focus of their amulet, it would have given him an advantage over his brother Demitrios. After they died, the amulets were scattered and hidden throughout the land. He must not be allowed to gain possession of even one of those amulets."

"But how would that be possible, Ronald? The Deluti War is hundreds of years in the past. Surely, Scorpios must have passed away a long time ago."

"Princess, the Deluti are not human. They are immortal beings, and can die only at the hand of another Deluti. It is said the High Lord still lives in the far northern mountains of Marlinor, and I have no doubt Scorpios lives far to the south of us in the Stagwood Marshe. Even the pirates avoid the evil that surrounds the

South Shore."

Ronald went to check on the horses and look for more coals for the brazier. He also wanted to give the Princess time to absorb what she had just heard before he shared his conclusions on the source of her power. When he returned to their corner, the confusion was still evident in her expression.

"I must admit, what Floanne carries could very well be one of those lost amulets, but what does that have to do with me?"

"The last thing written in the history I read was a foretelling by the High Lord himself. *'Many generations from now, the blood of the Deluti will return through the line of humans even stronger than before, and our time on this world will come to an end.'"*

Once again he stood, pulled his sword and held it point down as he knelt before the Princess, who shivered while searching his face for any sign of deceit.

"The power of the Deluti *is* in you. As long as there is life left in me, I will stand by your side to support you and be your friend, if you'll have me. In memory of my father, who gifted me this sword, this I swear to you, Princess."

"Never call me that again, Ronald," she whispered.

"The Princess is dead."

Just then, a bolt of lightning and the corresponding thunder shook the barn to its foundation. As the thunder continued to echo off in the distance, the two of them shared a look filled with trepidation and no little fear.

# CHAPTER SEVEN

# THE FIRST ARCH

Navon and Moonlight walked slowly along the paved streets of the deserted city. The forest disappeared to be replaced by a softly glowing mist. The palace that seemed so close when they first entered appeared to move farther away as they walked. It then materialized directly in front of them after they rounded one of many corners. None of the structures they passed resembled anything Navon had ever seen, nor could he imagine what their purpose might be.

As they walked, Moonlight shook her head and

sneezed several times. Through the tenuous rapport they shared, he got the impression something was different about the air around them. After a moment, he realized there were no smells, and no moisture. The air was just as pristine and sterile as their surroundings. On a whim, Navon re-traced their steps, this time taking a different street, but upon turning at a different corner, the palace appeared before them just as before.

"Looks like we have no other choice but to enter. Might as well get this over with."

His hand resting lightly on Moonlight's shoulder, the two of them entered through an opening in the nearest tower. In the center of a large courtyard stood three arches arranged so that their sides touched. Faint murmurings filled the courtyard, as if a large crowd of people whispered to each other, yet there was no one to be seen.

A spectral figure of white mist took shape before them. The apparition wore a single, sleeveless garment that hung from the shoulders in a seamless flow to just above the stones. Shoulder length white hair, and a beard that rested on his chest gave the impression of great age. However, the features of his face appeared both smooth and ageless.

The sound of whispering faded as a strong voice spoke directly into Navon's mind. *"Welcome to the Palace of Wistaglon, young Navon d'Roddell. We hope this image is pleasing to your eye and will provide some comfort. Are you prepared to begin your testing?"*

"Wait! I understand none of this. Where are we? Why am I here, and who are you?"

*"Has your mentor not explained to you who you will become, and why you must undergo the testing?"*

Navon's silence was his answer as he continued to stare at the figure before him. It still made no movements that he could see. Grateful for something to concentrate on besides the strange surroundings, the comfort he received from Moonlight continued to provide him with an anchor.

During his silence, the whispers increased in volume, then quieted once more.

*"We must ask your forgiveness, Navon. Our awareness of your world is not as it once was. When the spirit in your amulet called us, we assumed you had received your training, and were ready for your trials. Perhaps this is for the best. You are the first of a race that has never existed before; a joining of Deluti and Human. The old rules may no longer apply."*

So, his feelings all these years were justified. He *was* different. Navon's hands clenched into fists as his eyes squeezed shut to stem the tears that threatened to flow. The pain of years being shunned and bullied rose up on the inside to taunt him. How many times had he run to his big brother, unable to bear the hurt? Why had no one told him? Is this why Father had ignored him even when he excelled at his studies?

"Did my father know?"

*"Yes, your parents knew. We asked them not to show you any favor, or give you special attention. You had to learn to be independent, and not develop family ties that would interfere with your growth as a Deluti. Your life will be a solitary one as you must learn to rule without emotional attachments."*

dropped slowly to his knees next to Moonlight and held her close. The smell of her fur and warmth of her body provided a sharp contrast to the sterile atmosphere around them. Her feelings for him surrounded those hurtful memories and banished them. In their place blossomed love and confidence that filled him up and dried his tears. If the spirits were unaware of the love he felt for his brother and for Moonlight, they would soon learn. He rose to his feet to confront the vision before him.

"You said it yourself; the old rules no longer apply. I am human and if I am to rule, it will be in whatever fashion I see fit. Now, what are these trials you spoke of?"

Either the spirits realized how uncomfortable he felt addressing a motionless specter or they learned quickly. The figure now moved with a fluid grace as it raised an arm and pointed to an image of the amulet Navon wore.

*"The symbol of the Deluti uses three eyes to represent a vision of the power available through each one. One is for life, one is for death and the uppermost is the compassion to know when to use either. Each arch tests your ability to master one of those powers. The first one you must survive is the trial of compassion."*

"I don't understand. If the Deluti receive each of those powers through the amulet, why do I have to face these tests?"

"Only one of the new blood is required to face the Arches of Rineron. If you succeed, you will become the next Deluti High Lord."

Long moments passed as Navon let that revelation sink in. When Emma told him the power of the Deluti resided within the amulet, it all seemed so unreal. Now, he could not deny the reality of what he saw around him. Is this what he wanted for his life? And if Sebastian was to be believed, the Scarred Mage still lived and threatened the lives of all the Elder Races. Could he stand by and not do his best to combat that threat?

He glanced down at Moonlight who watched him with the same intensity as before. Whatever he decided, she would never leave his side. "What of the wolf?"

*"The bond between you was unforeseen, and cannot be broken. If you fail, she will die."*

"Then I will not fail."

*     *     *

Back in the clearing, the only sound to be heard was an occasional crackle from the fire. Emma and Sebastian alternated between looking at the path Navon had taken, and staring at each other. Eventually the silence became too much for Emma.

"Well, what do we do now?"

"We doing nothing be," he answered. "Amulet and pups him protecting. Wanting thinking time alone."

"That's easy for you to say, fur face. It's me the Old Man will hang from my toes if anything happens to Navon."

"I protecting you be, little one," Sebastian grinned at her from his place by the fire.

Before she could come back with a barb of her own, all the wolves sprung to their feet growling, and stared into the forest. Frantic howling could be heard in the distance, coming closer. The two male pups careened into the clearing, broadcasting terrifying images of a brilliant flash of light even Emma and Sebastian saw clearly in their minds. Silverstar and Drifting Snow were forced to clamp down on the necks of the pups to settle them.

Emma, who had a better rapport with the elder wolf than the pups, had to wait for a clearer image of what frightened the pups. What she did pick up from Silverstar made no sense. A white clearing with white buildings suddenly appeared on the trail, a voice that sounded in their minds, and then Navon and Moonlight disappeared along with the clearing. Emma knew this forest better than any other and there had never been a white clearing like they described.

All eyes turned to her. Once again, silence filled the clearing except for the quiet whimpers of the pups, and a low rumbling growl from Silverstar that Emma could feel.

Sebastian stood, then sat again, hand clenched on the

hilt of his sword. Slowly and carefully he spoke. "Little one, somehow we have failed. This is beyond any of us, and we need direction. Only you have the power to contact the Old Man."

Emma nodded and reluctantly reached inside her tunic to pull out the talisman she kept on a chain around her neck. The Ancient One had given it to her many years ago to contact him in an emergency. She had used it only once before in a fit of frustration, and received a tongue lashing for her actions. Even though this was an actual emergency, he would not be pleased at the interruption. At the touch of her finger along with a small release of power, a misty figure formed in the center of the clearing.

A deep, powerful voice filled the clearing as High Lord Demitrios faced Emma.

"This had better be important, little one."

"What, did I wake you from a nap?" she bristled. "Of course it's important, Your Ancientness."

Sebastian let his fangs show in a smile, and then quickly put on a serious expression as the image of the Ancient One turned to him.

"Sebastian, I am disappointed in you. I had hoped you would have her under better control. Now, I see all of you gathered here except young Navon, and what is most disturbing, I can no longer sense his spirit. What has happened?"

Sebastian could only shrug while holding his hands out to the side.

Emma approached the glowing figure, hands clenched at her side. "That's the problem. We don't see him either. According to the wolf pups, he and Moonlight have been taken away by your Deluti Spirits. You should have warned us."

"What do you mean? And who is Moonlight?" He stared off into the forest before turning to the elder wolf. "Silverstar, may I question your young ones?"

With a bark of command, the pups moved forward to sit at the feet of the old Deluti High Lord. He stared into their eyes for a short period of time, and then released them. They rose and returned to their parents, no longer whining.

The Ancient One paced back and forth with a look of concentration on his face as he pondered. "Which one of the Councilors inhabits the amulet that Navon wears? He is not ready. What is the purpose of the bond to the she-wolf? This changes everything."

"Stop babbling, old man, and explain to us what is going on," Emma demanded.

He turned to the ogre, as if he hadn't heard. "Sebastian, I must ask that you travel to the Capitol and present yourself to the King. Princess Sofia of Dahlian will arrive soon to fulfill an agreement between the two nations. My vision is unclear, but I sense that the Princess is next in line to receive an amulet. One of the Dukes is planning something, and I have to assume he is an agent of my brother. He will do anything to get his hands on one of the amulets. Tell the King I have sent you to be her personal bodyguard, and warn him of my brother's return."

He ignored the fuming Emma and turned to the elder wolf. "Silverstar, my old friend, the fate of your daughter and young Navon is now out of our hands. The Deluti spirits have activated the Arches of Rineron. We cannot interfere or aid them in any way." The Old Man paused as he raised his eyes and gazed to the south. "They must have passed through the first arch. I now sense Navon's spirit far to the south in the land of the Shadhuin Nomads. If he and Moonlight survive their trial, they will return to the north through the Shadow Mountains. Wait for them there."

Finally he turned to Emma with a look that caused her to step back. "And you, my favorite little tree climbing assassin, will accompany Sebastian to the Capitol, find out what the Duke intends, and then contact me again. Stay out of sight and stay out of trouble if you can."

Before she could respond, the image of the old man returned to her talisman, leaving her and Sebastian to stare at each other in consternation.

"That went well, don't you think," Emma beamed. "Did you hear him? He said I was his favorite! C'mon Sebastian, let's take care of the wagon and get going. The sooner we arrive at the capitol, the sooner I can find out what the Duke is up to."

Sebastian shook his head and chuckled as they broke camp.

*       *       *

Navon, Moonlight at his side, stepped through the first arch as the last words of the Deluti spirit followed him. *"Remember, young Navon, others will look at the world with a different eye than yours, but it does not mean they are without honor."*

The world they entered resembled nothing he had

ever seen before. Rolling hills of grass as far as the eye could see, with scattered stands of short, bush like trees. At this distance it was impossible to tell what kind of leaves they had if any. The sun shone directly overhead in a cloudless blue sky so expansive, Navon suddenly felt very insignificant.

Sweat formed on his brow, and he could feel beads of moisture trickle down his spine. Moonlight's tongue hung out, panting. A sweltering wind at their backs brought with it a sound like a blacksmith's forge combined with a stampede of cattle. Navon spun around to be confronted by the source of the noise. Fire! A wall of flame over ten feet in height stretched in both directions as far as he could see. In front of that wall were hundreds of animals of all shapes and sizes, running for their lives.

His legs had already reacted to the sight, and started pumping before Moonlight's mental image of running burst inside his mind. The faster animals pulled alongside and passed them by. Moonlight stubbornly stayed by his side even after several attempts to send her a command to run ahead and save herself. Not used to running in this kind of heat, Navon could already feel himself slowing down.

His lungs struggled to keep up, and his legs felt like burning stumps. Mixed in with the sound of the fire were the screams of the animals not fast enough to outrun the flames. The temptation to look behind was not enough to overcome the fear of what he might see, until Moonlight sent him a mental warning.

Navon took a chance and craned his neck around to look. Not far behind, a beast, larger than any bull back at the keep, bore down on him. He also saw that they were losing the race to the fire. The skin of the beast blistered and turned black as he watched. Somewhere he found the strength for another burst of speed, or did the ground begin to slope downward? Ahead of them appeared a solid line of dense vegetation with animals bunched up against it trying to force their way through.

The sound of screaming animals as they clawed at each other and at the barrier, combined with the roar of the flames behind him, threatened to overwhelm his mind. He could not think. Was this the end? If it hadn't been for Moonlight, Navon would have stopped and given up right there, but her constant mental encouragement kept him going. Maybe he could find a way to climb over the top without being trampled by the frantic animals trapped there. The forgotten beast behind him had a different idea. Just before they reached the hedge, the beast's nose appeared between Navon's legs and with a powerful thrust of his head, propelled Navon over the barrier to land in water.

Moonlight landed next to him with a splash, just as the fire blasted into the line of brush with a final flare that singed their hair. The sudden silence amplified the sounds of animals splashing, attempting to cross what turned out to be a small river. All around him the water filled with the bodies of animals who had outrun the fire, but had no strength left to stay afloat.

The spectacle of death slammed into his chest like a hammer blow, and ignited the fire of his anger. Navon stood up in the water, shook his fist at the sky and screamed. "Why! ...If I am to become some kind of powerful being, why could I do nothing to stop this senseless waste of life? All I did was run like all the others, only to be saved by a beast that probably deserved life more than I." The pitiful cries of the animals in the water spurred him to action. "By the Eyes, there will be no more death this day!"

He splashed back and forth, frantically searching for

animals, still struggling, he could carry back to shore. Moonlight already had a number of small animals clinging to her back as she returned to the bank. Several larger animals struggled aimlessly until he pulled them into shallow water where they climbed out on their own.

Something drove him to climb the small bank, squeeze through the blackened branches, and look for life. He pushed through right next to the bull-like beast who had saved him. Whether it had been on purpose or an accident was not important. Navon felt honor bound to do what he could for the animal.

Kneeling next to the beast, he soon realized he could do nothing. Burnt hip bones protruded past where the skin and flesh had melted away. Blackened and bleeding flesh covered the rest of the body. The only signs of life were small puffs of dust in the ash where the beast's muzzle lay buried. Laying his hand on the beast's head, overwhelming pain rocked Navon to the core of his being. Only the bond with Moonlight gave him the strength to pull much of the pain into himself.

The pain slowly diminished as the animal approached death. With a final shuddering breath, the spirit of the beast departed, but not before enveloping Navon in an embrace of peace and gratitude. Collapsing against Moonlight, sobs wracked the young man's body until he fell into an exhausted sleep.

After an hour, Moonlight woke him with the need to move. Not far away, they found the burnt body of another large beast. Navon cut away enough of the already cooked meat to last them for several days and converted the stomach into a vessel for carrying water. The safest option would be to follow the river, but he wanted to be prepared if they were forced away from it.

Navon watched as Moonlight devoured her portion of the meat, and realized they would soon have to find another source of food. The meat would not last long in this heat, and he at least needed something else for his diet, such as grain and fruit.

She growled a warning as her keen eyesight spotted a small group of riders approaching from the direction opposite the river. Navon pleaded with her to hide down by the water since he worried what their reaction would be to large wolf. She finally acceded to his request, but he felt her concern over his own safety.

He waited a few moments longer before standing up as if he had just noticed the approaching riders. He had no idea what sort of a picture he would present to them as his entire body was covered in soot and mud from the river. Hopefully they would not see him as a threat. As they came closer, Navon saw that none of the riders were using reins to control their horses. They rode with arms crossed except for two who held small horse bows at the ready. He had an uncanny feeling the horses were in control.

As the five of them approached, four slowed and stopped in perfect unison. The center horse continued until it was just a few paces in front of Navon. The young rider leaned forward to stare at him a moment before demanding.

"Who you? What you do here?"

"My name is Navon d'Roddell, and apparently I am a long way from home."

While the leader of the group paused to contemplate such a strange statement, Navon took a quick measure of the men confronting him. He judged that he would stand a head taller than the tallest one, and could take all five if it wasn't for the two arrows trained on his chest. Still, he had been trained how to fight against men on horses, and if he could keep one of the animals between him and the archers, he would have a chance.

Slowly inching his hand toward the hilt of his sword, he froze as the horse lowered its head and stared him directly in the eye. Navon received the unmistakable impression the horse knew what he planned and was ready to defend its rider. The odds had just changed, and not in Navon's favor.

Coming to a decision, the leader announced, "You slave. Steal long knife and bow. You with us come. The Maudwan will decide."

"I am no thief and no slave!" Navon shouted and made a grab for his sword, but the horse surged forward and knocked him to the ground, sword flying. Two of the other riders jumped from their horses, quickly pinned him, and tied his wrists together.

Now afraid for Moonlight's safety, Navon mentally begged her not to interfere and stay hidden, but follow at a distance.

His trial had truly begun.

# CHAPTER EIGHT

# THE SCARRED MAGE

For thousands of years, the Deluti fortress of Bryhom dominated the western shore of the Alegro River across from what had once been called the Stagwood Forest. The Fortress was the home of Scorpios, Dark Lord of the South. Built using dark grey, granite blocks from the nearby mountains, the one feature that set it apart from other fortresses was the massive tower located in the center. The iron clad, double doors were the only known way in or out.

At the end of the Deluti War, Scorpios lost control of

his power as he attempted to trap and burn his enemies. Being immortal, he lives forever changed by the hideous scars that cover his body. His loss of control also resulted in the complete destruction of the forest, now known as the Stagwood marsh. The evil he unleashed that ill-fated day still permeates the earth, and all life there became twisted and corrupt. The souls of those killed were forced to remain, and are constantly searching for a means of escape. Only Scorpios and a select few of his human sorcerers are able to navigate the marsh and reach the secret seaport on the south coast.

On this day, the massive stone blocks were outlined in a blue haze of the Lord's power as it crackled down the seams to ground out through the foundation. The pristine halls of the great fortress were eerily silent as the servants huddled in whatever hiding place they thought might protect them from the Scarred Mage's wrath. When the strength of his anger emanated from the walls in this fashion, the elders knew they would soon have to find another slave to serve him.

Scorpios, his gnarled hands resting on the waist high walls, stood unmoving at the apex of the massive tower. A soft breeze ruffled the wisps of hair that grew between the scars on his head, but it did nothing to cool the heat of his anger. With the intensity of his power directed inward, he knew the only way to prevent damage to himself was to allow some of it to bleed through his hands into the stone below.

The focus of his inner vision lay far to the east, penetrating the haze that shrouded the marsh. It ignored the ships that fought the wind and sea past the Channel Islands, and traveled the vast distance to the Shadhuin Plains where the last energies of a Deluti Portal slowly dissipated. What he *saw* ignited for the first time an infinitesimal spark of uncertainty in the core of his being.

He had underestimated the power of the Deluti Spirits and their ability to influence the world of the living. The appearance of the Wistaglon Palace in the natural world was a thing even Scorpios thought no longer possible. It seemed the spirits of the Deluti were active once again. Was this a sign their misbegotten plan to mix the blood of a Deluti with some pathetic human had failed, or was young Navon more powerful than they foresaw? Therein lay the foundation of his anger... uncertainty. He despised not knowing, and not being in control. His only consolation hinged on the fact Navon was now completely out of his brother's reach.

The invisible thread of life-force tied to his human sorcerer sent out to capture young Navon, had returned to him late last night, confirming the man's death. The young whelp must have had help! If any of those abominable talking animals were involved, he would soon find out. Those creatures constantly interfered with his plans, but once he acquired another amulet, a plan would be set into motion to rid the world of those obscene creatures.

Scorpios refused to acknowledge the incessant itching of his scars as he hurried down the stairs of the tower. Due to the power of his brother's curse, they would never heal, and were a constant reminder of his greatest failure. He forced his vision away from the past and focused on the future. Time was of the essence, and he could not afford any more delays.

A plan began to form as he descended the stone steps and solidified by the time he reached the door to a very special room. A room even his brother did not know existed. This room contained Deluti Mirror Portals tied to every ancient Deluti structure that still existed on both continents. Through these mirrors he could reach into any of those buildings and influence the weak minded to do his bidding.

It was time for a different approach, since a direct attempt failed to capture young Navon. A rapid mental inventory of his sorcerer corps brought up the image of the perfect young man to send to the Shadhuin Horse Lords and ensnare Navon through the guise of friendship. First, he must contact his slave trader in the port city of Argo, and then the unpleasant task of attaching another life thread. Unpleasant for the young sorcerer, but not for Scorpios.

*     *     *

The Royal apartments occupied the majority of the Iron Fortress's upper floor and were divided into separate units for the King and Queen, and each adult child. Prince Mathias made the familiar journey from his rooms to the King's suite unaware of his surroundings, or he would have noticed the faint layer of dust and the lack of shine on the wooden floor.

The monarchy had been in the hands of the d'Rodare family for many generations, and the interior of the Royal apartment reflected the conservative tastes of the long established family. Mathias announced himself as he entered, and then sank into the padded leather arm chair next to his father. A small fire burned cheerfully in the fireplace, and a bottle of wine with two glasses rested on the small table between them.

King Charles knew his son well enough to hold his peace until Mathias was ready to talk. A companionable silence fell over them until his son began asking his questions.

"Have you received word of Princess Sofia's departure from the Rose Palace, Father?"

"My network of contacts is not that good, Mathias," the King chuckled. "I do have an agent in Whitecliff who will send a pigeon when the Princess departs there for Seaside. From that point we will just have to wait until her ship is spotted entering the Bay of Salia."

Silence once again filled the room while Mathias rose and refilled their glasses. He stood for a moment staring into the fire, the glass forgotten in his hand, before turning to face his father.

"What kind of a woman do you think she is?"

The King was tempted to poke at his son's seriousness by asking, "Who?" but sensed that there was more to this visit than questions about the Princess. He would just have to be patient and wait for Mathias to reveal what was truly bothering him.

"I have heard that her beauty inspires bards and poets, but she has a temper and is not much interested in ruling."

"What do you mean?"

"It is reported she never appears at court unless it's required, but spends most of her time riding and practicing arms. If the last report is accurate, she has reached the level of a master swordsman."

The King chuckled when he saw the crestfallen look on his son's face, who was only an average swordsman. "Don't worry, son. It is highly unlikely you will ever have to face her in a duel. I have heard of your prowess in bed, so confine your battles to the bedroom and you should be fine."

Mathias snorted as he turned away to stare out the window facing the harbor. "Very funny, Father. No matter the battle, I have a feeling she will not be easily won over."

He returned to the armchair but perched on the front edge so he could face his father. "There is another reason I wished to speak with you."

"I suspected as much. What is bothering you, Mathias?"

Unable to sit, Mathias stood up and paced back and forth in front of the fireplace, marshaling his thoughts. "I don't know if I am jumping at shadows or just suspicious of change, but I have a bad feeling. Something is not right in the world, Father. Why this sudden change of heart by the Queen of Dahlian?"

"I imagine she is just as tired of this senseless war as I am," the King replied.

"It's not only that. What of the rumors being spread by the Elders? What if they are true? Even with our combined armies, we have no chance against the power of the Scarred Mage."

"If the Scarred Mage is truly still alive, then his brother will be also. The Ancient One defeated his brother once before, and will do so again."

"But at what cost in human lives?" Mathias whispered.

Their thoughts were interrupted by a knock at the King's door. After a command to enter, one of the new servants came in bearing a tray of refreshments, including another bottle of chilled wine. With the barest hint of a bow, the servant turned and left.

Uncomfortable with their present discussion, Mathias

took the opportunity to change the subject. "Have you noticed the increasing number of un-familiar faces among the guards and staff, Father?"

"Oh yes. It was brought up in council several weeks ago by Duke d'Lorange. He felt it would be to our advantage to rotate the guards and some of the staff with some of the outlying keeps. They will gain experience dealing with different situations and locations. The Council agreed. In another month we should see some familiar faces returning."

"Wherever these new guards are coming from, they are not being taught proper respect. I caught one of them making obscene gestures behind the Queen's back. I ordered two other guards to escort him to the holding cells for punishment, but he never arrived. All three have since disappeared."

"That is disturbing news, and I will have Marcus look into it right away. Surely, it was just a misunderstanding."

Mathias bowed to the King and turned towards the door. "I hope you are right, Father. About everything."

*     *     *

The promise of a glorious new day hung in the air, heralded by a faint glow on the eastern horizon. The rain overnight scoured all lingering odors from the air in preparation for the fragrance of morning flowers. Sofia filled her lungs as they rode out of the barn and felt some of the misgivings from the night before dissipate in the crisp air.

Ronald's continued grumbling brought a smile to her face as the memory of this morning's confrontation replayed in her mind. He had readily agreed that a clean shaven face would not help their persona of mercenaries, but when she ordered him to put dirt on his polished boots and actually scuff them, the look on his face was priceless.

"Now who's being surly, Ronald?"

He wisely kept any comments to himself as he carefully latched the barn door and mounted his horse. They had decided that mercenaries with re-mounts would stand out, so all the horses were released into the pasture behind the barn. Ronald reassured the Princess he would get a message to the guard in Whitecliff informing them of the farmer's fate.

Soon they were back on the main road to Whitecliff. The rain had washed away any sign of wagon tracks, but Sofia still felt the connection to Floanne pulling her toward the town. True dawn was fast approaching, and the air began to hum with the sound of insects and the call of the birds eager for breakfast. Squirrels scolded the pair as they passed by.

They traveled the first hour in silence until Ronald turned to the Princess and confided in her what had been on his mind all morning. "I have come to the unpleasant realization that my uniform and rank in the Queen's Guard determined my self-worth. Now that I have been stripped of all the fancy packaging, what sort of man remains? It pains me to think I may not be the right man to stand at your side."

This time, Sofia kept her comments to herself. She felt the same way, not about Ronald, but about herself. With the outer shell of a princess discarded, what sort of woman remained?

One thought had plagued her since they found the abandoned coach, and it had nothing to do with them. "Ronald? Not that I would have it any other way, but why have they kept Floanne alive and brought her along?"

Ronald glanced at her and then continued to stare straight ahead as he answered, "Despite the Guard's best efforts, the slave trade is alive and well in Whitecliff."

Sofia shuddered and urged her horse into another

burst of speed.

The sun shone down on them from directly above when the outskirts of town finally came into view. Ronald reined in and stared at the town a moment before turning to Sofia. "I may not know a lot about mercenaries, but what I do know is that we should stop at the first inn we come to, order a meal and ask the innkeeper if he knows of anyone hiring caravan guards."

"I have no intention of hiring on as a lowly caravan guard, Ronald. Why bother? This close, I can probably lead us right to them."

A smile flashed across Ronald's face as he imagined Sofia as a caravan guard. "Appearances, Sofia. If we ride in looking like mercenaries, and then don't act the part, word will spread like wildfire through the underground. Someone would then watch our every step. Come, we are probably being watched already."

The first buildings they passed belonged to the local woodcutters with stacks of building materials outside waiting to be delivered. Several butcher yards filled with sheep, pigs and cattle were scattered to either side of the road. They continued on past a number of small cottages with children playing in the yard, and dogs that barked a warning before they finally arrived at an inn.

Sofia hid a smile behind her hand as Ronald put on what he assumed was the attitude of a mercenary. The innkeeper gave no indication one way or the other whether he accepted their story, but disappeared into the kitchen to fetch them a pair of platters. After setting the food on their table, he hurried behind the counter, filled a pair of mugs with ale from the cask there, and set them on the table also.

When the innkeeper returned to polishing his mugs, Sofia leaned forward. "I don't know how convincing your story was, but I think the tavern accent you took on set him at ease. Where on earth did you learn to speak that way?"

Ronald smiled at her around a piece of meat and took his time chewing before he answered her. "I too have learned things you would be surprised to know. My father loved to frequent the local tavern, and mix it up with the locals. Once I was old enough, my mother made him take me along. She hoped it would keep him out of trouble."

"Did it?"

"Yes and no. No one wanted to fight a man who had his young son along, but I attracted all the ladies to his table. Some of the, shall we say, less discreet women used me as an excuse to get close to my father. Too close."

Sofia smiled to herself as she pictured the scene he described. They finished their meal in silence, and then stood up to leave since Ronald had already paid. They found the door blocked by a large bearded man, heavier than Ronald, and armed with a massive club at his side instead of a sword.

"You cannot leave. The guild here in Whitecliff will not allow women to carry a sword. She must be taught a lesson," he began, and then froze as a single drop of blood ran down from the tip of Sofia's sword where it rested against his throat.

Ronald folded his arms and leaned forward with a smile. "You are lucky, my friend. She has just completed her meal and no longer feels surly. If you had come any earlier, there would be more than one drop of blood. I suggest you and your brothers find other business while my partner and I complete ours and move on. If however, they decide to be stupid, it wouldn't be the first time we've left a trail of bodies behind. Now step aside or die."

The tip of her sword never left the man's throat until he stood pressed up against the far wall. She slowly wiped the blood off of her blade on his jerkin then let the tip drop until it pointed at his groin. Beads of sweat broke out on his forehead when he looked into her eyes and saw the glow of her barely contained anger.

"You are not the first man to feel the edge of my blade, but you are the first one to survive."

Sofia sheathed the sword in one fluid motion, then spun on her heel and left through the door Ronald held open. Once outside, they quickly mounted and headed into town at a trot.

"Lead the way, Sofia. I think we'd better find Floanne and leave this town as soon as possible."

She led them unerringly to the south side of town where they stopped in front of an abandoned livery stable. The faded sign over the padlocked door hung from a single hook, and the windows were boarded up. The large gate to the holding area lay broken on the ground inside the fence.

Ronald pointed to the gate where fresh wagon tracks could be seen entering the yard and ended at the closed door of the old livery. Quietly they dismounted, led the horses inside the fence to be tied off, and approached the smaller door of the stable where they heard arguing inside.

The moment the old livery came into view, the glowing embers of Sofia's anger burst into flames. She sensed Floanne's fear as a ghost hovering at the edge of her mind, and when that ghost began a silent scream of terror, the flames became a raging inferno, burning away all reason and caution.

Without waiting for Ronald, the Princess opened the door, completely ignoring the two men who stood there, her eyes locked on the man opposite them. The aura of power, laced with the echoes of the ancient evil that surrounded him, awakened the power buried deep within her soul. Here was an agent of her true enemy.

When Harlo first saw the Princess enter the livery, he smiled and thought how great his reward would be when he presented not only the amulet, but the Princess also to his master. The smile quickly froze, and his eyes narrowed in a vain attempt to dim the blinding light of her power, visible to his sorcerer's eyes.

"Don't come any closer, Princess, or I will be forced to kill your maid servant."

Her steps never slowed.

He conjured the largest fire ball he was capable of and sent it directly at her. It simply disappeared as if absorbed.

The Princess stopped just a few feet away, pulled her sword and held it pointed down and slightly to the side.

Harlo's smile returned, and he almost laughed out loud. *So this little slip of a girl wants to play with swords. She will soon learn swords are a man's weapon.* He pulled his own and advanced, prepared to teach her a lesson.

The sorcerer's first swing was intended to force her back and into a defensive position. She stood like a statue and never flinched. The tip of his blade left a slight trace of blood on her chin. His backswing was met with the base of her sword, and he watched in stunned amazement as the end of his weapon sheared off and clattered to the floor.

Sofia spun her blade and brought it down, severing his arm just above the wrist, and before his sword could fall to the ground, aimed a thrust just below his sternum. In the instant before his death, she became aware of the life thread to his master, and added a message of fire to the thread as it detached and sped away. Deliberately wiping the blood from her sword on the sorcerer's shirt, she turned and opened the large livery door.

Trembling with fear, Eric and Bron quickly mounted their horses, their dash for the open door shortlived. The horses snorted and pranced, unable to pass the Princess.

"Before I let you go, Eric, I have a message for my sister. Her life is now forfeit. I *will* return and see it done."

Long after their hoof beats had faded into the distance, and Ronald had freed a quietly sobbing Floanne from the back of the wagon, Sofia remained standing at the open door. Never before had she been this helpless in the face of her anger. The anger faded, only to be replaced by an equal fear of the path it had forced upon her.

# CHAPTER NINE

# SO IT BEGINS

Emma held Silverstar in a tight embrace, sad, knowing they would soon be parted again. The wolf quickly shared images of their youth, and the adventures they had experienced together. The love and respect they felt for each other engulfed those memories as he gently pulled away and led his pack into the trees.

She stared into the forest long after the wolves had disappeared until Sebastian softly placed his hand on her shoulder. Scrubbing the tears from her face with one hand, she squeezed his hand with the other, and then turned to gaze up at his hairy face.

"I wish I could go with them."

"I know. Come, little one, work we have."

A quick inventory of the wagons revealed that one was filled with items intended for trade. The sorcerer must have planned to use that as his excuse for traveling. They decided to use the wagon for the same reason. The coach and other wagon were pushed into the forest as far as possible, two of the horses were hitched to the trade wagon, and the rest set free.

With Sebastian in the driver's seat and Emma resting in the back, he pulled the team out on the road to Brighton Ferry where they would turn to the west and continue on to the Capitol.

"You are just full of surprises," Emma observed. "When did you learn how to drive a wagon?"

"It easy be," he replied. "I shake reins, say go, they go. I pull back reins, say whoa, they whoa. Simple."

Emma just shook her head at the ogre and secretly hoped the horses didn't develop any ideas of their own. Her thoughts soon turned back to Navon, and she couldn't help but worry. The Shadhuin Nomads were not known for their hospitality and shunned outsiders. She also worried about Moonlight since the nomads were extremely protective of their horses, and the young wolf could easily be mistaken for a threat.

Sebastian interrupted her thoughts when he leaned back and patted the seat next to him. She glanced up and down the road, but other than vast stretches of knee high grass and an occasional grove of small trees, the area was clear. The look on his face was all seriousness as she sat down beside him.

"Talk to me, Em. I need to practice my speech. The King must believe what I tell him, and he will not take me seriously if I sound like a talking animal," he said carefully.

She looked up at him and smiled. "You know, I like it when you call me Em." Matching her tone to his, she continued. "You're right, you must be able to speak clearly so there are no misunderstandings. What would you like to talk about?"

"Humans. I be..." he started, then growled and shook his head. "I have not spent as much time around them as you. How should I act? How will I be treated?"

"Just be yourself, Sebastian. You are a poor actor, and that is why humans will trust you. There is a saying among them, 'Honest as an ogre'. They will probably be respectful, yet a little afraid." She just couldn't help herself when she added, "You are a big, hairy, ugly beast, ya know."

He smiled down at her and let his fangs show. "Thanks, little one."

She wanted to punch him in the arm, but knew he probably wouldn't feel it.

They continued to talk until the outer wall of Brighton Ferry came into view, and Emma quickly jumped in the back to hide. As in all major towns, two of the King's guard stood watch at the gate. Sebastian pulled up to talk to one of them.

"Hello, friend ogre," the guard called out as he approached the wagon. "What brings you down from the mountains?"

"A desire to visit the Capitol, friend human. I have read the histories, and would like to see those places for myself," Sebastian replied. "If you would be so kind, I require directions to the West Gate."

"It would be easier for me to show you the way. Wait a moment while I get someone to take my place and I'll ride with you."

The guard disappeared inside a small building next to the gate, and returned shortly, followed by a young man in uniform. The new guard stopped to stare at the ogre before taking his post. The stare was not friendly.

Climbing the side of the wagon, the first man held out his hand. "Sergeant Fredrik Tuttle."

Sebastian's hand engulfed the sergeant's as they shook. "I'm known as Sebastian."

They rode along the first street in awkward silence while the ogre returned waves of greeting from friendly townsfolk, and tried to ignore the stares of those who were not.

After they turned down a street not as crowded, he faced the sergeant and asked quietly, "Is it not unusual for the guard to escort someone through town?"

Fredrik's eyes continued to travel up and down the street as he replied, "Is it not unusual for an ogre not to tell the truth?"

Sebastian slumped back on the bench, crestfallen. "Obvious be?"

"No. I've also read the histories, Sebastian. I would not have risen in rank without the ability to determine whether someone was telling the truth."

He was interrupted by a group of children of all ages that came alongside and began to pepper the ogre with questions. One of the youngest, in his innocence, asked if Sebastian had come to burn down the town like people were saying. He assured the little boy the ogres were too busy hunting & fishing and playing with their little ones to bother with burning towns.

He reached under the seat and pulled out a small bag of hard candy Emma had found in the supplies. He tossed it to the oldest boy who had been quietly observing the whole time. "By the Eyes, I charge you with the duty of seeing that everyone receives one of those, even the littlest among you."

Leaving the children gathered excitedly around the older boy, they continued on their way. Sebastian fixed his gaze on the sergeant, a questioning look in his eyes.

Fredrik glanced once at the ogre's face and sighed. "There you have the answer to your question, Sebastian. I'm escorting you personally because someone has been spreading stories that not only ogres, but all the Elder Races are going to attack the towns of the east, killing and burning. Fortunately, most townsfolk pay them no mind, but there are enough who listen, and that concerns me."

"So it begins," the ogre growled and stopped the wagon. "Look to your own safety, Fredrik. The Dark One is spreading his hate for the Elders among your people in the hope of turning them against one another."

The only sound was that of the horses shaking their harnesses as the sergeant stared in disbelief and fear. "So the rumors are true," he whispered. "The Scarred Mage still lives."

"Yes, and to answer the question you were too polite to ask, the Ancient One has sent me to give this message to the King. Be not afraid, Fredrik. The Eyes of the Deluti are returning to the world, and will give those chosen, the power to defeat him."

Sebastian snapped the team back into motion, his unease growing with the un-natural quiet around them. Turning at the next street, which according to Fredrik, led directly to the West gate, his fears were realized. A crowd of men with swords and clubs filled the street, blocking the gate.

"The Eyes watching over us be. Faith be having, Sergeant," the ogre murmured, and moved the wagon slowly forward.

*     *     *

With a wary glance at the horse, Navon struggled to his feet, surprised the two men actually helped him. The young man on the horse said something to the men which initiated a heated discussion. This gave Navon a chance to catch his breath and notice things he hadn't seen before. The horses and men were covered in soot just as he was, and the stains on their clothes appeared to be blood. The approach of a rider-less horse drew his attention away from the men, and put an end to the discussion.

The leader studied Navon for a moment before speaking. "Untie hands, you not run, yes?"

The newly arrived horse stood next to the leader, and Navon felt the intense scrutiny of three sets of eyes. Surrounded by horses and standing in the middle of a wide open plain, the idea of trying to run hadn't even entered his mind.

"You have my word. I will not run."

At a nod from the young man, they removed the rope from his wrists. The older man leaned in close and whispered, "I watch you." They returned to their own mounts as the new horse moved to stand next to Navon.

"Come. Much work to do. Our brother, Moshere, carry you."

He mounted in the same manner as the others, by grabbing the mane and then swung his leg up and over. The group turned and headed back in the direction from which they had come. Navon was an experienced bareback rider, and soon realized even an inexperienced rider would have no problem staying on this horse. Moshere moved in a way that prevented Navon from feeling off balance. He could only shake his head at the distinct impression the horse was pleased at his thought.

From the higher vantage point, Navon could see that the terrain was not as flat as he first assumed. They traveled across gently undulating hills that hid the main group from view until they crested the last rise. From this height, Navon could see the group had been working systematically across the burned out plain, gathering and butchering the dead animals caught by the fire. The others greeted them with joy and what sounded like some good natured banter. The work never slowed, and it appeared that everyone, including the horses, had a specific job to do. He also noticed that no women were in the group.

Navon was left astride his horse along with the leader and the old man as the rest of the men left to join the work in progress. The young man pointed to a group of horses dragging what looked like several large sleds towards a number of large beasts lying in a rough circle.

"Come. Not happy work we have."

Puzzled by the leader's words, Navon had no choice but to follow, once again reminded of the fact he was not in control. As long as he remained mounted on the horse, he went where the horse took him.

Once they reached the circle of burnt, adult beasts, he understood what the leader meant. The beasts had formed a protective barrier against the flames in an attempt to protect the lives of two calves. Unfortunately, without a mother to suckle, they would die regardless. Their pitiful cries touched something inside Navon's heart. The memory of the death of the large beast that morning filled his mind.

The three of them slid off their horses and approached the circle of animals. Navon stretched out his hand to stop the old man when he saw the knife in his hand.

"No... Wait... Please."

The two men shared a questioning look, but shrugged their shoulders and watched as Navon slowly approached the circle of bodies. The calves were huddled against the blackened body of the one who had probably been their mother. Two of the adults had fallen practically on top of the calves, pinning them inside the circle. They continued to cry while their fear filled eyes watched Navon grab the head of one of the beasts and pull it to one side. The presence of un-burnt grass under the calves was a testimony to the effectiveness of the adult's efforts.

Once a path was cleared, and with no more understanding of what he'd done earlier with the beast who had saved his life, Navon opened his spirit to their fear. In the same way he had learned from Moonlight, he projected a feeling of safety and caring into the calves. They ceased their crying and carefully stood, their eyes locked on him as he backed away from the others and sat on the blackened ground.

They followed, brother and sister, lay down on either side of him, and continued to gaze into his eyes. Navon filled their spirits with a feeling of peace and images of green fields with the presence of a cool spring breeze. The acrid smell of smoke and the stench of death disappeared as their spirits frolicked in the sun and rose higher and higher, while he gently drew the life from their bodies.

After a final goodbye, emptiness filled his spirit until he felt Moonlight fill it with her love for him. The little bodies now lay peacefully in his lap as his eyes flew open and the full force of his anger at the senseless killing of innocents focused on the two men who he felt were responsible. Fortunately for them, the sorrow over what he'd just done overwhelmed the anger as Navon buried his head in soot covered hands.

Quietly, and with surprising tenderness, the men approached and carried off the two calves. Navon didn't care where; they were now just empty husks of meat. The sound of the others as they arrived, and began the process of butchering roused him out of his reverie. He rose and ran to help several men who struggled to position one of the larger beasts. Nothing was said of what he'd done for the calves, but furtive and sometimes fearful looks followed him the rest of the day.

Work proceeded at a feverish pace since the meat would not stay fresh for long in this heat. Several small boys were just as busy as the adults, making sure that everyone paused for a moment to drink a cup of water from the small barrels they had strapped to their backs. Even so, the heat began to take a toll on Navon until the leader appeared at his side with a strip of water soaked cloth, and showed him how to wrap it around his head.

The relief from the sun was welcomed and Navon smiled his thanks. The young man merely nodded and turned back to his work.

The majority of the meat had been cut into strips and hung on racks above smoking fires by the time shadows stretched long, and the sun was a golden disk floating just above the horizon. Navon was given a blanket, a bowl of stew with a chunk of bread, and a cup filled with a bitter tasting drink that, surprisingly, left him feeling refreshed. Following the example of the others, he rolled up in the blanket and immediately fell asleep. Today had felt like the longest day of his life.

Navon woke to the presence of Moonlight in his mind, concern for each other foremost in their shared rapport. He tried to convey to her that he was safe, and that she should continue to stay away, undetected. Her presence faded when the older guard, from yesterday, approached carrying two steaming mugs. He sat up while the other settled to the ground on crossed legs and handed one of the cups to Navon.

"You work hard. No complain. Maybe not thief."

Navon met his gaze and nodded in thanks. "Maybe not thief."

The wrinkles around the old man's eyes deepened, and the corners of his mouth twitched as he nodded in return. "I named Jamar, and young leader named Lodorn. He son of Maudwan."

As they worked yesterday, Navon had realized the fire must have been planned. The group was too well organized to take advantage of a random event. His anger at the loss of life from the day before, returned as he swept his arm out to indicate the surrounding land, and picked up a handful of ash covered soil.

"You set this fire on purpose. So many animals died, and now there is nothing left for the survivors to eat. Why?"

Jamar listened carefully to his words, and stared off into the distance before turning his attention back to Navon. "Old and weak die. Young and strong live. Rain come soon and grass grow tall. This is right."

They were interrupted by the arrival of one of the boys and a colt who was loaded down with a basket of bowls and several pots wrapped in skins. The boy filled two bowls from one of the pots, and after a short bow to the elder, handed a bowl to each of them. He and his horse quickly moved on to the next group, and repeated the process.

The old man kept his attention focused on Navon and asked the question that had been on everyone's mind since yesterday. "You take away life of little ones. How?"

The amulet resting against Navon's chest began to chill as if to remind him to be careful how he answered. He already suspected that Jamar would see through a lie, so the basic truth would have to suffice. He returned the old man's intense look with one of his own. "It's just something that I can do."

Holding his stare a moment longer, Jamar nodded and turned his attention to the bowl in his hand.

They ate in silence as Navon savored the thick porridge, particularly the sweet taste of the blueberries mixed throughout. The boy soon returned to collect their empty bowls, and another ran by gathering up Navon's blanket.

The sound of a horse approaching from behind drew Jamar's attention, but Navon didn't need to turn around. Somehow he knew it was Moshere, the horse who had carried him the day before. He turned around and after a short bow, tried to project his thanks to Moshere in the same way he did with Moonlight. The horse nodded in return and turned so Navon could mount.

Jamar's eyes became hard once again as he regarded the pair. "Mystery, you Na-von of Roddell. Never a brother demand to carry slave. You trouble maybe, and I like trouble not."

Navon could only shake his head at Jamar's retreating back and thought, *"Neither do I, Jamar. Neither do I."*

# CHAPTER TEN

# ON TO SEASIDE

Gilfor breathed a sigh of relief after crossing the bridge, and the town of Vinebridge receded in the distance behind him. Distinctly uncomfortable wearing the uniform of a lieutenant, he'd felt sure someone would stop him and demand an explanation. But the Princess's plan appeared to be working perfectly. Everyone made way for him, and no attempt was made to impede his progress. Even the guards at the town gates waved him through.

This was pretty heady stuff for a young man recently come up from the country. He felt a momentary regret for the loss of his comrades, especially the sergeant who had taken Gilfor under his wing. He eased his mount back down to a walk as the sudden pain of guilt, of being the only survivor, forced his eyes closed until the ache subsided.

*You fool, you wouldn't have survived either if the Princess hadn't healed you,* Gilfor berated himself. She had entrusted him with an important mission, and he needed to keep a level head. Someone wanted the Princess, and everyone with her, dead. If he didn't play his part perfectly, he would join his fellow guardsmen in death, and the Queen would never know the truth.

A mile or so outside of Kiplar, the terrain took on a familiar cast and brought back memories of his walk along this road a little over a year ago. A young man away from home for the first time, he had searched for somewhere to change into clean clothes before approaching the Capitol city in hopes of finding a job. He still marveled at his luck in becoming a Queen's Guard. Slightly more overgrown, the path into the woods remained visible.

He dismounted and cautiously led the horse along the path, hoping no one had claimed the abandoned cabin he'd found last year. The fact he had to push through the thick undergrowth was promising.

The last year had not been kind to the cabin. Part of the roof now lay inside on the wooden floor, but the walls still stood. The corral appeared solid enough to keep a horse from wandering. The spring rains had made sure the water trough was full, and lush green grass covered the area. The horse should be satisfied until someone could come and retrieve him.

Gilfor carefully eased open the gate, and led his horse inside where he removed the tack and gave the horse a quick rubdown. He replaced the bridle with a halter he fashioned from one of the reins. He found a dry corner inside the cabin to pile the tack, and after changing out of the lieutenant's uniform, covered everything with brush. If all went well, someone would be sent to recover the horse and tack before they were discovered.

He grabbed a fallen branch and swept the path in an attempt to erase their prints as he made his way back to the road. A quick check to make sure the road was clear; he stepped out, polished boots now scuffed. Satisfied, he hurried toward the Capitol, a small travel bag over his shoulder.

Even though the Princess gave Gilfor exact directions

to the correct inn, he wandered up and down several streets, glanced into a few windows before apparently choosing an inn at random. The hazy interior revealed only two tables were occupied. A table against the wall, furthest from the others, caught his eye. Hiding his bag under the table, suddenly afraid he would say something wrong; he waited nervously for the innkeeper to approach.

The portly, bald headed man looked him over and nodded. "I've a bit of stew left, and a half loaf of bread I'll let you have for a tenpiece."

"I'll take it," Gilfor replied. "How much for a pint of Red River ale? I've heard it's old but sweet."

The only reaction from the innkeeper was a raised eyebrow. "I'll see if there's any left."

If he'd said the words correctly, a pigeon would soon be winging its way up to the Palace, and Master Horshall, the old arms-master, would make his way down to the inn. All he could do now was wait.

The young guardsman sat nursing his second ale when a hooded figure leaning on a staff, appeared at his table without a sound. "Put on your cloak if you have one, and if not, keep your head down and walk next to me."

They left the inn, and turned to walk along the line of

store fronts, now closed up for the night. After several blocks, the voice of the stranger whispered, "At the next corner, act like you're going to run and then flatten yourself against the wall as soon as you turn the corner. We're being followed."

Gilfor did as ordered, and sprinted around the next corner, followed closely by the hooded man. Faint footsteps could be heard hurrying towards them. The figure he hoped was the arms-master casually stepped out of the alley and confronted their pursuer.

"I do not take kindly to being followed," growled the voice from inside the hood. "Why don't you take that ugly face of yours back up to the Palace, and tell your master the next person I catch following me, dies."

Gilfor could see nothing except the old man, but the un-mistakable sound of a sword leaving its scabbard didn't need to be seen.

A deep voice chuckled, "Well now, old man. That's awful big talk, considering I have a sword and you have a stick. They told me to follow you, but they never said I couldn't cut you up a little for fun."

Apparently, the thug with a sword had never faced an arms-master wielding a staff. Three moves and it was over. One to disarm, a second left him gasping for air, and finally a blow to the side of the head. Gilfor rushed out to help the old man drag the body down the alley and sit it up against a barrel.

Gilfor was awestruck. "How did you do that?"

"A sword is only good for one thing, young Gilfor, and that is to kill. A staff can accomplish the same thing, but I have yet to face someone with a blade who I couldn't disarm and knock out."

"You know my name?"

"Of course. I know the names of every man in the Queen's Guard, especially the ones assigned to protect my Princess. Come, we will be safe now back at the inn, and you can explain to me why you are here and not at her side."

*       *       *

Embarrassed, Floanne pulled away from the Lieutenant's chest and rushed over to her mistress, prepared to kneel before her. Instead, Sofia pulled her maidservant into an embrace which initiated another flood of tears. The Princess whispered words of comfort until the sobs quieted once again.

Noting the traces of sheer terror that still lingered in

the corners of Floanne's eyes, Sofia held her at arm's length. "Are you hurt?" This close, she didn't need to ask about the amulet. It was like a presence felt, but not seen.

Floanne shook her head, and then nodded in the direction of the dead sorcerer. "That man, Harlo, stopped the others from killing me back at the barn. Did he have to die?"

"Yes," Sofia answered simply.

Ronald, who had moved to peer out of the door, returned. "We must leave, and quickly. I don't look forward to trying to explain the presence of a body." He gently led Floanne back to the wagon. "Sorry, Floanne, I don't have time to explain everything to you right now. From now on, you are a wealthy merchant's daughter, and we are two mercenaries hired to escort you to your new husband."

He assisted her up onto the driver's seat, led the team out into the corral, and shut the door behind them. Sofia tethered Ronald's horse to the back of the wagon, and then mounted her own as he joined Floanne in the wagon. A flick of the reins, and they left the stable behind. Even traveling slowly to avoid attention, they soon reached the southern gate and a lone guard.

Before they approached the gate, Ronald leaned over and whispered to the young hand-maiden, "Act bored and resigned. Remember, you are being forcibly escorted to a marriage not of your choosing."

"But I'm not ..." she began, then glanced at the both of them and nodded.

Ronald paused to tell the guard about the farm where they had stopped the previous night, and the murder that had been committed there.

"It's probably them blasted non-humans," he spat. "The Queen should do something before they kill us all."

After leaving the gate, they continued at a walk until a bend in the road hid them from view, and the lieutenant urged the team into a trot. When the team began to tire, he pulled them back to a walk as Sofia rode alongside. They took turns explaining to Floanne what had happened, and their suspicions of who was behind the attack.

Alarmed, she turned to face her mistress. "But shouldn't we go back? The Queen may be in danger!"

"Hopefully, the plan I have set in motion will assure the well being of both my mother and oldest sister. We must continue on to Marlinor and whatever safety we find there."

Floanne attempted to hide her giggles at the look on her Princess's face when Ronald shared the nick-name he had given her, and then laughed out loud as he stuck out his tongue when Sofia shared his.

He turned sober and asked Sofia, "What did you think of that guard's comment about the Elder Races? It struck me as very strange."

"I don't know, Ronald, but I sense that something is not right in the world. The Elders have always been our friends and allies."

The vista that appeared around the next turn took Floanne's breath away. As far as the eye could see, there stretched an expanse of dark blue water, along with the occasional white of a ship's sails, some near and some far away. The specter of terror finally left her eyes as they took in a sight she had never dreamed of seeing.

Soon, a moisture laden breeze, filled with a hint of salt, ruffled their hair. Glimpses of the natural harbor, and Seaside itself, appeared as the road descended. Once at sea level, the occasional stench from the fish processing houses assailed their noses, but never lasted long.

One last admonishment from Sofia preceded their entrance into the town. "Floanne, under no circumstances are you to address us as Princess or Lieutenant. Those two no longer exist, and don't act surprised when we address you as my lady."

The streets were filled with heavily laden wagons traveling to and from the docks, and workers either carrying large bundles or pushing them along in hand carts. The three of them made their way slowly toward the waterfront as Ronald kept an eye out for a particular type of inn.

He paused in front of a large, particularly gaudy inn with guards at the door, before guiding the team around the side and into the yard behind.

Floanne leaned over and whispered, "Why here?"

Ronald spoke without turning to her, keeping his eye on the stable boys as they approached. "A successful owner will advertise his ability to broker profitable deals. He receives a percentage of each transaction, and uses that to keep his establishment clean and hire extra guards. We should find what we're looking for here."

"I hope you're right," Sofia commented as she dismounted. "There is evil close by."

Ronald flipped a silver coin to the stable boys and promised another in the morning if the horses were well taken care of. Huge smiles lit up their faces as they swore the horses would receive the best care in town.

He had to touch Floanne's arm and give her a tiny shake of his head when she started to reach for their bags. She had a part to play. Head down in embarrassment for a moment, she turned for the door, a disinterested look on her face. The other two hurried to catch up.

Floanne entered the inn where she was confronted by a large man whose wide leather belt struggled to hold up a belly to be proud of. A long pony-tail, and a beard that partially hid a face only a mother could love, took her aback until she noticed the small apron that hung from his belt.

Floanne looked him up and down, and announced, "I require a room for myself and an adjoining room for my guards."

Unimpressed by her attitude, he returned her frank appraisal with one of his own. "That'll be five silver per room... m' lady."

With little experience at this sort of thing, she turned to Ronald and hoped she acted correctly. "Pay the man," she ordered.

Knowing that mercenaries rarely carried coin, Ronald

pulled out a small gem that he had pried loose from Sofia's jewelry, and handed it to the innkeeper. "Add three meals to that, and then return the remainder in coin."

The man pulled out a jeweler's glass to inspect the gem, and grunted in surprise. He set up scales on the counter, reached for his money chest, and counted out a stack of silver and gold coins. Placing the coins in Ronald's hand, he jerked his head in the direction of the stairs. "First floor, last two rooms on the right. There is a private dining room for the young lady, but you two will eat in the common room."

The coins safely tucked away in his leathers, Ronald led the way to their rooms. Floanne followed closely while Sofia brought up the rear. A quick glance inside the first room verified the existence of a connecting door. They continued on to the second door and entered the room together.

Opening the connecting door, Ronald tossed his small bag inside. "I will sleep in there, if that's alright. Anyone planning mischief will assume Floanne is in a room by herself, but will discover either me or Sofia." Turning to the Princess, he asked, "Do you still feel the evil presence?"

"It's not inside the inn, but close nonetheless."

"I'm hungry, and I imagine Floanne is starving. Let's eat and then come back here to discuss our next move."

They escorted Floanne to the private dining room, and took a table in the common room where they could keep an eye on her and the rest of the inn. Upon returning to their room, Floanne laid down and immediately fell asleep. Sofia and Ronald went round and round, trying to agree on what to do next. She wanted to maintain their disguises and depart in secret, but Ronald was concerned about the time it would take to find a ship.

Unable to come to a decision, they went back down to the common room where Ronald would approach the innkeeper, and Sofia would glean what information she could from overheard conversations. Floanne should be safe enough for the time being as the Princess felt their connection even stronger than before.

Ronald and the innkeeper had their heads together in hushed conversation at the counter when a sudden silence in the common room caused them to look up. Three men stood before the corner table where Sofia sat sipping her ale. The lieutenant moved to draw his sword, but the innkeeper stopped him with a look. A prearranged signal brought four guards from their places along the wall, joining the innkeeper as he approached the three men.

"I will not tell you again, Roushal. You and your lies and rumors are not welcome in my inn. If you force my hand, you will not live to trouble me again."

A young, well dressed man turned to face the owner. A forced smile twisted a handsome face as he sneered, "I will go where I please, and leave when I am ready, innkeeper. Maybe you will sing a different tune when word gets out that you are harboring agents of Marlinor and are in secret negotiations with non-humans."

Before the owner could respond, the sound of Sofia's chair scraping across the floor rang out, and her voice filled the room.

"Look closely my friends, for you are seeing the face of evil. The Scarred Mage is once again sending out his sorcerers to poison the world with his hatred."

Roushal spun to face the Princess, a mocking laugh burst from his lips. "Oh, come now! The Scarred Mage is a myth to scare children, and sorcerers no longer exist."

He swallowed his laughter as eyes, black as night, froze him in place, and his mage sight picked out the tendrils of power that writhed up and down her arms.

"Tell me sorcerer, how does your power compare with that of a Deluti?" At which point she raised a hand as if to attack.

A visible aura of power surrounded him in an instant as he sent one fireball and then another screaming toward her. Sofia calmly caught each fireball, joined them together, and returned a stream of liquid fire. A flash and a thunderclap followed. The sorcerer simply ceased to exist.

His companions shared a look of disbelief, then turned and ran from the inn. Ronald ran also, but in the opposite direction. He had seen the utter despair and fear that filled Sofia's eyes just before she squeezed them shut.

With an arm around her shoulders, he guided her toward the stairs. The gathered crowd parted to let them pass, as whispers of *"Deluti"*, and *"Scarred Mage"* began to circulate throughout the inn. Entering the first room, she sat down on the nearest bed while he sat on the other and waited.

After what felt like an eternity, she lifted empty eyes and focused on his. "Did you know my father, Ronald?"

"Yes, I knew him well. He and my father were very close, and I was there the day they died."

The fear in her eyes flared as she begged, "Please tell

me what happened, Ronald. Mother refused to ever speak of it."

"One of the reasons they were best friends was my father's ability to deflect the King's anger, and never take his words personally. It was rare for them to argue, but on that day, father was either unable or unwilling to back down, and the King killed him in a fit of rage. Your father fell to the floor, sobbing, lifted my father in his arms, and voiced a cry of anguish such as I've never heard from a human. Before anyone could move, he pulled a knife and slit his own throat."

"Oh Ronald, I am so sorry! I never knew." Tears streaming down her face, Sofia turned unseeing eyes to the window. "I am my Father's daughter, Ronald. That same rage burns deep inside of me. I lied to you when I said that I feared nothing. The fear that I will kill someone I love is second only to my rage, and just as strong."

The door to the other room opened as Floanne appeared with eyes closed, and a voice not her own ghosted from her lips. *"Master your rage, Princess, and the Eyes of the Deluti will be yours. If it becomes master, you will die and the amulet will go to another."*

Ronald rose from the bed as the door closed silently

behind Floanne, sat next to the Princess and took her hand in his. "You are not your father, Sofia. Believe me, I know. You are stronger than your father, and the anger. I will always be there until you find a way to master it."

*     *     *

Far to the south, high atop his tower, the Scarred Mage dismissed the vision with a wave of his hand, desire clouding his thoughts. The Princess's little message of rage, sent along with Harlo's returning life thread, had awakened a lust buried deep inside him for centuries. The loss of two minor sorcerers in one day was nothing compared to the prize revealed, a female Deluti. Let that pathetic Navon play with his animal friends, Scorpios now had a new focus. A smile literally cracked the skin on his face as plans began to form.

# CHAPTER ELEVEN

## AN OGRE AT COURT

As Sebastian guided the team toward the crowd of angry men blocking the West Gate, the villagers exchanged confused and uncertain glances. They were not expecting a single ogre driving a wagon with a sergeant of the King's Guard sitting beside him. Several large rivermen with clubs stepped forward to block the path of the wagon.

Emma carefully slipped out the back before the wagon came to a stop. She hoped the extra movement did not alert the sergeant, who was still unaware of her presence. A figure in a long dark cape, the hood covering part of his face, stood slightly apart from and behind the crowd. Her senses warned her that an agent of their enemy was present, but she needed to get closer to be sure.

Sebastian took a moment to watch her ghost through the crowd, unseen by all eyes except his own. He turned his attention back to the men who continued to smack their clubs against their palms. Careful not to make any move toward his weapons, he hoped Emma would control her constant desire to use those knives she was so fond of. Any injuries resulting from this confrontation would do irreparable harm to their mission.

Sergeant Tuttle leaned towards the ogre and whispered, "Remember, the truth," then stood to face the men.

"Is there a reason you men are interfering with the duties of the King's Guard?"

"By the Eyes, Sergeant! It ain't you we be interferin with, it's that vicious animal that be sitten next ta ye."

It took all of Sebastian's self-control not to smile and show his fangs at the man's compliment. Struggling to keep a straight face, he looked away and noticed a man in a dark cape making his way towards them, Emma at his side, unseen. The crowd parted as if a giant hand gently moved them aside. Sebastian turned back to the men blocking him to keep from laughing at Emma's antics as she mimicked every move the stranger made while making faces at him.

"I assure you," the sergeant retorted. "I am not in the habit of sitting next to vicious animals. Ogres have been honored citizens of our Kingdom for many generations, and are entitled to travel anywhere they desire without interference."

"Then why he be here now if not ta spy on us?" the largest of the men shouted.

Sergeant Tuttle started to answer, but was interrupted by the man in the cape.

"Let the spy speak for itself, if it's able."

Tuttle nodded to the ogre, and then jumped from the wagon, his attention on the stranger. From the reports he'd received, here was the man responsible for most of the rumors.

"I am called Sebastian, not animal or beast," he addressed the crowd. "I am sent by the Ancient One with a message and warning for our King. The Scarred Mage is alive and sending his sorcerers throughout the land spreading rumors about the Elder Races."

"Nonsense!" the man in the cape laughed out loud. "The Ancient One and his brother are long gone and sorcerers are a fairy tale made up to frighten children."

"Maybe you have forgotten that an ogre can sense those who use power. You, human, are a sorcerer and a liar!"

The stranger's face twisted into a mask of hatred as his hands shot out from under the cape, a ball of flame forming at his fingertips. Only Sebastian saw Emma stick out her foot to trip the sorcerer and the small flame that sprang from her finger to the back of his cape. He fell forward onto his own ball of fire while flames quickly spread over the cape. Writhing and screaming in agony, the sorcerer rolled back and forth in a vain attempt to extinguish the flames. It was over quickly.

Except for the crackling of the flames that consumed the body, silence hung over the crowd like the smoke from the fire. People began backing away from the corpse while the men blocking the gate moved aside.

The first riverman, to have spoken, handed his club to another and approached the wagon. Looking up at

Sebastian, the man offered up his hand.

"Your pardon, friend ogre. Ye be speakin da truth like all your kind. We will see to it all da folks in town know da sorcerer be tellin lies. May the Eyes watch over ye on yer way to da King."

Sebastian leaned down and engulfed the man's hand in his own. "Thank you, but be warned, there will be others like him."

The gate swung open at the sergeant's command as the ogre flicked the reins to get the team moving again. Sergeant Tuttle smiled and waved the ogre through the gate, both unaware that the children they had met earlier were already spreading the tale of the generous ogre and what had happened at the gate.

Just outside, Sebastian felt the wagon dip and glanced back to see Emma climbing into the back. She came up and sat beside him, a satisfied look on her face.

"You would think that a man who plays with fire would know better than to weather proof his cape with the most flammable oil around. I would rather have used a knife instead of my finger, though."

Sebastian shook his head and smiled at his blood thirsty partner. Thinking of the road ahead, he wondered what their reception would be upon arriving at the Capitol.

*    *    *

The forest gave way to more and more farms with an occasional orchard separating the fields. The number of folks traveling the road increased also. Most were friendly and wished them a good day, but a few eyed the ogre with suspicion and passed by quickly. With every unfriendly face, Sebastian's shoulders slumped a little further. Not looking down at the little assassin, he sighed.

"Worried I be, little one. What we do if guard not letting me see King? I only one ogre be, humans are many."

Emma ignored the 'little one' for now, knowing how upset he was. Sebastian had never experienced this kind of prejudice before. "I'm worried too, but we'll do what we've always done and find a way to complete our mission. Now quit slouching, you're an ogre and a good one, even if you are hairy and ugly."

The ogre sat up straight and smiled down at her. "Thank you, Emma. It is even more important now for me to talk right. Tell me more of these humans."

The sun shot up in to the morning sky, and soon hung directly over their heads. They had separated on uncertain terms years before, and took this opportunity to renew their friendship. An inn appeared strategically located halfway between the Capitol and Brighton Ferry. Seeing the look of apprehension on Sebastian's face, Emma grabbed his arm.

"C'mon, let's stop for a bite to eat. The more we learn about how people feel, the better prepared we will be once we reach the Capitol."

With a sigh, he guided the team into a field next to the inn where other wagons sat awaiting their owners. At the front door, Sebastian reached out to push it open, motioning for Emma to enter and quipped. "Age before beauty."

She stuck out her tongue, kicked him in the shin and then hobbled inside followed closely by the chuckling ogre.

A look of surprise crossed the faces of the patrons as the two entered, but no fear. The innkeeper rushed forward while wiping his hands on his apron. "By the Eyes, it has been too long! I'm honored, friend ogre. Be welcome in my establishment."

His hand engulfed by the ogre's, he turned to Emma. "You are also welcome, young woman. Are you here to speak for the ogre?"

"The hairy oaf can speak for himself. I'm here because I'm hungry."

Sebastian released the innkeeper's hand and reassured him. "Never mind my grumpy little friend, Master Innkeeper. I have studied long and hard to learn your language, and no longer need someone to speak for me. But it has been a long morning and I am hungry also."

"Of course. Of course, and I have just the place for you to seat yourself," the innkeeper said, leading them to a corner table. "My great, great Grand-Sire fought alongside the ogres during the war of the Deluti and had great respect for them. He commissioned this table and chairs for their occasional visits to the inn," he explained while wiping down the oversized table and chairs. "Make yourselves comfortable and I'll return shortly with your meal."

Sebastian eased back in his chair, pleased with how well it fit him, and tried desperately not to laugh out loud at Emma who looked like a child at the grown-up's table. One look at her face convinced him to keep his thoughts to himself or he might wake up in the morning missing body parts.

The patrons patiently waited for the pair to finish their meal before one of the men called out. "What news of the world, friend ogre?"

"Dire news, my friend. I am on my way to bring a message to the King from the Ancient One. His brother, the Scarred Mage, is once again spreading his hatred toward the Elder Races. His agents, including some sorcerers, are traveling throughout the country spreading lies. Already the rumors are turning some of the humans against us as we barely escaped from Brighton Ferry this morning. Fortunately, the sorcerer there revealed himself and fell to his own hatred."

The innkeeper pulled over a chair and joined the conversation. "Dire news indeed. Who would be foolish enough to believe those lies?"

"People have short memories, Harold," one of the men addressed the innkeeper. "Most have only heard of the Elders through the old tales."

"Aye, I been hearin' dem rumors myself," the elder at the table joined in. "What be putting a crack in me pots is da attitude o' dem new guards. They's mean and gots an evil look. Somthin tain't right, I tell ya."

Worried, Harold turned to the ogre. "Sebastian, do

you have a contact in the Capitol?"

After a quick glance at Emma, Sebastian turned back to the innkeeper and shook his head.

"After you enter the city, continue down the main street until you pass the stable yards and leather shops. Turn right at the next street and look for the Four Horse Inn. Ask for Aaron, the proprietor. He holds the same respect for the Elders as I do, and will take care of you."

Harold walked them out to their wagon where he shook the ogre's hand again. "It's been a pleasure, Sebastian. Good luck, and if I may offer another piece of advice, ask for Prince Mathias instead of the King when you reach the Palace. I've heard he is the most approachable of the bunch."

Emma and Sebastian spent the rest of the journey in silence, each lost in their own thoughts. As they approached the city, the traffic increased to the point where Emma once again hid in the back of the wagon. They had discussed this earlier and decided it would be best if she stayed out of sight.

Once inside the city, Sebastian followed Harold's directions and turned down the first street looking for the right inn. Before he could find it, four of the King's Guard surrounded the wagon, hands resting on their swords.

"If you can understand me, ogre, turn your wagon around and leave the city. Your kind is not welcome here."

Knives in hand, Emma shifted the light around her and stood up, ready to defend her partner.

Onlookers were drawn to the confrontation from all directions as word of an ogre in the city spread swiftly. Some in the crowd shouted encouragement to the ogre while others sided with the guards who found themselves in the position of keeping the two sides separated while Sebastian sat there in wonder. He would have turned the wagon around and left except for the crowd that hemmed him in. Before the situation could erupt into total chaos, a figure in royal attire, escorted by two of the Palace Guard, forced his way through the crowd.

"What is the meaning of this disturbance, Sergeant?"

"Just following orders, my lord," he tried to explain. "This crowd gathered and became unruly right after I asked the ogre to leave the city."

"I will find out who issued those orders, but for now, consider them rescinded. An ogre does not simply ride into the city without a good reason. Perhaps we should ask after said reason."

From the look on the sergeant's face, it was obvious he felt this was a waste of time. The Prince turned away, frustrated with having to deal with another of the new guard who had been brought into the city. Shaking his head, he addressed Sebastian. "Forgive me, friend ogre. There are still many here who welcome the presence of the Elder Races, myself among them. May I inquire as to the purpose of your visit?"

Sebastian bowed from his place in the wagon, having recognized Prince Mathias from the description given him back at the inn. "Certainly, Your Highness. I am called Sebastian, and have been sent by the Ancient One to bring a message of warning to the King."

"Sergeant, you and your men may continue your patrol. I take full responsibility for the safety and well being of our guest."

Some of the crowd had left once the Prince arrived, but a few remained, concerned over rumors they'd heard. "Is it true that the non-humans are preparing to attack our outer settlements?" someone called out.

Sebastian was genuinely puzzled by the question, and it showed on his face. He turned to face the direction the question had come from and held out his arms. "We are very happy with life in our homeland, and humans have nothing that we want. What possible reason would we have to attack?"

Those folks in front nodded in agreement after witnessing the confusion on the ogre's face and walked away satisfied there was nothing to worry about. Everyone knew an ogre couldn't lie. The Prince rode over to the side of the wagon and stretched out his hand.

"Well met, Sebastian. I am Prince Mathias, but I cannot imagine how you knew."

The ogre grasped the Prince's hand in his own, careful not to cause injury, and smiled. "Well met, Prince. You have a good reputation with the folks out in the country. At the last inn, they said I should seek you out once I arrived. Their description was very accurate."

"May I?" the Prince asked, indicating the empty spot next to Sebastian.

At the ogre's nod, Mathias tied his horse to the back of the wagon and climbed in, joining him. "I would offer you a place in the Palace but I would need to introduce you to my father first, and it's too late for that. Have you a place for the night?"

"I was told to seek out Aaron at the Four Horse Inn,

and that he would treat me kindly."

Mathias called out to his guard, "Richard, escort us to the Four Horse Inn."

"As you wish, Highness."

On the move once again, an enterprising street urchin trotted alongside the wagon and began his pitch. "If you be needin a guide in da city, Sir Ogre, Poppie be the man for you. I knows alla best places ta be eatin and buyin. Everyone knows Poppie and Poppie knows everyone."

Sebastian smiled down at the boy. "Little man, if you know a merchant who might buy this wagon load of supplies, send them to the inn this evening and there will be a reward in it for you."

"You can count on Poppie, Sir Ogre! Be seeing you at the inn," he yelled over his shoulder and disappeared down the street.

Prince Mathias glanced up at the ogre and nodded. "I wondered about the wagon, Sebastian, but I must admit that you have taken everything I thought I knew about ogres and trampled it under the hoofs of the horses. Never have I heard of an ogre driving a wagon like a merchant, and who speaks better than most learned men."

Sebastian laughed out loud. "The Ancient One would

have my fangs if I couldn't present his message to the King in a way that is easy to understand. As for the wagon, I know someone who would tell you that I am just a lazy ogre, but riding is much easier than walking."

"But what of the trade goods inside?"

The ogre hesitated before answering, unsure what he could say without lying, but without revealing too much truth either. "We ogre do not use coins as you humans do. It seemed a good idea at the time I acquired this wagon to sell the items inside to have the coins I would need to pay for lodging and food."

Before the Prince had a chance to ask Sebastian what he meant by 'acquired', they arrived at the inn and caught the innkeeper outside sweeping the entryway. Jumping down from the wagon, Mathias waved to the innkeeper. "Take good care of my friend, Aaron."

Back in the saddle, he rode up to Sebastian. "The main entrance to the Palace is only used for special occasions, so use the common gate instead. Anyone can direct you. When you arrive, ask for me personally and I will escort you in to see the King. Tomorrow is fortuitous since he will be meeting with the Council of Dukes, and they should also hear what you have to say."

Aaron lived up to his reputation and saw to Sebastian's every need. He also had a room big enough for an ogre, and didn't bat an eye when Sebastian requested two meals be served in his room. He probably assumed that the ogre would eat both when in truth the other meal was for Emma.

True to his word, Poppie showed up soon after with someone who, after some spirited haggling from the boy, agreed to buy all Sebastian had and also pay a small fee for the use of the wagon to transport the goods to his store. Poppie promised to bring the wagon back as soon as it was unloaded. Sebastian picked out one of the smaller pieces from the bag of unfamiliar coins and handed it to the boy not knowing it was actually one of the more valuable pieces.

The boy stared in wonder at the coin resting on his palm. If Sebastian had been able to read a human's expression, he would have recognized the dawning of hero worship. From that moment on, the ogre could do no wrong in Poppie's eyes.

Emma had been uncommonly quiet all evening. Sebastian walked over to stand next to her as she stared out the window, and reached down to squeeze her shoulder. She glanced up at him, placed her hand over his and shivered.

"I wish we could just turn around and go home. There is an evil here such as I have never felt before. It taints the world around me and it's coming from the Palace on the hill." Taking a deep breath, she squeezed his hand in return. "I am afraid for you, Sebastian."

Without a word, the ogre left her alone with her fear and lay down, rehearsing in his mind the words the Ancient One had entrusted to him.

\*       \*       \*

Making his rounds of the inn as was his habit before turning in for the night, Aaron found young Poppie asleep in front of the ogre's door. Taking a blanket from one of the rooms not in use, he covered the boy, and smiling, continued on to bed.

\*       \*       \*

Bright and early the next morning, Poppie proudly escorted Sebastian to the common gate of the Palace, and announced to the guards, 'Sebastian the Ogre' was here to see Prince Mathias and he was expected. The Prince arrived quickly and led the ogre through the Palace to a set of ornate double doors. After knocking loudly, he opened the doors and ushered Sebastian inside.

"Forgive the intrusion, Majesty, but Sebastian here has traveled far to bring you a message from the Ancient One, and requests permission to speak."

The Council member's initial irritation at being interrupted soon turned into wide smiles at the look of disbelief on the King's face. Duke Strumant guffawed loudly and smacked the table with his hand.

"There you are, Charles. An ogre in the Palace with a message from the Ancient One. Do you believe now? I think we need to hear what he has to say."

The King motioned for his son to approach, and handed him the Cup of Truth while attempting to regain his composure. He stood as Mathias handed the cup to Sebastian.

"Well met, Sebastian. Do you consent to the Cup of Truth?"

At Sebastian's nod, the King continued. "Then speak your message, and may the Eyes guide us in dealing with what you reveal."

# CHAPTER CWELVE

# THE OASIS

Navon felt sorry for those who had to walk and cover their faces to breathe. As the work party made its way to the next butcher site, they stirred the ash and dust into clouds that seemed to follow them. The dried blood on his clothes cracked and fell off in flakes, but the stench remained. Not for the first time did he wish for a fresh set of clothes, or at least be able to wash the ones he wore. Already, the rays of the sun had dissipated the cool night air, and what water they had would be needed for drinking.

Riding upon Moshere's back above the drifting ash and dust allowed Navon's thoughts to focus on the one so dear to his heart. His concern for Moonlight's safety continued to grow. The abundant meat available on the plains would soon spoil, and he had a feeling that when the group returned home, they would travel away from the river. She could probably survive without food for several days, but water would become a problem.

Riding next to Jamar, he turned to his guard. "How long will you continue to work?"

"One day. Meat go bad. Go home tomorrow."

"How far away is home?"

After scanning the area and sharing a look with his mount, Jamar answered. "Four days."

That look convinced Navon these men had developed a bond with their horses similar to the one he had with the wolf. He now understood why they called them Brothers. Was this something they were born with or did it take time to learn? Yet he never saw the young boys staring at their mounts in the same way as their elders, so the latter must be true. Moshere bobbed his head and the unmistakable echo of agreement touched Navon's mind.

Navon now had even more to worry about. If

Moshere was that aware of his thoughts, would he detect Moonlight's presence and alert the others? Thoughts of the young wolf were forced to the back of his mind as the group set up and Navon was once again busy helping out where needed. Like the day before, no one spoke to him, only sent guarded looks his way.

Work progressed at a feverish pace, with the noon break consisting of only enough time to down a cup of the same bitter drink that had been served the night before. Thankfully, no more living calves were found.

At a signal from Lodorn, the young head of the group, the butchering came to a stop and every effort was made to get the meat hung on drying racks. Smoky fires were lit under the racks and would be carefully tended all night with the dried meat salted and packed away in the morning. Those not directly involved with the fires were allowed to relax and gathered into several small groups, leaving Navon alone. Thoughts of Moonlight came flooding back to trouble him as he slumped to the ground, head resting on his knees.

One solution had presented itself as he worked. While most of the bones were used to keep the drying fires going, the skulls were discarded. Some were large enough to hold a fair amount of water. The meat was carefully guarded, but anyone could help themselves to the water barrels at any time. So far, no one seemed to notice as he poured his cup of water into one of the skulls after taking a sip for himself. He needed to figure out a way to carry several of the skulls as they traveled so he could leave one filled with water at every stop along the way.

Other than Moshere standing by him for awhile to provide some welcome shade, and the boys who brought him a blanket and a meal, Navon continued to be ignored. Later that night, as he lay staring up at the stars, Moonlight's concern for him filled his thoughts. He tried to project to her they would be leaving in the morning, and he would leave a skull full of water for her every day. Satisfied she would be all right for now, he closed tired eyes and let sleep overtake him.

In the morning, Navon rolled over and came face-to-face with a whiskered snout. Sometime during the night, Moshere had laid down next to him, either for protection or companionship. The two of them raised their heads and stared into each other's eyes. Without thinking, Navon projected a feeling of thanks and a good morning. Moshere nodded, and the distinctive feel of his thoughts merging with Navon's was unmistakable.

Unnerved, the young man rolled back to his other side to sit up and found Jamar sitting back on his heels, eyes narrowed in concentration and disapproval. Navon accepted the offered steaming mug and tried to ignore the suspicion in the old man's eyes. Moshere had moved a short distance away to shake off the dirt and soot then returned to stand behind Navon.

Jamar glanced up at the brother before he spoke. "You, Moshere, share heads, yes?"

With the horse now a constant presence in his mind, Navon could only nod.

Jamar sighed. "Not good. Only Shadhuin share heads with Brothers. Others are angry. Some afraid. Moshere is… how you say, highest of Brothers." He stood and frowned down at Navon as his own mount approached. "Old, old Shadhuin story from the elders say Demon come someday, steal head of highest Brother and kill Maudwan."

"I'm no demon," Navon said quietly at the same time Moshere snorted.

"You no Shadhuin, maybe not thief, and you say no demon. What are you, Na'von de Roddell?"

"A lonely young man, a long way from home," came his answer.

*     *     *

Nestled up against the base of Mount Baltok, where the Capitol of Kiplar had originally set down its roots, sat an old non-descript inn. Known as the place for late night meetings between discreet lovers, and those whose actions were best kept hidden, its innkeeper never lacked for money. No one remembered the inn's original name. Based on the faded sign above the door, that supposedly sported the likeness of the first Queen of Dahlian with two pints of ale pictured below, the name "The Queen's Jugs" had stuck. Only the innkeeper was aware of the irony of the name considering the identity of one of his patrons.

In a dark booth farthest from the door, two hooded figures sat in a lovers embrace. The pain of long-buried memories resurfacing threatened to overwhelm the Queen as she softly kissed the lips of the old arms-master, and gently traced the scars on his cheek with her fingers. The face of a young guardsman hovered before her as the past overcame the present, and she lost herself to the feelings she had buried for so long. He reached up to cover her hand with his as she pulled back, the flickering candlelight revealing a sad smile on his face.

"The memory of your soft lips has never left me even after all these years. Please believe me when I say I never stopped loving you, Olivia. i used to curse the Eyes for the position we found ourselves in, until I realized I could protect you better from the shadows than by your side."

"Oh Malcom, I've missed you so," she murmured while resting her head on his shoulder. "What happened to our love, my handsome young protector? Why have you chosen now to bring back painful memories from so long ago?"

The arms-master stiffened at her question and then let out a sigh heavy with regret. "The Deluti happened. It is also one of the reasons I needed to meet with you like this. The story I have to tell may not be easy for you to hear."

It was Olivia's turn to stiffen as she lifted her head and stared at him, the eyes of a queen replacing those of a young princess in love. "I'm listening."

Malcom paused to gulp down the rest of his ale and signaled for another, which gave him time to order his thoughts before answering. "On the day Sofia was born, I felt compelled to guard the door to your rooms. After everyone had left to allow you and the baby a chance to rest, a Deluti spirit appeared and had me under its spell before I could react."

He shivered as the memory of that night returned and he felt caught up in its grip once again. "It was like time had come to a standstill, and only the two of us existed. The spirit told me that soon the five Deluti Amulets of Focus would return to the world of men. The spirits had chosen a number of human children who would receive a portion of Deluti blood mixed with their own. Sofia is one of those chosen. The spirit then charged me with keeping that secret, and to protect her with my life until she left to be on her own."

He watched in admiration as the intelligent woman he knew and loved calmly sipped her wine while processing the information he'd just given her. It didn't take long before she leaned back, closed her eyes and blindly reached for his hand.

"Well, that explains a lot, particularly why you distanced yourself from me after Sofia was born, and why you insisted on training her in secret when she was old enough. It's also clear to me that you wouldn't be telling me this unless something has happened to her." At which point she squeezed his hand. "Please tell me she is safe."

"That Sofia is still alive I can almost guarantee, but whether or not she is safe, that remains to be seen." He hesitated before continuing, "Olivia, the repercussions from what has happened will ripple through both our countries, and the resulting consequences are too numerous for me to fathom."

Her only reaction was to open her eyes and narrow them in concentration. He then proceeded to relay everything young Gilfor had passed on the night before. He also assured her that men and wagons were already on their way to the ambush site to retrieve the bodies of the guards and to bury the attackers where they lay.

"So my daughter has the power of a Deluti inside of her?"

"Yes, and she has already begun to use those powers even if she isn't aware of it yet. With Ronald at her side, I believe they will be able to take care of themselves. What worries me is how the rumors are going to affect our people. What King Charles's reaction will be when he hears of the possible death of his son's betrothed is anybody's guess."

The Queen set down her glass of wine and pulled him close, a coy smile dancing across her lips. "Those problems will still be there on the morrow. Right now I need you to remind me how much you love me."

Malcom returned her smile with one of his own. "As Your Majesty commands."

*     *     *

Other than the heat and the constant worry over Moonlight's survival, Navon might have enjoyed the next several days. By the evening of the first day, they reached the edge of the burn, and he realized that out of the vastness of the plains, the area of the fire was actually fairly small.

As he had anticipated, they headed west away from the river, but to his surprise, each stop always included a well or spring. At least that eliminated his concern over Moonlight having enough water. Now he was able to use the empty skulls to leave her whatever food he could hide away.

An unintended side effect of riding Moshere, as the hours slowly passed with nothing but rolling grassland to capture his attention, was the bond between them grew even stronger. Words in the Shadhuin language began to have meaning, and he found that he could follow some of the conversations between the others. This was both a blessing and a curse.

Navon's feelings of isolation eased as the language became more familiar, but he soon realized the majority of the comments were about him. The closer they got to their home, the more fear entered into the quiet words spoken. Some were angry because a slave should not be allowed to ride, but with Moshere an elder among the Brothers, no one dared to interfere.

On the evening of the second day, as everyone settled in to wait for their meal, Jamar and his Brother approached and waited as Navon finished brushing the dirt from Moshere's coat. He acknowledged the elder with a respectful tilt of his head, but said nothing. He couldn't help but notice as they were traveling that Jamar spent the day talking to the other elders and Lodorn, their leader. No doubt the conversations had been about him and Moshere. Navon braced himself for whatever decision they had reached.

After the boy serving the evening stew handed a bowl to him, Navon, without thought, thanked the youngster in the same manner as he'd seen Jamar. The boy began to respond in kind then froze. Eyes wide, he stared first at Navon, and then turned to the elder. Jamar waved him away and the boy turned and ran.

Jamar folded his legs and sat in one fluid motion, narrowed eyes fixed on Navon. "So, now you understand the Shadhuin tongue?"

Navon didn't miss the fact that the old man spoke in his own language, but shook his head. "Only the little I've picked up by listening to others. I still don't understand much of what is said."

Jamar gave no indication whether he believed him or not, and changed the subject. "Tomorrow home. Much talk with elders about you. Some say send to slave market, but Moshere say no. I say no. Tradition say you go to Maudwan to decide, so you go."

Nothing more was said as Jamar finished his bowl and then left Navon alone with his thoughts and worries about the next day. It appeared he had a protector in Moshere, but how was he to protect Moonlight once they arrived at the settlement? As if she'd heard his thoughts, Moonlight's love and concern filled his mind. He missed her more and more each day, and reveled in the glow of their mutual concern. It was difficult for him to tell at this distance, but she seemed to be holding up well so far.

Moshere's presence in his mind now felt so natural,

the thought of trying to block him never entered Navon's thoughts. He held his breath as the horse and wolf met in his mind for the first time. Unable to follow what transpired between them, he only got the impression Moshere had reassured her. Whatever the intent, the result was that she became more at ease than at any other time since they arrived. In the morning, Moshere made sure they were the last to leave so no one would see Navon leave one of the skulls filled with stew.

By noon, the terrain took on the appearance of foothills even though there were no mountains close by. Some of the shallow valleys even hid stands of small trees, giving Navon hope Moonlight would be able to find some small game. A faint breeze sprang up to provide much appreciated relief from the stifling heat of the grasslands.

At the crest of the next hill, Navon was transfixed by the panorama spread out before him. He was at a total loss, unable to fathom what his tired eyes perceived. Moshere felt his confusion and stopped, trying to convey the meaning of what Navon saw, but their bonding was still too new. Frustrated, he cantered up ahead to join Jamar.

Once alongside the elder, Navon pointed back to the rise they'd just descended. "Up there I saw a blue haze that stretched in both directions as far as I could see, and the air felt different somehow. I don't understand Moshere when he tries to explain. What did I see?"

Jamar shared a look with Moshere and then faced Navon. "You see the big water."

Having never seen anything larger than a small lake and several rivers a person could easily swim across, he shook his head in disbelief and dismay. He was familiar with the map of Marlinor, and the known countries surrounding it, his father kept in his study. If what he'd seen turned out to be the Southern Sea, he was further from home than he had imagined. How would he return? There were no roads through the Shadow Mountains to the north, and Rogosh the Pirate controlled the waters of the south.

Hopeless despair wormed its way into Navon's thoughts and clouded his vision of the land they traveled. Had he made a mistake accepting the Deluti's challenge and placed not only his own life in jeopardy, but that of Moonlight's as well? How would she survive in an environment totally unfit for a wolf? Did he face a lifetime of slavery, alone?

A sharp mental rebuke from Moshere burned away the darkness and lifted Navon out of his despair. There were no words, but the message was clear. *'You are not alone or a slave, stop acting like one.'* His vision cleared as the entire group stopped on the crest of another hill. The silence was profound. Men and beasts stood rooted in place, all facing the same direction.

Navon lifted his eyes to a picture right out of a children's fairytale. Larger than the village of Twin Oaks, the Shadhuin buildings were constructed with brick and stone rather than wood. Rooftops were covered in brightly colored tiles, and banners like rainbows adorned every building, large or small. A patchwork of cultivated fields surrounded the city. No enemy could approach undetected by the watch towers placed on every side. Slaves could be seen working the fields as small bands of horses grazed the outskirts.

The whisper of a soft baritone voice floated on top of the breeze, and made its way down the hillside towards the city. Soon other adult voices joined in, accompanied by the higher pitched harmonizing of the young boys. The wind increased along with the volume of the song, eager to reach the ears of family members waiting for their return. The horses were the first to react as they turned and galloped in their direction followed by a flood of residents flowing from the city.

Through his bond with Moshere, Navon understood this was a song celebrating their return home, and the joy of once again being with loved ones. It was a song of peace and pride in their home. No one moved until the last note faded into the distance. His prior despair forgotten, Navon turned to Jamar, wonder filling his eyes and heart.

The elder smiled at him and then laughed out loud. "What you expect, Na'von, mud huts and tents?"

# Chapter Thirteen

# Truth and Rumors

"Ronald, I destroyed that man with just a thought. How is that possible?" Sofia asked quietly, eyes still focused on the darkness outside the window.

Rather than answering right away, Ronald got up and poured a cup of water from the pitcher on the washstand and handed it to her. He returned it to the stand after she had her fill and sat back on the bed, taking her hand once more.

"I have no idea. Legends of the Deluti are filled with all manner of amazing feats they were capable of, so what you did doesn't surprise me. I am really glad you did though. Even I could sense the evil he represented."

"But it wasn't really me who killed him! It was the anger that took control and held me in its grasp. I was completely powerless."

He placed his hand on her shoulder and gently turned the Princess to face him. "No Sofia, it was you. The anger is part of who you are. It's the fear of the anger that gives it power over you. Embrace your anger. It's what makes you strong."

She stood with a tired smile and squeezed his hand before releasing it. "Discarding the trappings of a lieutenant has revealed something even more rare."

"What's that?"

"A true friend." And with that she headed for the room she shared with Floanne. Hesitating at the door, she turned back. "What happened tonight will surely start rumors and cause problems for us."

"For now, I plan to get a good night's sleep. We will just deal with whatever comes up in the morning, and make our plans then," he replied, unbuckling his armor.

As Sofia had predicted, trouble arrived at their door early the next morning when someone stopped outside and began pounding on it. The three of them had already risen and were gathered in Ronald's room. He grabbed his sword and cautiously approached the door.

"Who is there?"

"The innkeeper," he shouted. "You and your partner need to come down right away and deal with the crowd that has filled the inn and the surrounding streets. Any damage to my inn and you will pay dearly."

"Tell them we will be right down," Ronald shouted back.

As the innkeeper's footsteps retreated down the hall, Sofia and Floanne joined Ronald at the door, the former handmaiden's hands gripped tightly before her. He reached down to pick up the helm Sofia had been wearing, but she shook her head and unbraided her hair instead. She locked eyes with her new friend until an unspoken agreement was reached. Ronald smiled, and with a flourish, opened the door for her.

Fear and uncertainty shrouded Floanne's voice as she stared at Sofia's retreating back. "What do you want me to do?"

Arm around her shoulders, he guided the young handmaiden through the door. "Just be yourself. It appears the Princess has one more act to perform before we leave our home."

The increasingly loud conversations between the people inside the inn came to an abrupt halt when Sofia set foot inside the common room. Folks nudged their neighbors and pointed while something in her eyes caused those in her path to step aside. Awed whispers of "The Princess" followed close on her heels, and the innkeeper rushed to open the front door, bowing as she passed. The crowd outside had already quieted, forewarned by the sudden silence from within.

The Princess stepped out onto the wooden platform that fronted the inn, Ronald and Floanne to either side and slightly behind. Those in the crowd who recognized her dropped to one knee in a show of respect. She inclined her head in recognition, and then motioned for them to rise.

"As some of you may have heard, I have been betrothed to Prince Mathias of Marlinor to seal a peace agreement between our two nations. However, two days out of the Capitol we were ambushed. Myself, my handmaiden and Lieutenant Marton are all that is left of our company. Unfortunately, three of the attackers survived also and escaped to report that we still live."

She had to stop as angry shouts rang out from the crowd, some loudly denouncing the Marlinorians. She raised her hand and the people quieted once again.

"Only someone in the Palace with prior knowledge of our exact travel times could have organized an attack with such precision. I am no longer safe here. That is why the three of us disguised ourselves and plan to travel on to Marlinor."

Someone called out, "Your Highness, what of the rumors from the inn last night?"

Sofia stiffened and a look of uncertainty crossed her face as she glanced back at Ronald. He inclined his head slightly and smiled in encouragement. Emboldened, she turned back to face the people.

"Long ago, at the end of the Deluti War, High Lord Demitrios prophesied that one day the power of the Deluti blood would return to this world mixed with the blood of humans." She hesitated, closing her eyes. "That prophesy has been fulfilled."

The Princess stood a little taller and raised her voice to reach those in the back. "The man you knew as Roushal was a sorcerer sent out by the Scarred Mage to spread his evil lies and to turn the people against each other and the

Elder Races. And yes, I destroyed him last night, as I will anytime I confront evil."

Frightened murmurs of uncertainty began to circulate through the people. Stories of the Scarred Mage had descended into the realm of myth and were used to frighten unruly children. The idea that he still lived was not well received. Sofia waited patiently for the people to quiet once again when one of the men in front stepped forward to address her.

"Your Highness, if everything you say is true, what are we to do? None of us has the power to stand up to a sorcerer."

She made eye contact with as many as she could while carefully choosing her words. "Do nothing. Live your lives as best you can while ignoring their lies, as I'm confident more agents will be sent. If anyone asks about me, tell them a different story each time. Confusion will only serve to protect me."

She glanced back at Ronald before continuing. "But, I want you all to hold this thought close to your hearts. As a Princess of Dahlian, I promise as long as there is breath inside me, I will find a way to return to fight this evil and to discover my betrayer."

The Princess returned the many waves of the townsfolk as they made their way back to their homes or work amid calls of "Be safe," and "Return soon".

Ronald touched her arm and then held open the door into the inn. "Come back inside and we can discuss what to do next over a hot meal."

They chose a table against the front wall of the inn where Ronald could watch over the street outside while Sofia kept an eye on the door. The innkeeper rushed over, unsure how to address them.

"I have a much nicer table in the other room, ah, Highness."

About to respond with one of her typically biting remarks, she took a deep breath and smiled at the innkeeper instead. "My friends call me Surly Sofia, innkeeper. What do your friends call you?"

Put at ease by her smile, he straightened up and returned the smile. "I am called many things, but I answer to Cedric."

Sofia laughed out loud. "I can just imagine, Cedric. For now, we are just three hungry patrons of your fine establishment. When we leave, it will be as we arrived; two mercenaries guarding a young woman."

"Well I certainly cannot have word get out that I let my patrons starve. I will return shortly." He couldn't help himself and bowed once more before turning towards the kitchen.

From the time they left their rooms, Floanne had not said a word, and now sat at the table with eyes downcast. Ronald reached out and gently raised her head with a finger under her chin. He felt her quiver, and tried to address the fear he saw in her tear-filled eyes.

"I imagine you wish we could just go home, but I hope you realize that is no longer possible. Sometimes life puts us in a position where all we can do is our best to survive. I know there is a strength deep inside of you that will rise up when needed." He released her chin and sat back. "Besides, you are in the presence of two of the meanest, nastiest mercenaries this side of the Straits of Durmont. What could go wrong?"

Ronald was rewarded with a smile as Cedric returned, along with one of the serving girls, loaded down with steaming bowls, and mugs filled with a tart but refreshing fruit drink that filled the air with its aroma. The three of them dug in with a renewed sense of purpose and were almost finished when an explosion outside shook the inn down to its foundation.

Several chairs crashed to the floor as patrons jumped to their feet and ran out the door. Clouds of dust rained down from the ceiling, ruining their food and drink. Sofia and Ronald stayed seated, but with hands on the hilts of their swords waiting for word of what happened. Floanne covered her mouth and trembled.

Soon, a young man stumbled into the inn shouting, "The Silverfin exploded and sank. Two other ships and the pier are on fire. Hurry, everyone is needed to fight the flames." He left quickly and continued down the street, shouting his message.

Ronald recognized the flash of anger in Sofia's eyes and carefully laid a hand on her arm. "Your sister?"

"Her blood debt continues to grow. If she kills so easily, what of the Queen and Francine? Should we return?"

He squeezed her arm in understanding. "If Gilfor reached the arms-master, I can guarantee Master Horshall will do everything in his power to protect them. Right now it is only the two of us against an unknown number of your sister's agents. We need allies, and hopefully they will be found in Marlinor."

The innkeeper appeared at their table and leaned down to whisper. "Quickly now. Grab your packs and head straight for the stable. The wagon and your horses should be ready when you arrive. Take the north shore road out of town and look for an old pier and buildings about a mile up."

As the three jumped up from the table, he explained. "An old friend of mine there has a two-masted schooner he uses for fishing, but claims it's the fastest ship on the coast. Tell him Cedric sent you, and if he gets you safely across to Marlinor, I will consider his debt to me paid in full."

They rushed through the now-empty common room, up the stairs and to their rooms. After packing and ensuring that nothing was left behind, they made their way down the back stairs to the stable where they found the innkeeper harnessing the wagon. Sofia tossed her bag into the wagon and approached him.

"You are a good man, Cedric. Watch yourself. My enemies will not hesitate to kill anyone they believe helped me."

"Don't worry Prin... ah, Sofia. I've been watching out for myself for a very long time, but thanks for the warning. One more thing. There ain't room on his ship for your horses and the wagon, so I will send someone to bring them back. What should I do with them?"

"When we rode into town yesterday, I couldn't help but notice a number of hungry children wandering the streets. Someone should do something about that."

A large smile pulled at the scars on his face as he bowed one last time. "I like the way you think, Sofia. I have not said this in a long time, but may the Eyes protect and guide you on your journey."

A short time later, two people in a wagon followed by a single rider on horseback could be seen slowly making their way out of town on the coast road. Once over the first small rise and out of sight, the horses broke into a run.

\* \* \*

Still reeling from his whirlwind journey through the castle, Sebastian struggled to absorb the images of luxury he'd seen. The Ancient One's secret fortress in the Mountains of Mists was nothing like this. Here the stone floors were covered in colorful designs made with small tiles, and large murals depicting scenes of battle lined the walls, alternating with tapestries attuned to the seasons.

However, his sharp eyes picked up the subtle signs of neglect in the faint layer of dust and the occasional wilted flower among the many vases lining the halls.

The faint echo of a familiar power surrounding the Cup in his hands brought him back to the present. Sebastian realized with a start that the King had already resumed his seat, Prince Mathias standing beside him, and both waiting for him to speak. Before him sat four of the most powerful humans in this part of the world, and they must believe the truth of his words.

Carefully holding the Cup where all could see, Sebastian cleared his throat and began the well rehearsed message. "Charles d'Rodare, King of Marlinor. High Lord Demitrios of the Deluti sends his greetings, and the hope that you and yours are in good health and fare well. As an ogre, I was chosen to deliver this message so you would know that no sorcery was involved and you could trust my words as true."

Pausing to draw a deep breath, the ogre continued with the part of the message that concerned him most. "The Scarred Mage has spent several lifetimes raising a cadre of well-trained sorcerers to spread his evil and hatred toward the Elder Races throughout the world. He

has begun sending them to all parts of the country. I be..."
he slipped and started again after regaining his composure.
"I can personally attest to the success of his plan as I
barely escaped Brighton Ferry with my life, and was met
with hostility when I arrived here in the Capitol. If not for
Prince Mathias, I might not be standing before you now."

Following that statement, the King turned to his son.
"What happened, Mathias?"

"I heard a disturbance near the main gate and rode to
investigate. I found Sebastian being detained by the City
Guard, and surrounded by an angry crowd. The Sergeant
explained he had orders to keep all members of the Elder
Races out of the Capitol, but before Sebastian could turn
his wagon around, a large group of people had gathered."

"Some were on the side of the ogre, and the rest had
already heard the rumors. The look on Sebastian's face
when someone asked why the Elder Races were planning
to attack the human settlements convinced most everyone
the rumors were untrue."

Duke Benjamin al'Fortuna, who oversaw the area
including Brighton Ferry, leaned forward. "Majesty, I just
received word this morning from my man in Brighton
Ferry and he mentioned an ogre in the city. He originally

intended to write how he was concerned about the mood in the city, but that changed after the death of the sorcerer. Apparently, the man not only used his words, but also some sort of power to affect the people. When he died, it was like a dark cloud had lifted from the city."

He turned back to the ogre and smiled. "It appears Sebastian here has a way with children also. After he left, groups of youngsters roamed about the city proclaiming how good and kind ogres were."

Sebastian shuffled his feet and shrugged as he faced five sets of raised eyebrows. Remembering the rest of the message, he faced the King again. "One more thing, Your Majesty. The Ancient One is aware of your attempt to pursue peace through the betrothal of your son to Princess Sofia of Dahlian and he approves. However, he is concerned that there may be some on either side of the water who do not agree. Therefore, I am to offer my service as a personal guard for the Princess once she arrives."

The four men slumped back in their chairs and shared looks of surprise and dawning apprehension. Charles motioned his son to retrieve the Cup of Truth from Sebastian, and rose to address the ogre formally.

"Sebastian, as King of Marlinor, I accept this unprecedented offer on Princess Sofia's behalf, and if she is not aware of the honor bestowed upon her, then I will be sure to explain."

Looking at the concerned faces of his councilors for a moment, he turned back to the ogre. "Your words have served not only to warn us, but also to remind us of the power of the Deluti. If the Ancient One is aware of our plans, then it must be assumed the Scarred Mage is also. On a personal level, you have dispelled any doubts I had as to the intelligence of ogres, and I would be pleased if you joined me for further discussion at a later date."

Sebastian bowed to the King and answered. "It would be my pleasure, Majesty."

Prince Mathias, knowing a dismissal when he heard one, approached the ogre, and escorted him from the chamber.

After the door closed behind the Prince and the ogre, King Charles set the Cup in the center of the table and searched the eyes of his dukes. "Thoughts, my friends?"

Duke Marcus d'Lorange picked up the Cup and held it up before his face, slowly turning it round and round as if he'd never seen it before. "I had originally planned to wait for further clarification on the message I received from one of my contacts this morning. In lieu of the ogre's warning, perhaps it's best I share it now."

The Duke glanced around at the others before fixing his gaze on the King. "Charles, it pains me to report that apparently the Princess and her escort were ambushed on their way from their capitol to the port city of Seaside. It is still unknown whether anyone survived, but someone claiming to be the Princess was seen at an inn there, but then disappeared. Unfortunately, we must entertain the idea that someone in the Queen's court, or the Queen herself has been influenced by the Scarred Mage, and the overture of peace was an attempt to get us to lower our defenses."

Duke Strumant lurched forward and grabbed the Cup out of Marcus's hand. "I told you we couldn't trust those witches, Charles. They could already be on their way to attack our shores! We must deploy the army to protect the coast and send all our ships out to sea so they don't get trapped in the harbor."

King Charles sighed and sat back with his eyes closed. After a moment, he looked up and appealed to his most trusted advisor. "Marcus?"

Duke d'Lorange quickly dismissed the smile he'd been hiding behind his hand and faced the King with an appropriately serious expression. "Anthony has a valid point, but we should proceed with caution and secrecy. Also, I think it would be wise to continue preparations for the betrothal so as not to alert any agents the Queen may have in the city."

"Very well. Begin sending troops to the garrisons along the coast as soon as they are ready. Have the ships in the harbor leave one at a time, but have them stay close. I don't want the Capitol left undefended. Also send a message to all units to be on increased alert without giving a specific reason why. As you said, Marcus, we don't want to alert any agents here or elsewhere."

The King stood, followed closely by the others, bringing the council to a close. "Let us hope these precautions prove unnecessary. I have been a fool believing the Scarred Mage no longer concerned us. I'm afraid we will need the Blessings of the Eyes more than ever."

As the men filed through the door, Charles stopped his old friend. "Marcus, you will contact me as soon as you hear word of the Princess?"

"Of course."

*　　*　　*

Sebastian waited patiently outside the common gate for Prince Mathias to arrive with his horse. Why anyone needed a horse to get around the confines of the city was a mystery to him. He was not lonely, however, as Poppie had met him at the gate. The boy kept up a continuous chatter on the wondrous sights available in the Capitol, and how Poppie was just the person to guide the ogre.

Mathias soon arrived leading the horse and noticed the surprised look on the ogre's face, and laughed. "What, you think Princes are too good to walk?"

"Then why the horse?"

"I may be called back to the Palace at any time and need to return quickly."

Sebastian nodded his head as if he understood while struggling with the decision of how much he could trust this human. Em always accused him of being too trusting, and admittedly, it had gotten them into trouble on occasion. He didn't have as much experience with humans as she did, but there was something special about this young man.

At this time of day, the streets of the Capitol were

mostly deserted, and the few folks about gave them a wide berth. Sebastian felt it would be safe to speak of certain things except for the pair of ears attached to the little man who proudly skipped at his side.

"Poppie, would you run ahead and inform the innkeeper me and the Prince will be arriving soon, and some refreshment would be appreciated?"

The boy smiled up at the ogre, "You can count on Poppie!" and took off.

Subtlety not being a part of an ogre's nature, Sebastian turned to the Prince. "Mathias, can you be trusted?"

They continued to walk on in silence while the Prince considered the ogre's question. When the inn came into view, he looked up at Sebastian. "I don't have an answer to your question, Sebastian. What I can tell you is my family and this kingdom are more important to me than my own life. I suspected there was more to your message than what you were willing to share with the entire council, but I claim the right to use that information to protect the ones I love."

The honesty in the young man's statement was more important to Sebastian than the answer to his question.

"Understood."

Having made his decision, the ogre led the way into the inn and directly to his room where he ushered the Prince through the door. "Come, we have much to tell you."

"We?" Mathias hesitated and then froze as Emma suddenly appeared in the middle of the room.

"Yes, we, Princeling. Now sit and listen."

Fear and uncertainty robbed the Prince of all control as he practically fell into the nearest chair and stared at one of the deadliest assassins known. A whisper involuntarily escaped his lips, "An Elintrian Light-Shifter."

# CHAPTER FOURTEEN

## JEWEL OF THE PLAINS

Jamar slid off his mount along with the others, and motioned for Navon to do the same. The Brothers trotted away in the direction of those who had first spotted the work party. The men began a slow progress down to their waiting family members, followed closely by the draft horses pulling the heavily-laden wagons.

Lodorn walked up carrying Navon's weapons. He handed the bow and quiver to Jamar, but kept the sword. "Come. Must see Maudwan. Rumors start."

The crowds of family members stared at the three of

them, and then parted to let them pass. Painful memories of the ridicule Navon experienced while growing up different from his brothers, threatened to strip away his fragile confidence. Only Moshere's parting thought of well-being and courage kept Navon's head up while he matched the older men stride for stride.

Banishing old feelings, he concentrated on studying the people they passed and the city that waited. No wonder they stared. His sun-burned skin and long, pale hair set him apart from all those gathered. What captured his attention, however, were the colorful clothes worn by both men and women alike. He had never seen cloth that flowed as a person moved, or billowed at the slightest stirring of a breeze. Their clothes looked so much cooler than what he wore. Hope arose that he would be allowed to wear something similar.

Unlike the people filling the path into the city, the workers in the fields ignored them and the celebration going on over the return of the men. These must be the slaves Jamar talked about. They also wore the same rust colored clothing as the men who had gone out to harvest meat, which only made sense. Why take a chance on ruining the brightly-colored outfits they normally wore?

He quickly rejected the idea he might end up as one of them.

Navon would have paused to stare, as they approached the city, if he had not been flanked by his captors. The outer stone buildings, some several stories high, formed a wall that appeared to encompass the entire city. The only openings on the ground floor were arrow ports. He shivered at the thought of being part of an attacking army. It was just as much a fortress as a city.

Jamar and Lodorn greeted the two guards at the heavy gate that led through the buildings on this side and into a short tunnel. They were the first men Navon had seen dressed as warriors. They reminded him of his brothers back at the Keep, heavily armored and bristling with weapons.

They reached the end of the tunnel and all came to a stop, but for different reasons. Navon stared in awe at the large body of water that filled the inner courtyard, surrounded by stands of odd looking trees. Tall, graceful trunks topped with a crown of over-sized leaves, resembled nothing he'd ever seen before. A large jumble of boulders stood piled at one end where water gushed from the top and cascaded into the lake below. A cool, moisture-laden breeze teased the tips of his hair, a welcome respite from the heat outside.

The men raised their bowed heads and whispered together the words, "Chrystolos de la Palma."

Navon tore his gaze away from the image of serenity and life to raise an eyebrow towards his guardians.

Jamar smiled, and with a broad gesture, proudly indicated the oasis before them. "The Jewel of the Plain. In the long ago, many tribes fight to control. The Brothers came and forced peace. In all history, the water never stop. Plenty for all, and for the fields. Many search for riches, but this our treasure."

For the first time, Navon felt the spirit of his amulet reach out to him. It gently guided his awareness to the presence of a power deep beneath the oasis. The young man knew than this was not an accident of nature. The demonstration of the Deluti's power, and if Em and Sebastian could be believed, a power he possessed, sent a shiver coursing through his body.

Lodorn, mistaking the shiver for fear of their meeting, touched Navon on the arm. "Come. Maudwan fair and merciful. This way."

They led him to a modest, stone building near the

base of the rocks. Jamar knocked quietly and then led them inside. Heads bowed in respect, they waited for their eyes to adjust to the muted light until a youthful voice called them.

Unsure, Navon kept his eyes lowered as they stepped forward, until Jamar held out his hand. He waited while the two men continued on, and returned after a moment without his weapons. The murmur of voices, one the voice of the youth, and the other a labored rasp, accompanied the sound of Navon's sword being pulled from its sheath and slowly returned.

Lodorn was called forward, and then Jamar. Even though Navon had learned a number of their words, the hushed conversation prevented him from understanding, but Moshere's name rang out clearly several times. Jamar's voice rose in anger and then quieted at a soft rebuke from the youth. Whether he was arguing for or against Navon was impossible to tell.

The conversation came to an end. In the ensuing silence, Navon heard the weak voice of the Maudwan call his name. With a deep breath, he stepped forward and raised his eyes. The emaciated body of a man rested on a raised platform, his upper body propped up by a collection of colorful pillows. The young man hovered near his head while Lodorn and Jamar stood at the end of the platform. The distant sound of cascading water filled Navon's ears.

These details barely registered on the young Deluti's awareness as the image of a golden chain wrapped tightly around the Maudwan's neck, digging into flesh, filled his vision. A chain identical to the one around his own neck with an amulet attached, and it was obviously killing the man wearing it. Navon resisted the urge to reach up and check his own. Was it getting tighter? Would this happen if he failed his test?

No. He must not fail. Moonlight's life depended on it. Dropping his arm and standing a little taller, he shoved his questions aside.

The Maudwan had watched him through narrowed eyes, and when the young man beside him started to speak, he was stopped by a gesture.

"My sons and Elder Jamar see enemy and danger." He stopped to draw a ragged breath before continuing. "I see lonely young man lost in strange land."

Navon opened his mouth as if to argue, then let his shoulders slump and looked away.

"Yes, I still see good," the Maudwan smiled and

closed his eyes. "Brod."

"Father," the young man answered and addressed Navon. "Na'von de Roddell no slave, but hunt on Shadhuin land and not ask. Must work for Shadhuin thirty days. No trouble, will get weapons and go free. Elder Jamar help and show what work to do."

Navon's shoulders drooped even further. Thirty days? How would Moonlight survive that long? There was only one who might help. "Will I see Moshere?"

Brod sighed and shook his head. "Moshere do what Moshere do. He decide."

Jamar pointed to the door. The meeting was over, and Navon hadn't had a chance to explain. But then, what would he have said? Even he wasn't sure how they'd arrived here or why. How much did these people believe in the Deluti? At least he was no longer considered a slave, but what if they had decided he was a demon? Would he have been willing to hurt these people if they had tried to kill him? That question settled to the pit of his soul and would torment him for a long time.

Outside in the bright sun, they had to wait for their eyes to adjust before Jamar led him away. "Come, Na'von. Much work still to empty wagons. Then wash, clean clothes, and eat."

Navon lost himself to the work at hand, and to the promise of a meal and clean clothes. The heavily laden wagons were already positioned near the openings to the storage areas, which turned out to be large underground caverns. The horses that had pulled the wagons were long gone, and the work of unloading well underway. The blessed coolness of the caverns helped refresh his body, but did nothing to quell the anxiety that tormented his mind.

After the work was complete, the Elder led Navon to his home in a building where he lived alone. There was an extra room that had belonged to his son Navon could use. Opening the shutters, Jamar pointed to a chest at the foot of the bed. "Many clothes. Some maybe fit. Wash, put on clothes, we go eat."

The clothes were so loose that Navon wasn't sure if they fit right or not, but they were as comfortable as he had imagined. Already, the heat was less oppressive, and the soft fabric a nice change from the coarse woolens he was used to. Feeling a little conspicuous in the bright colors, he relaxed when Jamar only glanced and offered a rare smile. They walked down a long hall to a communal dining area where the Elder choose a spot at the end of a long table.

Several women moved among the tables bringing plates of food and pouring cups of water. While the stew he'd eaten out on the plains had been filling, this food excited taste buds in ways Navon was unused to. Although Jamar's expression never changed, Navon could tell by the twinkle in the elder's eyes, his amusement every time the young man called for another cup of water. Tiny beads of sweat formed on his brow.

While the faces he recognized from the work party no longer glanced at him with fear or hostility, being ignored was almost worse. Maybe it was the strong feeling of being alone that triggered it, but Moshere's thoughts suddenly flooded his mind. Foremost among them was the desire to see Navon and make sure he was alright.

Jamar recognized the far-off look as his charge stopped with his spoon poised halfway to his mouth. He set down his own spoon and sighed.

"Moshere?"

The startled look and downcast eyes were all the conformation Jamar needed. "Good time show you work for tomorrow. Take care of Brothers. Maybe not so hard."

They made their way out of the city to an area devoid of fields and designed specifically for the care of horses. Numerous covered areas with water troughs and containers for feed lined the path outside the gate. Navon's job would be to keep the water and feed troughs filled, and to help the elder in charge if any of the Brothers became ill or were injured.

Moshere arrived at the end of the path, tossing his head. Jamar watched the young man hurry out to where the leader of the Brothers waited patiently, mount and then gallop away. No matter what the Maudwan said, a heavy sense of foreboding filled his heart. There was something going on here he couldn't fathom, but nothing good could come of it.

Navon tried to answer Moshere's concern over what the Maudwan had decided. He inadvertently let slip his recognition of the power that fed the oasis, and the possible link to the hidden amulet worn by the Maudwan. Moshere never altered his stride or gave any indication the observation bothered him, only that he felt the decision was as fair as it could be.

Navon could almost feel the smile in Moshere's thoughts as he teased the young man with the idea of a special surprise in store for him. They crossed over a ridge and down into one of the small valleys out of sight of the city. There, a large, four legged animal peered cautiously out from behind a bush. Navon fell off Moshere's back before they came to a full stop, and ended up on his hands and knees. Moonlight pounced playfully, rolling him over on his back where she covered his face with licks and nipped at his nose.

Laughing and crying in equal amounts, Navon grabbed at her fur in an attempt to pull her down, but she had grown. Their shared thoughts swirled in a whirlwind of love and happiness as each tried to make sure the other was alright. She finally lay down beside him, muzzle on his chest as they stared into each other's eyes. No matter what else was wrong in the world, for now, Navon was at peace.

Moshere watched the display of youthful joy and innocence, shook his head, and trotted back to the crest of the ridge to keep guard. He was much older than anyone knew, and was quite aware of the amulet the Maudwan wore and the power it contained. His family had been recruited to help hide and protect the amulet when it had first been entrusted to the nomads.

Early on, when they still roamed the plains and lived in tents, it was decided a small wooden box could too easily be lost. The tradition evolved where the youngest son of their leader would wear the chain around his neck. Unfortunately, since they had no Deluti blood, the chain wouldn't grow as the young man grew, eventually choking him to death. At that point, the chain would fall loose and then be placed around the neck of the next youngest son. And so the cycle continued.

As with many of the Elder Races, Moshere was able to see past the illusion that hid the amulet Navon wore, and he could sense the power of a Deluti which surrounded him. He also knew if the Amulets were once again appearing in the world, it meant that war would soon be upon them again.

As much as he loved his Shadhuin brothers, he knew with their prejudices and distrust of anything different, it would be difficult to protect the young Deluti and his companion. Moshere understood that if something were to go horribly wrong, Navon had the power to destroy the city and all within. The uncomfortable feeling that he was making a mistake ate away at the confidence he'd held for so many years.

Emma stood before the Prince and challenged him, hands on her hips. "Yes, an Elintrian Light-Shifter, and don't be a fool. That you can see me and are still alive means you have nothing to fear. However, you have everything to fear while living in the Palace."

Sebastian laid his hand on Emma's shoulder and spoke quietly. "All is well, little one. We can trust Mathias."

Shaking off his hand, she went back to stare out of the window. A position she'd been in since the ogre left, drawn to the evil coming from the direction of the Palace.

Sebastian let his arm drop as he followed her movement. Sighing, he sat on the edge of the bed and faced the Prince. "Forgive me, Mathias. I am still learning the ways of humans and should have warned you. It seems I also made a mistake by not letting Em know I was bringing someone."

The Prince leaned forward, reached up to hook his shoulder length hair behind an ear, no longer fearful. "No forgiveness needed, Sebastian. Your friend is right. I was being foolish to think you would lead me into danger. With all the changes and uneasiness I feel in the Palace,

I'm afraid I'm more on edge than I thought."

Emma turned away from the window and moved to stand in front of the young man, patting the ogre on the knee as she walked past. Searching the Prince's face, she stuck out her small hand. "Well met, Mathias. I am Emma. The fact that the evil in the Palace bothers you convinces me more than words of your honesty. Please tell me more of those changes you spoke of."

Mathias held her hand in his, unseeing as his sight turned inward. "Evil... yes, now that you've named it, that is exactly how it feels. Ever since the new guards started arriving, the feeling has grown. Unfortunately, my father doesn't feel it the way I do."

Sebastian asked from his place on the bed. "The men who stopped us were new?"

"Yes. One of the Dukes felt it would benefit the Kingdom if guards were rotated between the different Keeps and the Palace. Not only the guards in the city, but most of the servants also. Some of the new men are more like brigands than guards."

They were interrupted by the sound of someone kicking the door as Emma quickly disappeared. Sebastian opened the door revealing a struggling Poppie, tongue sticking out of the side of his mouth. A loaf of bread, wedge of cheese, and slices of meat covered a large platter with a tall bottle of wine and a stack of glasses balanced precariously on the edge. The ogre rescued the bottle and glasses as the boy entered and placed the platter on their small table.

"Poppie do good, yes?" he announced proudly, smiling up at the ogre.

Sebastian, however, was not smiling and towered over the cowering boy. "Why are there three glasses, Poppie?"

"Ahh... Poppie go now," he exclaimed and made a dash for the door. The door slammed shut as Emma appeared in front of it, knives drawn. Sliding to a stop, his arms dropped to his sides as his features began to shimmer. Emma's eyes grew in surprise and then narrowed. The changes were subtle, but a young man now stood before her.

With a flourish, her knives disappeared as she stood there, hands on hips and frowning. "Cousin Roll. What are you doing here, and does your mother know?"

"No one except the Ancient One knew I was here, until now," he retorted. "And don't you dare tell mother. Did you think you were the only one tired of living in trees? I'm not as good at light shifting as you are, but the old man taught me how to make small changes to my appearance. I've always been a good actor, and no one pays attention to me when they talk to others. How do you think the High Lord found out one of the Dukes is up to something?"

Mathias relieved Sebastian of the wine and proceeded to fill the three glasses. The ogre declined, sitting back heavily on his bed, mumbling to himself. The cousins gratefully accepted. The Prince studied his wine before taking a sip, and turned to face them. "I used to believe employing spies was less than honorable, but I'm beginning to rethink my ideas. It's obvious we need information that isn't available any other way."

Sitting next to Emma on the bed, Roll asked for a refill. "I understand, Prince Mathias. There are those who would use spies to harm others, but sometimes it's the only way to get the information you need to protect those close to you."

Uncomfortable being the only one standing, Mathias pulled his chair over to the table and took advantage of the food. Tearing off a chunk of bread, he pointed it at Roll. "What can you tell us, and why do you suspect one of the

Dukes?"

"Prince Mathias, I don't know where these new men are coming from, but most of them have never been guards before. They complain constantly about having to play a part they despise. I must also assume they mean Duke d'Lorange when they refer to the one who is paying them as the 'local duke'. Whatever they are planning, it centers around the arrival of the Barons. I've overheard a number of them talking about taking their revenge at that time."

The Prince jumped up and began pacing the floor. "By the Eyes! If all the guards are loyal to him, it would be easy to threaten all the royal families and force them to name him King. But Marcus is the King's oldest and dearest friend and counselor. Even with proof, my father will never believe me. This is much worse than I imagined."

Sebastian roused himself and asked, "Mathias, how long will it take for all the Barons to get here, and when do you expect the Princess to arrive from Dahlian?"

The young prince paused to think. "Some of the Barons have a long way to travel, and will probably take almost a week to get here. As far as I know, Princess Sofia should arrive within the next several days, depending on the weather in the Straits. Why?"

Emma jumped down and studied the Prince. "Because, human, we need time to gather information and allies. I'll pinpoint the source of evil and follow the Duke's movements."

Roll joined her. "And I'll go down to the docks to get a feel for which way the wind blows."

At the door, Emma turned back to Mathias. "Every keep I've been in has a secret escape built in. I can't imagine the Palace wouldn't have one also. If you don't already know its location, I would find it and make sure it's still usable. We'll return here tonight to discuss what we've found."

After the door closed, the Prince turned to Sebastian, a grin on his face. "Is she always like that?"

"Always," the ogre laughed. "I'm surprised she didn't give me orders also."

His grin fading, the young prince downed the last of his wine and headed for the door also. "As much as I hate to admit this, it's probably because she knows you are not safe outside of this inn. I'm sorry, Sebastian."

The ogre took Emma's spot in front of the window

and tried to grasp the enormity of what he saw. Truth be told, he didn't want to leave the inn. He had no intention of sharing with the others, especially Em, just how intimidated he was being around so many humans. If they ever turned against the Elder Races, there would be no stopping them.

# CHAPTER FIFTEEN

## BROTHERS

The sand covered north road out of Seaside was vastly different than the roads they had traveled so far. The shifting sand dunes threatened to swallow up the road in several places forcing Ronald to slow as the horses struggled to pull the wagon through the loose sand. Eerily quiet, the pounding hoof beats and the rattling of the wagon could barely be heard over the distant roar of waves crashing against the shore.

Sofia estimated they had traveled at least a mile already, and began to wonder if the innkeeper was as honest as he seemed. Who would be fool enough to build a pier along this stretch of coast? After cresting another tall dune, a wide channel appeared before them which caused the road to angle sharply inland.

It followed the channel and became more solid the farther they traveled. Soon, several buildings came into view with a short pier that jutted out into the channel. As they got closer, the Princess could see only one building still sported a roof while the others had fallen in upon themselves. The skeleton of a ship thrust blackened fingers skyward amongst a jumble of scaffolding and supports at the water's edge.

She was no expert on ships, but the one that rocked gently alongside the lone pier didn't inspire any confidence in how long it would still float, much less sail. Ronald jumped down from the wagon and headed for the ship as Sofia rode up and stopped alongside Floanne who sat with slumped shoulders in an attitude of defeat.

She raised somber eyes to her former mistress. "Has the innkeeper betrayed us?"

"I don't know, but we won't learn anything sitting here. Come, we might as well hear what the captain has to say for himself."

Regardless of Cedric's reassurances, Ronald knew a smuggler when he saw one. They weren't much better than pirates, and were notoriously secretive, especially with strangers. It wouldn't surprise him to be confronted by loaded crossbows as he approached the ship, and hoped the women would have a chance to escape if things got ugly.

As he stepped onto the pier, details of the ship's condition emerged even to his untrained eye. What appeared from a distance as a derelict ready to sink at any time, proved to be quite the opposite. Not a speck of rust or corrosion was evident on any of the metal. Rather than being polished to a shine as on other ships, these fittings were carefully greased or oiled.

If the ship had ever been painted in bright colors before, there was no evidence of that now. New wood was oiled to look old where the ship had been repaired. The intentional deception only increased his suspicions, yet none of the crew members he could see working on the ship even bothered to look up. Either he was being watched by someone he couldn't see, or they had complete confidence in their captain's ability to handle a lone stranger.

He may not know a lot about them, but Ronald knew you didn't walk onto another man's ship without permission. Standing at the foot of the gangway, he called out.

"Hallo the ship. May I come aboard?"

The nearest sailor glanced up at the sound of his voice, but appeared to be looking past him. Turning around, Ronald spotted Sofia with her arm around Floanne already at the foot of the pier. Berating himself over his foolishness in thinking he could protect the Princess, her frown let him know she wasn't happy with his decision.

He turned back to the ship as shouting could be heard inside. One of the deck hatches slammed open followed by the reddest hair he'd ever seen on a man. Using the hook on his right arm, the old sailor heaved himself up on deck and quickly looked them over before speaking.

"Hallo yourself. What is it you want from me?"

"We need transportation, and have a proposition for you from Cedric the innkeeper."

"Well now, a proposition from that old thief is it? The last time I took him up on one of those I ended up with this," he replied, holding up his hook. "Very well, come aboard. Would this have anything to do with the smoke rising from Seaside's harbor?"

"Let's just say someone doesn't want us to leave."

The captain turned and started aft towards his cabin leaving them to negotiate the narrow gangway on their own. Ronald had to take Floanne by the hand and guide her as her eyes were tightly shut. Once onboard, they hurried to catch up with the captain as he stood over the open hatch, bellowing. "Bernard! Finish up down there and then report to my cabin."

"Aye, aye, Captain."

Glancing back to see if they were following, the old man continued on to his cabin where he opened the door and ushered them inside. The low ceiling forced everyone to duck, except Floanne. The Captain sat behind his desk, and the others found seats on chests along the walls. With steepled fingers, he leaned back and studied them before speaking.

"I seen a fair number of mercenaries in my travels, and if you two are truly what you make out to be, I'll give up my ship and take up farming." Pointing a finger at Ronald, he continued. "Military, and probably an officer unless I miss my guess, and your partner would feel right at home in a palace ballroom, me thinks."

Shifting his attention to Floanne, he leaned forward, a frown barely visible behind the red beard. "What a pretty little lass is doing with the likes of you two is a mystery to me. I'd almost be willing to give up the sea if I had someone like you to come home to."

Blushing, Floanne lowered her eyes and shrugged.

Sofia leaned forward, hand on the hilt of her sword, the heat in her eyes reflecting the burning fire of her anger. She pulled the Captain's eyes away from her handmaiden.

"Keep your observations and your hands to yourself, old man. You'll live longer. And since you've ignored the common courtesy of exchanging names, ours will remain a mystery also."

"Maybe there's a reason the Captain doesn't want his name bandied about," Ronald remarked after studying the old sailor. "I remember a story that circulated among the taverns many years ago about two brothers who had a falling out over the family business, and possession of a particular ship. The older brother disappeared along with the ship while the other changed his name to Rogosh the Red and vowed to sail the straits until the ship was once again his."

The Captain slumped back in his chair gently

caressing the surface of his desk with his fingertips, and looked up as if seeing the entire ship through the roof of his cabin. "This ship is my life, and it would be over if I lost her. Maybe he has become so famous; he is no longer interested in an old ship."

"Be that as it may," Sofia spoke up. "We have urgent need of you and your ship to reach Marlinor, preferably the Capitol of New Bratan. Cedric promised that if you could accomplish this, he would consider your debt to him paid in full. My concern is, with the tensions between our countries, how will it be possible to enter the country safely?"

A smile broke out on the old man's face as he pulled a Marlinor flag from a drawer. "Now why would an honest, properly registered Marlinor merchant have any trouble sailing into New Bratan harbor?"

Ronald laughed, took one of the Princess's gems and set it on the desk. "I have no idea what your debt to the innkeeper is, but a man needs to make a profit. That should cover it. So, do we have a deal?"

"Aye, that we do," he agreed and stepped from behind the desk to shake their hands, except for Floanne's. He tried to raise her hand up to be kissed, only to have his hand slapped by Sofia. Floanne left the cabin giggling.

"Just one more thing," he stopped the other two at the door. "If my brother does catch us, he will probably try to save this ship, but won't hesitate to kill us."

Sofia turned to stare at him as the temperature in the cabin rose sharply.

"He can try."

*       *       *

After the council meeting, Duke d'Lorange spent the rest of the day half-heartedly attending to the needs of the Capitol, his mind elsewhere. By late afternoon, his work finally done, Marcus strode purposefully through the halls of the Palace on his way to the family mansion across the square. Oblivious to the nods of the guards now loyal to him, the events of this morning's council meeting replayed over and over in his thoughts. While the results from his announcement the Princess had been attacked were exactly what he'd planned, his thoughts kept returning to the ogre.

Damn that meddlesome Prince Mathias for countermanding his orders to the guard, and allowing that animal into the Capitol. The message to him was clear. Regardless of what the ogre actually said, the Ancient One was aware of the Duke's plans, and the presence of the ogre was a warning. Why wouldn't the old man just die and leave the world of men to those with the power and ambition to rule it?

His thoughts scattered when he opened the door and was greeted enthusiastically by his son.

"Father! Is it true?"

"What?"

"Rumors are all over the city that an ogre spoke at the council meeting this morning. Did it actually speak? What did it say?"

The Duke turned away to pour himself a glass of wine which he quickly downed before pouring another. What else did the rumors say? He shook off the sudden unease and turned back to his son.

"What the ogre had to say was meaningless. He's just an animal taught to mimic the speech of men. Forget about him."

Rafael grabbed his favorite history book from the table where he'd been reading, and held it up like a shield. "But Father, an ogre's honesty and loyalty are legendary. Their intelligence has never been questioned, only their ability to learn to speak properly. According to this, they were instrumental in winning the war against the Dark Lord."

"Nonsense," Marcus retorted and tossed back the second glass of wine. "Men made up the back-bone of that army while the animals were just in the way. Whoever wrote that book must have believed the Deluti lies."

Recognizing the look in his son's eyes, he decided to put an end to the argument before it even began. He didn't have time for this. "And to prevent you from getting any ideas, I expressly forbid you talking to that ogre. Now tell your mother and sister I am not to be disturbed. Is that understood?"

Marcus sighed as his son stormed from the room, slamming the door behind him. Tempted to pour another glass of wine, he refrained, knowing that no amount of alcohol would diminish the pain he was likely to experience from what he had to do.

Fumbling with the lock on the door to his study, Marcus took a deep breath and turned to face the tapestry on the wall and what was hidden behind it. Even without the cloth covering, it would take more than a casual inspection to discover the near invisible seam outlining the door. Wiping the sweat from his brow, he stepped behind the tapestry and lightly touched the wall with his fingertips. A section of wall, barely wide enough to pass through, swung open soundlessly and then returned after he'd stepped through.

He'd learned long ago not to assume what his master knew or didn't know, and just reported the events as he saw them. By the time he'd mustered enough courage to speak the words of calling and watched the great eye in the mirror disappear, beads of sweat once again covered his brow.

The scarred face of his master soon appeared in the mirror. Those hate-filled eyes always made him feel like he had to confess something, anything. But he would not soon forget the consequences of speaking before being given permission, and used every bit of his resolve to keep his mouth firmly closed.

After an eternity, the Dark Lord's lips twisted into a parody of a smile as his eyes froze the blood in the Duke's veins.

"Listen very carefully, my little Duke. Plans have changed. I am aware of the attack on Princess Sofia, and her sister will pay dearly for attempting to cross me, but none of that matters to you. What matters to you is that

Princess Sofia now belongs to me. If by chance she makes it to the Capitol and you discover her, do nothing except contact me. She is not to be touched. Is that understood?"

"Understood, my Lord," Marcus answered. Worried about his own plans, he asked without thinking, "What of the betrothal?"

Slammed up against the wall, every bone on the verge of shattering, the Duke stared in horror as the scarred visage of his master appeared to emerge from the mirror just inches from his own.

"Maybe I didn't make myself clear, my pathetic would-be King. There is no more betrothal. The Princess belongs to me. Now, I hope for your sake, you had a good reason to call me."

Released from the wall, and unable to control the tremors that wracked his body, Marcus struggled to remain upright. Afraid to speak, but afraid not to, he forced a word past the tightness of his throat.

"Ogre."

"What did you say?"

"An ogre addressed the council this morning," he gasped. "He claimed to have been sent by the Ancient One, and issued a warning."

"Didn't I order you to ban all non-humans from the Capitol?"

"Yes," the Duke rushed to explain. "I gave specific orders to the guard, but that meddlesome Prince Mathias intercepted the ogre at the gate and reversed my orders. The Prince welcomed the ogre to the Capitol and accepted full responsibility for Sebastian's safe ..."

The tiny room plunged into darkness as Marcus held his breath. What did he say? Faint blue tendrils of power surrounding the mirror were the only things visible. He soon realized he couldn't draw a breath even if he'd wanted to, but no longer had the capacity to care.

Slowly the Duke became aware of the returning light and his body had resumed the process of breathing. His master's face had returned to the mirror, and Marcus didn't miss the splatters of blood caught in those hideous scars. The voice that hissed from those twisted lips was barely recognizable.

"Kill the ogre."

"But ..."

Once again, the Dark Lord's face hovered inches from his own.

"Find a way, human. Your life depends on it."

269

The Duke collapsed to his knees as the face was replaced by the eye in the mirror and the door opened on its own. He managed to crawl out of the room and onto the chair at his desk, his master's last command consuming his thoughts. Once able to stand and fortify himself with another glass of wine, he unlocked the door and pulled the servant's rope. A plan began to form as he waited for his aide to arrive.

"How may I serve you, my Lord?"

"Set someone to watch the ogre that arrived at the Palace today. I want to know where he sleeps, who he talks to, and every move he makes."

"It will be done as you say, my Lord."

\*　　\*　　\*

Emma slipped through the door on the heels of the servant and fled the Duke's mansion. In an alley not far away, she doubled over and lost the contents of her stomach. The evil that infused her spirit like a decaying corpse would not be purged so easily. A fear like she'd never experienced before gave strength to her legs as she ran to warn Sebastian, and even though she would never admit it, she needed the comfort of the ogre's presence.

# CHAPTER SIXTEEN

## BALANCE

"Bernard!" the Captain yelled before noticing his first mate leaning up against the ladder outside, watching the two women as they crossed the deck.

The wiry, leather skinned sailor turned back to his old friend with a crooked smile and a gleam in his eye. "Ya think she be know'n how ta use thet sword?"

"Don't be a fool, Bernard. Maybe if you'd been check'n out her hands instead of other parts, you might've noticed the faint scars. I don't think she got them doin needle point. Now, roust out the men and get the ole lady ready to sail. We leave in an hour to catch the tide."

Back inside the cabin, Captain Gerrad fell back against the closed door. Memories, long buried, filled the room. The specter of his brother appeared before him to replay the argument they'd had all those years ago: who would take over their failing family business. Failing because of Rogosh's habit of gambling away their profits. The scent of acrid smoke filled his nose as it had that night when his brother returned and set fire to the yard.

If not for the suspicions of an enterprising young innkeeper, who had arrived earlier in the day to "Protect his investment", Gerrad and his men would have been lost. As it was, nothing could be done about the flames that ravaged their storehouses or the partially completed ship resting in the dock. He'd fought for his life and to protect his ship. Gerrad lost his hand to his brother that night, and Rogosh's words after being driven back were as fresh as if they'd been spoken yesterday. *"You owe me more than a hand, big brother, and someday I will collect."*

The vision dissipated as quickly as it had formed, leaving the Captain gasping for breath and shivering. He stumbled over to the desk and fell into his chair, resisting the urge to scratch the phantom itch on his missing hand. The sparkle of the gem resting on his desk mocked him, daring him to pick it up and inspect it. Was it fake? He didn't think so.

Leaning back with eyes closed, he let the familiar sounds of his crew readying the ship bring him back to the present. In his mind's eye, the Captain watched as barrels of water and crates of supplies were loaded into the hold. Men scampered aloft preparing the sails, lines were snaked out on deck, and he could feel the heavy booms being swung into position.

The excitement he normally felt prior to getting underway eluded him. Gerrad knew this was just the calm before the storm, and the storm wore leathers with a sword at her hip. The moment he had looked into the young woman's eyes, he knew his life would be forever changed. The mantle of death covered her like a cloak, and if he wasn't careful, it would cover him as well.

Ronald and Sofia waited by the wagon, Floanne having decided to stay onboard and not attempt the narrow gangway again. They watched while some of the crew swarmed the ship doing things the two of them could only guess at, and others moved stores from the one building to the ship. The quiet precision displayed by the men helped to banish Ronald's apprehension over the upcoming voyage. Their professionalism rivaled any military unit he'd seen.

"I don't think we could have found a better ship and crew to get us to Marlinor." He turned to Sofia when she didn't comment. She no longer watched the ship, but stared far into the distance. He imagined what she must be feeling, as he felt it also. Once they left, there was no turning back, and both would be faced with a totally unfamiliar world.

"Are we doing the right thing, Ronald?"

"What else can we do? Anyone could be our enemy here, and I'm convinced if we return now, we will die. Our only hope is to leave and then return with allies."

She turned her eyes on him and searched his face. "How can you be so sure?"

Ronald returned her look and reached out to touch her arm. "I believe in you, and I believe in the Deluti spirit that guides you. There are four more amulets somewhere in the world, and more like you with Deluti blood running in their veins. My hope is that we will discover another amulet wearer in New Bratan. At the very least, we can reach out to Prince Mathias for help."

Two sailors approached, putting their conversation on hold. "We was sent ta help ye load yer packs onboard. The amidships cabin be cleaned out fer ye. It be a mite snug fer three, but beats sleep'n on deck."

They followed the men up the gangway, and to what looked like a miniature house in the middle of the ship. Inside reeked of tar and hemp, but appeared clean. Floanne huddled in a corner, her face painted with an expression Sofia recognized right away. First things first as she inspected the interior and turned to the sailors.

"I see no beds. You expect us to sleep in here?"

The one sailor laughed out loud until his partner slapped him in the arm, and then turned to the Princess. "Aye, and dis be da best place ta sleep in a storm. Yer beds be hang'n there on the bulkhead." He pointed to three canvas bags hanging from hooks. "We be cast'n off soon, and the Capt'n asks ye stay here until across the breakwater."

Ronald went to inspect their supposed beds while Sofia went over to sit next to Floanne. She gently pried apart her former handmaiden's clenched hands and placed them in her own.

"I promised to always protect you, didn't I?" At Floanne's cautious nod, she continued. "We survived leaving the Palace, we survived the attack, and we will survive this. Now, tell me about that grandmother of yours. She sounds like the kind of woman I would have liked to know."

A little hesitant at first, Floanne soon became more animated as she shared some of the family's most popular stories of her favorite relative. The slight angle of the deck, as the ship swung out into the channel, went completely unnoticed by either woman.

*    *    *

Chaska watched from the rail of the pirate ship as the Port of Argo appeared in the distance. His initial excitement over being chosen for this mission by his master, the Scarred Mage, faded as the reality of his situation came into view. He would have to act the part of a slave, but what exactly did that mean?

From his earliest memories, he'd been treated with respect and given special treatment because of his potential. Three years ago, when that potential finally burst forth and his true power manifested itself, even the Dark Lord took notice. He was still required to perform his duties and work alongside the other apprentices, but he soon eclipsed them in their studies and level of control.

None of that would serve him now. His master had made it very clear while attaching the life-thread; Chaska was not to use his power in any way. His sole purpose was to befriend the young man from Marlinor and gain his confidence. As powerful as he was, a sorcerer was no match for the young Deluti. He would have one chance, and one only, to snare Navon in a moment of weakness. He would either succeed or die.

The Captain bellowed out orders for the crew to prepare for entering port. Satisfied with the level of activity he observed and confident in the ability of his first mate, the Captain turned the ship over and approached the young sorcerer. In his hands was a pair of chains and shackles.

"I don't know what you did to deserve this, and I don't want to know. I learned long ago not to question the orders of Lord Scorpious. From this moment on, your life will change." He snapped the cuffs over Chaska's wrists, and then bent down to attach the ankle chains. "You will wear these chains until you reach the city of the Shadhuin. They are a rigid, close mouthed lot, but I've heard they treat their slaves well."

Chaska struggled to control a surge of panic when he realized the chains effectively cut him off from his power. He doubted the Captain was aware these were a leftover from the Deluti Age used to control enemy sorcerers. A final calming breath allowed him to speak.

"They will remove these chains?"

"Of course. The chains are only to prevent you from running away while in the port. Once you reach their city, attempting to run would be foolish unless you can outrun a horse."

*Unless I'm on a horse of my own,* Chaska thought, returning the Captain's smile.

The Captain checked the attitude of the ship and the distance to the port with a quick glance, and turned back to the young man. "Come, we will be docking soon, and our contact will be waiting for you on the pier. He has been told the reason for your captivity is for a debt you were unable to pay. The Shadhuin will assume that debt, and you will work for them until they feel the debt has been repaid."

The first mate gauged their approach perfectly. Lines were tossed to the pier and the ship docked with barely a bump. The Captain led Chaska over to the gangway and helped him step up.

"Remember, work hard, watch your tongue, and your ordeal will soon be over."

As the young sorcerer carefully made his way down the narrow gangway to the burly man waiting there, he was afraid the Captain's words might be true in more ways than he could imagine.

*    *    *

Navon's days quickly fell into a routine of trips back and forth from the lake to the water troughs outside the city, ensuring all the animals had feed and keeping the area clean. His sense of isolation continued to deepen as the opportunities for conversation with Jamar were few. At least he had a place he could think of as his own since the elder reassured Navon the room was his for the duration of the sentence.

Their respective schedules left time for nothing more than the occasional greeting. Navon would rise in the morning before Jamar, since the elder sometimes stayed away late into the night. Even Moshere had only stopped by twice to see how he was getting along. Navon's new master, Elder Atora, kept him busy most of the day caring for both the Brothers and the many beasts of burden. Not that the elder displayed any sign of disdain toward the young man, he was concerned for the animals under his care and had no time for the problems of others.

Every time Navon approached the lake to fill his buckets, the memory of the incredible vision shown to him by the Amulet would enter his thoughts. The constant physical labor freed his mind to pick at the details of that memory. If he let his senses wander and then focus on a particular object, details not visible to the eye would emerge. The grain of the wood used to make the buckets emerged revealing the health of the tree. Cracks in the stone, invisible to the eye, became like fissures in his sight.

He spent more time now with the other Brothers than ever before, opening his awareness of their thoughts a little more each time. In the morning and evening, when he replenished their bins with hay and grain, it was like walking into a crowded room. He was aware of conversations all around, but not quite able to pick out the individual speakers. Moshere was not surprised at Navon's increased sensitivities and took it all in stride.

Early in the morning, Navon began to fill the first

buckets of the day in the endless chore of keeping the water troughs full. Buckets in hand, he was about to return to the stable outside the city when a scream of pain and terror flooded the young man's mind and forced him to his knees.

He was up and running before being aware of the destination, and quickly identified the cry as coming from one of the Brothers and not a human. The mental voice carried the feel of youth behind it and came from somewhere near the stables. Overriding the pain was a fear so powerful, Navon had to fight the urge to curl into a ball and hide in a dark corner.

Exiting the city, he not only had to force his way through a wall of sadness and anger, but also the Brothers who crowded the area projecting those emotions. Many were reluctant to let him pass. He continued to push his way through, ignoring them as best he could. His entire being was focused on the mind of the young Brother somewhere ahead.

Elder Atora's deep voice, alternating between anger and pleading, led Navon directly to a scene he never expected. The elder, knife in hand, confronted an animated Moshere who stood protectively over a colt lying motionless on the ground. Both the colt's forelegs lay at an unnatural angle. How that had happened was only a fleeting thought as Navon's own anger erupted.

"Everyone, stop!"

The silence that resulted from his command, both verbal and mental, was quickly broken by Elder Atora who turned his blade on Navon and began hurling what sounded like accusations and threats. The words came too fast for the young Deluti to fully understand as his attention was focused elsewhere.

The moment Navon locked eyes with Moshere; he fell into a maelstrom of emotions and visions that stirred up the power resting deep inside his soul. The elder Brother broke contact, shaking his head. Atora looked on in disbelief as Moshere turned back to Navon and went down on one foreleg. For the first time, Moshere's thoughts were clear and carefully expressed to ensure the young man understood.

"Elishere is my only son. Heal him or guide him into death. You have the power. Never should he feel edge of blade."

The amulet hanging from Navon's neck awoke and made him aware of an imbalance in his life. He had taken the lives of two innocents out on the plains and must restore life in order to compensate. Whether the power and confidence came from the amulet or rose up from inside him no longer mattered.

Motioning Moshere to rise, Navon hugged his friend around the neck, turned to the silent elder and addressed him in perfect Shadhuin.

"Put away your blade, Elder Atora. It will not taste blood this day. Now, either assist me in restoring Elishere's legs, or stay out of my way."

Either the command in the young Deluti's voice or the power that blazed from his eyes sent the elder rushing to bring water and blankets. Navon sat on the ground next to Elishere and laid his hand on the colt. Opening his senses to the young one, he drew the fear and pain into himself and then passed them on to Moshere who stood nearby. Once the colt was calm and pain free, he began.

Navon's newfound ability to un-focus and then focus inside, guided him as he carefully lifted the first leg onto his lap and began the arduous task of knitting together the ragged edges of shattered bone and torn muscles. Bone fused to bone, returning to the proper alignment. The outside world faded into darkness as the amulet guided him deeper to touch and repair severed nerves and broken blood vessels.

It was fortunate Elishere was in excellent health as Navon drew on the colt's energy reserves to drive his body's natural healing. He also drew strength from Moshere and several other volunteer Brothers, pressing on until not even a hint of a fracture remained in either leg. It took Navon a moment to realize the amulet no longer guided, but was encouraging him to un-focus. Once he did, oblivion overtook him.

The onlookers drawn to the scene that morning had departed long ago. There was nothing to see, and they certainly didn't understand what was happening. Atora sent someone to find Elder Jamar as soon as Navon fell into a trance-like state. One or the other elder was always at the young man's side as they watched in fear and awe.

Neither could detect the movement of Navon's hands, but move they did. Hours passed as first one foreleg and then the other returned to normal. The swelling diminished and the ragged edges of the break, which showed through the skin, smoothed out and disappeared. The elders shared a look of concern when first Moshere, and then the other Brothers, sank to the ground, their bodies deflated, while Elishere's filled out and glowed.

Jamar was the first to reach out; catching Navon as the young man's hands dropped and he fell to one side. Elishere raised his head, gently pulled his legs off of Navon's lap and stood. Several experimental steps later, he bent down to nuzzle the side of his healer's face. He hurried over to Moshere and lay down next to his sire, resting his head on the elder Brother's chest.

The two men watched and then turned to stare at each other in wonder. Elder Atora started to speak, but Jamar silenced him with a curt headshake.

"Don't ask, Atora. I do not know the answers to your questions. What I do know is that the young man will need to sleep. Come, help me get him back to his room, and then we'll care for the Brothers."

As they walked back to the city, supporting Navon between them, Jamar worried. *I may not know the answers, my old friend, but I'm afraid our lives will never be the same.*

# Chapter Seventeen

## Acceptance

". . . and then Grandmother said to him, *'Majesty, if you didn't want me to gaze upon the magnificence of your royal manhood, you shouldn't be traipsing around like a little boy who's forgotten his pants'.*"

Laughing, Ronald threw back his head and bumped it against the bulkhead. "Ow," he muttered, his sheepish grin setting off another round of laughter.

Floanne's excellent imitation of an old woman, and her descriptions, made it easy for Sofia to picture the scene. Struggling to regain her composure, she gasped,

"What did Mother have to say after that?"

"After the Queen sent him to their room with a smack on his bare cheek, she hugged Grandmother. Still laughing, your mother said, '*I've never seen him so red faced and speechless at the same time. Thank you*'. Of course, she told Grandmother never to tell anyone."

"Well, she must have told someone." Sofia pointed out; slightly offended one of the servants had disobeyed the Queen.

"Oh, Grandmother had to tell Mother and me so we wouldn't be caught in the same situation. Please forgive me. I thought enough time had passed that I could share the story with you."

The Princess leaned back, closed her eyes, and let the gentle motion of the ship, and the sounds that penetrated their small cabin, bring her back to the present. Straightening, she laid a hand on her former maidservant's knee. "It's alright, Floanne. All that is in the past, and I must look to the future now. But tell me, did your grandmother ever explain to you why you shouldn't leave the Palace?"

Floanne shook her head. "No, she never had the chance. It's strange; I remember when I was very young her telling me she had an important family secret to pass on when I got older. At breakfast on the day she died, she said it was time and to come see her that night."

"Wasn't that when she was in charge of my sister, Darnelle?" Sofia asked, struggling to remember.

"Yes, Grandmother was very unhappy then, but wouldn't tell anyone why. It's still a mystery how she died. They found her face down on the floor in her room, and the Palace physician was at a loss as to what had happened."

The ship dropped sharply and began a slow rise. Floanne, eyes wide, stared at Ronald and whispered, "Are we sinking?"

The former lieutenant sprang to his feet, stumbled with the movement of the ship, and headed for the door. "I don't think so, but I'll check."

He returned a short time later, smiling. "The ship is fine. One of the sailors told me that as we get farther out into the Straits, what he called a deep swell will occasionally come along, raise the ship high up and drop us way down. The water actually looks pretty flat. Care to look?"

Floanne's emphatic head shake made it clear she

wasn't moving, so Sofia got up to join him outside. They made their way to the rail and stood quietly watching their homeland diminish behind them. Eventually it would be lost to sight altogether. It wasn't until they glanced down at the water flowing past that the speed of the ship became real. Sofia craned her neck to stare up at the tapestry of sails humming in the wind. She couldn't help but fill her lungs with the crisp, moisture laden air.

"Did you ever dream of being a sailor, Ronald?"

"No, not really. Oh, I fantasized swinging from one ship to another, sword in hand to battle the evil pirates. I soon realized I'd rather have solid ground under me, or better yet, a strong horse. You?"

"I wasn't allowed to dream."

Turning away from him, she spotted the first mate approaching, envious at how easily he moved with the ship. She had questions and hoped the man had answers.

"Bernard, right?" she asked before he could speak. "If we are attacked, how do we fight back?"

Taken aback by her forward manner, the first mate paused and searched the young woman's face. The fire smoldering deep inside shone through her eyes and sent a shiver down his spine.

"Well now, thet not be likely, but Rogosh, he be wantin dis ship. If he attacked, maybe a couple shots from his ballista ta hole our sails, but for sure, grappling hooks ta be pullin da ships together."

"Will many have swords?" Ronald asked, hand resting on the pommel of the weapon at his side.

"Naw, mostly clubs, knives, spikes and chains. Now thet Rogosh, he fancies his two short swords and knows howta use em."

A sudden tilt in the ship's deck forced both Sofia and Ronald to grasp the rail while the old sailor took it in stride. Frustrated, Sofia glared at him. "Bernard, if we are to fight from this Eye forsaken deck, you must share the secret of how you keep your balance."

"'Tis no secret," he replied. "Keep yer knees bent and let da deck move under ye."

They practiced under the watchful eye of the first mate until most of the awkwardness passed.

"Now, afor I ferget, da Captain asks ye to join him in his cabin fer a bite ta eat."

As they walked aft towards the Captain's cabin, keeping their knees flexed, Ronald remarked. "Reminds me of riding a horse."

The Princess laughed, shaking her head. "Now why doesn't that surprise me?"

Before he could respond, they reached the cabin where the Captain greeted them with an outstretched hand. "Please let me apologize for earlier. The name's Miles Gerrad, and be welcomed aboard *Moon's Shadow.*" He held the door for them. "Come in. Come in."

"Thank you, Captain Gerrad. I'm Ronald and this is Sofia."

Miles paused and caught her eye. "As in Princess Sofia Salidoris?"

"A Princess no longer, Captain, and you would do well to forget that name. You'll live longer."

Nothing more was said as each filled a plate with meat, cheese, and a chunk of bread. Miles pulled out a bottle of wine, and filled their heavy cups half-way. Handing out the cups, he raised his in a toast.

"Here's to an uneventful crossing."

Downing the last of her wine, Sofia stood and addressed the Captain. "Thank you, Captain Gerrad. If it's agreeable, we will return later this afternoon. I have some questions, and I'll try to answer yours, but right now, Ronald and I have things to do."

Out on deck, Ronald followed her to an open area just aft of the mainmast, his question un-asked as she turned to face him.

"Ronald, do you remember the no-touch exercises Master Horshall taught you?"

"It has been a while, but yes, I remember. Why?"

"Maybe I've become too cynical, but I don't share the Captain's belief in a safe crossing. We should practice while on this moving deck or our sword skills will be useless. We'll start out slow and move faster after we've warmed up."

Several sailors paused in their work to watch, but soon lost interest. The familiar ring of steel striking steel occurred several times in the beginning, and each time, they stopped and repeated the exercise. It was slow and repetitive, but eventually the moves were completed in total silence. After fifteen minutes, they stepped back for a quick break and shared a water skin provided by one of the sailors. Now they were ready to practice in earnest.

The first mate turned to his Captain where they were watching from the top of the pilot house. "I'm not understanding. Why they blades no touch?"

"Watch and learn, my old friend. If they be using

wooden practice swords, you would hear much contact, but that's solid steel in their hands and one mistake could kill or maim. It takes a might more skill not to touch than to hit. You are about to witness a thing few have ever seen; a sword dance between masters."

Sofia and Ronald faced each other once again and began. Soon the movements of their blades were too fast to follow, and became a blur with only an occasional glint of steel. Every sailor quit what they were doing and gathered in a circle to watch. The two fighters never stopped moving, circling each other and constantly changing positions. The deadly grace of the dance held the crew spellbound. The hiss of the ship slicing through the water and the sighing of the wind could not hide the unmistakable ring of sword against sword. The two froze, stepped back, and raised their swords in salute. The dance was over.

Smiling, Gerrad turned to his first mate. "Well, Bernard. Any question about her skill with a blade now?" Slapping him on the back, the Captain walked away, leaving his first mate speechless.

Floanne surprised them when she accepted the Captain's invitation to dinner that evening. She answered the question on Ronald's face. "Sharing stories of Grandmother reminded me how strong and fearless she was. I want to be like her."

Holding tightly to the lieutenant's arm, she gazed about the ship with a new determination. Sailors stood and nodded when they passed on their way aft. Once inside the cabin, Bernard was uncommonly quiet while passing out portions of the food brought up from the galley. With a final apprehensive glance at the Princess, he excused himself saying he would return later for the dishes. The meal was simple yet surprisingly tasty. The three companions dug in with gusto.

"I know this isn't what you're used to, but I try to feed my crew a decent meal."

"You'd be surprised at what I'm used to, Miles, and Ronald spent much of his youth eating in taverns. My compliments to your cook, however. The venison is tender, the potatoes are just the way I like them, and the mixed vegetables are crisp. I have no complaints."

Captain Gerrad pushed away his plate, sat back and studied them again over steepled fingers. "So, tell me. Will I have to take up permanent residence in Marlinor for helping the three of you escape?"

Sofia and Ronald shared a look. They proceeded to tell the Captain what they felt he should know, and left it up to him to decide. Some things, like Sofia's new found power, were best left untold. Wanting an early start in the morning, they excused themselves soon after and left.

Later that evening, as the three of them prepared for sleep, Ronald unhooked one end of his hammock and stretched it out to attach to the opposite wall. He stood staring and then fiddled with the folds in the canvas.

"Did you ask directions from one of the crew on how to use that?" the Princess asked.

"Well no, but I've read about them. How hard can it be?"

Sofia turned to Floanne and mouthed the word '*men*', eliciting a giggle that she quickly covered with her hand.

Ronald grabbed the sides of the hammock and attempted to climb in. Losing his balance, the bed flipped and dumped him to the deck. The women couldn't contain their merriment at his situation, and laughed even harder at his glare. He tried again, this time lifting a leg up and over, except it tangled in the cords at the end. He finally joined in their laughter while hanging upside down, his foot caught.

"A little help here, please!"

Between their laughter and tears, the women struggled to free the Lieutenant. Rubbing his backside, Ronald watched as Sofia approached her hammock, carefully sat in the middle, grabbed both edges, and then swung her legs up while lying down at the same time. Floanne turned to hers, copied Sofia's actions and snuggled right in.

Grumbling, Ronald unhooked his hammock, wrapped it around him and curled up on the floor. "There must be something wrong with mine. It's not like I've never slept on the floor before."

More comfortable than she would have imagined, Sofia soon drifted towards sleep. It had been a very long day. Just prior to oblivion, a voice in her head stole her smile. *'Beware the storm.'*

Early the next morning found Sofia and Floanne at the ship's rail, refreshed after a sound sleep, while Ronald walked the ship's perimeter trying to work out his stiffness. Neither Floanne's excitement over watching the sun rise above the water's surface or Ronald's complaining managed to lift the darkness that had filled Sofia's thoughts since last night's warning.

Captain Gerrad joined them at the rail. "Beautiful, isn't it? I never grow tired of watching the rays of the sun shoot into the sky overhead just before it crests the water's surface. If this weather holds, we should reach New Bratan tomorrow."

The lookout called down from above. "Sails ho, Captain, dead astern!"

Miles shouted back, "What color?"

"White."

"Bernard! Set full sails. I don't want that ship catching us before we reach Marlinor."

"Aye, Captain!"

Sofia turned to him, confusion etched on her face. "White sails? What other color would they be?"

"Rogosh runs red topsails. He believes they strike fear into the hearts of his intended victims."

"And do they?"

"Yes."

Turning away, he motioned for them to follow and headed for his cabin. Once inside, he unrolled one of his charts and pointed to an area near the middle of the Straits. "I plotted our position last night. We are on course, and with this increase in speed, we may reach the Bay of Salia tonight. Once there, we will be safe and can drop anchor for the night. It's too dangerous entering New Bratan in the dark. Arriving early in the morning is best, anyway."

Before anyone could respond, Bernard burst through the door. "Captain. Sails directly ahead. Red sails."

Miles grabbed his distance viewer and sprinted out the door, the others hard on his heels. Standing atop the pilot house, the Captain didn't need the viewer to see that Rogosh's ship was near, and closing fast.

"Curse you, Brother. May the Eye of Death consume your soul." Turning to the others, he explained. "Somehow he knew we were coming, and used the other ship to drive us right into his cursed arms. He waited to set full sails, knowing we wouldn't see him until it was too late."

"Can you outrun him?"

"No. Any move we make, he can counter. We are too close."

Sofia locked eyes with the Captain, and in a quiet voice, decided. "Then we will fight. The longer we delay will give the other ship time to catch up and engage."

Miles struggled to pull his eyes away from the fire that threatened to engulf him. Maybe it was his imagination, but the world suddenly appeared darker. He managed to nod once before turning away.

"Bernard, stay on course. Station the men and be ready to strike the sails on my command."

Afraid to face the Princess, he continued as if talking to himself. "When we strike the sails and slow, he will have to maintain full sails in order to close on us. Once in range, several lucky shots from our ballista should ruin his mainsail and give us a chance to get away."

The ships closed on each other like two bull elk in rut. A large projectile left the bow of the pirate ship, followed shortly by the distinct sound of a ballista being triggered. Captain Gerrad gave the command to strike sails, resulting in an immediate reduction of speed. As he had predicted, the other ship continued on with sails full.

Ronald had taken Floanne back to their cabin amidships, and would stand guard outside while Sofia remained with the Captain. It felt right for her to face their enemy by Gerrad's side. Unexpectedly, the pirate ship turned directly into their path.

Miles bellowed the command, "Hard to port," followed immediately with, "Fire!"

Sails on Rogosh's ship tore as the ballista shots ripped

through them, but nothing could prevent the two ships colliding broadside. The impact sent many of the crew tumbling to the deck as a dozen grappling hooks found purchase on Gerrad's ship. The lines snapped taut, spinning the ships in a circle.

The number of pirates that rushed onboard easily outnumbered their crew. Miles drew his sword and turned to Sofia. "I hope you are prepared to die, Princess."

"Not this day, Miles. Not this day."

Her ever-burning anger gave her strength as the two of them repelled the first wave of pirates attempting to swarm the pilot house. Ronald appeared to be holding his own, but the rest of the crew were soon overrun. Out of the corner of her eye, she saw one of the pirates manage to get behind Ronald and raise his club. Before the attacker could deliver a blow, Floanne burst out of the cabin, screaming. Holding Sofia's crossbow like a club, she struck the pirate in the back of the head.

That turned out to be a terrible mistake as two pirates immediately broke off and grabbed her by the arms. A voice rang out from the other ship. "Bring the Princess to me and kill the rest!"

Sofia's anger exploded. Her spirit cowered in a corner

of her mind as the anger raged totally out of control. Day became night as black clouds materialized along with howling winds. The sea rose up in mountainous spires, and an incessant rain of lightening pummeled both ships. Splinters of wood rocketed through the air as the two ships were flung against each other repeatedly. Ronald and Floanne clung desperately to each other, his free hand clutching ropes at the base of the mast.

Ronald's words to her whispered from afar. *"The anger is part of who you are. It's the fear of the anger that gives it power over you. Embrace your anger. It's what makes you strong."*

Drawing on a separate power, the power of her humanity, Sofia's spirit rose up in her mind and shouted, "I am not my father!"

She embraced the anger as it threatened to overwhelm her. Laughing, she realized she was just fighting herself and filled her soul with anger's power. Reaching for the sky, Sofia pulled the lightening to her outstretched arms. The darkness and the wind fled as the seas calmed once again. Tendrils of blue lightening writhed up and down her arms as she dropped them to her sides.

Ignoring the destruction around her and the pirates

who scrambled out of her way, she approached Floanne and a smiling Ronald. Her eyes locked onto her former maidservant. The eyes that stared back belonged not to Floanne, but a spirit of indeterminate age. The ancient voice filled the air.

"So, you have embraced your anger. Congratulations. The amulet is now yours. Wear it with compassion."

The amulet appeared in Floanne's hand and she held it out for the Princess. Sofia placed the chain around her neck where it snapped shut; the amulet emitted a golden glow, and then vanished.

The spirit raised Floanne's arm to point at Sofia's chest. *"This young woman is now free to live her life as she pleases, and her true heritage will soon be revealed."*

The mark branded into Sofia's flesh, the day they left the Palace, lifted from her body and passed through her leathers to land on Floanne's open hand. *"No longer are you her guardian, and the link between you is removed. Never forget, Princess. The storm can destroy and it can cleanse. It is up to you to decide. You are the storm!"*

# CHAPTER EIGHTEEN

## SECRETS AND MYSTERIES

Prince Mathias spent most of the afternoon visiting with his family, thinking the logical place for an escape route would be somewhere with easy access to the royal family. He entered each apartment on the pretext of asking how they felt about the new servants while casually surveying the walls for anything out of the ordinary. The suites were almost identical in layout and design. Nothing odd stood out between them.

He was afraid to ask anyone, especially his father who was the likeliest to know, because of the inevitable question: Why do you want to know? He hadn't come up with a suitable answer to that yet. So Mathias wandered the Palace halls, peeking behind tapestries and cabinets when no one was around. No secret doors were to be found. After supper, not ready to give up, he headed for the Palace Library.

With no idea where to look for the original plans used to build the Palace, he went first to the sealed cabinet containing all the old histories. One at a time, he gently removed each volume and sat down to skim the stories looking for any mention of a way to escape the Palace.

Behind him, the sound of the door closing intruded on the hushed atmosphere of the library. He continued reading, there was only one person he knew who would seek him out here.

"There you are. What are you doing hiding in the library?"

Mathias spun around and smiled up at his old friend. "I am not hiding, Rafael. With all that's going on, I felt I'd better read up on the Elder Races since I know so little about them. What are you doing in here?"

The Duke's son came around and sat across the table from the Prince. "Looking for you, and don't bother with those old histories. I've already read them and there isn't much in there about the Elders."

"You and your love of history," Mathias laughed. "I should have remembered and come to you first. What can you tell me about them?"

"Not much more than you already know," Rafael retorted, and then leaned forward, his voice filled with excitement and longing. "But you actually spoke to one! What is he like, Mathias? Is he as fierce and savage as they say?" Slumped back in his chair, his tone became wistful. "I would give anything to actually speak to an ogre."

"Sebastian certainly looks fierce, but savage he is not. He's well mannered and speaks as well as you and me. Why don't you go speak to him and find out for yourself?"

"What, and be disowned by my father who has forbidden it? By the Eyes, Mathias, the Duke is getting harder to deal with every day. Something is bothering him, but he refuses to talk about it."

The Prince slowly closed the ancient tome, returned it to the cabinet, and made sure the doors were sealed tight. Once again in his chair, he hooked a loose strand of hair behind his ear, crossed his arms and studied the son of their enemy.

"Rafael, do you remember the secrets we shared as children?"

A smile broke out on Rafael's face. "Hah, do I ever. Some of those secrets would have earned us a sound beating, I'll wager."

"I'm afraid a beating is nothing compared to what might happen if what I'm about to share with you gets out. I hate to involve you, my old friend, but there are few I can trust. I need your help."

Rafael lost his smile and leaned forward again. "Is this about the rumors? Are the Elder Races really going to attack?"

Mathias shook his head. "No, but that is what we are meant to believe. The Scarred Mage has sent his agents out into the world to spread those lies. Unfortunately, too many people are beginning to believe. There is something else afoot that will put everyone in the Palace in danger."

Without hesitation, Rafael asked. "What can I do to help?"

"The Palace must have a secret escape route or tunnel somewhere, and I need to find it. If you help me, I'll do what I can to set up a meeting for you with Sebastian."

Rafael lowered his chin and closed his eyes, deep in thought. A moment later he raised his head to stare at his friend. "I seem to remember an old story where someone went down to the lower storage level to check on something they didn't want others to discover."

The two sprang from their chairs, boyish grins lighting up their faces.

"Well, what are we waiting for?"

The years flew away as two boys once again embarked on another great adventure. Mathias in the lead, and Rafael keeping an eye out behind, they snuck along the hallways and stairs, peeking around each corner before proceeding. The lower storage level revealed a dimly lit hallway with a row of doors down one side.

With a shrug, they each grabbed a spare lantern from the rack. After several failed attempts with the new striker, they lit them using the one already burning. Mathias opened the first door and jumped back as a cascade of broken furniture tumbled out into the hall. Grumbling at the laziness of servants, they shoved the bits and pieces back into the room. Rafael held everything in place while Mathias carefully closed the door. Both had to push to get it to latch.

The next room held more promise. They could actually enter and walk along the walls looking for anything unusual. Shaking his head, the Prince left the room and started for the third door. "It would help if we knew what to look for."

"I know, but hopefully we'll know it when we see it."

The next room was identical to the last, but Rafael had a puzzled look on his face when they returned to the hall. Turning around, he stepped back inside, followed closely by Mathias. He stared at the wall to the left and then to the right. Carefully measuring his steps, he paced the distance from the door to the right wall.

Back out in the hall, Rafael paced out the same distance and had Mathias stand where he stopped. He disappeared into the second room, returning moments later and stepped out a distance from the second door. He stopped and stared at his friend. There remained a gap of roughly six feet between them.

The Prince broke out laughing and they shared a triumphant smile. "Rafael, you never cease to amaze me. How did you know?"

"I didn't, but I remembered the doors to all the other

storerooms are centered in the room. These two were just enough off-center to look wrong."

Excited, they peered closely at the wall and soon found the outline of a door hidden in the vertical wood pattern used throughout the Palace.

"Leave it to the Deluti to hide a door in plain sight, but how do we open it?" the Prince asked.

"Run your fingers over the wall. Maybe the latch is hidden in the pattern also," Rafael suggested.

When their inspection turned up nothing, Mathias slammed his hand against the wall in frustration.

"Wait! What did you just do?" Rafael exclaimed and leaned forward studying the wall. "Do that again, only this time push instead."

The Prince laid his hand against the wall and pushed as instructed, but nothing happened. Setting his feet, he tried again with both hands, adding his weight to the effort. A grinding sound emerged from the floor as the mechanism protested centuries of neglect. His section of wall slowly depressed while the wall in front of Rafael swung outward.

"There's a lip here I can get my fingers behind. Help me pull," his friend gasped, struggling to hold on.

Together they managed to open the door, despite the groaning of the pivots, until a barely discernible click was heard. The putrid reek of dead air forced them back, inadvertently releasing their hold on the door. It remained locked open.

Covering his mouth and nose with a cloth, Rafael cautiously peered inside, holding the lantern at arm's length. "It must use a counterweight to hold the door shut, and there is a latch here that probably unlocks it. Just to be sure we can open it from the inside; I'll let it close and then try to open it again."

He released the lever, and the door swung closed much faster than it opened. Soon it opened again, Rafael pushing from the inside until it locked.

"What now, Mathias? The smell isn't as bad as it was, but I'm afraid of what we'll find."

The Prince joined his friend inside the passage and released the door. "Unless I know where this exits the Palace, it is of no use to me. Come on."

They had only walked a short distance when Rafael stopped to stare at his friend's back, the meaning of his words now clear. "You never intended to use this as an escape, did you? Who are you planning to smuggle into the Palace, Mathias?"

The Prince hesitated, and then motioned his friend forward. Ignoring the question, he pointed ahead with his lantern. Lying alongside the wall was a skeleton, and just past it, another door. Sharing a look, they bent down for a closer examination.

"Well, whoever it was, they died a long time ago," Rafael observed. "The clothing has turned to dust, and look, a sword but no sign of armor."

"Rafael, that is the blade of a royal."

"Unless he stole it."

"A mystery to solve another day." Standing, Mathias handed his lantern to Rafael. "Douse the lanterns. I don't want their light to draw anyone's attention."

He pushed against the door, but there was no movement. Rafael felt his way next to his friend, and on the count of three they pushed as hard as they could. The door jerked, moved several inches and stopped. It was jammed.

The Prince laid his hand on Rafael's shoulder. "I think we just solved part of the mystery."

*    *    *

With the wind and waves having fled the entangled

ships, a deathly silence remained, interrupted only by the occasional moan of an injured sailor. Both Gerrad's crew and the pirates held their collective breaths, afraid to draw Sofia's attention. What they had just witnessed was only whispered among those who were familiar with history. What else was she capable of?

Sofia reached out to lift Floanne's bowed head so she could look her in the eye. "Never again will you be a servant of another. You now have a new destiny."

The Princess marshaled her human emotions, yet a rebellious tear still managed to escape the corner of her eye. Facing the still smiling Lieutenant, she held out both arms. Ronald captured her hands in his.

"What can I say to you, my dear friend? I owe you my life. Your words were like a light to lead me out of the darkness. I am not my father, but I had to finally accept he is a part of me."

"I am happy for you, Sofia. Sometimes we look to others for the truth that lies inside us." He squeezed her hands. "Now, you better address the men so they can breathe again."

She returned the gesture and smiled. "Still giving orders, Lieutenant?"

He shrugged his shoulders, and she released his hands to turn to the men. "Gather the wounded here and begin treating their injuries until I return," she ordered, pointing to the deck. Heading for what was left of the ship's rail, she beckoned to Captain Gerrad. "Miles, if you would join me."

Clearing the distance between the ships easily, Sofia led the way to where Rogosh stood, still clutching a sword in each hand. A black-robed figure stood motionless beside him.

"Lower your hood in the presence of a Deluti, sorcerer."

Satisfied with his compliance and the resignation she saw in his eyes, she turned to the pirate and pointed at his left hand. The fingers convulsed and began to shrivel, useless, dropping the sword.

"Balance has now been restored. How you conduct yourself from now on is between you and your brother. Captain Gerrad and his ship are now under the protection of the Deluti. Any attack on him will be seen as an attack on us and will be dealt with accordingly. War is on the horizon, Rogosh, and you will have to choose a side. Choose wisely."

"What of my crew?"

"They will return once all have been healed sufficiently to survive their injuries."

Miles led his brother away, both ignoring the sword left lying on the deck. Alone with the sorcerer, Sofia asked. "What is your name?"

"Thomas, Your Highness."

She studied him for a moment before reaching out with her new awareness and carefully untangled the life bond linking him with his master, revolted. "Of all the Dark Lord's accomplishments, the life thread is the most foul. Thomas, you are now free to live your life as you wish. If you decide to return to Scorpious, we will meet again, and I will not hesitate to kill you as I have the others."

He closed his eyes, shivered, and then stared at her in wonder. "The link is truly gone. I have never felt freedom such as this. Thank you, Princess. In return, I must warn you, Scorpious is now obsessed with your capture. Second only to his hatred of the non-humans is his desire for a female Deluti at his side."

"He is not the first man to want me by his side. I doubt he will be any luckier."

Sofia returned to their ship where she went down the line, healing each man only enough to ensure their survival. The pirates pried loose their grappling hooks and jumped the expanding distance between the rails. As the ships slowly drifted apart, the Captain and Bernard, who had a bandage wrapped around his head, inspected the damage and set the crew to repair what they could.

The Princess waited outside the amidships cabin and watched the sorcerer out of the corner of her eye. He had requested permission and jumped onboard at the last minute, clutching a small travel bag. Thomas explained he had family in Marlinor and wished to visit them. Even though she had released him from the Scarred Mage's control, it would be a long time before she would fully trust any sorcerer.

Miles appeared from below decks, looked up at the sky, and then approached her. "Princess, what repairs can be done be complete soon. One of the masts is cracked so we no have full sails. But without wind, we no be going anywhere."

Closing her eyes, she sent feelers out into the sky searching for the wind that had fled along with her anger. Opening her eyes as a breath of air teased the ends of her hair, Sofia smiled at him. "Raise your sails, Captain. You have your wind."

As she turned away to enter the cabin, he asked. "My brother. Will he ever regain the use of his hand?"

She paused, "Will you, Miles?" and shut the door behind her.

Once inside, Sofia found Ronald trying to comfort a distraught Floanne who immediately appealed to her former mistress.

"What am I to do if I can no longer be a maidservant? I have no other skills."

The Princess sat opposite them and sighed. "You are destined for a position much higher than a servant, Floanne. I will try to share the memories revealed to me by the amulet."

She paused, waiting for the sound of sails being rigged to quiet. The ship's deck tilted as the approaching wind stretched tight the expanse of canvas and propelled them toward their destination. Eyelids fluttering, Sofia's voice took on the cadence of a master story-teller.

"During the reign of Harold d'Tomorin, King of Marlinor, one of the Deluti Council of Five resided in the Capitol City. Many were against the King's involvement in the Deluti War, and the Dark Lord successfully planted agents throughout the city and Palace.

Unable to continue protecting both the King and herself, the ancient Deluti Councilor transferred her spirit into her amulet and entrusted it to the King's son and daughter. The Prince, acting as decoy, drew the enemy agents away into the Palace while the Deluti's servants smuggled the Princess onto a ship bound for Dahlian. Deluti spirits guided her to the Royal Palace where they charged her and future generations with the task of protecting the amulet."

Sofia's eyes refocused and she sat next to Floanne, who stared wide eyed with her mouth agape. Taking her former servant's hand, the Princess willed the truth to fill the emptiness in Floanne's heart.

"This is the story your grandmother planned to pass on to you. The amulet no longer needs protecting. Your family's charge has ended. You are descended from a Marlinor royal family and equal to any princess."

Unable to speak, Floanne glanced first at Ronald, then Sofia, and back to the Lieutenant, who smiled and wrapped his arm around her shoulders.

"I would believe her if I were you. You know how she

gets when anyone disagrees with her."

Floanne managed a weak smile when Sofia stuck her tongue out at him. In a voice filled with wonder, she whispered, "I may be a Princess?"

Sofia slumped back against the wall, overwhelmed herself by the events of the day. "Not yet, but I have a feeling the Deluti spirits are not done with you."

They arrived late that night at the anchorage in the Bay of Salia, and then proceeded into port early the next morning. Many eyes were upon them as the ship slowly drifted past. No one challenged Captain Gerrad's right to moor at the head of the pier. As is normally the case with sailors, rumors abounded on the Captain's true identity, and the nature of his business.

The fact the ship displayed signs of severe battle damage, and had survived a possible pirate attack only added to the mystery. The dockside taverns would be abuzz with rumor and speculations tonight.

Miles told the Princess he didn't plan on returning to Dahlian anytime soon, and would be here if she needed him. After taking their leave from the Captain, they stood on the pier not sure what to do next. A young boy ran up and greeted them.

"Welcome to New Bratan. If you be needin' a guide in da city, Poppie be da man for you. I knows alla best places to be eatin' and sleepin'. Everyone knows Poppie and Poppie knows everyone."

Sofia shared a look with Ronald. Some things never change, no matter where you are. She nodded in agreement. There was something familiar about this little man, and she planned to find out what.

Ronald waved the boy onward. "Lead on, Poppie. First order of business is someplace to take a hot bath, and then eat."

"Follow Poppie. Poppie knows just da place!"

# Chapter Nineteen

## Emma's Fear

Chaska shuffled alongside the man from Argo, the chains around his ankles long enough for a normal stride, but too heavy to try and run. He glanced at his large, quiet companion, confused. A slave newly arrived at his master's fortress would have been beaten by now. This man was neither friendly nor abusive. Apparently, he was only part of a business transaction, and the man was just doing his job.

The apprentice sorcerer relaxed enough in the presence of the slave trader to take in the unfamiliar world spread out before him. Even this close to the sea, the hot, dry air burned his throat. A person certainly wouldn't survive for long in this country without water. Several buildings sported clumps of flowering bushes, but nothing tall enough to be considered a tree.

The rainbow of color adorning the people in the street, some in combinations that hurt the eye, did nothing to offset the drab buildings. The billowy, loose-fitting clothing must be cooler than the wool and leather he wore. No one appeared to sweat the way he did, so hopefully he would be given something similar.

They reached the center of the city and a large open market with the first stone building he'd seen so far. Voices proclaiming the uniqueness of their wares echoed off of the surrounding walls with an undertone of spirited banter over prices. The spicy aroma of cheap meat pies struggled to overcome the pungent odor from the livestock pens.

Senses reeling, Chaska was led past the market and into the large stone building. Once inside, the temperature dropped significantly, and as his eyes adjusted to the dim light, a row of iron-barred cells appeared along the back wall. One of those would be his temporary home until the

Shadhuin buyer arrived.

Locking the door to Chaska's cell, the trader pointed to a jug of water sitting on a shelf by a narrow cot. "Drink much, stay strong. I bring food."

He returned shortly carrying a steaming bowl full of stew that smelled similar to the meat pies outside, and another jug of water. The stew was indeed spicy, but good, and the water, cool and refreshing. Chaska lay on the cot to wait, surprised at how comfortable it was, and soon fell asleep. None of this was what he had expected.

He awoke after a short nap feeling refreshed, and drank water as instructed. The silence was profound, and such a departure from what he was used to. The unending competition with his fellow apprentices, and the constant threat of violence had consumed his life for as long as he could remember. Unbeknownst to him, the Scarred Mage had instructed the slave trader to ensure Chaska was the *only* slave available to the Shadhuin when they arrived.

The power whispered to him from across the barrier of the shackles and forced him to his feet, pacing, unable to answer its call. In desperation, his thoughts raced down paths he'd never dared to tread before. What would become of his life should he lose the power forever? The

Dark Lord certainly would no longer have any use for him other than as a true slave. His only other passion was caring for the animals kept in the fortress. He'd always felt a kind of peace while in their presence.

At some point, the trader returned with more food and a jug of water. The gloom surrounding Chaska's cell never changed and made it difficult to determine the time of day. Apparently, it was time for the evening meal. He thanked the man and asked, "How long must I stay here?"

The trader nodded in response to his word of thanks and answered. "Not long. Maybe tomorrow."

Completely alone for the first time, Chaska spent the remaining hours immersed in thought. Normally he would have taken the time to practice his spell-casting, but that was denied him for now. Instead, he thought about the things he had seen, and compared them to what he had been told. What if some of those were untrue? If this Navon was as evil as his master claimed, how would he befriend him? Would the Deluti kill him out of hand after learning what he was?

In the morning, a thoughtful, yet apprehensive sorcerer's apprentice arose to meet the brightly dressed Shadhuin Horse Lord who approached his cell.

The dark-skinned elder studied Chaska's face closely before speaking. "You horse, care for?"

The words were broken, but the young man thought he understood and answered simply. "Yes."

A quick conversation ensued between the elder and trader until agreement was reached. Chaska was released from the cell and followed the Shadhuin outside to a small wagon. He stumbled as if the heat and bright sunlight had struck him a physical blow.

The elder retrieved a length of cloth from under the seat, deftly wrapped it around the apprentice's head, and helped him into the back of the wagon.

Chaska marveled at how much protection the simple length of cloth provided. He was cooler and the sun didn't glare as much as before. The road was smooth, and he might have enjoyed the fast pace if it wasn't for the weight dragging on his ankles and wrists. The memory of riding in a similar wagon as a small child, along with others his age, made him frown. He'd always known he had been abducted, but the knowledge never bothered him until now. Surviving in the Scarred Mage's fortress left little room for past memories.

They arrived at the Shadhuin city where the elder

stopped the wagon just outside the southern entrance. An elderly woman shuffled out to meet them. She produced a small key, unlocked the shackles, and motioned for Chaska to climb out. He picked up the chains, thinking they might be too heavy for her to lift, and was amazed at their light weight. *Interesting.* The heaviness was only an illusion fueled by his own power. He placed them under the seat as directed and followed her inside.

She led him to a room filled with shelves of drab clothing, and began assembling an assortment of shirts and pants.

"They not as pretty as Shadhuin wear, but why wear and get dirty every day? Come in evening for clean and leave dirty in baskets."

Leaving there with his arms full, she showed him the common dining area and then took him up to the third floor. A large room filled with bunks along each wall, some with a small chest at the bottom, occupied the entire floor.

"Some beds not used, pick one. Clean yourself and change clothes in washroom at back, then join others for the mid-day meal. Someone will come for you after."

She turned to leave and then turned back. "What your

name?"

"Chaska."

"Means 'man of strength'. You need it."

"Why?"

She pinned him with her eyes. "The man you work with. They say he demon."

*     *     *

Sebastian turned from the window at the sound of his door opening. Emma stood there for a moment, breathing heavily, and then purposefully grabbed her travel bag from the end of the bed. The hint of tears on her cheeks contrasted with her actions as she began stuffing items inside the bag.

"Pack your things, Sebastian. We're leaving."

"Why?"

"You delivered the warning to the King like the Ancient One commanded and now we're done. Let the humans deal with their own problems now."

The ogre reached out and gently turned his partner to face him. "I not leaving be, little one. Evil here."

She stared up at him, tears beginning to form once again. "But... but, they're going to kill you!" she cried, wrapped her arms around him, and then buried her face in his chest, sobbing.

Sebastian awkwardly patted her on the back and let her cry. This was unlike the Emma he knew, and he wondered what could have scared her so. She began to pull away with only an occasional sniffle, and he carefully lifted her onto the bed. Not caring how silly it looked, he pulled over one of the chairs and sat on it.

"Talk to me, little one. Listening I be."

"Miserable, hairy beast," she grumbled. "Why do you have to be so loyal? And don't call me 'little one'."

The ogre's expression never changed as he waited for her to wind down. They had been partners so long; he knew she would have to overcome her fear before speaking.

"Who frightened you, Em?"

Eyes wide, she stared at Sebastian and tried to speak. Her mouth moved, but no words came out. Taking a deep breath, she squeezed shut her eyes and whispered, "Scorpious."

The ogre jerked forward, the groaning of the chair masked by the snarl that rumbled past bared fangs. Barely able to form words, he rose up and towered over her. "Dark Lord, here?"

Raising her hands defensively, she shook her head. "No, no. Only his voice!"

Confused, Sebastian collapsed back on the chair which creaked ominously. "Voice?"

Emma hurried to explain. "The Duke has a secret room in his office. When he opened the hidden door, the evil that poured out made me ill, and I dared not enter. However, even with the door shut, I could just hear their voices through the tiny crack."

Shivering, she hugged herself, eyes locked on the ogre's. "Sebastian, Scorpious sounds just like his brother, the Ancient One, except his words are like honey covered in fire. When the Duke mentioned your name, the Dark Lord's hate drove me to the floor. He ordered the Duke to kill you, or his life would be forfeit. I barely got out of the way when the Duke crawled out of that room."

"Kill me? How?"

"I don't know. All I know is he is sending someone to watch your every move, but I don't know why."

Sebastian sat motionless for a long time, calming himself and mulling over what Emma had told him.

She slid off the bed, poured a glass of wine for each of them, and after handing one to the ogre, downed hers in a single gulp. Looking out the window, she continued with the rest of what she'd heard.

"I'm sorry, Sebastian. I let my fear control me. As much as I hate to admit it, you're right. We must stay and help fight this evil. I heard Scorpious call him, 'my would-be King', so our assumptions were correct. How we are going to fight so many of the Duke's men, I don't know."

The chair finally gave up the fight as Sebastian heaved himself up; ignoring the pieces left behind, he moved to stand behind her.

"We are forewarned and have you to thank. You must find this watcher, and it will be up to us to make sure they see only what we want them to see." He turned her away from the window, and continued, "If the Duke be planning on being King, the Royal Family is in danger, and we must warn Prince Mathias before he arrives tonight. If the watcher already out there be, we don't want them seeing the Prince."

A knock at the door sent Emma into the shadows while Sebastian moved to stand by it, hand on his sword. "Who's there?"

"Poppie, Sir Ogre!"

Sebastian jerked open the door and grabbed the young man by the arm, almost lifting him off his feet as he pulled him inside. Emma appeared beside them.

"Cousin, we are being watched, but don't know where and by whom. Quickly now, we must find Mathias and warn him before he arrives."

"But…"

"But nothing. You can share what you've learned later," she ordered, pushing him out the door.

Once in the hall, the young man called out, "You can count on Poppie!" and left the inn, confident Emma was right behind.

*    *    *

"By the Eyes!" Mathias cursed and slammed his fist against the stone. "Many lives may be lost if we cannot find a way to open this door."

Between his eyes adjusting to the darkness, and the faint light that trickled past the jammed door, he could see his friend sitting on the floor. "What are you doing down there?"

"The strikers on these lanterns are broken. That's why they were left on the lower level. If I can fix one of them, we won't have to stumble around in the dark."

A little envious of his friend's knowledge of so many different things, the Prince busied himself running his fingers around the edge of the door. There must be something holding it closed. He had already thought of a number of men outside the Palace he could count on to sneak inside and help him protect his family. Trying to get them inside any other way would be next to impossible.

Rafael grumbled a curse as one of the lanterns flared to life, and he stood sucking on a finger. "Well, that wasn't what I had planned, but it worked."

"Sometimes you scare me," Mathias joked, shielding his eyes from what looked like a bonfire after the darkness. "Bring your light over here, wonder boy. I felt something between the door and the wall here at the bottom."

Rafael dropped back to his hands and knees, held the lantern up and peered into the crack. "Just as I suspected. It's a knife blade, and a poor one judging by the amount of rust. It was probably jammed in higher up and then fell as the rust ate away at the metal."

He set the lantern out of the way and leaned against the door. "Come on. Help me push the door closed. If we can fish that blade out, the door should open."

At first nothing happened, but with their combined weight it finally jerked back into place. Mathias pulled his knife and got down on his knees this time, trying to reach the rusty blade. After several minutes of reaching and scratching, he sat down and sighed. "It's no use. It must have moved with the door and is now out of reach. We need something longer."

"What about that old sword?"

"It's probably too thick, but it wouldn't hurt to try. I don't think our bony friend is going to care."

Rafael reached down and carefully worked the sword out from under the pile of bones. Straightening, he stopped and stared, then ran his hands reverently over the intricately formed and jeweled hilt. Words of wonder passed his lips in a whisper.

Curious, the Prince got up and joined him. "What is it?"

Rafael turned to his friend, excitement and awe dancing in his eyes. "Mathias, I've seen a drawing of this sword in the history books! It's a Deluti sword, and the only one known to have been gifted to a human monarch. I don't remember the name as that was during the Deluti War, but I'm sure I can find it again."

"That's interesting, Rafael, but will it work to free the door?"

Rafael sighed, a hint of disappointment shading his voice. "You don't give a whit about history, do you?"

The Prince shrugged and turned back to the door. "Right now, it is the future that concerns me. The past will still be there when we have time to study it. Hand me the sword, please."

The slender blade fit easily into the gap, and Mathias made short work of pushing the rusted knife out of the way. He handed the sword back, motioned his friend to douse the lantern once again, and pushed on the door. It opened smoothly.

Latched fully open, both men peered cautiously out into the gloom. Rafael turned to his friend, his eyes full of wonder. "Do you know where we are?"

Mathias returned his smile. "It's the blind alley behind the Palace where we used to hide as children. Now we know why it doesn't go anywhere." Searching for a way to remember the location of the door in the featureless wall, he noticed a worn symbol etched into the stone at its base. "This is perfect. You can go home from here, and I can go to my meeting without having to sneak back through the Palace. Leave the lantern and the sword and close the door."

"But…"

"Think, Rafael. How far will you get on the streets of New Bratan carrying a sword like that? And what if the servants or your father see you?" He laid a hand on Rafael's shoulder and reassured him. "I promise, in the morning I will return, retrieve the sword and hide it in my quarters for safe keeping."

Reluctantly, and with great care, the young historian placed the sword on top of the pile of bones and released the latch. The door shut smoothly. He hurried to the entrance of the alley, peered around the corner, waved and then disappeared.

Mathias took his time, waiting and listening for footsteps that might indicate someone following his friend. Patience exhausted, he stepped out and hurried on toward the inn. Halfway there, a small figure detached from the shadows and beckoned. Hand on his knife, he followed the shadow into the narrow space between two buildings. The little man lowered his hood. He looked like Poppie, but spoke like Roll.

"Prince Mathias," he whispered. "The Duke set

someone to watch Sebastian. If you wish not to be seen, put on this cloak and raise the hood. The watcher is sitting in a corner of the common room with a view of the stairs."

Donning the cloak, the Prince followed him back out into the street. They were met at the back door of the inn by Aaron, the innkeeper, who led them through the kitchen. At the door leading into the common room, he bid them wait.

Aaron confronted a bored looking young man sitting at a corner table, blocking his view. Roll tugged on Mathias's hand, and they hurried up the stairs where he knocked a discreet pattern on Sebastian's door. It quickly opened and they slipped inside.

The somber mood inside drained away the Prince's excitement over sharing his good news. The ogre sat on the floor while Emma picked pieces of wood up off the floor. Accepting a glass of wine from Roll, Mathias sat on the remaining chair and asked quietly, "What have you learned?"

Emma threw down the broken pieces, kicked them under the bed and faced the Prince, her eyes aflame. "Duke d'Lorange has a hidden portal of some kind in his office where he can speak directly to Scorpious, the Dark

Lord. The evil and hate emanating from there is being felt throughout the city. He has definite plans for becoming King, and I can only imagine he plans on using force to accomplish it."

She stopped and turned away, the muscles in her jaw tightening. With a sigh, she continued. "What's more, the Scarred Mage ordered Sebastian's death. If the Duke fails, he forfeits his own life. That is why the watchers both inside and out."

Roll stood next to his cousin and quietly added, "I'm afraid my news isn't much better. The Navy has been loading troops from the local garrison onto ships and leaving port."

"Leaving only men loyal to the Duke here in the city and Palace," Mathias guessed. "At least I have some good news. Rafael and I found the escape tunnel in the lower levels along with the remains of someone who died there around the time of the Deluti War. The question is, do we smuggle people in or out?"

He stood to leave and faced the ogre. "Either way, friend ogre, with only the few men I know I can trust, some of us will not survive what is coming."

"Have faith, young human," Sebastian told him.

"Good always seems to find a way. Something will come along; we just need to be ready."

The Prince turned to the door and beckoned the cousins to join him. "Come, I'll show you where the door to the tunnel is located in case something happens to me."

At the door he stopped and turned back to the ogre. "I almost forgot, Sebastian. Rafael wishes to speak with you and I promised I would ask."

"And who is this Rafael?"

"My best friend since childhood who spends his time reading history books, and... he is the Duke's son."

The ogre stood and looked down at the Prince, their eyes met. "Do you trust him?"

Unflinching, Mathias answered. "With my life."

"Very well. I assume his father would not approve, so we will meet tomorrow night in secret."

And with that, Sebastian was left alone once again to ponder their fate.

# CHAPTER TWENTY

# A DELUTI ARRIVES

Gilfor chuckled quietly at the situation he found himself in. Here he was, doing the same thing that drove him away from home over a year ago, mucking out stalls and caring for animals. At least these were the royal stables inside the Rose Palace, and he was here for a special reason. Master Horshall wanted someone near who was loyal and could be counted on.

For the first time in his life, Gilfor felt good about himself. Not only had he accomplished the charge set before him by Princess Sofia, the old arms-master had been impressed with his resourcefulness and taken the guardsman under his wing. Master Horshall showed him the secret passages that intersected the Palace, and had begun teaching him how to defend himself with whatever was at hand. He hoped someday to wield a staff as well as the arms-master.

Maybe it wasn't as glamorous as parading around in a shiny uniform, but he understood his new position was just as important, if not more so. He had determined to do everything asked of him, to the best of his ability, for the sake of the Princess. He owed her his life. It was a little scary, though, being a secret player in the vicious game of power between those above him.

Unable to sleep, worried about a terrible sore on the foreleg of one of his charges, Gilfor had slipped down to the stables to check on the mare. It appeared to be healing nicely with the salve the stable-master had applied. About to rise up from his inspection, he froze at the sound of approaching footsteps.

Gilfor had learned enough by now to know someone coming to the stables this late at night wouldn't want to be discovered. He quietly curled up in a corner of the stall and pretended sleep. The footsteps ended in the empty stall next to him, and whispered voices drifted over the separating wall.

"She will not be happy, Eric. I don't like this. We should have just taken the chest and run."

"Shut up, you fool. If she threatens us, we will kill her and then run. Just keep your mouth shut and let me do the talking."

Lighter footsteps sounded a moment later, followed by a woman's demanding voice. "Do you have it?"

"Yes, Highness. It's safely hidden in the city below."

"Find a way to have it sent to my rooms tomorrow. What of my sister?"

The man hesitated before answering. "Unfortunately, the Princess and the Lieutenant escaped our trap, but," he quickly added, "They were seen by the docks in Seaside just before her ship went up in flames and sank. My contact also reported another ship left there soon after. Either they are dead or left the kingdom, and not likely to return."

An ominous silence followed his confession. Gilfor shuddered at the venom shading her voice when she spoke again.

"That is not what I ordered. If she returns, you will

both suffer. But I will give you one more chance. My older sister, Francine, must die, and soon. Accomplish that and you will be rewarded."

Her footsteps sounded again, and then paused. "Do not fail me again, Eric."

Long after she was gone, the other man spoke again. "You didn't tell her what Sofia said."

"That's her problem, not ours. Come, we've got plans to make."

"Wait."

The voices were clear, no longer blocked by the wall, and Gilfor knew they must be standing at the end of his stall. Resisting the urge to hold his breath and peek, he tried making gentle snoring noises instead.

"It's just some straw-head from the farm more at home sleeping in the hay than a real bed. Leave him to his dreams of fleas and horse farts," commanded the voice belonging to Eric.

Their voices receded as the other man argued. "We should kill him."

"And do what with the body, fool?"

Gilfor lay there for a long time after they were gone and thanked the Eye of Life for protecting him. It would do no good trying to find Master Horshall at this time of night, so he would have to wait till morning. One thing he was sure of, he would never forget the sound of Princess Darnelle's voice.

*     *     *

Early the next morning, Roll left the inn and headed the short distance back to the waterfront. Anything that took him farther away from the Duke's mansion was a relief. He may not possess the same abilities as his cousin Emma, but he had special abilities of his own. All the Elder Races shared an awareness of power and evil in others. For Roll, that awareness was amplified.

The Ancient One explained to him that all creatures affect the reality around them, some more than others. For most, the affect was minimal, but the more power a creature possessed, the easier it was to detect. Being in the presence of the Ancient One was like standing in the middle of a dream. Roll knew of two young sorcerers in the city who were probably not even aware of their gift since he'd never seen them attempt to use it.

This heightened awareness guided him to the docks this morning just as it had led him to the Ancient One's secret palace in the mountains so many years ago. At the head of the main pier, he froze and stared along with all those around him. Reality held its breath as a dark ship entered the harbor and cut through the water, headed directly for him.

The young man knew nothing of ships, but there was a lethal grace to the shape and movement of this one. All was not perfect as the top of one mast leaned to one side, a yardarm hung out of position, and there was obvious damage along the rail. They had seen battle and survived. From the whispered stories he'd overheard in the local taverns, it could only be the *Moon's Shadow*, a ship that had long captured the imagination of local sailors, along with respect and a little fear.

But it was not the ship that held Roll rooted to the dock. It was the distortion of reality surrounding the *Moon's Shadow* that caused it to fade in and out of his sight. A Deluti rode that ship, and buried in the aura was the weaker signature of a sorcerer. Both hope and fear paralyzed him.

Who was this Deluti, and why were they traveling with a sorcerer? Would they be willing to help his friends, or were they here to support the Duke? Was the Ancient One aware? Thoughts of High Lord Demetrious helped calm his thoughts and make a decision. He was sent here to gather information for the High Lord, and it was up to him to determine the truth.

Fortunately, his years with the elder Deluti had taught him how to mute the extra burden on his awareness, but it was difficult to do and maintain his illusions. The sorcerer left the ship as soon as the gangway slid out, and ignored Roll when he passed. The faint remnant of evil surrounding the man was odd. Out of habit, he committed the man's face to memory.

He soon forgot the sorcerer when three people appeared at the rail. A strikingly beautiful young woman stepped up on the gangway, forcing Roll to struggle with his control. Her eyes passed through him while the amulet hanging from her neck blazed like the rising sun. Dressed as a mercenary, of all things, with a sword at her hip and a travel pack over her shoulder, she strode down the gangway with purpose.

The man, also dressed as a mercenary, helped the other woman negotiate the narrow path to the pier. Hers was a softer beauty, but no less striking. Who these two were held little interest for him, but of one thing he was sure, Princess Sofia, a Deluti, had just arrived in New

Bratan. Emma was going to kill him.

Drawing a ragged breath, he stepped up and began his well rehearsed act.

"Welcome to New Bratan. If you be needin a guide…"

*     *     *

"May the Eyes protect us!" Emma exclaimed from the window. "Sebastian, I'm afraid our lives just got a lot more complicated."

The ogre looked up from the book he was trying to read and bared his fangs in a smile. "What can be more complicated than living with you?"

Hands on hips, she gave him *that look*. "Very funny, fur face. For your information, a Deluti just arrived at the docks, and it isn't Navon." She turned back to the window. "And they're coming this way"

Sebastian shrugged and returned to his book. "Amulets returning be. They find us. You stay here."

She climbed back onto the bed to help him with some of the words, and wondered if being found was a good thing.

*     *     *

Sofia hung back and studied their little guide. There was something about him that worried at the edge of her new awareness. He had volunteered to carry one of the heavy bags Ronald struggled with and casually slung it over his shoulder. The more she concentrated, a sort of double vision set in and the image of two persons appeared.

Angry at the deception, she was about to walk up and confront him when she noticed Ronald and Floanne hanging on to each other, walking like they'd had too much wine. The Lieutenant had just finished whispering to Floanne as Sofia hurried to catch up.

"Is there something wrong? Are you sick?" the Princess worried.

"No, we'll be fine," Ronald assured her as he stumbled again. "Bernard warned me this might happen. After being on the ship for several days, our bodies would need some time to get used to solid ground again. It feels like the earth is moving." He glanced at her out of the corner of his eye. "It doesn't bother you?"

Sofia shrugged and walked up ahead to their guide, who now looked like a young man. She waited until the street cleared of passerby's before commenting. "You are not who you appear to be."

Roll nodded to himself, her statement proving what he already knew. Only a Deluti would see through his illusion. Without breaking stride or glancing up at her, he made his own observation. "Neither are you, Highness."

She slowed, but he quickly shook his head and urged her to continue. "Please don't stop, Princess. The situation here is dire, and what you wear around your neck acts like a beacon to anyone sensitive to its power. People will be attracted to you and not understand why. Let's get you and your friends safely off the streets and into your baths. We will try to answer your questions afterwards."

They walked on in silence until the inn came into view. Roll turned to her and kept his voice low enough that only she could hear. "Princess, I know you have no reason to, but please trust me. The innkeeper's name is Aaron. Tell him Poppie sent you and he'll take care of you. He will accept your Dahlian coin or anything of value, but don't let others see. I will return shortly, but there is someone who absolutely needs to know you are here."

"And who might that be?"

"Prince Mathias."

Before she could object, he dropped the bag, waved and sprinted off down the street. Ronald and Floanne caught up walking normally again.

"You know, there's something not quite right about that boy," he observed.

"You're right, Ronald, and we'll deal with him later. Right now I have a rendezvous with a bath tub." Picking up the bag Poppie had left, she led them inside.

*     *     *

Mathias arrived at breakfast wearing one of his longer cloaks, complaining of a chill. His mother commiserated, upset the servants no longer kept her rooms comfortably warm. His older brother and sister had their heads together in an animated discussion involving potential marriage prospects among the arriving Baron's sons and daughters.

Preoccupied, the King ate quickly, glanced at his son and hesitated. It only lasted a second and then he got up, patted Mathias on the shoulder, and hurried from the dining room. His father was keeping something from him, and it probably had to do with the Dahlian Princess. She should have arrived by now, but every time he asked, the King dismissed his concerns and told him not to worry.

Mathias worried anyway, along with his other

concerns, but right now he had a promise to keep. Kissing his mother on the cheek, he excused himself from the table, ignoring his siblings. Out in the corridor, he noticed a guard leaning casually against the far wall, and headed for the stairs. On a whim, the Prince turned a corner and ducked into a room, leaving the door open just enough to peer out.

A moment later, the sound of approaching footsteps reached him. The guard hesitated at the corner, but then continued on down the hallway. Was the guard following him, or just going about his rounds? Not wanting to take a chance, Mathias took off in the opposite direction, and headed for the lower levels by another route.

He searched for and found two working lanterns and carried them hidden inside his cloak. At the last set of stairs, he hesitated and listened. Hearing nothing, the Prince berated himself for an over-active imagination. Why would anyone want to follow him? He hurried down to the hidden door, sighing with relief when it opened easily. Not bothering to latch it, he slipped inside, lit one of the lanterns and left the other hanging from a peg by the door.

He hurried to the end of the tunnel and knelt down to

retrieve the sword. In his haste, he brushed up against the skeleton and the fragile bones collapsed. The pelvis shifted revealing a glitter of gold. Amongst a pile of ancient coins lay a misshapen ring. It appeared to be only half formed with a clear stone attached. Intrigued, he dropped it in his pouch and stood, wrapping the sword in his cloak. Lighting one of the broken lanterns, he left the good one hanging from another peg at this door.

He returned to the other end and froze at the sound of angry voices outside.

"You gotta believe me. I followed him down here and he disappeared."

"What I believe is you lost him and dragged me down here for nothing. Now go find him before I have to report you to the Duke."

Knife in hand, Mathias waited long after the footsteps faded before opening the door, unsure whether he'd heard one set of boots or two. The hall was empty, but out of the corner of his eye, he saw one of the storage room doors move. Blood pounding, he raced up the stairs and around the corner where he flattened up against the wall, and steeled himself for what had to be done.

The guard appeared and never had a chance to cry out

before the Prince's knife slipped in under his ribs and into his heart. The man's look of surprise quickly melted as his lifeless body slumped to the floor. Pulse still racing, Mathias dragged the body down to the tunnel, opened the door, and hid it inside. Leaning against the wall, his head spun while he tried to catch his breath.

Returning to his room with the sword was out of the question. With a new destination in mind, he picked up the bundle and headed for the only place he thought would be safe. Opening the door to the library, he almost ran over his friend.

Rafael staggered back, opened his mouth to ridicule his friend, and then saw the bundle in Mathias's arms and the look on his face. No questions were needed as he closed the door and led him to a far corner of the room. He began pulling books from a shelf and neatly stacked them.

"I found this extra space behind these books a long time ago. The sword should be safe in here as long as I return the books to their proper order."

He pulled the bundle from his friend's unresisting fingers and placed the sword inside, returning the books to their original places. Leading Mathias back to where he had left a book lying on the table, they sat down next to each other. Rafael studied his friend closely and thought, *there is a story here I'm not sure I want to hear.*

"What happened, Mathias?"

The Prince closed his eyes, but jerked them back open, not liking what he saw, and took a deep breath. "I killed a man, Rafael. I've never had to kill like that before, and hope to never do it again."

"The body?"

"Inside the tunnel. He followed me there."

"Why would anyone follow you, and what is so important about that tunnel you would kill to keep it secret?" Rafael demanded, and then narrowed his eyes. "What are you not telling me?"

As the Prince struggled to find a way to tell his best friend what they suspected, Rafael stood and slowly paced the floor. Bits of overheard conversations, comments made, and arguments at home over the past year fell into place like pieces of a puzzle. It all made terrible sense.

Shoulders slumped, his head down, unable to face his old friend. "It's my father, isn't it? No wonder you were afraid to trust me completely."

"Come sit down, and let me explain."

Rafael sat and stared at the ancient history book

before him.

"Look at me, please. Never have I doubted your loyalty or friendship, otherwise I would not have agreed to your meeting with Sebastian. I was so afraid of hurting you before I was sure of the truth. We have discovered the Scarred Mage is able to contact your father. Ignoring his influence would be difficult for anyone."

"It's in his office. It must be. He goes in there and locks the door for hours at a time. No one is allowed in there now." He frowned, "but what has he done?"

"The Duke put forth the idea of rotating servants and guards with the other keeps so they would learn the ways of others, and Father agreed." Mathias hesitated, his eyes searching for a place to land other than on his friend. "Rafael, every servant and guard in the Palace has been replaced by those loyal to your father, and not the King. The heads of all the ruling families will soon be gathered here for the Betrothal even though the Princess has yet to arrive. Can you think of a more perfect time to eliminate all opposition and gain absolute control of the nation?"

Horrified, Rafael stared wide-eyed at his friend. "He wouldn't dare!"

"The old Duke... probably not. But one under the

influence of the Dark Lord, would."

The young historian began absently turning pages in the large book before him and mused, "It's happening all over again."

"What is?"

"Here it is," he said and pushed the book over to Mathias. "This is the drawing of the sword I remembered seeing. It was given to King Harold d'Tomorin by the local member of the Deluti Council of Five in recognition of his support for the Deluti in the war. His Dukes conspired against him, and he died at the same time his son and daughter disappeared. He was publically executed, so the remains we found in the tunnel probably belong to the Prince. It worked for the Dark Lord back then, why not try it again?"

Before Mathias could respond, a guard poked his head in the door, sighed and approached them. "Prince Mathias. The boy, Poppie, waits for you at the common gate. He says he's found what you were looking for and to come quickly."

"I'll be right there." But before he could thank the man, the guard had already spun on his heel and walked out.

Shaking his head, Mathias turned to his friend. "I must leave. If you still wish to speak with the ogre, come to the inn around midnight."

"Mathias, before you go," Rafael stopped him while pulling his shirt over his head. "Trade me shirts."

"Why?"

"Because there are blood stains on yours."

Left alone with his thoughts, Rafael absently turned back a page and found a small drawing he hadn't noticed before. Peering closer at the page, he muttered, "What a strange looking pair of rings."

# CHAPTER TWENTY-ONE

# THE ANCIENT ONE

Navon awoke without opening his eyes; instinctively allowing his senses to roam free. The faint scent of down feathers filtered through fresh linens, and the familiarity of the surrounding walls told him where he was. He was not alone. A whisper touch confirmed who it must be, and that the elder slept.

About to reach out to Moshere in what had become a daily greeting when he woke, the memory of what he'd done the day before, forced him upright in bed staring at his hands. What had happened was impossible. It must have been a dream. In desperation, he reached for the elder Brother and found him and his son sleeping peacefully. Moshere stirred just long enough to greet Navon and thank him for saving Elishere's life.

He swung his legs out and sat on the edge of the bed, head hung down and hair falling forward to hide his face from Jamar. Puzzled, the young man slowly ran his fingers through the fall of hair. It had never been dark, but now it almost appeared white. He looked up when the elder stirred and spoke.

"Yes, your hair is lighter than it was before. The question is why?"

Elder Jamar sat cross-legged in front of Navon's door preventing entry, but Navon was afraid the elder had no intention of letting him leave either. Suddenly uncomfortable, he hoped to change the subject by glancing at the window.

"I wonder what time it is?"

Jamar's eyes penetrated Navon's soul and held him captive. This was the moment the young Deluti had dreaded from the beginning.

"What time is it? It is time for the truth, Navon d'Roddell."

Unable to pull his eyes away, Navon fidgeted. "But I have been telling the truth."

The elder's eyes narrowed and refused to release their hold. "Half-truths. Maybe you are hiding the truth from not only me, but yourself also."

Rocking back and forth, his head shaking, Navon again stared at his hands. That was it. All those years of hating his differences, and wishing he was like his brothers so others would like him. And now, those differences were not only imagined, but real. How long would he hide from the truth?

"Navon, look at me. Some slaves decide to stay and live here after their debt is paid, but even after many years, they have trouble with our language. What language have we been speaking?"

Eyes wide, staring at the elder, Navon's mouth opened, but nothing came out. Recognition numbed him.

Jamar nodded. "You speak our language as if born and raised Shadhuin, and what you did yesterday is not possible for a human. What are you?"

Navon squeezed his eyes shut and froze. The amulet sent a gentle touch of support and encouragement at the same time Moshere's thoughts entered his mind. *You are who you are for a reason. The world needs you to counter the evil that spreads once again.* He thought of his bond with Moonlight, and the final barrier crumbled. He sat up straight, faced the elder, and in a slightly deeper voice, answered him.

"I am Deluti."

Jamar collapsed back against the door and sighed. "It is as I feared. The Deluti are returning as foretold, and our lives will be forever changed."

Rising to his feet, he studied the young Deluti. "So be it. Come, it is after the mid-day meal, but hopefully there is something left to eat, and then I will introduce you to your slave."

Navon jumped to his feet, confused. "My slave?"

"Yes. Fortunately, Elder Atora cares not what you are, only for the welfare of his animals, and the Brothers. You will no longer waste time hauling buckets of water and feed, but concentrate on caring for our companions."

As they approached the common room, Jamar turned to Navon with another question. "Why have you come to the Shadhuin, Deluti?"

"I am being tested."

"And if you fail this test?"

"I die."

The elder stopped and searched the young man's face. "Stay strong, Navon. I fear if you fail, your life will not be all that is lost."

*      *      *

The innkeeper lived up to Poppie's guarantees, and treated them with the utmost respect. Sofia had already picked out the watcher, before Aaron, while quickly hiding their Dahlian coin, nodded in the direction of a man sitting in the corner and whispered, "Can't be too careful."

The inn had separate bathing rooms for men and women. Aaron suggested they eat while the water heated for their baths. Sofia's stomach was still a little unsettled, but Ronald and Floanne professed to be starving. The food was similar to what they ate at home, only the difference in seasoning marked it with a slight change in taste. After several bites, she fell into it with the same gusto as the other two.

The few patrons displayed only a casual curiosity, and no one gave her sword a second glance. Ronald admitted he was concerned over the hardened leathers they wore. He knew nothing of how mercenaries acted in this country, and worried their ruse would soon be uncovered.

That was the least of Sofia's worries with the evil eating at the edge of her awareness.

The innkeeper had given them two rooms on the second floor where they retired after a long, enjoyable bath. Ronald knocked on the adjoining door and poked his head in. Sofia sat with her back to Floanne who carefully wove the Princess's hair into a single braid. Sofia had changed into a wide skirt with a high necked blouse hiding the amulet and chain.

"Come in, Ronald. We're as decent as we'll ever be, or at least Floanne is," the Princess quipped.

He entered and bowed in mock admiration. "If it's complements you're fishing for, m'lady, sorry I've used them all up. It is nice to see there is still a woman behind the armor, but where is your sword?"

She wrinkled her nose at him and held up a hand with tendrils of blue lightning dancing between her fingertips. Standing, Sofia patted him on the cheek. "I don't think I need it anymore."

Floanne giggled at the look on Ronald's face and took the brush to her own hair, but left it hanging loose. He joined the Princess where she stood staring out of the window.

"What's wrong?"

"You may yet regret your decision to follow me, Ronald. There is an evil here such as I've never felt before. I believe now the betrothal was a ruse from the very beginning. Someone here only interested in obtaining the chest with the amulet inside, and they will be furious when it doesn't appear. The question is whether the King and Prince Mathias were aware, or if they are being manipulated also."

He turned to her, the sincerity in his tone unmistakable. "I will never regret that decision, or with what may happen. As for the rest, hopefully we will learn the truth if Poppie actually brings the Prince. Until then, what should we do?"

Sofia turned back to the window. "We wait."

They did not have long to wait before their door opened and closed on its own. Floanne's hand jumped to her mouth, stifling a scream while Ronald reached for his sword. Sofia grabbed his arm and shook her head.

The air shimmered, revealing a boyish looking woman, her eyes downcast, and hands outstretched, palms up. She raised her eyes to the Princess, and the notion of youth was crushed by the weight of years buried there.

"I am Emma Greenleaf, Lightshifter and Master Assassin, from the tribe of the Shadow Mountain Elintria, an Elder Race of Marlinor. I welcome the Deluti in the name of High Lord Demitrios, last surviving true Deluti."

Time stalled and held its breath as the new Deluti and the Elder locked eyes, each aware of the other's legacy. Sofia nodded and responded in kind as time gasped, marching forward once again.

"I am Sofia Salidoris, former Princess of the Kingdom of Dahlian, now Deluti and Mistress of the Storm. I accept your welcome."

Emma broke out in a huge smile. "Wait till I tell the old wind bag he doesn't know everything! Well, never mind. May I bring my partner so we can try and explain what you've walked in to? He's big, ugly and hairy, but gentle, unless you make him angry of course."

Sofia smiled at the little woman's enthusiasm and nodded. Emma returned a moment later leading a reluctant ogre, who ducked coming through the door.

Sebastian faced the Princess and bowed. "I am Sebastian, a mountain ogre. My heart sings with the return of the Deluti to our world."

Before she could respond, there was a knock at the

door. Emma disappeared and Sebastian stood against the wall behind the door. Ronald, hand resting on his sword, approached and quietly asked, "Who's there?"

The voice outside could barely be heard. "It's Poppie, with a friend."

Opening the door, the Lieutenant stepped back as the little man entered followed by someone whose face was hidden deep inside a hood. The man quickly reached up to uncover his head, and studied the strangers before looking down at Poppie and mouthing the question, "*Princess?*" The little man glanced at Sofia standing by the window and nodded.

Mathias approached the woman he had already determined was the Princess. Regardless of the simple outfit she wore, there was an aura of power and confidence surrounding her that wouldn't have diminished even dressed in sack cloth. It was the quiet beauty and simple grace of the young woman seated that tugged at his heart. Their eyes met, and he almost stumbled before she hastily lowered hers with a shy smile.

When he turned back to the Princess, the twinkle in her eyes vanquished the little composure he had left. Shoulders falling, he appealed to her. "Forgive me,

Princess. This has been the worst day of my life, and may be the last time we will get to meet. Can we just sit and I'll try to explain, from my side, the impossible situation here."

"Please do, Mathias, and call me Sofia. Princess is a title I no longer answer to. My companions are Ronald, a former Lieutenant in the Queen's guard, and Floanne, who is actually descended from one of your past Kings."

Her last remark almost turned the Prince's eyes in Floanne's direction, but he wisely kept them on Sofia. He was having enough trouble ordering his thoughts. They settled on chairs, the bed, and in Sebastian's case, the floor. The ogre asked a question that had been on his mind since the Prince walked through the door.

"What has happened, Mathias? The scent of human blood covers you."

Mathias, the haunting in his eyes plain for everyone to see, faced his new found friend. "I had to kill a man this morning, Sebastian. In cold blood."

Ronald spoke up for the first time. "Killing a man is never easy, even if it's necessary."

"I'm sure Mathias wouldn't have done so if it wasn't necessary, Lieutenant," the ogre replied in defense of the

Prince.

Grumbling, Emma jumped to her feet and stood in the center of the floor, glaring at the men. "You men! Killing is easy. Living is hard, and will get harder if we don't find a way out of this."

She turned away from them and addressed Sofia. "I will make this as short as possible. The evil you sense comes from a portal in the Duke's mansion tied directly to the Scarred Mage. The Duke wants to be King, and the Dark Lord wants you. Duke d'Lorange replaced every Palace Guard with men loyal only to him. I believe your betrothal to Mathias was just an excuse to bring all the ruling families to the Palace and eliminate them."

"Surely the families will have their own personal guard. Besides, how would he accomplish such a thing?" Sofia asked.

"I'm afraid I can answer that," Mathias replied. "The main audience chamber is the only space large enough to accommodate all the guests. It can easily be secured from the outside, preventing escape. As a young boy, I discovered galleries on either side that look down upon the chamber. They've never been used in my lifetime. A handful of archers up there could pick off their targets at leisure."

While they were talking, Roll made himself useful by bringing up a couple bottles of wine, and passed them around along with goblets. He paused in front of Ronald who watched him with narrowed eyes. "Sorry, Lieutenant. I may not be able to shift the light like my cousin Emma, but I change my appearance for protection." He then handed a goblet of wine to the Prince and asked. "Why don't you tell them about the tunnel you found with the skeleton in it?"

Mathias gulped down his wine and hurried to explain. "We found an ancient escape tunnel in the lower level of the Palace leading to a blind alley in the city. The skeleton must have been there for centuries since a Deluti sword remained there also. Rafael, my oldest friend and a lover of history, found a drawing of it in one of the old history books. It had been given to the King during the Deluti War, but it and the King's son disappeared about the same time. We believe the skeleton must be the remains of the Prince."

Floanne leaned forward eagerly, her eyes bright and hopeful as she glanced back and forth between Mathias and her former mistress. She summoned the courage to ask the question foremost in her mind. "Highness, did this history of yours mention a daughter and name the King?"

Puzzled by the expression on her face, and the question, he answered. "Yes it did. Actually, the Princess disappeared at the same time as her brother. The King's name was Harold d'Tomorin. Why do you ask?"

The slight change in Sofia's voice fixed all eyes on her as she began to speak. "Prince Mathias. The spirit who inhabits the amulet I wear is the Deluti Councilor who gifted her sword to the King for safekeeping. After giving up her life to fuse her spirit into the amulet, it was given to the Princess. While she escaped the city by ship, headed for Dahlian, the Prince acted as a decoy drawing the Dark Lord's agents away into the Palace. Floanne is a direct descendent of the Princess and bears the name, d'Tomorin."

Mathias almost lost himself to the possibilities if they could prove those claims, and gazed at Floanne in a whole new light.

"That's all very nice and historical," Emma cut in. "But it does nothing to help us. Mathias will be required to attend the banquet which leaves four of us to try and sneak into the Palace to do what? Eliminate forty or fifty guards without alerting the Duke? I may be good, but I'm not that good."

In the silence that followed, Sebastian cleared his throat and addressed Sofia. "Would your power be of help to us?"

She shook her head. "Not in such a confined area, and certainly not quietly."

The ogre nodded and fixed his eyes on Emma. "It is up to you, little one. You know what you must do."

"Oh no. Oh no! Don't make me do that, Sebastian. You know how he gets."

"But I thought you were his favorite?"

Emma stared at him a moment before a smile lit up her face. "He did say that, didn't he? Fine, but if anything goes wrong, I'm blaming you."

With a heavy sigh, she turned to the others. "Brace yourselves, and let's hope he's in a good mood. You are about to meet High Lord Demitrios, the Ancient One."

She pulled out her talisman and touched it with a finger, releasing a trickle of power to energize it. At once, a column of mist formed in their center and solidified into the vision of a tall, powerful man. Flowing white hair and beard framed a face surprisingly smooth for the number of years laid upon it. Eyes like polished steel pierced the diminutive Elintria who stood defiantly before him, and his mouth opened to speak.

Instead, he slowly turned and faced the Princess from Dahlian, surprise his only emotion. He cast down his eyes and bowed.

Eyes aflame, Sofia arose, and the spirit of the amulet spoke through her for all to hear. *"Don't you dare bow to me, Demitrios, Son of Tar. Because of your failure these children are now faced with the evil and hatred of your twin. They have the power and the passion to prevail, but lack knowledge and experience. Guide and instruct them. If they fail, your spirit will be forever banned from the Gates of Wistaglon."*

Sofia shook off the effects of the Deluti spirit, her eyes softened with compassion and then resolve. "I can almost feel sorry for you, Lord Demitrios, as one day I will have to face my sister, but the spirit is correct. We need your help and or suggestions."

Unexpectedly chastised, the High Lord's stature and youth diminished as the weight of centuries pressed down upon him. The face of a tired, old man regarded her.

"Very well. With your permission, it will be faster and

less confusing if you allow me to view your thoughts. I will only read the surface, so bring to mind anything you think I should know."

Receiving a nod of acceptance from everyone, he proceeded to stand before each one, and ended in front of Emma, scowling. "Old wind bag, is it?" He reached down, gently raised her head and smiled. "I don't know how Sebastian puts up with you, but yes, you are still my favorite."

She smiled back and immediately turned to stick her tongue out at Sebastian who laughed, his fangs glistening.

The High Lord turned and met the eyes of each human before continuing. "Remarkable. Not only has the blood of the Deluti returned, but the old blood of humans as well. Every one of you carries the blood of some of the most courageous men and women I have ever known. It gives me hope."

He gazed out of the window in the direction of the Duke's mansion, gauging the power and influence of the evil there.

"Sofia, your abilities are too chaotic to be of use within the confines of the Palace, but you can use your power to shield the others from my brother's influence.

What you need are men, and I can think of none better than those who fight for the d'Roddell name."

Demitrios began pacing as the possibilities came together in his mind, and finally turned to Emma. "Run like the Eye of Death is at your heels, little one. There is an ancient path that leads straight to the keep from an old inn halfway between here and Twin Oaks. I know you will find it easily."

"And what makes you think that stubborn son of the Baron will listen to me?" Emma grumbled, heading for the door.

The old man began to fade, and then returned. "Young Navon should face his trial soon, and if he survives, I have asked the spirits to deliver him to his home. He will convince his brother, and should provide the distraction you need to secret the men into the tunnel."

He faced the Prince and inclined his head. "Forgive me, Prince Mathias. I took the liberty of pulling from your memory the location of the tunnel and the entrance to the galleries. I have placed them inside the minds of the others so no one gets lost."

"If this Navon does not survive his trial, what then?" Sofia asked quietly.

Demitrios hesitated, unwilling to acknowledge the possibility. After a moment, he faced her with tired eyes full of sorrow. "If he fails, the High Lord of the Deluti will return to the world of men and create the diversion you need."

With that, the vision collapsed down to a single point of light and winked out.

# CHAPTER TWENTY-TWO

## THE ANGER WITHIN

.

The dining room was uncommonly quiet with just the two of them sitting across from each other. Jamar had managed to convince the grumbling cook to put together a meal for them from leftovers. Even though Navon felt hungry, he ate without tasting what went in his mouth. His thoughts continued to focus on the admission the elder had forced from him earlier. Already, the way he saw himself was changing. People would either accept him for what he was, or not. It no longer mattered.

His heightened awareness now hung at the edge of his

sight, ready to be accessed with just a thought. Not only could he penetrate the world around him with his eyes, his other senses had also blossomed. Navon could separate the smells coming from the kitchen and identify each vegetable or meat being prepared along with the individual spices applied. Every sound was quickly identified as to their source. He raised his head and caught Jamar's eye as the whisper of his name floated to the edge of his mind.

The elder nodded. "Our histories say the High Lord Demitrios commanded the army through his thoughts." Having caught Navon's full attention, he cautioned. "Beware, Navon. Some thoughts are better left unheard."

Still reeling from this latest revelation, Navon turned at the sound of someone approaching. An elderly woman bent down to whisper in Jamar's ear, never looking in Navon's direction. She rose up and froze, accidentally catching the Deluti's eye, then bowed and left quickly.

The elder stood and picked up his plate. "The new slave waits in the common room of their quarters. His name is Chaska."

The moment Navon stepped into the common room, he knew a sorcerer sat there. A hint of evil hovered there also, but was confined to the silvery thread attached to the man. It could only lead back to the Scarred Mage. *Interesting.* Why would the Dark Lord send someone without a trace of iniquity, and guessing from his age, only an apprentice? Navon would have to be careful. Something here didn't add up.

Chaska stood as they approached, his fair complexion, short blond hair, and medium build typical of a Dahlian male. He had some filling out to do, but then so did Navon as they were of an age. The apprentice's eyes widened when they met the Deluti's, and then quickly lowered.

Jamar introduced them. "Chaska, this Navon. You help care animals. He show you." Turning to Navon, he switched to Shadhuin. "Show him quickly. Elder Atora is anxious for you to look at several of the Brothers."

Navon nodded, but kept his eyes fixed on the sorcerer who glanced back and forth between them until Jamar turned to leave. The Deluti motioned for him to follow. "Come on, Chaska. The work isn't hard, just tedious."

"You understand him, yet you are not Shadhuin."

"No I am not," Navon replied, and left the implied question unanswered.

Once they reached the center of the city, the apprentice slowed to a stop and stared at the lake. "Is this real?"

"Very real. A gift from the Deluti long ago to persuade the Shadhuin to give up their nomadic life and settle in one place." Navon looked around and smiled. "Apparently it worked."

They waited while a group of slaves filled their buckets and headed out to the fields. Navon and Chaska grabbed two buckets each, dipped them in the water and started walking towards the north end of the city.

"Always return the empty buckets to the lake for others to use. When you have all the troughs filled, find me and I will show you which feed boxes to keep full for the Brothers, and which ones to put in only a measured amount."

"Brothers?"

"They are one of the Elder Races, and share this land with the Shadhuin. The two formed a partnership of mutual protection long ago. The Brothers are built like horses, but are as intelligent as humans, live long and communicate with their minds."

"They can hear my thoughts?" the apprentice

murmured.

"You will find out when you meet one. They can converse with Deluti, Shadhuin, and," Navon turned to face him, "sorcerers."

Chaska stumbled, suddenly afraid as that word coursed through his body. Had Scorpios sent him here to die? This Deluti was no older than him, yet even his words held power. He hurried to keep up, his eyes lowered pretending to watch his step.

*　　*　　*

Moonlight, nose to the ground, eagerly followed the scent of an animal hopefully larger than a rabbit. Moshere had shown her a source of water nearby, but food was becoming a problem. He warned her to stay clear of the area surrounding the Shadhuin city. Unfortunately, she was in a growth spurt and the small rodents available here were not enough to satisfy her hunger.

Her concern for Navon mounted. She hadn't seen him or felt his presence in days, except for a momentary surge of anger and frustration broadcasted yesterday. Was he in danger? His absence was an ache in her soul she didn't understand.

Following the scent up and over a rise, she stopped

and raised her head at the sound of approaching hoof beats. Hope and joy soared in anticipation of seeing Navon riding on Moshere's back. Too late she realized her mistake. The trail had led her far into Shadhuin territory, and three men on horses closed quickly, weapons raised.

Too late, Moonlight spun around as pain exploded throughout her body driving out every though other than to run. One hind leg soon began to drag as it no longer obeyed her, but she continued to run. Unable to breathe, she slowed and finally collapsed. Her last thought was a desperate call for Navon.

*       *       *

Navon left to find Atora and quickly dealt with the concerns the elder had for several of the Brothers. A feeling of unease suddenly fell upon him. It was nothing he could identify, yet something was wrong, somewhere. Straightening up from his last inspection, he felt a playful nudge in the back and the presence of a certain young colt in his mind. Navon spun around in mock anger, and took several menacing steps toward Elishere who pranced away, mane and tail flying. The little Brother hadn't developed the ability to communicate with words, but his emotions came through loud and clear.

His mind filled with joy and happiness, Navon held out his arms as the colt trotted up and nuzzled the Deluti's chest. Navon wrapped his arms around Elishere's neck, projecting to him how brave and strong he had been, but please be more careful in the future. With a vigorous nod of his head, the little Brother pulled away and ran off to join his friends chasing each other out on the plain.

Navon watched them play, looking forward to the time he would spend with Moonlight later. He turned away and had to chuckle at the look on Chaska's face who stood wide eyed, nose to nose with Moshere. The elder Brother would give the young sorcerer an "ear" full on the proper behavior while in service to the Shadhuin.

After Moshere finished and left, Navon came over. "I see you've met the true power of the Shadhuin."

Chaska stared at him in confusion and a little fear. "If you both know what I am, why am I still alive?"

"We do not kill someone for what they are, only for what they've done to deserve it." Turning the apprentice in the direction of the storage rooms, Navon continued. "Come, I'll show you where the grain is stored and help you feed everyone properly."

Navon and Chaska headed back into the city at the

end of the day, returning the empty buckets they had taken earlier. Next to the lake, they came across three of the Shadhuin guard being confronted by Jamar. They must have just come in from patrol as all three still had their weapons about them. As the two got closer, Navon caught the elder's angry words.

"No matter the size of the beast, Shadhuin do not leave an animal to suffer and die!"

"We had planned to follow, Elder Jamar, but as soon as the first arrow struck, our Brothers bolted and ran back to the city," the first guard explained.

"It was like they were afraid," added another guard. "But they refuse to talk to us to explain why. Besides, all three arrows hit their mark. Surely the beast must be dead."

Fear and apprehension churning in the pit of his stomach, Navon's voice quavered as he asked the lead guard, "What did this beast look like?"

Surprised at being addressed in his native tongue, the guard turned from Jamar, faced the young Deluti and held out his hands. "About this tall, covered in grey and white fur, and a muzzle with large fangs."

The buckets dropped from Navon's clenched fists, the

rope handles smoldering where they had burned through. The waves of heat radiating from the Deluti's body forced the men back, and the water at the lake's edge began to steam. The city groaned as a tremor swept through its center, chunks of stone falling from the surrounding buildings.

He sent out a desperate call for Moonlight and found nothing.

"Nooo...!" The verbal and mental cry of anguish reverberated through the men's souls as the sorcerer fell to the ground, more sensitive to the power than anyone else.

Anger and sorrow pulsed inside of Navon with every beat of his heart. The men should die for what they had done, but yet, how could they have known? They were only protecting their own.

Navon ran for the nearest city gate. The power of his anger broke free and reached deep into the earth to slam shut the conduit feeding water to the lake. Another tremor rocked the city, causing people to cry out in fear and flee their homes. Reining in his anger, it found another target and turned inward. It was his fault she was dead. He should never have brought her along to face unknown trials.

The crops in the fields, and then the grass out on the plain, shriveled and fell smoking as he ran past. Dark clouds began to form on the horizon. The wind came from all directions as if confused while the ground continued to tremble.

As he ran calling out her name, the anger turned to hate; a hatred for what he'd become. He reached up, undid the chain around his neck and threw the amulet to the ground. If anyone deserved to die, it was him.

Why? Why did this have to happen, and why to Moonlight?

Navon stumbled to a stop and fell to his knees. No matter how far he ran, he would never find an answer or Moonlight's body. He knew he could only lose his life to another Deluti, but could he kill himself? He was determined to find out.

*    *    *

Prince Mathias shook off the feeling of awe that had settled on him while in the presence of a man considered by many to be only a legend. The revelation that Sofia was also a Deluti put the idea of a betrothal out of reach. Deluti had always kept themselves separate from the world of men, and rightly so.

The heaviness of despair lifted to be replaced with hope. They now had a chance, but Emma would have to leave quickly.

"Emma, before you go, a suggestion. If you manage to convince Altair d'Roddell to provide us with men, have them stop just out of view from the city gate. Men on foot, two or three together, should have no trouble entering. The guard will not allow a large, armed force to enter, and you would have to fight your way to the Palace. Someone will meet them at the first street crossing and lead them here. Aaron will know what to do."

Emma kissed him on the cheek and laid her hand on his arm. "Stay strong and have faith, young prince. Sebastian and our new friends from Dahlian are a small army themselves. I'm sure they will do whatever is necessary to protect you and your family." She nodded to the others and disappeared.

The silence hung heavy in the room. Sebastian pulled one of his smaller knives, turning it over and over in his large hand. Ronald had his sword out, quietly running a stone along the edge of the blade.

"How far is this d'Roddell Keep, Sebastian?" Sofia asked quietly. "Can she make it in time?"

The ogre leaned back against the wall and closed his eyes. "Emma, human not be. Reach Keep tonight." Grumbling under his breath, he leaned forward and faced the Princess. "Whether the men on horses can return in time depends on how soon they start."

Mathias stood and bowed to the Princess who, along with the others, rose from their seats. "I must go, Sofia. I regret not having more time to spend with you, but my mother is set on making this a grand occasion even though you haven't officially arrived yet. I believe she expects you to make a royal appearance at any time."

"Truly, I plan on making an appearance, but I'm afraid it won't meet with the Queen's expectations," she retorted, and shared a smile with Ronald.

The Lieutenant reached out to clasp Mathias's hand. "Well met, Prince Mathias. You're a good man, and I promise we will do everything in our power to stop the Duke."

Mathias nodded his thanks and turned to look up at the ogre. "Sebastian, my friend. I feel I have learned so much from you in such a short time. As a favor to me, would you stay behind tomorrow? The passage to the galleries is too narrow for you, and I fear you would only become a large target for our enemy's crossbows. If things go badly, someone will have to warn the Elder Races."

"I will stay out of the Palace, if that is your wish," the ogre promised.

Lastly, Mathias approached the woman who had made a place for herself in his heart. The Prince lifted her hand to his lips as they gazed intently into each other's eyes. "Lady Floanne. This may sound old fashioned, but I truly believe the spirits have brought us together for a reason. When this is all over, I would like to spend some time getting to know you, if that's agreeable?"

Blushing, she whispered. "I would like that, Highness."

A smile lit up Mathias's face as he released her and made for the door. "Come on, Poppie! You have work to do, and I must speak with Aaron." He paused at the door. "Tomorrow, the watchers will be blinded."

"Roll, wait," the ogre called out, handing the small knife and sheath to the Elintria. "Tomorrow maybe not safe for little man. Take this, stay alive."

Emma's cousin stared at the knife, and then up at the ogre. "Thank you, Sebastian. Hopefully I won't have to use it."

After the two had left, Ronald filled the wine glasses and handed one to Sebastian, who was shaking his head. "Lieutenant, does this mean Prince Mathias cares for Floanne?"

"Uh huh."

"Humans are so strange," the ogre remarked, to which Ronald laughed out loud.

Sofia had wrapped Floanne in her arms, and wiped the tears of joy from her face. "I told you the spirits weren't done with you yet."

The two women surrounded Ronald, each grabbing an arm. "How would you like to escort two ladies around the streets of the Capitol? I may know the inside of the Palace, thanks to the Ancient One, but I want to get a feel for the city."

"It would be my pleasure," he replied, grinning, and followed them out the door.

Sebastian, alone again, took the bottle of wine to his room. He sat on the bed to read, and waited for the Duke's son to arrive.

# Chapter Twenty-Three

## Hope Revived

Moshere shook off the disorientation caused by Navon's mental cry, struggled to stand and ran towards the city where the cry had originated. He could think of nothing that would cause Navon so much anguish unless it involved Moonlight. The Deluti ran past, completely unaware of the Elder's presence, power pulsing from him in waves of heat. There was nothing Moshere could do. He needed help.

The guards at the gate dove out of the way as Moshere galloped through headed for the city center.

Sliding on the paving stones near the lake, the first thing he noticed was the quiet. The constant sound of water cascading over the rocks into the lake was absent. Only the faint tremors still echoed through the city. Would that be the extent of Navon's retribution?

Three wide-eyed guards stood transfixed, and stared at the sight of a Brother inside the city walls. Elder Jamar muttered angrily to himself while assisting the sorcerer to his feet. Chaska swayed and almost fell again, clutching his head.

Years of anger and frustration dealing with the stiff-necked and narrow-minded Shadhuin burst forth along with his mental voice. *"You fools! What have you done?"*

The guards exchanged nervous glances, afraid to answer. Jamar ignored them and turned to Moshere. "These three shot and killed a large beast they felt threatened our herds. Navon overheard. I hope I never come that close to the Eye of Death again." He shivered at the memory. "What I don't understand is why he reacted that way."

Moshere's worst fear had come to pass, and he berated himself for the decision to keep Moonlight's existence a secret. But there was still hope.

*"The great beast you shot is Navon's* bonded *partner and companion. If you had truly killed her, this city would be nothing but a pile of rubble."* Focusing on the guards, he ordered, *"Find her, now! And pray to the Eye of Compassion that she still lives. Her name is Moonlight. Tell her, Navon is on his way."*

As the guards ran for the stables, the two elders faced each other and shared private thoughts. Jamar was the first to speak. "I'm afraid we both made mistakes with what we knew or suspected. Navon values life too much to come back and destroy us, but will probably blame himself and turn the power inward."

"He has already done so. Have Elder Atora bring a large cart and be ready to bring her back here while Chaska and I try to rescue the Deluti from himself."

Left alone with the confused slave, Moshere worried if this was another mistake, but what choice did he have? Reaching out for the mind of the apprentice, the Elder Brother shared a memory of Navon and his companion. *"I need you, sorcerer. Where Navon go, I not follow. You have power call him back. Decide."*

Touched by the images of Navon and Moonlight frolicking in the grove, and the obvious affection they held for each other, Chaska once again began to doubt what he'd been told about the Elder Races. Unable to follow the earlier conversation, and then being knocked to the ground by Navon's mental cry, it was now clear something terrible had happened to Moonlight, and the Deluti blamed himself. It was time Chaska believed what he saw and felt, and not what he'd been told.

Grabbing a hold of Moshere's mane, the sorcerer hoisted himself onto the Elder's back. "I will do what I can."

The path of unintended destruction was easy to follow once they left the city. The dust cloud from the guards could be seen already far to the north. It was clear Navon had fought to control his anger as areas of dead plants and smoking fence posts alternated with areas untouched. A strong wind had arisen, and the farther they traveled, the fiercer it became, eventually forcing Moshere to a slow walk. Head down, straining against the wind, he spotted the amulet and chain and stopped.

Chaska, who had attempted wrapping part of his head covering over his face to protect it from the abrasive dirt and debris, carefully opened his eyes and realized why the Elder had stopped. There lay the one thing his Master desired more than anything else, the amulet of another Deluti.

*"You pick up,"* Moshere ordered.

A shiver of fear coursed through Chaska as the words of his Master replayed in his head. "I cannot! I will die."

"Dark One lie. Pick up."

The sorcerer put aside his fear, fell from Moshere's back, gingerly picked up the amulet and sighed when nothing happened. Unable to pull himself back up with one hand, he held on to the Elders tail and blindly followed. If he'd seen what they strained towards, he might have given up.

The wind formed a vortex that reached up into the sky. Dark clouds sped from the horizon to be swallowed up in the mouth of the vortex. Lightning flashed along its length, unheard above the roar of the winds. At the base knelt a solitary figure seemingly untouched by its power.

Moshere fell forward and Chaska was jerked to his hands and knees just feet away from the specter that was Navon. They had reached an area of calm surrounding the Deluti, cracks in the ground radiating out from the center like spokes in a wheel. On his knees, with arms raised above his head, Navon's eyes were open, but only the whites showed.

The young apprentice sat cross-legged before Navon, the amulet resting on his lap. His thoughts scattered at the display of unfathomable power. Never had Chaska felt so insignificant.

Moshere's voice rang out in his head. *"Attack, sorcerer. Now!"*

Knowing it would be a useless gesture, Chaska still brought up the most lethal spell he knew, reached out for the energy to power it, and gasped. Not only had Navon drawn to him the power of the Deluti, the power used by sorcerers had amassed alongside it. Without hesitation, the apprentice forced more power into his spell then he thought possible, and hurled it at the unsuspecting Deluti. Chaska experienced a moment of fear. Certainly, no one could survive what he had just unleashed.

The resulting concussion knocked the sorcerer back several feet. Moshere lay on the ground, stunned. An ominous silence followed as the vortex slowed to a stop, the winds diminishing. Chaska hurriedly crawled forward to where he'd started and held out the amulet. Pain began to pulse through the life thread to his hands, smoke curling up from burning flesh.

The vortex suddenly collapsed into a roiling sphere of darkness directly over Navon's head, his arms now pointing forward. Pupils appeared and focused on the sorcerer. About to destroy the apprentice, Navon hesitated at the sight of the tear stained, dirt covered, and ravaged face before him. The acrid smell of Chaska's burning flesh drove the Deluti to look at his own blistered and burnt hands, the only sign of his failed attempt at self-destruction.

The apprentice's strained voice, forced through clenched teeth, brought Navon back from the edge of the precipice he'd longed to jump from.

"Take it, please. He... is... killing me."

Navon focused on the power pulsing along the life thread and knew there was no better target for his anger. With deft precision, he painlessly disconnected the thread, and with the speed of thought, sent the sphere of raw power and emotions chasing the thread back to its source.

Chaska still held out the amulet to him. Navon studied the sorcerer before asking, "Why?"

"The world needs you, Navon. They cannot fight this evil alone. And if you'll have me, I would fight by your side."

Navon placed the chain around his neck once again and took Chaska's hands in his, healing them.

"Thank you, but what of your own hands?"

The Deluti starred at hands that no longer bled, but were covered in ugly scars. "A reminder to never doubt myself again."

Moshere reached out to the strongest of the Brothers accompanying the three guards. They had found the wolf, but she was unresponsive. He lowered his head and confessed. *"Forgive me, Navon. I must share the responsibility for what has happened to Moonlight, but now that you have returned, I can tell you there is a chance she still lives."*

Navon surged to his feet. "She still lives? But how?"

*"Apparently, being bonded to you gives her the strength to endure injury, but we must hurry."*

Navon's smile pushed away the last of the darkness as he vaulted onto the Elder's back and held out his hand to the apprentice. "Chaska, ride with me and I will teach you why sorcerers were first created."

Chaska climbed up behind Navon, but was concerned for Moshere after their struggle to reach the Deluti. "Do you think he can carry us both?"

The Elder snorted and broke into a run. *"Do I look like horse?"*

*     *     *

Covered in the blood oozing from burns that had never healed, Scorpios painfully levered himself up on one elbow and stared at the destruction around him. Several small fires still ate at the remains of his shattered furniture while the charred body of his Master Sorcerer lay crumpled in the far corner.

It could have been much worse if he hadn't been so intent on punishing that traitor, Chaska, and felt the power release. How dare the apprentice go against direct orders and hand the amulet back to Navon? The Dark Lord had been able to deflect the majority of the attack to his underling, but the ferocity stunned him.

An emotion kept buried for millennia awoke, and the worm of fear began to wiggle and squirm in the pit of his soul. He had no defense against the human emotions of suffering and sorrow infusing the power of the new Deluti. Its strength came from pain; the pain of compassion.

*     *     *

Rafael stepped out into the darkened hallway and

paused to listen. His sister had stayed up later than usual, excitedly discussing choices of dress for the banquet tomorrow with their mother. The flickering shadows on the wall from the single lantern brought back memories of his childhood. He and Mathias would sneak out late at night and meet in the alley behind the Palace. Most of their adventures ended in big trouble for both of them. He hoped this wouldn't end up the same way.

At the bottom of the stairs, he could see light still coming from under the door to his father's office. Anger rose up inside him at the thought of what his father had planned for tomorrow. His hands clenched into fists and he started for the door. Frustrated, he turned away. What could he do? The Duke would never listen to him, and he didn't want his father to find out anyone else knew. Besides, plans were already in motion and it was too late to stop them now.

Rafael had made up his mind to protect the Prince's life with his own if needed, but right now, he had a meeting with an ogre.

From the looks of it, the old door in the back of the pantry hadn't been used since the last time he'd snuck out. Quietly moving old barrels and crates out of the way, he opened the door, peered out and jumped down into the alley. Reaching back in, he put everything back and shut the door. It couldn't be opened from the outside, but wasn't a problem. When Rafael returned, the guard at the gate would assume he had left earlier when another was on duty.

He'd never been bothered on the streets at night, but kept a hand on his knife anyway. A short figure leaned out of an alley up ahead and waved. Curious, Rafael slowly approached the opening and peered inside to find Poppie beckoning him.

"Poppie, what are you doing here?"

"The ogre send Poppie to warn you. There is a man inside the inn watching. Be careful. Come, follow Poppie."

The boy led them to the back entrance of the inn where he stopped and whispered. "Sir Ogre is on the second floor, far room to the left. Knock once and enter."

Rafael waited until he saw the man sitting at the corner table turn to talk to Poppie before slipping out of the kitchen and hurrying up the stairs. Reaching the last room, he knocked and opened the door.

A deep, quiet voice called out. "Welcome, Rafael

d'Lorange, friend of Prince Mathias. I hear you are interested in history."

Hours later, in between yawns, the new friends called it a night and made plans to get together again. Rafael opened the door prepared to step over Poppie who Sebastian said had a habit of sleeping in front of it. He glanced down the hall, but the boy was nowhere to be found. Shrugging, he slipped down to the common room which was empty also. He left through the front entrance so as not to disturb the cook.

The guard at his home nodded and smiled as expected, but the red faced Duke who confronted him just inside the door was not.

"How dare you disobey my orders to stay away from that filthy animal!"

Rafael was just tired enough, he no longer cared to play his father's games. Unblinking, he met the Duke's glare and answered softly. "Sebastian is a respected member of the Elder Races, not a filthy animal. The father I once knew would never have given that order in the first place. As soon as I am able, I will move out and you won't have to worry about me disobeying your orders ever again."

The twisted smile that spread over the Duke's face sent shivers down Rafael's spine. At a signal from his father, two guards appeared to either side of the young man.

"Escort my son to his room. He is not to leave until I give the order."

Rafael called back over his shoulder as they led him away. "This isn't over, Father."

The Duke laughed out loud. "After tomorrow, it will be for the ogre."

# CHAPTER TWENTY-FOUR

## THREE LEAVE AS ONE

The two men clung tightly to Moshere as he flew over the last rise and plunged down the slope into the valley where Moonlight lay surrounded by the three guards and their Brothers. Even at this distance, the physical condition of Navon's beloved partner flooded into his heightened awareness. Her body had already begun to cool, and any signs of life were fading fast.

Two of her wounds were the result of arrows imbedded in muscle, and the guards had already removed the shafts and dressed those injuries. The third shaft protruded from her chest where it had punctured a lung. Wisely, the men had left that one untouched.

Navon refused to acknowledge the fear and panic threatening to rise up inside him, and fought the tears blinding his sight. He slid from Moshere's back, pulling Chaska with him. They knelt at Moonlight's head.

"Open yourself to me, Chaska. Sorcerers were originally created to be healers, and trained to work closely with the Deluti. Watch and learn. I need your help if we are to save her."

The Deluti opened his heart and sent his spirit deeper than ever before, searching and calling her name. A tiny spark of life flickered in the distance and whispered his name. Navon reached out and captured her before she could escape the world of the living. Enveloped in the warmth of his love, and fed by his passion for life, the spark grew into a flame. He drew from Moshere the strength needed to bring Moonlight's spirit back and anchor it to her body once again.

"Watch closely, Sorcerer. Once I clear the blood from her lung, it will be up to you to keep it clear while I attempt to remove the arrow."

Navon began to dissolve the blood, used the energy

released to feed her body, and encouraged it to replenish the blood lost. Once the lung was clear, and her heart slowly began to beat again, Chaska fumbled for a moment before settling into his role. Now Navon could concentrate on removing the shaft while repairing the damaged tissue left behind.

At one point he faltered, but then strength flowed into him from another source. More Brothers had arrived along with Jamar and Atora, and volunteered to support him. Soon, all of Moonlight's injuries were healed, and even her coat regained its original luster. Navon released Chaska from their rapport and collapsed against her side. The rhythm of her beating heart matched his own.

Raising his head, Navon searched the faces of the three guards, wanting to understand. "Why?"

The three shared a look before one answered. "We reported to the Maudwan tracks from a large predator were discovered just north of our range. He ordered us to track down and kill the animal." He gazed at the young wolf and whispered. "We had no idea."

The Deluti lowered his head and sighed. Now he understood.

The Elders had brought along a cask of the drink used

by the workers while out on the plain. Each man received a cup while bowls were set out for Moonlight and the Brothers. It still had the same bitter taste Navon remembered along with the feeling of being refreshed.

He helped the wolf into a position where she could reach the bowl, and watched as Chaska stood and moved away from them, ignoring the cup in his hand. Moonlight urged him to find out what was troubling the young sorcerer. Sharing her concern, Navon sighed, let go of her neck and approached the apprentice.

"You should drink. It has a bitter taste, but will refresh and restore you."

The Deluti couldn't help but smile at the face Chaska made after taking a sip, but the apprentice continued to stare into the distance, and didn't comment. Navon knew he would have to find a way to get through to Chaska and determine what was wrong. Too much depended on the sorcerer's loyalty.

"Thank you. Not only did you place your life in danger to rescue me from myself, I would not have been able to save Moonlight without your help. For that I will be forever grateful. I believe you are on your way to becoming a great sorcerer."

Chaska spun around to face him, the anger in his voice at odds with the tears that welled up in his eyes. "And what sort of sorcerer shall I become, Navon? I've spent the last ten years of my life studying how to kill, destroy, and twist the minds of others to do my will. I reveled in the praise as I strove to become the best. In a few short hours, you opened up a whole new world for me that exposed the evil I'd been taught. I can't unlearn what I have learned."

Navon studied the face of the young man and carefully choose his words. "No, you cannot. Learn to balance the evil with the good, Chaska. Until Scorpios is defeated, you will need those skills you've learned, especially if you accept the new responsibility I wish to place upon you." He turned away and returned to Moonlight's side.

The elders had brought along a tarp they carefully positioned under the wolf. Together, the men lifted her into the cart. Navon jumped in to hold Moonlight's head in his lap while Chaska rode Moshere. Jamar and Atora guided the cart along the smoothest path they could find. A soft breeze fanned their faces as the sun dropped toward the horizon. It would be dark by the time they made it back.

A crowd of angry and frightened families met them at the northern entrance to the city. Navon stood up in the cart and waited for them to quiet. The people exchanged surprised looks when he addressed them in perfect Shadhuin.

"Some of you believed I was a demon, yet you accepted me and even treated me with respect. That meant more to me than you'll ever know. There is no excuse for my loss of control putting all of you in danger. I apologize. What I can tell you is I am no demon, I am Deluti."

They stared at him in stunned silence until someone called out, "We are afraid to return home." Another asked, "What happened to our water?"

"Your homes are safe, and the water will return before I leave."

Most of them took him at his word, but several were unsure and approached the elders with quiet questions. A man Navon recognized as one of the harvesters after the fire, looked up at him and asked. "Why you lose control, Navon?"

The young Deluti studied him for a moment and then

asked his own question. "What would you do if you thought someone had killed your Brother?"

"I would kill anyone who took the life of my Brother."

Navon nodded and jumped down to face him. "I am bonded to the she-wolf in this cart as you are bonded to your Brother. I had the same reaction when I thought Shadhuin scouts had killed her. I lost control, and for that I am sorry. It will never happen again."

The man peered into Navon's eyes and saw nothing but regret and truth. After glancing at Moonlight, he reached out to grasp the Deluti's forearm. "Understood. It is good your partner still lives. Fare you well, Navon Deluti." Turning away, he gathered up the rest of the people and herded them into the city.

Moonlight was now a constant presence in his mind, as it should be. Never again would he be foolish enough to let them be separated. Right now, hunger was foremost in her thoughts.

"Elder Atora, I would be grateful if you would take Moonlight and feed her as much as she can stomach. I'm afraid our time here is coming to an end."

As Atora led the cart away, Navon turned to Jamar

411

and Chaska. He spoke in the common tongue for the sorcerer's benefit. "Walk with me, both of you. The Maudwan will be waiting for me, and there are decisions to be made."

By the time they reached the Maudwan's hut, Chaska had agreed to stay and protect the Shadhuin. Jamar, with the approval of the other elders, would assist the sorcerer in finding and training others. The knock on the door sounded unnaturally loud in the eerie silence left by the absence of cascading water.

Navon waited just long enough to hear the word 'Enter' before he slammed open the door and stormed in. That was the only courtesy he was willing to extend at this point. The perpetual gloom no longer a deterrent to his heightened senses, he approached the raised bed and glared down at the emaciated man lying there. The heat of his anger flared, driving the son back while beads of perspiration gathered on the Maudwan's face.

"You knew!"

"Yes."

"I could have destroyed part of this city and taken the lives of innocents. Why would you order such a thing?"

The old man struggled to sit up and glared back at

him. "Because I want to die! I can't continue to live like this. You could have destroyed the city, but you didn't. You came here to kill me just as I hoped."

Before anyone could move, Navon lunged forward and wrapped his hands around the Maudwan's neck. The golden chain flared at the Deluti's touch and began to grow, loosening it's strangle hold. Navon quickly healed the bruised and deformed flesh, allowing the old man to speak and breathe easily again. The glow diminished and the chain lay normally around his neck.

Navon stood back, crossing his arms, the lack of respect for the man evident in his voice. "As Moonlight still lives, so shall you. Whether the Shadhuin wish to have a coward continue leading them is something they will have to decide. Another will return soon to claim what is rightfully theirs. Only they will have the power to remove the amulet from your neck. At that point, the charge set before the Shadhuin long ago will be complete."

Navon turned away and left the hut, walking past a frowning Jamar, Chaska hurrying to catch up. Standing next to the lake, he sent his sight deep into the earth to slowly re-open the channel feeding water to the city. As the sound of water cascading over the racks returned, people appeared and began to cheer.

Concerned by what he had seen, Chaska whispered. "What if Scorpios finds out there is another amulet here?"

"I'm afraid he already knows, Chaska. The power needed to unlock the chain was also a signal to summon the chosen bearer of the amulet. That person should already be on their way here, but the Scarred Mage would have sensed it also."

Jamar left the hut and slowly closed the door behind him. Glancing at the flowing water, he nodded and then approached the two young men. He looked Navon in the eye and sighed. "Forgive us, Navon. What he has done goes against everything the Shadhuin stand for. The elders will decide his fate."

"Every man has a breaking point, Jamar. The Maudwan found his." Time was growing short, and the pull to return north intensified. "The Dark Lord will not hesitate to send his men and sorcerers against you now that he knows an amulet is here. I would stay to help, but the Spirits are calling me and I must leave."

Navon headed for the apartment he had shared with Jamar, the elder and Chaska walking alongside. Neither man spoke while he changed back into the wool and leathers he had arrived in. Jamar left for a moment, returning with the weapons that had been taken from Navon earlier. As they left the building and headed for the stables, Shadhuin began gathering along the way, some nodding, some bowing, and others holding torches to light their way.

The Deluti nodded and bowed in turn, and made eye contact with those he had worked alongside. A smile lit up his face when they left the city and found Moonlight and Elishere standing side by side in the flickering light. The wolf's love for him was echoed by the emotions coming from the colt. Navon returned their mental greeting, knelt down to gently hug Moonlight, and then faced the two men he would have to leave behind.

He reached out to grasp Jamar by the arm. "Elder Jamar, I will never forget the patience and understanding you displayed towards a lost and confused young man. It was an honor learning from you and your people."

"Till we meet again, Navon Deluti," the elder responded, grasping Navon's arm in return.

Navon then turned to the young man who had succeeded in his mission to befriend him. "The title of apprentice no longer fits you, Sorcerer. Defend these people as best you can."

"I will, and thank you."

A bright flash caused everyone to blink and stare as a glowing white archway appeared in the road. Resting his hand on the wolf's shoulder, Navon and Moonlight started for the arch when Moshere stepped out of the darkness and blocked their path.

The elder Brother locked eyes with the Deluti, and then bowed his head. *"I no longer have a purpose here. The bond we share is not the same as your bond with Moonlight, but is strong nonetheless. I wish to continue that bond and join you."*

The initial fear Navon had felt when taking Moonlight into the unknown rose up inside him, but was quickly replaced with his newfound confidence. *"I would be honored, Moshere."* He smiled at the Brother, *"Besides, you run faster than I do!"*

Moshere snorted and moved to stand beside him. Navon turned back one last time, and carefully repeated the words of respect and thanks he had picked up from the boy out on the burnt plains. He sent it out as a mental farewell, and from the startled looks, it must have been successful.

The archway widened to allow them to walk through side by side, and then disappeared.

*    *    *

Emma broke into a steady run as soon as she left the inn, a pace she could maintain for hours thanks to the talisman from the Ancient One. This time of day, there were still crowds of people going about their lives, and she had to stay alert. They might not be able to see her, but would certainly feel it if she accidentally ran into someone.

Already, Sofia's influence had lessened the impact of the evil emanating from the Duke's mansion. Emma could see it in the spirits of those she passed. There was a lightness to their steps while smiles and friendly greetings abounded.

Emma's mind began to wander once away from the Capitol and out on the deserted road. A sudden turn of her thoughts almost brought her to a standstill. It was all coming true at last. The Deluti were returning and the final confrontation with the Dark Lord was imminent. The fate of her people and all the Elder Races hung in the balance. Would they survive?

Another thought she had tried to push aside kept returning. Sebastian. How had the overgrown, furry oaf managed to breach her walls of indifference and uncaring? He meant more to her now than she would ever admit to anyone. It was unwise for an assassin to grow attached.

Sebastian was too trusting. Emma pictured him as a sheep in wolf's clothing. The humans would use and then discard him. She hoped one of the others convinced the ogre to stay at the inn and out of sight. Tears welled up at the thought of losing him.

Her cheeks had dried by the time she reached the Halfway Inn, and decided to stop. While the talisman would keep her going, she still needed to eat. Besides, help from the locals would be vital if their plans were to have a chance. The common room was deserted except for the one table with the same old man and his friends. Emma chose the table next to them and hoped her trust wasn't misplaced.

The innkeeper hurried over. "Emma, nice to see you again. How is our friend, Sebastian?"

"In grave danger, along with the entire royal family, Harold. We need your help. But first, I've been running for hours and need to eat. A plate of food would be welcomed, and I'll explain as I eat."

Harold returned with a heaping plate, a pitcher of water, and joined her at the table. He and the others had the common sense to hold their questions. A cup of water and half a plate later, she paused and looked each man in the eye.

"One of the Dukes fell to the evil of the Scarred Mage, and is planning to overthrow the King tomorrow evening." She turned to the old man. "Those guards you complained about last time are all loyal to the Duke and share his ambition. There are too few of us to fight them so I'm on my way to Baron d'Roddell's Keep for help. We'll return on horses, but the guards will never allow armed horsemen into the city. Would you men be willing to ride with us and take care of the horses after we dismount and continue on foot?"

The men at the table sat back and stared at each other as the innkeeper leaned forward. "Emma, you still have a long way to go. How will you reach the Keep and then return in time?"

"I was told there is an ancient road along here that runs straight to the Keep."

The old man exclaimed. "By the Eyes, Harold! She

means the old Deluti road. It's one of the reasons your ancestor built the inn where he did."

Harold stared at Emma and shook his head. "That road hasn't been used in my lifetime and is impassable. The road itself is overgrown, and the forest on either side is old and thick."

She stood, ready to leave. "I am Elintria, Harold. I run faster through the trees than you do on the ground. Now, where is this road?"

Harold jumped up to run to the kitchen. He returned with a small package and handed it to her. "Here. Several meat pies to see you on your way. The road begins behind the inn where some paving stones can still be seen. When you return, we will help in any way we can."

Surprised and heartened by his simple gesture, she jumped up on the chair and kissed him on the cheek. "Thank you."

Headed for the door, she stopped and faced them again. "One more thing you must know. The Deluti are returning, and I hope you understand what that means."

The old man downed his ale, stood and bowed. "Yes. War is coming. May the Eyes watch over you, Elder."

Emma returned his bow, nodded to the others and

faded from sight.

# Chapter Twenty-Five

# Navon Returns

Navon and his companions stepped through the arch, and he stood once again in the courtyard of the Wistaglon Palace, home of the Deluti spirits. Both Moonlight and Moshere began sneezing at the dry, lifeless air. Navon's anger rose up inside him as the figure of the Deluti spirit materialized and offered greeting. Hands clenched at his side, the young Deluti ignored the greeting.

"I survived your test, Spirit of the Deluti, but the cost was almost too high. Many lives could have been lost if I had failed. Even successful, one life was almost ended because of your test. Have the Deluti forgotten the compassion they once held for the other races of this world?"

"Any loss of life is unfortunate, but sometimes necessary. It is also unfortunate you have gained another companion. The test of life will certainly result in their deaths. But that is a decision for another day."

The spirit then turned away and floated toward one of the entrances to the courtyard. *"Come, there is trouble in your kingdom. Lord Demitrios requested we delay your testing and deliver you to your home."*

"So, Demitrios has the power to influence the activities of the spirits?"

"As High Lord, the spirits are required to accede to his requests whenever possible."

The mist surrounding the perimeter of the city resolved into the fields outside the d'Roddell Keep. The city street they were on ended at the path to the Keep. Conflicting emotions filled Navon with joy and apprehension at the thought of facing his family. But what did the spirit mean by trouble in the kingdom? Resisting the urge to run from the city of the dead and return to the world of the living, He paused and turned back to the

Deluti spirit.

"When I become High Lord, the role of the Deluti in this world will change."

The love and support coming from his companions put a smile on Navon's face as he spied Altair coming down the path with Emma, of all people, beside him.

*     *     *

Emma breathed a sigh of relief as the forest thinned and the ancient keep came into view. Not many remembered it was originally a Deluti fortress. The meat pies were history, and hunger had become a constant companion. She hoped Altair wouldn't make her beg for food, but she would if necessary.

It was just not her way to knock at the door. She waited impatiently for someone to open it and slipped inside unseen. As the oldest, Altair took his responsibilities seriously in the absence of the Baron, and was still in the office writing in a ledger. Several lanterns lit up the room, and a brazier near the desk kept the night chill at bay.

Emma tip-toed into the room and eased up onto the padded chair directly in front of him. The warmth from the brazier was welcomed as her body began to cool. Her mouth began to water at the sight of a platter full of bread, meat and cheese sitting untouched at the edge of the desk. Sighing, she released the beams of light shifting around her.

Altair glanced up from his ledger, lifted an eyebrow and continued writing. "I'll be with you in a moment, Elder."

"An offer of food would be nice, Altair d'Roddell."

Without looking up, he nodded toward the platter. "Help yourself."

Emma didn't hesitate to pour herself a glass of wine and climb back in the chair, the platter on her lap. Not used to being ignored, she fed her frustration with meat and cheese.

Setting aside the ledger, Altair leaned forward, elbows on the desk. The corners of his mouth threatened to turn up into a smile when he saw the empty platter in her lap. "It's late, and I doubt you came here just to eat my dinner. How may I help you, Elder?"

Emma refused to be embarrassed or feel sorry she'd eaten his meal, and returned the platter. Hands on hips, she faced him. "The name's Emma, and you would be hungry too if you'd just run all the way from the Capitol. And I can guarantee it's not in my nature to do such a thing unless lives were at stake. We need your help."

Altair stared at her without blinking. She seemed sincere enough, even with her attitude, and he could think of no reason an Elder would come here late at night and make up stories. He decided to hear her out. "I'm listening."

"Duke d'Lorange has been infected by the evil of the Scarred Mage, and is using it to fuel his ambition. He will stop at nothing to become king. The Palace and City Guards have been replaced by men loyal only to him. The Banquet was a ruse to gather all the ruling families in one place. Whether the Duke intends murder or use the threat of it is unclear. What is clear is the King will not survive. We are too few to fight them and need help. The Ancient One sent me here believing you would supply the men we need."

The Baron's oldest son leaned back in disbelief. "I have never trusted that honey-tongued Duke, but I can't believe even he would contemplate such a treasonous act. What proof do you have?"

Emma sat back down and returned his stare. "Only the word of an Elder who has no reason to lie to you, and the fact I heard the words straight from the Duke's mouth."

Altair stood and went over to study a map of the Kingdom hanging on the wall. Hands clutched together behind his back, he turned to face her. "The Banquet is to be held tomorrow evening. Even if I agreed to supply you with men, we would need the power of a Deluti to reach the Capitol in time."

A white light, brighter than the sun, burst through the window and filled the room. Altair and Emma squinted at the window, their mouths hanging open in shock. A smile covered Emma's face as she jumped down from the chair. "I believe that power just arrived!"

The sound of pounding boots was followed by a guard sliding to a stop outside the office door. The young man, eyes wide in fear, stared at Emma and managed to stammer, "Altair... a city... in our fields."

Emma headed for the door. "Come on, Altair. Let us go and greet your brother."

He turned from staring at the window and looked down on her, confused. "Brother?"

"Yes, silly. Your brother, Navon Deluti."

Altair's face lit up with a smile as he followed the

diminutive Elder down the path to the gate. Eyes filled with wonder, he looked out over the city of the spirits. Legends come back to life, and his little brother was a part of it. And there was Navon, walking the streets of the white city, a wolf and horse at his side. Altair hurried to catch up with Emma.

Navon and his companions stepped from the white cobblestones of the city onto the dark gravel of the path. The city flashed once again and vanished from existence, leaving the after-image etched in their minds. No one had thought to bring a lantern, and they were plunged into total darkness. A ball of soft light appeared above Navon's outstretched hand, and slowly rose to illuminate the area.

Altair hesitated and hung back a moment. The legends also said the Deluti had held themselves aloof from the Elder races and humans, and the confidence surrounding Navon was unmistakable. How much had he changed? His concerns evaporated as he watched his brother greet the Elder with joy.

Navon lowered his head in a bow to Emma, but she grabbed him instead and planted a kiss on his lips. Laughing, he lifted her up and spun in a circle.

"Put me down, you big oaf," she mock grumbled.

"Why is it, all the males in my life think they can pick me up anytime they want?"

Still laughing, he stole another kiss and set her down. "That's because we all love you!"

Altair stepped up and grabbed his brother by the shoulders. "Look at you! I always knew you were special, but a Deluti?"

Navon reached up and squeezed his brother's arms. "I may not be able to fly, big brother, but I have learned a few things," he smiled, glancing up at the light. "Come, I want you to meet my companions."

Emma and Moonlight didn't need introductions, but the Elintria was taken aback when Moshere introduced himself to her mentally. Altair bowed to both, suitably impressed. Navon became aware of another presence hovering at the edge of the shadows and shook his head.

"Looks like I have more introductions to make," he announced and sent a mental request for the others to join them.

Emma squealed with delight as Silverstar and his pack padded into the circle of light. Moonlight's brothers came running, their entire bodies wagging. It was obvious she had not only outgrown her siblings, but gained maturity as well. She calmly put up with their antics.

Navon's smile faded as he surveyed the familiar faces gathered before him. "That we are all here cannot be a coincidence. The Ancient One asked the spirits to bring me home because there is trouble." He glanced from Altair to Emma. "What has happened?"

Altair made his decision and turned to Emma. "You will have the fighting men you requested. I'll leave it up to you to explain the situation to Navon. I need to roust out the men and get them ready to travel."

"Make sure they bring hooded cloaks," she called after him. Emma pierced Navon with those crystal blue eyes he remembered so well. "You must get us back to New Bratan before tomorrow evening, or the King dies."

\*    \*    \*

Sebastian slowly opened his eyes and stared at the drifting specks of dust sparkling in the rays of sunlight streaming through the window. It was later than usual for him because of his late night with Rafael. What an interesting young human. The ogre looked forward to spending time with him in that library he spoke of so fondly.

He let his eyes wander to the rest of the brightly lit,

but lonely room. It was too quiet. Emma had been gone less than a day and already he missed her. What a change from how he'd felt a year ago. It appeared the world was changing in more ways than he could imagine.

Where was the little man? Normally, Roll would have brought up a plate of food for the ogre by now. Even though the folks in the common room always treated Sebastian with respect, he felt out of place and was more comfortable eating in his room. He also enjoyed his conversations with Roll when the little man wasn't pretending to be Poppie.

Rolling onto the floor, he stood and returned the mattress. The bed was too short for him to sleep comfortably, but with the mattress on the floor, it was tolerable. Concern for his friend sent him out to knock on Ronald's door.

"Poppie gone be."

It took a moment for Ronald to make sense of the ogre's words, but he soon nodded. "That isn't like him, is it? I haven't seen him since last night either." He ducked back inside and returned buckling on his sword. "Have you eaten?"

The rumble that erupted from Sebastian's stomach

gave answer.

"I'll join you in the common room for a bite to eat, and we can ask the innkeeper if he knows anything."

The common room was empty. The watcher was also gone as the Prince had promised. Aaron shook his head as Sebastian and Ronald seated themselves at a table against the wall.

"Poppie? No, I haven't seen him since late last night. A man showed up just after midnight and said he had a message for Poppie from a friend. They left together through the back."

Eyebrows raised, Ronald asked. "Isn't that unusual?"

"Not really. Poppie is well known, and can find almost anything, no matter the time."

Ronald and the ogre shared a look of concern as the innkeeper left. He returned shortly with several platters laden with eggs, bacon, and the largest steak Ronald had ever seen. Sebastian's fangs sparkled as he smiled and dug in.

Aaron sat down and faced the Lieutenant. "Just so you know, I've known Prince Mathias since he was a boy, and he has been a positive influence on the lives of many. Myself and a number of others will join you this evening.

Most can handle a sword and all want a chance to protect the Prince and his family."

The sincerity in the man's eyes told Ronald everything he needed to know. "Thank you. Hopefully, the men we are expecting will arrive in time, but if not, you and your friends will be welcomed. What I worry about is the number of City Guards. Will we have to fight our way out of the Palace?"

Aaron leaned forward, smiling. "You won't have to worry about the guard. They have made many enemies here, and will find their hands full come this evening. It didn't take much to convince a group of bored sailors to join in the fun."

The front door slammed open, and four of the City Guard marched in. One remained at the door, and one ran to the kitchen entrance, while the other two approached the table. Aaron jumped up from his chair, hands clenched at his sides.

The Sergeant of the Guard raised his hand to him. "Stay out of this, Innkeeper. It doesn't concern you."

His movements stiff with distaste, he placed a small, cloth covered bundle on the table and flipped open the covering, watching for Sebastian's reaction. Revealed was a small dagger covered in blood.

"Do you recognize this, ogre?"

"Yes. It be a knife I give to Poppie, for gift." He growled and then demanded, "Where you find?"

The Sergeant took an involuntary step back as the ogre stood, fangs openly displayed in a snarl. "The knife, along with a blood soaked cloak already identified as belonging to the boy, Poppie, were found in an alley this morning. Since you are the last one seen with the boy, I will have to bring you in for questioning."

At Sebastian's look of confusion, Ronald spoke up. "The ogre has been in his room all night."

The Sergeant's eyes never left the ogre as he sneered. "And of course you can prove this."

Ronald hesitated. He would be walking a thin line here if he said anything else. Sebastian would never betray Rafael's trust be revealing their meeting, and if the lieutenant brought it up, more questions could be dangerous for all concerned.

Aaron tried to come to the ogre's defense. Arms crossed, he informed the Sergeant, "Sebastian was not the last one seen with the boy. Poppie left the inn after midnight with someone else."

"I see. Who was this someone?"

The innkeeper's arm fell back to his sides. "I don't know. His face was hidden inside a hood."

A triumphant smile filled the Sergeant's face. "Well, when you find out who this someone is, be sure to tell me right away. In the meantime, the ogre will be locked up to ensure the safety of the good people of this city."

The look of despair and resignation on Sebastian's face when he turned to Ronald sparked an anger in the lieutenant he had never felt before. The completely innocent ogre would sacrifice his life so the others had a chance.

"Tell Emma, I sorry be." Sebastian whispered as he ducked through the door and was gone.

Ronald slammed his fist on the table. "I swear by the Eye of Death, the Duke will feel the sting of my blade before this day is done!"

Aaron quietly pulled out the chair he had abandoned earlier, sat down and studied the face of the man from Dahlian.

"Who is Emma?"

# CHAPTER TWENTY-SIX

## RACE AGAINST TIME

This time, Navon countered the force of Emma's stare with steel grey determination of his own. He did not look away.

"I've never been to New Bratan, but I know it is at least a two day journey, even by horse. While I have gained abilities since we last parted, I have no idea how to accomplish what you ask."

A smile slowly spread over her face, matching the twinkle in her eye. "Yes, you have, and more than you know. But, I would not be here if I thought the task was impossible. I left the Capitol early this afternoon and arrived in time by using an old Deluti road that bypasses Twin Oaks."

"Show me."

She led him to the edge of the fields where his enhanced sight picked out the line of the ancient road where it cut through the forest. Kneeling, he scooped away handfuls of dirt, exposing a paving stone buried beneath. A soft glow emanated from the stone as he placed his hand upon it.

For the first time, the spirit of the amulet spoke to him directly, as a dispassionate voice entered Navon's mind. *"Unlike the aquifer far below the Jewel of the Plains, this road needs constant attention. Feed your power into the mortar binding the stones together, human. The plants will wither. Use the energy released as they decay to feed power into the road ahead."*

Something in the tone of the spirit's voice raised the hairs on the back of Navon's neck. *"You don't like me. Why?"*

"You are human. I am Deluti. I am not here to like or dislike, only to provide you with knowledge you couldn't possibly discover on your own."

Sensing he would get nothing more from the spirit, the young Deluti did as instructed. He watched, fascinated, as a wave of destruction began to flow away from his hand. Plants of every size and description withered and died as the wave passed. In its wake, the stones continued to glow, marking the edge of the road.

Attuned to his mood, Moonlight approached from behind and laid her muzzle on his shoulder, watching the glow as it sped into the distance.

Her touch and the simple word of congratulations from Moshere was all Navon needed to cast off the words of the spirit. Tilting his head against hers for a moment, he stood and hurried towards the keep, Emma trotting at his side.

"See, I knew you would figure it out."

He glanced down at her, but said nothing.

By the time they entered the Keep, men were already gathering in the main dining hall. The aroma of a hastily prepared meal drifted through the door from the kitchen, and reminded Navon of how long it had been since his last meal. The cook's apprentices set out stacks of bacon and eggs as fast as they could fry them. Travel pouches were also being filled with meat and cheese rolls wrapped in flatbread, along with fruit, and water skins.

The Baron maintained a force of twenty men-at-arms, and it appeared Altair intended to send them all. The Keep's healer arrived, smiled and clapped Navon on the shoulder on his way to the tables. The jovial old man never missed a chance to eat. All the others greeted the Baron's youngest with curiosity, but held their questions. Altair finally returned carrying his gear and a bundle of folded clothes.

He stopped in front of his brother and handed him the bundle. "The clothes you are wearing no longer suit you, either in fit or function. This is an outfit made for me long ago and only worn once. You are now Deluti, and what you wear should proclaim that. Here, try them on."

Navon remembered the special occasion clearly, and the outfit his brother had worn. He had dreamed, someday, he would have one as well. This gift meant more to him than he could find words to express. Speechless, he hurried upstairs to change in the privacy of his old room.

He carefully laid out his new outfit on the bed and stripped off the old leathers he'd worn for so long. Navon knew he should hurry, but couldn't help admiring his brother's gift. The soft, cream colored shirt brought back memories of the Shadhuin garments he'd just given up.

The black pants shimmered and fit perfectly. When he finished securing the ties on the front of the jacket, just a hint of lace perched above the collar and peeked out from the ends of his sleeves. He dusted off his pair of black dress boots, slipped them on, and kicked the old walking boots into a corner. On a whim, he positioned the amulet outside his shirt where it nestled in the gap at the top of his jacket perfectly.

A hush fell over the hall as he entered. The patterns of gold trim sewn into the dark red coat came alive in the reflection of the flickering lamps. The Eye of the Deluti glowed, matching the golden patterns. A stripe of similar color sewn into the seams of his pants added an illusion of height.

With one accord, Altair and the men stood up and bowed. Emma approached, smiled up at him in approval, and winked. She turned to address the men.

"This is a momentous time for all of us, as the world is changing." She glanced at Navon and then his brother. "While the name d'Roddell will always hold a treasured place in Navon's heart, he was brought into this world to bear another. As a member of the Elder Races, I present to

441

you, Lord Navon Deluti."

Altair, a smile threatening to split his face, clasped his brother's hands, ignoring the scarred flesh. He leaned forward and whispered. "Is she always like this?"

Navon glared down at her and whispered back. "No. Sometimes she's worse."

Both laughed out loud when Emma stuck out her tongue and turned away grinning.

Everyone quieted once again as she jumped up on a chair and faced them, all traces of merriment locked away. The first words out of her mouth insured their attention.

"The King and your Lord, the Baron, are in grave danger. That is why we are here. I will tell you what I have witnessed myself and what we believe to be true. We have also come up with a tentative plan, but please hold your questions until I am done."

Soon after, the men of d'Roddell left on the best horses available with Navon and Emma up front carried by Moshere. The wolves ran alongside with grim determination foremost in everyone's mind.

*       *       *

Prince Mathias paced the length of his sitting room for the hundredth time that morning. He checked the hourglass again, just as he had every other time he reached that end. Was the sand still flowing? Could time possibly move any slower? He now had a greater appreciation for how a prisoner must feel knowing he is scheduled for execution.

The portrait of the King, hanging over the mantle, mocked Mathias every time he glanced up at it. That his father was going to die was a foregone conclusion. If the Duke planned on becoming the new King, the old King would first have to be eliminated.

What could he do? Tell Father his most trusted friend and advisor since childhood planned to murder him tonight, and maybe he should don his armor before going to the banquet? The King had already scoffed at the idea of wearing their swords, saying it was a celebration of peace between the two kingdoms, not a declaration of war.

Mathias stopped and stared at his door. He had to leave this room, but where would he go? The disappearance of the guard the day before had set off a flurry of activity and concern. Now, every hallway was watched by a guard at both ends. Did they suspect him?

Returning to the large audience chamber would accomplish nothing. He already knew exactly how every table and chair was arranged. Thanks to spending hours with his mother and siblings last night going over seating for the guests, he knew where each potential victim would be seated.

While his mother worried about seniority and political standing, his brother and sister concerned themselves with which eligible bachelor should sit next to which available daughter. The whole time, Mathias couldn't stop wondering who would be targeted first.

The Queen finally dismissed him, disgusted by his sour mood. She told him his mood would change once he met his new bride. He almost blurted out the truth, but wisely kept it to himself. It would change nothing. Mother still believed the Princess would be presented at the banquet as a surprise. That thought forced a sardonic smile to tug at the corners of his mouth. He could just imagine his mother's expression when Sofia actually arrived.

The Deluti. What did he really know about them? If he survived tonight, he would need to learn has much as possible, and quickly. With a destination in mind, Mathias headed for the library hoping he might find Rafael there. He needed a friend to talk to, and it was a good way to pass the time.

Disappointment added to the already crushing burden of worry when he entered the empty library. Shoulders drooping, the Prince dragged his feet over to the cabinet and pulled out the two volumes of history Rafael had shown him. Even though it was strictly forbidden to remove the ancient texts, he decided to bring them back to his room. Who would care?

Hours later, Mathias sat back from the history he had just read and sighed. Glancing at the hourglass, he cursed. "Damn, it does work."

*    *    *

Ronald continued to sit at the table long after Sebastian was gone. He quietly explained Emma's abilities and relationship to the ogre as Aaron listened in wonder. The innkeeper would find out eventually anyway. The time for secrets was over. Unable to eat, Ronald pushed away his plate after what felt like a lifetime of trying to convince his stomach it wanted food.

He still fumed over his inability to help the ogre. Even though he knew there was nothing he could have done, the look on Sebastian's face, when they led him away, still burned in the Lieutenant's memory. He had always prided himself as a patient man, but this time it was different. He had a score to settle.

Ronald glanced up at the ceiling in the direction of their rooms and took a deep breath. The women would have to be told sooner or later, it might as well be now. He knocked on their door, announced himself and entered when he heard Sofia's call. He closed the door behind him and stood there, unable to put his anger into words.

Floanne sat at the table, occupied with a needlework project she had brought along. Sofia stood in her favorite spot staring out of the window. When he didn't speak, she turned away from the view, saw the look on his face, and came to him. She had seen that look before when they found the farmer and his wife murdered.

"What has happened?"

Ronald closed his eyes and forced himself to calmly tell her. "Roll is missing. They found his cloak and the knife Sebastian gave him, in an alley this morning. Both were covered in blood. Because Sebastian admitted the knife was his, they arrested him for the murder of Poppie and took him away."

"Did you say anything?"

The Lieutenant threw up his hands and started to pace. "I couldn't say or do anything! I was afraid the guard would start asking questions I dared not answer. Nothing would please me more than to run into that sergeant this evening and wipe the smug look off his face."

Sofia grabbed her cloak and headed for the door. "We can't do anything for Sebastian or Poppie right now, and I can't take waiting in this room. I want to speak with Captain Gerrad. He has a way of finding information that might help us." She turned to Floanne. "Will you be alright here alone?"

Without looking up, Floanne shook her head. "I'll be fine. Say hello to the Captain for me."

As they approached the *Moon Shadow*, Captain Gerrad hailed them and led the way to his cabin. Once seated inside, he got right to the point. "I wanted to warn you, there will be fighting in the streets tonight. The people of this city are fed up with the guard, and I don't blame them. Those men are mean as snakes and don't act like professionals at all."

Ronald and Sofia shared a look before she nodded to the Captain. "Thank you for the warning, Miles, but we were already aware. There will be other things happening tonight and that's all I can tell you."

Miles sat back and smiled. "So you're telling me I shouldn't be surprised if a couple lightning bolts appear over the Capitol."

"I sincerely hope it doesn't come to that," she muttered, unable to share his humor. "We came here to ask you a favor."

"Very well."

"Do you know the boy, Poppie?"

"Of course. Everyone knows Poppie."

"And Poppie knows everyone," Ronald and Sofia recited together, this time bringing a smile to her face.

"Yes, well, the guard claims Poppie was murdered, but they have no body. We think they are using it as an excuse to charge a friend of ours with the crime. We hope the boy is still alive and being held by the guard somewhere."

"If he is in one of the guard stations, we'll find him. By the way, there is something else I wanted to tell you. A ship, known to do business with the Scarred Mage, pulled into port last night, but no one has come ashore. Very unusual."

The two got up to leave. "Thank you for the information, Miles. Keep an eye on that ship, if you can.

We'll check back later, and Miles, watch yourself."

# CHAPTER TWENTY-SEVEN

# A DELUTI AT THE GATE

For Navon, the night passed quickly as they traveled the ancient road. He and Moshere discussed possible actions they could take upon arriving at the Capitol. Moonlight, through images passed on from her sire, provided a glimpse into the abilities of the wolves. At the same time, he monitored the health of the horses, and provided a boost when necessary. All the while insuring the road ahead continued to clear.

Several hours after they had begun their run, the spirit voice of the amulet once again entered Navon's mind.

*"Your control is impressive, for a human,"* he admitted, grudgingly. *"But if the community of spirits intends for you to become the next High Lord, there are things you must learn."*

The spirit proceeded to grill the young man on the proper attitude of a Deluti. Navon learned how to infuse words with power to accomplish his will, how subtle shifts in body language would influence others, and above all, the importance of remaining aloof. *"The bonds you have formed will weaken you. A Deluti must never form an emotional bond, with anyone. You will spend eternity watching them grow old and die."*

Navon rode in silence, mulling over what he had learned, before addressing the spirit. *"I appreciate everything you have taught me, but in one thing you are wrong. I am not like you and never will be. I am human. The bonds I have formed give me strength. Without them, my body may continue to live, but my soul will die."*

When next they stopped to rest the horses, he spent the time with his arm around Moonlight, reassuring her of his devotion. They continued on in silence.

Navon woke up Emma and urged Moshere to slow when the back of the inn came into view. If he never had to travel like that again, it would be too soon. The pace he had set was steady but grueling. He released his hold on her and grimaced as the feeling slowly returned to his arm. Emma stretched and yawned, and then waved to the men coming out of the inn, who waved in return.

"The innkeeper's name is Harold. I never had time to learn the others. They are all good men, and I believe will help anyway they can."

Altair rode up alongside as they reached the inn and all dismounted, the men walking their mounts. Navon slid off Moshere's back and reached up to lift Emma down. She smiled in thanks, and the three of them turned to face the innkeeper.

The whole time, Harold watched in wonder as the pack of mountain wolves drank from the water trough and then laid down in the shade. He whispered to one of the men who ran back inside the inn.

"You made it!" he beamed. "We heard you coming, and have prepared a light meal. I will have something for the wolves shortly."

Rubbing the sleep from her eyes, Emma yawned again and shrugged her shoulders at Harold's knowing smile. "Thank you, Harold. That wasn't necessary, but is greatly appreciated." She turned to the young man at her side. "Let me introduce Lord Navon Deluti, who cleared the road for us, and his companions, Moonlight and Moshere."

The innkeeper didn't hesitate to bow to all three, and then reached out to shake Altair's hand.

"Altair d'Roddell, and these are my men. Your thoughtfulness will be repaid, innkeeper. You have my word as a Roddell."

Navon glanced up at the sun, and then shared a look with his brother who nodded in unspoken agreement. "I'm afraid the plan must change. There is not enough time for the men to walk to the city." Moshere and the wolves gathered behind him. "We will continue on now. Follow as soon as you are ready, and ride straight to the inn. Emma, if you would, please ride with Altair and guide them."

"But Navon, what of the men guarding the gate?"

He pulled himself up on Moshere, and in a grim voice, replied. "They will either leave or die, their choice. Now, how do I find the Palace?"

"Follow the evil."

\*     \*     \*

The noon meal sat on the table, untouched, and the

remains of the hourglass lay shattered inside the fireplace. Time no longer had meaning for Mathias as he stared up at his father's portrait.

"Sorry, Father," he whispered. "I've done what I can, but I'm afraid it won't be enough to save you. One thing I can promise, I will protect Mother with every breath I take."

The chain mail he'd secreted beneath the finery of his outfit weighed down not only his shoulders, but his soul as well. It and the knives he had hidden would provide little protection from arrows or swords, but he would fight with dinner plates if he had to.

Was this how his life was slated to end? Cut down in his home like a sheep at the slaughter?

He returned to the table and looked down, unseeing, at the page of history. The Deluti had failed long ago to save their King, or defeat the evil of the Dark Lord. Was history about to repeat itself? Had the Elintria succeeded in her mission, and if so, would they arrive in time?

The face of the Lady Floanne filled his vision, and he lost himself in fantasies. If they could only find a way to prove her heritage. The knock on the door shattered his dreams.

"Enter."

The guard opened the door, leaned in and nodded. "The Queen requests your presence in the audience chamber to great the guests as they arrive. It is time."

Mathias stared at the closed door long after the guard was gone. The man had actually smiled while shutting the door.

*　　*　　*

Moshere slowed to a stop at the pinnacle of a slight rise in the road, New Bratan spread out before them. The wolves lay down, panting, and Navon took the opportunity to go to each one. Soon they were up on their paws and ready to continue.

The sun hung poised above the horizon, its refection rippled on the surface of the water. Lights came to life throughout the city as daylight fled the darkness. Sitting atop Moshere, who still had not moved, Navon silently nudged his friend. *"Moshere?"*

The Brother brought his head around to face the young human. *"Is this city filled with members of your tribe?"*

At Navon's nod, Moshere shook his head and broke into a run. *"Eyes help us!"*

Four guards blocked the city gate, crossbows at the ready, and showed no sign of moving. Moshere stopped in a single beam of sunlight that had found its way around the tall buildings. Using what he had just learned, Navon stared at a point above their heads and added a touch of power to his words.

"You dare impede the progress of a Deluti Lord?"

Two men shared a look and lowered their weapons until a sharp command from the officer in charge snapped them back to attention. With narrowed eyes, he studied the well dressed young man who sat on a horse with no reins or saddle, and the pack of wolves sitting calmly to either side.

"I have my orders. No one is allowed through this gate, especially the non-humans."

Navon focused his mind on the officers' and asked. *"Are your orders worth dying for?"*

Eyes wide and struggling to hold his bow steady, the officer turned to the man next to him. The guard dropped his weapon and sprinted back through the gate.

Out of time, Navon urged Moshere forward and called out to the men one last time. "Flee or die."

Three bows loosed as one. The bolts disappeared in a

flash of light, steel heads falling harmlessly to the road. Their leader pulled his sword, but flew backward as a ball of flame struck him in the chest. The last two took off, stripping the uniform coats from their shoulders as they ran.

Navon passed through the gate into the city at a slow walk. Even blind, he could have followed the beacon of evil streaming from the vicinity of the Palace. He also sensed the circle counteracting that evil, and resisted the urge to turn toward the presence of another Deluti. It could only be the Princess from Dahlian. He sent her a word of greeting and continued on.

The gate behind him was now open for his brother and the men. Navon's next objective was to draw as many of the guard to him, so his friends would have a chance to reach the Palace unseen.

*     *     *

Sofia had changed back into her hardened leathers, and returned to the window to stare. The evil coming from the Duke's mansion could almost be felt. As the High Lord had suggested, she used her influence to push the taint from the area of the inn. Being in constant contact with its foul touch turned her stomach, making it impossible to eat.

She and Ronald had spent time practicing in the close quarters of his room. Sofia would have to rely on her skill with a blade in the upcoming confrontation. She was too new to her power, and the spirit of the amulet was less than forthcoming with answers to her questions. She could feel the power of the storm curled up inside, ready to strike. How many people would die if she lost control?

For the hundredth time, she laid a hand on her former servant's shoulder, taking comfort in watching Floanne weave needles in and out of the etched design. It was a moment of peace in her otherwise tumultuous life.

From what little Sofia knew of Deluti, it would be near impossible for her to die, but what would happen to Floanne and Ronald if she failed? How long would they survive if she had to flee back to Dahlian?

Ronald checked the edge of his blade one last time and stood, sliding it back in its scabbard. Glancing at the window, he buckled on the sword. "It is time, Sofia. We can wait no longer."

Sofia's hand fell away from Floanne and her body stiffened. Wonder and light flashed in her eyes as she smiled at Ronald. "He is here."

"Who?"

"Navon. He is in the city and drawing the guard to him. The others will not be far behind."

They ran to the window at the sound of horses outside. Two dozen riders filed past heading for the back of the inn. Sofia and Ronald quickly hugged Floanne and picked up their helmets, ready to meet the men downstairs, when the door crashed open.

Frantic, Emma searched the room and then looked beseechingly at the Princess. "Where is Sebastian, and my cousin?"

"Roll is missing, and Sebastian has been arrested."

"I must find him!" she cried and spun away. She froze in the middle of the doorway as the power in the Deluti's voice lashed out.

"Assassin!"

Body quivering and tears running down her face, Emma faced Sofia, eyes blazing.

"You have pledged your life to the Deluti, have you not?"

The Elintria nodded and forced the words past the constriction in her throat. "If Sebastian dies, the pledge is forfeit." She turned and walked out.

After the door closed softly behind the Princess and Lieutenant, Floanne returned to the table and picked up the needlework. She stood there, unmoving, her eyes blinded by tears.

*     *     *

The wolves fanned out ahead, and to either side, passing along images to Navon through Moonlight. Thanks to them, he was prepared when they turned a corner and faced a hastily constructed barricade of overturned wagons. Without slowing, Navon blasted the center wagon. They rode through the flaming gap in the abandoned barricade, Moonlight and Moshere shaking off the smoldering bits of wood raining down.

The bodies of two men, unlucky enough to be near the wagon, lay some distance down the street. The wolves surprised him with images of guards being attacked by groups of locals. Hopefully, that meant Navon would have fewer to face once he reached the Palace.

The force that greeted him by the steps to the main gate was smaller than he had feared, but made up of hardened, older men who would not be easily moved. Navon ignored them as a lone figure in a dark red robe stepped forward. One of the Scarred Mage's senior sorcerers.

Navon searched out Sofia's presence and sent her a terse message. *"I hope you are close to the galleries. Things are about to get loud."*

"Your game of pretend is at an end, Navon d'Roddell. I will be richly rewarded when I present the amulet to my master."

The sorcerer possessed power equal to Chaska's, but more importantly, he was older and wiser, with experience the former apprentice lacked. Navon had no time for word games, and focused on the powerful shield the man had already surrounded himself with.

Afraid he would regret his decision later, Navon pulled out the amulet. A bolt of lightning appeared out of the cloudless sky and struck the weakest point in the shield.

He found out why they called them amulets of focus. The sorcerer simply no longer existed, and the resulting concussion toppled the nearest section of wall circling the Palace. The men who could, stumbled away from the gaping hole left behind. Moshere galloped up the steps while thunder continued to echo throughout the city.

# CHAPTER TWENTY-EIGHT

## SWORD OF A DELUTI

Rafael sat at his favorite window listening to the sounds of the city and watching the lengthening shadows creep across the rooftops. His thoughts as dark as the narrow alleys below, he closed his eyes and sighed. Was this the end for his best friend, Mathias? His father's last words returned to haunt him. If only there was a way he could warn Sebastian.

Hours had passed while he made and then discarded plans to escape. Attempting to climb out of his upper floor window was out of the question, and he wasn't a good enough fighter to get past the guard outside his door.

A flash of light in the distance, near the city gate, drew his attention. Not long after, an eruption of flames shot up well inside the city, followed by a boom.

Rafael sat up and concentrated on the area of the fireball when shouting erupted out in the hall. Rushing to the door, he pressed his ear against it, listening. Nothing. He cracked open the door and peered out. The hall was deserted.

He didn't hesitate. Jerking his cloak from the rack, he sprinted down the stairs and out the back door. His only thought was to get to the inn and warn Sebastian before his father could carry out his threat.

He wasn't the only one out on the street, and had to hide behind a barrel as a group of hooded men jogged past. Were they the men who Mathias planned on using the tunnel into the Palace? If so, Rafael sent the blessing of the Eyes after them.

Not caring who saw him, he burst through the front door of the inn, and headed for the stairs. His footsteps echoed in the empty room. At the end of the upstairs hall he pounded on Sebastian's door and called out. When the ogre didn't answer, Rafael opened the door and glanced inside. No candle was burning, and it was clear the room had been empty for some time.

Unsure what to do next, he turned back to the hall to find a young woman awkwardly holding a small crossbow pointed at his chest.

"Who are you and what do you want with Sebastian?" she demanded, her voice trembling.

"I'm Rafael, and I need to find the ogre. He is in great danger."

"You are too late. The guard arrested Sebastian earlier today and took him away."

"Damn my father," Rafael cursed and tried to think. "There must be something I can do," he muttered, and started to run past her.

Floanne reached out and grabbed his arm. "Wait! Are you Mathias's friend? Do you know where they took Sebastian?"

Surprised she knew the Prince, he answered simply, "Yes."

"Then I'm coming with you. I can't stay here, alone, not knowing." She ran back in her room and returned shortly wearing a cloak, hiked up her dress, and they started to run.

"I'm Floanne, by the way."

He nodded, and then noticed her empty hands. "No crossbow?"

"I don't really know how to use it. Do you?"

"No."

Out of breath, they safely reached the open door to the secret tunnel and paused at the other end, listening.

She whispered, "Shouldn't you have a weapon?"

"Yes, and I know just where to find one. Come on!"

*　　*　　*

When Sofia and Ronald entered the common room, men were tying strips of red cloth around their upper arms. Harold handed them each a strip. "Most of the men we will face are in uniform, but we know some of the servants are loyal to the Duke as well. Also, we don't all know each other, and the less confusion, the better."

Sofia scanned the group of men and made eye contact with each one. "Since there are two galleries, I suggest we split into two groups. Emma will lead one, and I will lead the other. We have abilities you do not."

Altair spoke up. "Agreed, Princess, but if you are now Deluti, why do you wear a sword?"

She sighed and answered him honestly. "Altair, I have

had a sword in my hand since I was a little girl. It is like an extension of my arm. I have only recently come into my true power and don't trust my control. In the tight quarters of the Palace, I could do more harm than good."

The two groups left the inn and traveled separate, but parallel routes to the Palace. Emma and Altair reached the alley with the hidden door first, and with his size, Navon's brother had no trouble opening it. The putrid odor of a decaying body forced them back.

Sofia hurried up and asked, "What is wrong?" and then wrinkled her nose. "Stay back from the door and I'll deal with this."

At the other end of the tunnel, she found the body Mathias had hidden. The Princess let a little bit of her anger seep into the fire that engulfed the dead guard. A strong wind rose up and quickly scoured out the smoke and odor.

Sofia returned to her group as Emma and Altair entered the tunnel. At the far end, Emma nodded to him and then disappeared. He shoved with all his strength and the door slammed open. Two surprised guards sprinted for the stairs, but soon fell victim to the diminutive assassin's skill.

Emma reappeared next to Altair and whispered. "That those men were here waiting means the halls are being watched. Give me a few moments to clear the halls, and then run as fast as you can. I'll meet you at the gallery entrance."

Sooner than Sofia thought wise, Altair shouted for everyone to run. He answered her unspoken question. "No one can outrun an Elintria. The second man she reaches will be dead before the first one hits the floor."

The body of a guard littered each floor they came to. About to ascend the last set of stairs, Emma reappeared motioning them to stop.

"There are three men with bows guarding the entrance to each gallery. They have illuminator candles that will unmask me when I get near."

She was about to ask for suggestions when Sofia ran to the top of the stairs, and looked toward the front of the Palace, her eyes narrowed.

"By the Eyes, no," she muttered, and turned back to the others. "We are out of time! Navon is at the Palace and forced to do something that might have unintended consequences. Hurry!" she shouted and ran.

They rounded the last corner in view of the guards

when a tremor rocked the Palace to its foundation. Struggling to her feet, Sofia watched the guards get up, rush into the gallery and slam the door behind them. She had just made it to the door when the screaming began.

*     *     *

Rafael paused at the first set of dead guards. "If the others are headed for the audience chamber, there may still be guards where we have to go. We need to be careful."

Twice they had to hide at the sound of men running. Once inside the library, Rafael rushed to a back shelf and began throwing books to the floor. He reached in behind them and pulled out a bundle.

Floanne gasped in wonder as he un-wrapped the weapon inside.

"The sword of my forefather."

Rafael stared at her in confusion. "Your forefather?"

"Yes. When Mathias told us about the skeleton and sword you discovered in the tunnel, a Deluti spirit related the story of the brother and sister who were entrusted with the safety of a Deluti amulet. The Princess escaped to Dahlian with the amulet, and I am her descendant."

The young historian grabbed her hand and headed for

the door, shaking his head. "I would really like to meet this spirit someday."

They reached the door to the holding cells, and Rafael peeked inside. The room was empty, but more importantly, the keys to the cells lay out on the table. He smiled at Floanne in triumph, took a step inside, when the floor under their feet jumped and a loud boom echoed through the halls.

Eyes wide, they shared a look and then rushed inside, Floanne checking the cells on one side while Rafael grabbed the keys and yelled. "Sebastian! Where are you?"

"Here," came the answer as Rafael spied a large hand stuck out between the bars of a cell at the back of the room. Fumbling, he managed to unlock the door and swung it open. "Hurry, we must leave right away!"

"But Rafael, won't you be in trouble? I'm innocent, and I'm sure they will release me soon." the ogre protested, unsure.

"It doesn't make any difference, Sebastian. Father intends to kill you whether you are innocent or not."

"That's right, and we are here to do just that," came a voice from the door.

Rafael and Floanne spun around in surprise and stared

at the two men standing just inside the room, loaded crossbows held steady. Rafael raised himself up and addressed the men.

"I am Rafael d'Lorange, the Duke's son, and I order you to put down your weapons and release the ogre."

One of the guards laughed. "Sorry, boy. We only take orders from the Duke himself."

The other growled and raised his bow. "Just kill the animal so we can get out of here."

"Nooo…!" Rafael shouted and jumped in front of the ogre. One bolt struck Sebastian in the shoulder while the other imbedded itself in the young man's chest. Sebastian caught Rafael's limp body, laid it on the floor and then charged, his fangs bared in rage.

Swords out, one of the guards evaded the ogre's charge and focused on Floanne, a wicked gleam in his eyes. She reached for the sword lying next to Rafael and instinctually raised it to block the man's swing. He stared in shock as his blade sheared off when it struck the Deluti sword. Bellowing in anger, he lunged for her and impaled himself on her sword.

Floanne jerked her hand away from the sword as the man's body slumped to the floor. In shock, she stood there, her body trembling.

Sebastian returned, held her tight, and then bent down to retrieve the sword. He handed it back to her. "Sword save life. It yours be."

Without another word, he gently lifted Rafael's body in his arms and headed for the door. Sobbing, Floanne followed, the sword like a viper in her hand.

Out in the hall, she barely noticed the wolf. It barked once at the ogre and turned, leading them away.

*   *   *

Marcus circulated among the families gathered, smiling and laughing at their stories. They were all fools, and soon he would be rid of them. What use did he have for Dukes and Barons when he became King. His guard would keep the peasants in line, and governors loyal to him would have control over their assigned areas.

Charles was the biggest fool of all. The King believed every lie and ridiculous story Marcus had dreamed up. Replacing the guards with men loyal to him had been so easy. And using the other's distrust of the Dahlians played right into his hands as his rumors of the Queen's secret agenda spread.

Everything was proceeding exactly as he had planned.

In a short while, the guests would all be seated in their assigned places. His men wouldn't even have to search for their targets. Then one of his guards would call him outside to deal with a problem. Once he left, the doors would be locked from the outside and the arrows would fly. He smiled up at the galleries from where his men would ensure the deaths of those he despised.

His smile slipped when the King came up from behind and slapped him on the shoulder.

"You must be proud, Marcus. All of your hard work has culminated in this day. A day that will be long remembered as peace finally comes to our two kingdoms."

The Duke forced a smile as he turned to his old friend. "It was my pleasure, Your Majesty. But you must be proud of you son also, agreeing to marry the Princess Sofia. I hear she can be difficult."

The King's eyes narrowed slightly as he studied the face of his closest friend and advisor. "You would be surprised at the things my son has done that I am proud of." He noticed the Duke's smile falter and nodded to himself. "Speaking of the Princess, shouldn't she be making her appearance soon?"

"Very soon. The guards will alert me as soon as she

arrives at the Palace."

Charles clapped him on the shoulder again and moved away in the direction of Prince Mathias. Marcus watched the King, a grim smile now on his face. *So, my old friend, you suspect something, but it's too late, especially for you.*

The Duke raised his arms, about to call everyone to their places when the room shook violently, knocking decorations off of the tables, and paintings fell from the walls. Silence filled the room after the last booming echo faded. People picked themselves up and glanced at each other in fear.

The silence didn't last as a volley of arrows rained down on the crowd and women began screaming. Marcus ran for the door, pounding on it and yelling for his guards to open up.

Even if they could have heard him, they faced a problem of their own.

# Chapter Twenty-Nine

## The Cup of Truth

Sofia pushed through the smoldering ruin of the door, Ronald right on her heels. They almost stumbled over the body of a guard shredded by wood splinters. Once inside, the nearest guard turned to fire, but a bolt of lightning lanced out from the tip of Sofia's blade and knocked the man over the gallery wall. When Ronald appeared at her side, the remaining men threw down their bows, grabbed the heavy curtains, and vaulted over the wall.

The Princess, a storm dancing in her eyes, yelled. "Come on, Ronald. Time to follow your dreams!"

Grabbing a length of curtain, she leapt over the wall and disappeared into the chamber below.

He thought, *'Hanging from a curtain isn't really the same as swinging on a rope from ship to ship,'* but he shrugged and joined her anyway.

On the other side, Altair made short work of the door, and jumped aside as two bolts flashed by and passed over Emma's head. Before the first guard had a chance to draw his sword, she dropped him. Altair charged the next man, picked him up and threw the guard into the chamber below.

The rest of the guards decided to join their friends below, and clamored out of the gallery. Altair followed suit, the curtain anchor ripping away with his bulk.

Emma felt a presence in her mind and hesitated. She faced the rest of her group. "The other group has already joined the fight below, but Navon and the wolves need our help eliminating the men guarding the entrance to the chamber. What say you?"

"Lead on, Elder!" the men shouted.

They sped down the nearest stairs to the lower level, and fell on the guards just as the young Deluti and his friends attacked.

*    *    *

Moshere remained at the entrance to the Palace, guarding their back. Navon hurried down the nearest hallway, ignoring the rich, opulent surroundings. The growing taint of evil guiding him. At the far end of the hallway, a set of large, golden doors covered the far wall. The ornately carved images depicted on the doors announced the entrance to the Grand Audience chamber. From behind those closed doors came the sounds of fighting and screams.

The men arrayed before him were many, but thankfully, there were no sorcerers among them. Navon tried one last time to dissuade the men and sent thoughts of uncertainty and fear into their minds. It had little effect. These were desperate men and had nothing to lose.

Afraid to use his power in such a confined area, he sighed and drew his sword while the wolves spread out to either side. He hoped his years of training would serve him now.

Two older men smiled when Navon raised his sword, and stepped forward to challenge him. Just as he parried their first swings, Emma and the Keep men charged out of a side hall and attacked. The wolves, howling, joined in the fray.

*     *     *

Mathias struggled to his feet after the shock, and watched in resignation as his father fell, the first volley finding its mark. Duke Strumant reached down to snap off the shaft of the arrow lodged in his leg, and accepted one of Mathias's extra knives. Shouting, "Use the chairs as shields!" the Prince searched for the Queen and found his brother, Richard, already had their mother and sister protected in a corner.

A man from above crashed down on the table, his sword clattering to the floor. Mathias bent down to grab the weapon, avoiding the swing from a man who landed next to him. The Prince swept his sword low and took the man's legs out from under him. Mathias looked up and smiled in spite of the situation as Sofia swung down from the gallery. Curtains in one hand, and her sword, covered in dancing blue whirls of lightning, in her other, she engaged the guards. *'Nice entrance, Princess!'*

Hard pressed by two guards, Mathis was forced back until Sofia appeared at his side, and they made short work of men no better than street thugs.

When more of the experienced family members

acquired swords, the odds began to swing in their favor. Even the Baroness LaFontaine, blood flowing from a gash on her forehead, stood with sword in hand guarding a group of girls huddled against one wall.

Mathias spotted three men advancing on his brother at the far end of the room. They probably had orders to eliminate the royal family at all costs. He nudged the Princess and pointed. She sprang up on one of the long tables and started running, Mathias not far behind.

Several men jumped up to intercept, but she swept them aside without slowing. The noise of glass and plates crashing to the floor drew the attention of two of the men who spun to meet them.

Richard had never been proficient with a sword, and was down on one knee, blood running from a deep cut in his arm. His opponent raised his sword for the killing stroke. Mathias spun around his man, exposing his back, and ran his brother's attacker through from behind.

Expecting the same from the man behind him, Mathias spun in time to watch in wonder as Sofia dispatched both men in a storm of sword strokes. Well, the rumors were certainly true. He would never match her skill with a blade.

Searching for more attackers, the Prince lowered his sword as a hush fell over the chamber. The sound of fighting was replaced by quiet sobbing, and the moans of the wounded. Duke Strumant and others, collapsed onto chairs, adrenalin no longer able to compensate for the loss of blood.

Everyone turned to stare as the doors finally opened, and a young man dressed in fine clothes entered. Emma followed him in and shut them behind her. Marcus backed away, the tip of the man's sword resting just beneath his chin.

*    *    *

Navon continued to advance until the Duke was forced up against a table. He fought an internal battle as the Deluti side of him raged against the evil this man represented and wanted his death. His humanity won out.

"Duke Marcus d'Lorange, I am here as representative of the Deluti in search of the truth. You are accused of conspiring to murder the royal family for the purpose of gaining the crown. What have you to say?"

"Deluti?" the Duke laughed. "You may have fooled others, young man, but you don't fool me. The Deluti are long gone. Now, seeing as the King is dead, and I'm the senior surviving member of the council, I'm ordering you to lay down your sword and leave."

"I'm not dead yet, Marcus," came a pained voice from the floor where the King struggled to rise. .

Tears of joy pouring from his eyes, Mathias rushed over and fell to his knees, wrapping an arm around his father's shoulders. "How?' he demanded, and then glimpsed the shining edge of chain mail under the King's shirt.

Smiling, his father traced the line of a slice across his son's chest, exposing the metal links. "The father learns from his son. I may not be the total fool you believed me to be, but I'm more of a fool than I could imagine. I suspected Marcus was planning something, but had no idea he would go this far. Help me up, Mathias." Groaning in pain and taking shallow breaths, the King stood as straight as he could.

"Easy, Father." Mathias cautioned. "The chain may have stopped the arrows, but I would be surprised if you didn't have several cracked ribs."

Charles grimaced at his son, and then searched the face of his oldest friend, who stared, unbelieving. "There is only one way to determine the truth beyond question.

Mathias, hand the Cup of Truth to the Deluti, please."

The Prince retrieved the golden cup from a shelf where it was stored, and brought it back to Navon. The young Deluti concentrated a moment, nodded, and then handed it back.

"You see, Marcus," the King continued. "I have always known the cup lacked true ability to encourage its holder to speak the truth. It derives its power from the Deluti." Nodding to Navon, his eyes bored into the Duke's. "It now has that power."

Beads of sweat formed on Marcus's brow as his eyes jerked back and forth wildly. He jumped along with everyone else when the door burst open and slammed up against the wall.

Sebastian stood in the doorway, his eyes locked on the Duke. Rafael's body lay cradled in his arms, and Floanne stood at his side, a bloody sword in her hand.

Emma moved to go to him, and then hesitated. She had never seen tears on the ogre's face before. Afraid of what he might do, she motioned for everyone to stay back, including Navon.

The ogre entered and turned to the nearest table. Guessing his intent, Navon swept it clear with his sword.

Sebastian carefully laid Rafael on the table, and then approached the Duke.

Marcus trembled violently as he looked up into the eyes of death, but froze stiff when the ogre gripped the Duke's lapels and lifted him till they were face to face.

"Your son died saving my life, but it was the evil of your ambition that killed him," Sebastian growled. The ogre's eyes continued to bore into the Dukes' as he carefully set the man back on his feet.

Marcus squeezed his eyes shut against the flow of tears when Sebastian released him and stepped back.

"Who is the animal now?"

Ignoring Navon's offer to remove the bolt and heal the wound in his shoulder, the ogre walked out of the audience chamber, Emma at his side.

The King and Duke Srumant took the sobbing Marcus to a far table and began questioning him. Cup in hand, the Duke, a broken man, had no choice but to answer.

"Navon!" Altair called out. "Come quick. It's Father."

The young Deluti rushed over and knelt at his father's side where they had laid him on the floor. The Baron had numerous wounds, the worst being the one in his side which bled heavily.

"Navon... "

"Hush, Father, and let me work." Navon was concerned. He had healed more serious injuries, but only with the help of others.

A sudden quiet fell over the room, punctuated by sharp intakes of breath, as Moonlight bounded into the chamber. The sound of hoof beats echoed through the halls shortly after when Moshere entered and opened himself up to his companion.

Navon drew power from both the wolf at his side and the Brother standing nearby, and began the task of healing his father.

The previous battle to enter the Palace had taken its toll. Even with the extra strength provided by his companions, he faltered, losing the fight against the continuing flow of blood. A sudden rush of power flooded his senses. He stared up into the storm flashing in the eyes of the woman kneeling across from him. By unspoken agreement, she took over healing the multitude of minor injuries while Navon, with grim determination, concentrated on the wound in his father's side.

The Baron healed and sleeping peacefully, Navon selfishly pulled a little extra energy from her to refresh himself and his companions. He hoped she wouldn't mind. Taking her hands in his, he helped her rise and marveled at the shared rapport.

Navon tore his eyes away and faced Altair. "Let Father sleep as long as he needs, and then feed him. He will be weak when he wakes."

Her hand still in his, Navon focused in on her spirit. *"Walk with me?"*

Eyes wide at the presence of his voice in her mind, Sofia nodded. They walked out to the Palace entrance where she stared at the hole Navon had created, and then turned to look back at the wolf and horse following. "Do you command the Elders?"

He shook his head and wrapped an arm around Moonlight. "They are my friends, and something more. Moonlight and I share a bond I cannot explain, and Moshere accompanies me of his own free will."

Having made his decision, Navon hugged the wolf tight, and then wrapped his arms around Moshere before turning back to Sofia and taking her hand. "Sofia, my time is short. The Deluti spirits are calling me, and I must leave to continue my trials. Even though I would not have survived my first trial without help from my companions, the spirits have made it clear they will not survive the next. Therefore, I must continue alone."

Moonlight began to whimper while Moshere shook his head as the young Deluti spoke. "More than anything, I want to stay and help you return to your home and explore the rapport we shared. I promise you, when I complete this next trial, I will come back to help in any way I can."

Sofia squinted at the bright light heralding the arrival of a white arch on the steps below them. She squeezed his hand before letting go. "What are these trials?"

"I don't have time to explain. Ask the spirit in your amulet," he called out before entering the arch.

Another flash of light, and he was gone. Moonlight lifted her head to the sky and howled. Moshere lowered his head in silent resignation. The Princess waited until the after-image faded from her sight before returning to the audience chamber where the King and Queen stood waiting.

"It's unfortunate you no longer wish to be a princess, but the title of Deluti fits you better," the King observed. "Marcus has told us of your sister's plans, and his part in them. You have risked your life for us, and I can do no less than offer you whatever help we can."

Smiling, the Queen glanced at her son and Floanne standing close to each other, and then held out her hand to Sofia. "I was afraid Mathias would be disappointed, but it appears he has found someone else. Thank you for saving his life and ours. We would be honored if you and your partner remained in the Palace tonight."

"Thank you both, but the Palace is no longer my place. Ronald and I will return to the inn and come back tomorrow."

Sofia turned away from them to deal with the question on Altair's face.

"My brother?"

"Gone. The Deluti spirits have claimed him again."

"Curse the spirits! How much more will they put him through?"

Sofia shuddered when the spirit in the amulet whispered in her mind. *"You cannot even imagine."*

.

# About the Author

Mr. Boykin is retired and lives in the Northwest surrounded by family and pets. His goal is to write stories that entertain and inspire. To find out more, you can visit his blog: www.rolandboykin.blogspot.com or check out his profiles on Google and Facebook.

Made in the USA
Lexington, KY
06 April 2017